Corrupt City Saga

Corrupt City Saga

Tra Verdejo

www.urbanbooks.net

Urban Books, LLC
97 N18th Street
Wyandanch, NY 11798

ISBN 13: 978-1-62286-916-9
ISBN 10: 1-62286-916-8

First Trade Paperback Printing July 2015
Printed in the United States of America

10 9 8 7 6 5 4 3 2 1

Distributed by Kensington Publishing Corp.
Submit Orders to:
Customer Service
400 Hahn Road
Westminster, MD 21157-4627
Phone: 1-800-733-3000
Fax: 1-800-659-2436

Corrupt City Saga

Praise for Tra Verdejo

"Tra Verdejo's sophomore novel, *Corrupt City,* is such a great read. I haven't enjoyed urban literature with so much suspense in a very long time. Tra has penned a phenomenal page-turner." —Rukyyah J. Karreem Author of *Princess & Princess II*

"Breathless, explosive, exhilarating. *Corrupt City* is the perfect combination of spine-tingling and heart-pounding suspense. Tra Verdejo is definitely an author to look out for." —Silk White Author of *Tears of a Hustler* and *Tears of a Hustler 2*

"A peek into the reality of the streets. Tra Verdejo will take you directly there. A man on a mission, he is determined and enthusiastic about 'keeping it real.'" —Jennifer Robinson, Expressions Book Club

Dedication

I would like to dedicate this book to all the innocent lives lost at the hands of police officers with quick triggers. Also to all the police officers killed in the line of duty while protecting us. Rest in Peace.

Acknowledgments

Peace to the Gods and Earths.

I first want to thank everyone who purchased this book. Thank you for the support. I mean that from the bottom of my heart. I will always put in 100 percent. Love is love.

Without a doubt I have to thank my mother, Mirta Davila. I hope you are resting in peace. I want to thank the second most important woman in my life, Purified Earth. You complete me, and thank you for two beautiful boys, Omighty and Destin. Everything I do is for them, my family.

I also want to thank my father, Pedro Verdejo, the man who taught me how to work hard. Next, I want to thank my sister Ana, who is holding it down on her own. Single parents, stand up. My little sister Nichole, I'm so proud of you, doing your thing and running your own business, too. My eldest sister, Tee, what's good? I want to shout out the future of our family tree, my nieces and nephews Ray, Destine, Tyler, Nelly, and Kenya.

I also want to thank Freddy "Tone" Garcia. Many thank God for their second chances; I would like to thank this man for my second chance. Love you, Brah. You already know that. Melissa Edwards, I remember telling Eric when we were younger I would buy you a house. Trust me, I haven't forgotten that promise. Thank you for stepping in there and providing shelter when I needed a home. I will love you forever. I also want to thank my entire family in Puerto Rico, especially my *abuela*, Carmen Alomar.

Now it's time to show love to my other family, Remy Rich, Ray Rocca, and Daddio (Wagner Projects, stand up). Peace to the God-born Knowledge. I love you, Brah. My cousin Ruddy. My CNS family—Snypes, Ron, DB, Smoke, Last Breath, Buddha Bride, Ill Murda, Kauso, Lizzy Long, Boo Bizzy, Rob-U

(RIP), and Gutta (RIP). And 119th Street and Lexington Avenue, stand up, baby!

Now the literary love. I first want to thank all the authors who believed in my vision and were part of the 2009 Sexy Scriptures calendar. Those authors are Kwame "Dutch" Teague, K'wan (good looking for all the love), Deshaun "Jiwe" Morris, Sexy, Julie Ojeda (BX Bookman, what's good?), Kerry "Mr. Wagfest" Wagner, Dex, Shani Greene-Dowdell, and my Bronx connect, Iesha Brown.

I can't forget all the beautiful models. I want to thank Mrs. January. Tish Love, for helping in finding most of the girls and our locations. I only had a few slots for the calendar, but there are a bunch of authors in the game I break bread with, and I have to shout them out as well. Authors Rukyyah J. Karreem, Silk White, Maxwell Penn (Peace God), Dex, Antoine "Inch" Thomas, Tenia Jamilla Conrad Glover (let's make this movie). I also want to send love to authors like Ingrid, Winter, Robert T. Sells, Don, Dashawn Taylor & the many others who have done book signings at my spot in Baltimore.

To all my book vendors and distributors, good looking for the love, especially the ones that pay up front, Black & Nobel (Philly, stand up), BX Bookman, Purgo on 149th Street and Third Avenue, Black Star in Harlem, Charles in Baltimore (the Wise brothers), Shane by Lexington market, Cliff at Expression bookstore in Baltimore, African World Book, and the list goes on. I really appreciate the love.

On the other hand there are a lot of bookstores and vendors with bad credit and reputations. I'm not going to blast you, but please stop bull$hitting. I want to send a shout-out to all my covendors at the Patapsco Flea Market in Baltimore. Love is love.

I also want to thank two ladies, Jeannie Hooper and Helen Andrews. We spend a lot of time critiquing books. I gave these ladies the opportunity to read and review my book first. I also want to thank my weekly supporters who stop by the flea market. Thanks for the love.

Shout-out to Flowers High in Largo, MD, whose seniors did a book report on my first book, *Born in the Streets But Raised in Prison*.

Acknowledgments

I also want to thank all the people who have hated on me. Yah are the reason why I stay motivated and work so hard. I know it must burn inside watching my success blossom the way it has. Get used to the feeling because I'm just getting started. Many thought my first book was just a one-hit wonder. I'm sorry to burst your bubble. But please remember one thing—Yah could kiss my Puerto Rican A$$.

Chapter One

10/22/2003

"Damn, we have been out here for like forty-five minutes, Toothpick. What's taking them so long?"

"I don't know. Maybe they changed their minds."

"Changed their minds? We have a bag filled with money. How can they change their mind? It's too late for that. They got fifteen minutes, or we out."

Cash and Toothpick had placed an order for two kilos of cocaine and four guns, two of which were semiautomatic rifles. They were getting a bit nervous waiting for the drop. All kinds of scenarios ran through their heads, and they were hoping they weren't being set up.

"I hope they're not trying to pull any funny moves, 'cause I have a full clip," Toothpick added.

They both took a deep breath and leaned back on their seat, both exhaling like two little bitches. They were in the Hunts Point area of the Bronx, parked in an empty parking lot behind a large agriculture warehouse between Garrison and Longwood Avenue. It was close to midnight on a breezy Friday night, and there wasn't a soul in the area. That's how cold it was. But it still felt strange because, usually, you would see at least a few crackheads roaming around. To the criminal-minded, it was one of those perfect opportunities to pull off a hit—no witnesses, and in the middle of nowhere.

After another twenty minutes went by, they finally decided to leave. In all honesty, they both were nervous and thought it was a bad idea to meet there, anyway.

"Fuck this! They're not coming. Let's go," Cash said as he turned the car on.

"Wait. Look. Here they come."

Cash looked to his right and saw headlights approaching. The lights blurred both their vision, and they couldn't see the car. Both Cash and Toothpick placed their hands on their guns, just to be on the safe side. As the car got within twenty feet, they finally had vision on it but couldn't see inside because of the dark-tinted windows.

After the car pulled up parallel to theirs, the passenger lowered his tinted window and told Cash, "Follow us."

"First of all, who the fuck is you?" Cash shot back. "And where is Scratch?"

The window from the back started to roll down, and that's when Toothpick pulled his 9 mm. He cocked it back so quickly, the window only rolled halfway down and stopped.

"Chill, Toothpick. It's me, Scratch. I'm in the backseat. It's all good. Put the gun away. Just follow us. We know a safer place. This shit here looks too creepy."

Toothpick lowered his gun and told Cash to follow the car. For a moment there, it almost got ugly. Toothpick was seconds away from pulling the trigger.

While they were following the car, both of them were quiet, their minds were heavy with suspicion. Not knowing where they were going added to the suspense. They could be driving to a setup where more goons with guns could be waiting for them. This criminal life was full of surprises, and your reflexes had to be quick in order to survive. Second thoughts would get you killed in this game. Your first instinct was the first and only rule to live by.

Toothpick and Cash both knew something was wrong, but they were both strapped with loaded guns, so they risked it anyway, knowing the odds were against them. They knew it was a big mistake, but once you've committed and you've passed a certain point, there is no turning back.

They got off at the Castle Hill Avenue exit. They parked across the street from Castle Hill projects and both looked at each other.

"Toothpick, how in the fuck is Castle Hill projects safer?"

They both laughed.

"I don't know, but we about to find out. These cats are fuckin' amateurs, but keep your eyes open. Don't even blink."

As Cash was parking, Scratch jumped out and walked up to their car.

"Toothpick, you come with me. We're going in this building behind me."

"Scratch, what's up with all these last-minute changes? You sure you have the bricks and the guns? Don't fuck with us."

"Toothpick, just trust me on this one. Calm down. We're going inside to my cousin's apartment. That way, you get a chance to check everything out while I count the money."

"A'ight, cool. C'mon, Cash, grab the money."

"Just you, Toothpick. Your boy has to wait in the car."

"C'mon, Scratch, that's my partner, we roll together. I'm not going upstairs alone."

"Listen, either you come alone, or the deal is dead. It's your decision. My driver is also waiting in the car. Don't worry, your partner will be okay."

Toothpick looked at Cash and waited for his approval. Once Cash nodded his head, he jumped out of the car with a bag of money. Toothpick kept looking back as he walked with Scratch, making sure no one was following.

As soon as they got in the building and pressed for the elevator, two gunmen emerged from apartment 1B. It happened so fast, Toothpick didn't have time to react or reach for his weapon. They pulled him inside the apartment, took his gun, and threw him on the floor.

Scratch leaned over him as he pressed the cold barrel against his cheekbone and asked him, "How long have you known your boy outside?"

"What the fuck is going on here, Scratch? Are you crazy? We are boys. What's going on? Why are you asking about Cash?"

Before he could answer, about five to six shots rang out. Toothpick knew those shots were intended for Cash. He wanted to break loose and reach for his other gun, but he had to play it cool and wait for the right moment. There were three people in that apartment with guns in their hands. He wasn't stupid.

"Were those shots? What the fuck is going on here?" Toothpick asked with a clueless expression, trying to work his way out.

"Answer my question. How long have you known Cash?"

"Not for long. My cousin set me up with him when I came home two years ago. Why?"

"Cash is police. He's undercover. Please tell me you are not a cop as well."

"A cop? Get the fuck outta here. Cash can't be police, and if he is police, your boy just shot him. Why the fuck is you still here? That means police was either following us or on their way here. We need to bounce the fuck outta here. Let me go. You know I'm not a fuckin' pig. Get off me, nigga. I'm not trying to get locked up today. Let's bounce and handle business another day."

Scratch looked into Toothpick's eyes for about four seconds and couldn't read any lies. He believed him and decided to let him go. "My bad. I had to make sure," he said, helping Toothpick up and giving him his gun back, but with the clip and the bullet in the chamber. "Nowadays, you never know who's undercover. Wait about fifteen seconds after I leave before you bounce. We'll make the deal another time. Keep your money. No, as a matter of fact, give me this fuckin' money. Next time, pick a better partner," Scratch said before running out.

Toothpick waited for about five seconds before he reached for his second gun and ran out. He kicked open the front door of the building so hard, he got the attention of Scratch and his boys. By the time they realized where the noise came from, Toothpick was already approaching, shooting rounds from his 9 mm Glock. Instantly, he dropped two of them with single shots to the head. Now it was just Scratch and his driver left.

It was an all-out war at one o'clock in the morning in the middle of the streets in the Bronx. Half the neighborhood was up watching the action from their windows, some ducking bullets. These projects were known for their high crime rate, but neighbors never saw anything like this.

Toothpick was in the battle of his life. He had to run for cover behind a parked car when Scratch's driver pulled out a MAC-11 and emptied the entire clip at him. Bullets were flying all around Toothpick. All he could do was stay put and pray they didn't go through the car and hit him.

He caught a break when the MAC-11 went silent for a few seconds because it ran out of bullets. As soon as he heard a pause in between shots, Toothpick jumped up, quickly let off two shots, and ducked back down. He'd shot the driver in the neck and shoulder.

Scratch realized he'd lost his crew. Now it was just him left. But he was still hanging, going out like a soldier, letting off rounds from his .40-caliber. When he noticed Toothpick reloading, he jumped in the car and tried to make a quick getaway.

Before he was able to switch gears, Toothpick ran up on him and pressed the hot barrel on his temple and yelled, "Freeze, muthafucka! You are under arrest. You have the right to remain silent. Anything you say will be used against you in a court of law—man, fuck that! And fuck you!"

Toothpick, whose real name was Donald "Lucky" Gibson, shot Scratch twice in the head then quickly ran toward his partner, praying for a miracle.

"Nine-one-three, nine-one-three. Officer down! I need a bus, and I need it now, goddamn it! Now! Officer down, I repeat, officer down. I'm on Castle Hill and Randall Avenue!" he yelled.

When he got to Cash, real name Michael "Tango" Scott, he was still breathing, but there was blood everywhere. He noticed Tango had been shot a few times in his chest. When they took this undercover assignment, they knew they couldn't wear a vest. Tears overcame him because he knew his partner's destiny.

Tango kept mumbling for Lucky to call his wife. "Please call her. I want to hear her voice before I die."

"You are not going to die. Help is on the way. Hang in there," Lucky replied, reaching for his cell phone.

Lucky started dialing the number, the phone rang once, and his wife, Tammy, answered. When he went to pass the phone over to Tango, he was already gone. He didn't know what to do. Should he hang up or tell Tammy what happened? He couldn't hang up because Tammy knew his phone number.

"Hello," Lucky said, sounding like a scared little boy.

"Hello, Lucky? That's you? What's going on? I hear sirens in the background. Where is Michael? What's going on, Lucky?"

"Tammy, I'm sorry. I'm so sorry," a teary Lucky said.

Tammy became hysterical because she knew it only meant two things—he was either in critical condition or dead. "Lucky, goddamn it! Tell me the truth. What happened to my husband? Is he okay? Oh, please, God, help me. Please, God."

"I'm sorry, Tammy, our cover was blown, and Tango, I mean Michael, didn't make it."

The phone went dead.

Tammy had yanked the cord from the socket. She was throwing a tantrum at the house. Her twin boys, only eight years old, woke up asking their mother what happened and why she was crying. She was speechless. She didn't know how to tell them their daddy was never coming home.

Meanwhile, back at the crime scene, Lucky, still in shock, was trying to put the pieces of the puzzle together. Two questions kept bugging him. *How did they know about Tango's identity? And why was it taking so long for backup to arrive?*

Lucky was starting to get a major headache and was feeling weak. He dropped to one knee, and that's when another cop at the scene noticed Lucky had also been shot. They rushed to his aid and treated his wound on the spot.

He was hit on the side of his stomach, a flesh wound, nothing serious. His adrenaline was running so high, he'd never felt the shot. After a fifteen-minute conversation with his captain, he finally agreed to get in the ambulance and head to the hospital as a precaution.

The Present (2006)

Lucky woke up sweating and out of breath. He was dreaming about the night, Tango, was killed. That was one memory he would carry with him for the rest of his life. Till this day, he suspected it was foul play that led to Tango's cover being blown.

Today was a big day for Lucky. He turned on the TV and listened to the news reporter, while getting dressed for court.

"Today, June 21, 2006, the biggest case against the State of New York is set to hear the prosecution's main and last witness, Donald Gibson, a former, fifteen-year veteran police officer, was one of the four officers present the night Perry Coleman, a twenty-five-year-old Black man, was gunned down by the NYPD. The other three officers are all being charged with murder.

"Perry's case has drawn national attention, and the entire state of New York is behind the Colemans. New Yorkers, already sick and tired of thugs roaming the streets, don't want to have to worry about these trigger-happy rogue police officers running wild in their community.

"Even the great Minister Al Muhammad has joined the family and their legal team. We all know the minister's reputation for bringing attention to police brutality cases.

"Today, the jury will hear the shocking testimony of Mr. Gibson, where he indicates Perry Coleman was murdered on the night in question for no apparent reason. The courtroom will be filled with supporters, police officers, and politicians. Everyone is anticipating what will take place today.

"Rumors are circulating that Donald has been hiding under his own protection, without the help of the government, because he knows how crooked the system has become. In another forty-five minutes, we will finally hear what happened the night Perry Coleman was murdered. I'm Destine Diaz, live from the courthouse, Channel Five News."

Those three officers were confident the charges would be dropped until Donald "Lucky" Gibson reappeared and agreed to testify.

Meanwhile, it was pandemonium outside the courthouse. There were news stations parked everywhere, and reporters were interviewing anyone who wanted to get in front of a camera. The crowd was asking the same questions over and over. "Will this be the case that will rock the state of New York and shine the spotlight on police brutality? How many more innocent bodies need to drop? Better yet, how many more minority bodies need to drop?"

Inside the courtroom, there were barely any seats available. The NYPD tried to take up most of the seats to prevent supporters and protesters from entering the courtroom. Court officers had to ask police officers to move to the right side of the courtroom or exit.

Police officers were not happy, and some even argued their point. The police department knew their future relied on the verdict of this case. Though the evidence against these three cops was not in their favor, they strongly supported their own. The cops involved were all suspended with pay, which was nothing but a paid vacation.

The people demanded more severe punishment, not a slap on the wrist. However, Mayor Ralph Gulliano and Police Commissioner Brandon Fratt made it their business to point out that Perry Coleman had a criminal record on file and the people shouldn't rush to judge and crucify these officers who were doing their job. Both the mayor and police commissioner received harsh criticisms for their stance. Blacks and Hispanics were not shocked, because the lack of support in their communities had always been evident.

The mayor tried to smear Perry's image. Perry Coleman had been working at the same job since he was nineteen years old and had no record of felonies or misdemeanors. They were referring to a juvenile robbery charge. Perry and a few of his high school friends got caught running out of a store with jewelry when he was fourteen years old. Part of his plea bargain was that his record would be sealed, which meant closed, and would never resurface again, after he completed eighteen months of probation. But the following night after Perry was killed, newspapers were already printing stories about his juvenile record, hoping the court of opinion would at least convict him of being a thug.

The public didn't care about what he did when he was fourteen. He turned out to be a good human being and role model to others. Perry was a manager at a furniture store and was a year away from earning his bachelor's degree in business communication. He was survived by his wife, Kim Blackburn Coleman, and their three-year-old son, Perry Coleman III. Perry's family promised that his name would never be forgotten and that his story would be told across the world.

Perry's mother, Laura, said it the best. "You can't change destiny, but you sure can change your life. My son is a prime example that one mistake shouldn't ruin your future. Perry was a great son, father, and husband. He worked extremely hard to stay positive and keep his family happy. Now, because of racist, trigger-happy cops, my son is no longer alive. We will carry the torch from here and educate the world, not just on police brutality, but on racism as well, because it's still alive in our communities, in our everyday lives."

Chapter Two

Lucky's Testimony

Around 8:15 a.m., the judge, who had a reputation for handing out harsh sentences, walked out of his chambers. He was six feet, five inches tall and weighed about two-sixty. His white beard matched his old, white, long hair. He barely smiled in a courtroom. A lot of protesters were against him hearing the case because he was rumored to be a racist, and Perry's family was concerned they wouldn't get a fair trial.

"All rise," the bailiff said. "The Honorable Judge Henry J. Lewis presiding." A few seconds later, he added, "You may all be seated."

"Good morning to all. Counselors, are we ready? Mr. Johnson, you may call your witness."

District Attorney Jonathan Johnson had over fifteen years of experience and had worked on more than a few high-profile cases in the past. He was considered a celebrity. He once graced the cover of *Essence* magazine, and was ranked number two on the top ten of single Black men in law. The smooth-talking prosecutor was the lead counsel on two cases that brought down The Young Kingpins, a million-dollar street gang in Spanish Harlem. He'd also taken down a few mob figures and dirty politicians. His resume had Perry's family feeling confident. If anyone could get a conviction, it would be this man.

Mr. Johnson had a history of going for the maximum penalty without a second thought, and barely offered deals to offenders. In his first public statement about this case, he made it known he hated dirty cops.

African Americans all felt they had the right prosecutor. Whites, on the other hand, were bitter and had mixed feelings.

Ever since the trial started, it had been a racial war. The courtroom was packed with angry supporters from both sides. Yet people of all colors were rooting for a guilty verdict. With the anger and tension across the courtroom, the smallest thing was going to set it off.

District Attorney Johnson got out of his seat and said, "Your Honor, I would like to call the state's last witness to the stand, Mr. Donald 'Lucky' Gibson."

The courtroom exploded, some cheering and clapping, others yelling and using obscene language.

"You fuckin' nigger rat!" an officer in uniform yelled.

"How could you betray the brotherhood? We should hang you," a White man dressed in a three-piece suit yelled.

A few supporters on Perry's side were yelling at the officers. They couldn't believe the trash coming out of their mouths.

The judge started banging his gavel so hard, court officers came marching in.

"Silence in my courtroom!" a furious Judge Lewis said. "Officers, get the crowd under control immediately. Whoever doesn't obey my order, escort them out of my presence. I will not tolerate this behavior in my courtroom. I'm extremely shocked at the police department's outburst. I'm sure Commissioner Fratt will be embarrassed when he hears of this. Any more interruptions and I will clear this courtroom. Mr. Johnson, will you please proceed?"

Extra security was on hand because of the high media attention. In fact, the media had been coming down hard on the NYPD. And some experts were saying the outcome of this verdict was meaningless because the court of opinion had already convicted the police officers.

It took about five minutes to get the courtroom back in order after a few were escorted out, one in handcuffs, but none of the officers were thrown out. Perry's family was heavily protected by the Nation of Islam security, the FOI, the Fruit of Islam, known to provide excellent protection.

Perry's mother, not rattled by the mini outburst, sat there motionless as she held her husband's hand. She didn't even look toward the altercation. Her only concern was getting justice for her baby who was gunned down by those dirty cops.

Once there was silence, the trial proceeded.

"I would like to please the court and call my final witness, Mr. Gibson, to the stand," Johnson said nervously, hoping another outburst didn't occur.

Lucky came in the courtroom from the back, from where inmates entered. As he walked to the stand, you could tell he was a buff brother. Lucky's suit didn't hide his biceps, which were huge. He was known as a weightroom rat, and it was obvious. He didn't have that prototypical cop look. At six foot, one, and weighing about two hundred and twenty pounds, he looked more like a professional athlete going to a business meeting, or a superstar rapper. His jewelry and swagger gave the impression he was a street cat, not a detective. Which was probably why he made one hell of a detective. His thuggish appearance was so believable.

As he was walking with swag toward the stand, he turned to the crowd. He couldn't believe the amount of people in attendance. Then he turned toward the defense table, where his former partners were all sitting. He slowed his walk and gave each one of them eye contact. He read through their eyes. He knew they were all nervous. Lucky smirked at them because he knew his partners had searched hard, hoping they could kill him and prevent this day from ever happening. But he laid low right under their noses. He'd never left New York. He was hibernating, cooking up a plan of his own.

"Mr. Gibson, we don't have all day," the judge snapped. "Please sit down, so we can proceed."

After Lucky sat down, a few police officers stood up and walked out as he was being sworn in. One of them said, "Die in hell, rat!"

The DA waited for the officers to exit before he began his questioning. "Can you please state your name, for the record?" Mr. Johnson asked.

"My name is Detective Donald Gibson, but everyone calls me Lucky," he said as he slouched on the chair. Lucky had a laid-back demeanor about him, like an old-school pimp, but without the funny-looking hat. His body language was hard to read.

"Why do they call you Lucky?"

"In this line of work, I've brushed death a thousand times," he replied as he looked at his former partners. "I'm lucky to be alive right now."

"Tell us about your resume, Detective."

"I have worked for and dedicated my life to the NYPD for the past fifteen years. I started in 1991 as a streetwalker. I was a rookie straight out of the academy at twenty years old. I'm now thirty-five. I've always wanted to be a cop. It was a childhood dream of mine. I was hoping by being an African American police officer, I could change the bad image in my community.

"After my second year on the force, I was promoted. I was transferred from the Twenty-fifth Precinct to the Twenty-third Precinct, still in Spanish Harlem. I was assigned a new partner and given a new police cruiser. After four years of protecting the streets of East Harlem, I finally made homicide detective in 1999. After I solved a few murder cases in Queens and I received guilty convictions in all, I was assigned to a special elite unit called Operation Clean House."

"Mr. Gibson, can you please explain to the court the qualifications needed in order to be even considered for such an elite team?" Johnson asked.

"Sure." Lucky turned toward the jury. "To be honest, the qualifications are not written in stone. I was told, because of my excellent performance, great attitude, distinguished record, and high conviction rate, it made me an easy candidate. Like I stated earlier, I dedicated my life to the badge. For me it was a way of life, not a job to pay bills."

"So, is it safe to say before you joined Operation Clean House, you were an honest police officer?"

"Yes."

"I object, Your Honor. He's leading the witness," Defense Attorney Matthew shouted it.

"Overruled."

"Thank you, Your Honor. Donald, for the past three weeks, the jury got an in-depth explanation of why we are here. Today, they will get a chance to hear the truth about what happened to Perry Coleman."

"I object, Your Honor. Is this necessary? Are you going to allow the counsel to make a mockery of your courtroom?"

"Mr. Johnson, please ask your question. Save any additional comment for your closing statement."

"Donald, do you consider yourself a dirty cop?"

"I object!" Matthew interrupted again. "He's leading the witness."

"Overruled. Mr. Matthew, I'm eager to hear the truth."

"What kind of police officer are you?" Johnson asked again.

"By the book, until I joined Operation Clean House. I mean, I'm a man, and I take responsibilities for my actions. I knew what I was doing was wrong. Operation Clean House was like a crackhouse. It's impossible to live in a crackhouse and not smoke. I became part of the environment."

"Donald, let's start from the beginning. Take us back and tell us about your first day in Operation Clean House."

Lucky reached for the cold water in front of him and slowly sipped it, hoping it would prevent the sweat from pouring down his face. He was about to commit suicide by testifying against his former employers. He finished the glass, cleared his throat, sat up, and began talking.

"I remember my first day on the job. I received mixed feelings from my new partners because I was the only Black guy on the team. They didn't hide how they felt about my presence either. I extended my hand out to all four men in that room, and only one of them shook my hand, Detective Michael "Tango" Scott. Tango became my closest friend on the squad but died in the line of duty. His cover was blown in one of our many dangerous assignments. My other partners are all sitting right there." Lucky pointed at the defense table. "Captain William 'Tuna' Youngstown, Steve 'Loose Cannon' Stanley, and Jeffrey 'Speedy' Winston."

Captain William "Tuna" Youngstown had been in the police force for close to forty years. He was six foot three and weighed two hundred and ninety pounds. He had long blond hair, which he kept in a ponytail, and evil dark brown eyes. He looked more like a bouncer at a nightclub than a police captain.

Detective Jeffrey "Speedy" Winston, a ten-year veteran, was five foot nine and barely weighed a hundred and sixty pounds. He was built more like a sprinter than an officer. His low-cut hair and clean-cut attitude gave away his military upbringing.

Detective Steve "Loose Cannon" Stanley, a seventeen-year veteran with tattoos all over his body, didn't look like a cop. Just less than six feet tall, he looked more like a biker or the leader of a dangerous gang.

"My first assignment was taking down a notorious heroin gang called M&M, which stood for Murderers and Millionaires. The captain wanted to throw me in the fire quickly and test my ability. Since we were going after a Black gang, I was made the lead detective, even though I was basically a rookie on the team. I guess they wanted me to fail and throw me off the team.

"Michael and Jeffrey were going in as undercover drug addicts, and my job was to infiltrate their operations. M&M was making about twenty to fifty-thousand dollars a day in the Bronx. They called their product 'cliffhanger.' Fiends were dying off this powerful drug. There was no cut—straight, raw dope. A violent drug war started behind the success of cliffhanger. Bodies were dropping daily because other drug dealers were losing profit. The city was losing control on the war. The mayor called our captain and told us to take down M&M at whatever cost."

"The mayor of this city said, 'at whatever cost'?" Johnson interrupted.

"I object, Your Honor. That's hearsay, third-party speculation."

"Sustained. The jury will ignore that last question. Counsels approach."

After counsels approached the bench, the judge said, "Don't you dare implicate our great mayor through a third-person statement, Mr. Johnson. Your action could lead to contempt of court, and you could be disbarred in the State of New York. Are we clear?"

"We're clear."

Johnson didn't like that the judge came down hard on him, but he understood. This case wasn't about the mayor. He walked back to the center of the courtroom and proceeded.

"Let's get back to M&M. Please continue, Mr. Gibson."

"M&M was a gang that was well organized. Their leader, Money Mike, was a smart criminal. We label these individuals as organized thugs. He ran his operation out of one building on 139th Street and Third Avenue. He had so many lookouts, his team barely got arrested. Tango and Speedy, I mean Michael and Jeffrey, never got a chance to buy from the dealers directly. M&M would have the neighborhood kids deliver the drugs back and forth from the building and serve the addicts.

"These kids were making anywhere from one to three hundred dollars a night. That's more than what an average cop makes today, or even their own parents. These kids were not going to school. M&M basically ran a twenty-four-hour operation. Anyway, after ten months of surveillance, we had nothing on M&M, not one wiretap, only a few photos. We arrested a few members with bogus charges, but they didn't talk. That was strange because usually there is always one who wants to talk, but not this crew. Not even the little kids we arrested would talk. We were up against one of the most loyal organizations in history.

"This made our job a lot harder because we rely on information to solve at least ninety percent of our cases. From the intelligence we gathered on M&M, we only knew who was calling the shots, but there were six to seven other members who were still a mystery. We didn't know their ranks or true identities. Truth be told, we could have been wrong about who was calling the shots. We needed to come up with a better strategy. Meanwhile, the crime rate was rising like the sun. This is when I first learned that our department worked under a different set of rules."

"What do you mean by 'a different set of rules'?"

"We did as we pleased. We didn't report to no one. Don't get me wrong, we were good at our jobs. We just took the law into our own hands, even if that meant planting drugs, tampering with evidence, assault, or murder. Whatever it took to get the job done, we did it."

"Murder? Do you mean others besides Perry were innocently murdered as well?"

"Yes."

You could hear the *oohs* and *ahhs* all across the courtroom.

"The only reason why this case is getting national attention is because Perry didn't have a criminal record and was a working parent. Had he had one felony, forget about it."

Matthew quickly stood up. "I object. The witness is using the stand as his personal platform to speak for his personal feelings. I move that the witness be removed, and I ask that his testimony be made inadmissible. It is obvious his intent is personal."

"Overruled."

"Your Honor, but this witness has a personal vendetta against my clients."

"I said overruled," Judge Lewis shot back in a slow, loud voice. "Your objection was heard and denied."

"Okay, let's get back to M&M. Donald, please continue," Johnson said.

"Since we couldn't get close to M&M, we decided to set up one of their key members. M&M ran Patterson Projects, but they had beef with their neighbors, Mott Haven Projects. We did a sweep one night in Mott Haven Projects and locked up about ten members of the RSB, which stood for Red Slab Boys, a crack gang. That same night, we pulled over Money Mike's black Mercedes Benz, and one of M&M's key members happened to be driving his car.

"We later learned he was the captain of the crew. His name was Derek Bailey, better known as Thirty-eight. He loved and used his .38 handgun so much, that became his nickname.

"That night when we pulled him over, we didn't care about the gun or drugs. Around that time, a gun charge against a high-profile criminal was like a misdemeanor charge. Money Mike would have spent good money on attorneys to get his captain out and charges dropped. All we wanted was for Thirty-eight to spend one night in jail, so we made up a story about an arrest warrant, took him to Central Booking, and we locked him up. I was undercover in the cell waiting for him, so were the ten RSB members we picked up. The plan was to drop Thirty-eight off in the cell, and when all hell broke loose, I'd jump in and help him out.

"The plan was perfect because not a minute went by after the CO closed that cell before one of the Red Slab Boys approached Thirty-eight and started swinging. Ten against one is no match for any one, so within seconds, Thirty-eight was on the floor getting stomped. Since they all had their back toward me, I jumped toward them and pushed the whole pile toward the metal bars, and Thirty-eight was able to get back on his feet. We were both swinging to save our lives. After the correction officers saved our butts, the RSB boys were moved to a different cell, and Thirty-eight thanked me. He wanted to know why I helped. I told him because that's how I get down, and by his reaction, I knew I had him in my pocket.

"The following morning right before Thirty-eight's court hearing, we had a few COs from Rikers Island come in and scoop me up, making it seem like I got transferred to there. Before I left, Thirty-eight told me to look him up when I got out. I told him once I posted bail I would. I waited a week before I went to Patterson Projects, looking for him. When I got there, it was like they were expecting me. They were showing me a lot of love for helping Thirty-eight. That same day, I was introduced to Money Mike and the rest of the crew, and Thirty-eight spoke highly of me.

"Within days, I knew their whole operation. Five months later, I had a wiretap on the whole organization. With my intel, we were able to identify all the top members and their ranks. We knew where the stash house was located, their connections, plus drop-off and pickup locations. I had so much information on them, we didn't need a snitch for this case. It was a slam dunk."

"Impressive. So what happened next? Did all the members from M&M get convicted?"

"No."

"What do you mean? I can't believe you. Why not?" Johnson fired back with a puzzled face.

"Deals below the table were cut. Information was leaked about how we illegally arrested Thirty-eight. A lot of charges were dropped, and my evidence was not admissible in the court of law."

"You mean to tell me the wiretaps were not accepted?"

"I had Money Mike on tape ordering hits and talking about his operation. I recorded meetings between all the members and Money Mike. They were all incriminating themselves, talking about murder, kidnapping, and money laundering. You name it, they talked about it on my wiretap. We all heard the tapes together."

"Donald, can you please clarify for the court who you mean by 'all of us'?"

"I'm referring to my partners sitting over there. We all heard the tapes together. We played those wiretaps over and over, like a Marvin Gaye record."

"So everyone from M&M walked, how?" Johnson asked.

"Not everyone. Money Mike only did eighteen months, and four others were sentenced to only two to six bids. I don't know how, especially with all the evidence we had, but you would have to ask my former employers sitting over there why." Lucky pointed at his former partners.

"So you are testifying today that there was foul play?"

"I object, Your Honor. This testimony has nothing to do with the current case. This is an irrelevant testimony."

"I agree. Counsel, get to the point," the judge stated.

"I'm just trying to bring to light the criminal behavior of these police officers, including Donald Gibson himself. Donald, you may continue," Mr. Johnson said.

"I recorded those wiretaps myself. I felt betrayed. Everyone in my department turned their heads. I risked my life, and it seemed like no one cared. A few days later, our captain called a meeting to discuss our new target. I tried to ask about the M&M case, and he snapped at me. They wanted me to turn my cheek like they did. At first I couldn't, but after a while, it became old news, and I just went with the flow."

"So just like that, you were given a new target? Who was the new target?"

"This delivery service company located in Manhattan, called Mr. G Express. We got a tip they were delivering cocaine all over New York."

"Who provided the tip?"

"We used to pay all our informants lots of money if they provided good information."

"How much did it cost for this tip?"

"Around twenty thousand dollars."

"Twenty thousand? Wow! Where did the money come from?"

"Like I said, we were governed by a different set of rules. We never once turned in drug money we seized, not once."

"I object, Your Honor," Matthew yelled. "This is all speculation."

"Overruled."

"Go ahead, Donald, finish what you were saying," a cocky Johnson said.

"We never turned in confiscated drug money. We created our own budget. For example, once we paid this informant on a tip about a Dominican crew smuggling drugs through fifty-four-foot trailers coming up from Miami. We infiltrated the buy. We confiscated 450 kilos of cocaine, over fifty brand-new guns, and 1.5 million dollars in cash. We only reported the 400 kilos and the guns. We never turned in the money."

"What happened to the money and the fifty kilos of cocaine?"

"We split the money. Tango was no longer with us at the time. We each took $200,000 for our personal use. We put the other $500,000 in the budget along with the drugs. In our line of work and how deep undercover we worked, we needed to produce cash, drugs, and guns quickly, so I will say at times, it was necessary to have that amount of money and drugs. We abused the system, using and keeping a lot of money for our own personal use."

"No one ever questioned your team or made you guys follow guidelines?"

"No. It was like we were given the green light to do whatever we wanted."

"Whatever happened to M&M?" a curious Johnson asked.

"Karma. Money Mike was murdered, and his crew fell apart."

"What about the Mr. G delivery business? Who led that investigation?"

"Loose Cannon—I mean Steve. I don't know how or why, but I kept my mouth shut. We didn't call him Loose Cannon for nothing. We spent about four months trying to find a lead, but we couldn't. We really thought we were taken for a ride by the informant. We followed every delivery boy on foot, bike, and car. We had nothing, until we illegally got access to Mr. G's computer and his network."

"What do you mean by illegal access?"

"I object, Your Honor. Witness is testifying to a third-party conversation."

"Overruled. This is all credible testimony."

"I don't know how Steve got the access. I just know he showed up with a disk full of information. Mr. G's computer became our personal informant. His company seemed legal, at least to the naked eye. We couldn't digest all the computer language, and he had a bunch of codes and passwords, so we hired an ex-con computer geek, and he was able to hack the files. We'd found the break we needed.

"One of the first things we noticed was, Mr. G had another warehouse we didn't know about. This warehouse was located in Long Island City, Queens. That same night, Jeffrey, Steve, and I watched the new warehouse all night. About four in the morning, the main gate opened up, and a white van with tinted windows drove out.

"We followed the van all the way to East Harlem. The van stopped at 110th Street and Lexington Avenue. We parked on 111th Street. Five minutes later, we noticed a Hispanic man walk up to the van, and an exchange was made. We thought we were following the van because they were making a drop. Come to find out, the driver was a heroin addict just out buying a quick fix. We pulled the van over right before he jumped back on the FDR Drive on 116th Street and Pleasant Avenue. We arrested the driver, and if my memory serves me correctly, his name was Robert, yeah, Robert. We were hoping the van was dirty, but it wasn't. All we had on Robert was the few bags of heroin. He was not cooperating either. We needed him to talk, so we started offering him all kinds of deals."

"What kind of deals?" Johnson asked.

"Money. We started at a thousand and offered as much as five thousand, but he didn't want the money. All he wanted was his heroin, so Steve went into the captain's office. Ten minutes later, they are letting Robert shoot dope right in the interrogation room."

"Donald, you mean to tell me you guys let a heroin addict shoot up just to get information out of him?"

"We did whatever it took to solve a case. I didn't agree with it, but it worked. Robert gave up all the information we needed. Even though we had Mr. G's files, we still couldn't read them correctly. Mr. G had a very large clientele list, and Robert helped us figure out who were the cocaine customers and who weren't. His VIP customers either owned or ran Fortune 500 companies. He was averaging about one million dollars a week, since he didn't deal with small-time customers. To buy drugs from him, you also had to use his mailing services. That's how he was able to stay under the radar and make his business look legit. We also learned he made out-of-state deliveries as far as California and Las Vegas. He was larger than what we'd originally thought. Robert agreed to wear a wire, but things got ugly quickly. Two days later after our meeting with him, he was found dead in an alley, and Mr. G disappeared."

"What do you mean, he disappeared?" Johnson asked.

"He was gone. After Robert got murdered, Mr. G and his files disappeared."

"Wait a second, Donald. How can your main suspect, his operation, and all the evidence you had on him disappear?"

"That's a good question."

"What do you think happened?" Johnson asked.

"I object, Your Honor. He's not an expert witness. He is asking him for his opinion."

"Overruled. Though he's not an expert, he was part of the investigation and has firsthand knowledge on the matter. I think his opinion does count in this matter."

"When we started to carefully read the list and check out some of these VIP customers, too many important names were surfacing. We're talking CEOs, VPs, and politicians. My honest gut feeling, these people were able to pay their way out."

"I object, Your Honor. Witness is speculating, based on hearsay."

"Sustained."

"You didn't make any money off these deals?" Johnson asked.

"Not off the Mr. G case. I never received one dime. I was told to erase the whole operation from my mind."

"By who? Who said erase it from your mind?"

"My captain." Lucky pointed at William.

"How much money you think they made?"

"I object, Your Honor!" Matthew shouted.

"Withdrawn, Your Honor," Johnson shot back before the judge gave his ruling. He walked back to his desk and consulted with his assistants. He was getting ready to ask about the night in question.

Lucky took advantage of the break and poured himself another glass of cold water. He knew the heat was coming.

Johnson waited for Lucky to finish his glass of water before he proceeded with his case.

"Mr. Gibson, tell us about the night Perry Coleman died. What really happened? Do you remember that night?"

"How can I forget? It still haunts me at night. Anyway, we were all having drinks at this strip club called Tops Off. We normally hang there when nights are slow."

"Were you guys drinking while on duty?"

"Yes, we arrived around seven p.m. It was Captain William "Tuna" Youngstown, Steve "Loose Cannon" Stanley, Jeffrey "Speedy" Winston, and me. We didn't leave till we heard the call. We were drunk and high off cocaine. All of us were."

"While still on duty, you guys were high and drunk?" Johnson asked as he turned to the jury.

"Yes, that was a regular routine for us. We got a call about a robbery on 103rd Street and First Avenue. By the time we arrived at the scene we didn't see any perps. We had a description on the suspect, a young Hispanic male in his early twenties, wearing a red shirt with blue jeans.

"We drove around the area for about fifteen minutes, but we came up empty. Steve was pretty upset about it. He was having a blast at the strip club and didn't want to leave. He kept repeating to himself, 'Someone is getting locked up, and I don't care who.' While we were sitting at the light, he yelled, 'What's that?'

"We all looked toward our left and we saw this Black male wearing a white shirt with black jeans walking out of the store. He was reaching for his cell phone, not a gun, and he clearly didn't fit the description. I was driving, Captain was shotgun, and Steve was sitting behind me with Jeffrey to his right. Steve and Jeff were the first ones to jump out of the car, with the captain right behind them. All three had their guns drawn, yelling for Perry to get down on the ground."

"Wait a second, Mr. Gibson. Are you saying that Perry never shot at the officers first?"

"Correct. Perry never shot at us, because he never had a gun."

The courtroom erupted again. This time, it took about fifteen minutes to control the crowd. Everyone who supported the Colemans was on their feet, demanding and screaming for justice. The police officers in attendance were still sticking up for their brothers and began arguing with a few protesters.

Through the ruckus, you could see Perry's mother still in her seat, her head down. She was in tears and crying out for help under her breath. "Why, sweet Jesus, my Lord and Savior, why did you have to take my son away?"

By the time the mayhem was over, the courtroom was half-empty. A few more protesters were arrested.

During the disturbance, Lucky had looked over at his old partners and read the lips of his former captain.

"You are dead."

Lucky just smiled and gave him the middle finger.

Once order was restored in the courtroom, the judge banged his gavel and said, "This will be my last warning. One more, and I will empty the courtroom and postpone this case. Mr. Johnson, you may continue."

"Thank you, Your Honor. Lucky, please continue. What happened next?"

"I parked the car right in the middle of the street. When I jumped out, I noticed Steve approaching Perry and he was discharging his weapon. The captain and Jeffrey followed like a domino effect. They were also firing their weapons. As I'm running toward them, I was able to stop both the captain and Jeffrey from shooting. Steve stopped only because he ran out of bullets. I was in complete disbelief because I knew we messed up pretty bad. As I'm yelling at the Cap and Jeff, Steve, who I thought had had enough, was trying to reload his weapon. The Cap tackled him to the ground and was able to calm him down for a few seconds.

"Meanwhile, Jeff ran back toward our unmarked car to retrieve a .357 revolver we kept in the trunk for dirty work. The serial number was scratched off. He took about four to five steps back from the car and shot at the back driver-side window twice. He then ran back over to Perry and placed the .357 in his hand. As soon as I approached Jeff about his actions, other units showed up to the scene. It was too late."

Lucky stopped to wipe a tear coming down his cheek. He looked around and Perry's family was also in tears. A few jurors had watery eyes as well.

"Mr. Gibson, did you discharge your weapon?"

"No."

Matthew shouted, "I object, Your Honor. Our forensic witness made it clear that there were other shells found on the scene. This witness is committing perjury."

"Your Honor, their witness also confirmed those shells did not come from Donald's service nine-millimeter weapon."

"Overruled."

"And are you positive Perry never had a gun that night?" Johnson asked.

"I'm positive. We planted the gun. We shot him first and continued to shoot him while he was on the ground."

The crowd started whispering. Lucky's testimony was firing them up again. Even the judge thought another eruption was about to take place, but everyone kept their cool this time.

"What made you come forward?"

"Even before the shooting, I was having a hard time sleeping. It almost felt like I was in too deep to turn back. I wanted out, but I couldn't find a way. This case here is my way out. When Perry was killed, I realized then how important it was for me to stand up and come clean. These past few years, I have nothing to be proud off. I wanted to give back to New York. I have taken so much as a dirty cop. Hopefully now, I'm able to rest in peace in the afterlife."

"No more questions, Your Honor. The State rests its case," Mr. Johnson said.

Judge Lewis looked at his watch. "It's now eleven-thirty in the morning. Let's break for lunch. I will see everyone back in here at one p.m. Mr. Matthew, you will get a chance to cross-examine the witness then."

Chapter Three

Lucky's Roots

Lucky was led back to the holding cell for his own protection. He had just made himself a whole new set of enemies with his testimony. It wasn't just police officers who felt betrayed, but correction officers as well. Even the prisoners hated him. They didn't care that he was helping Perry's case. He was still a dirty cop and a snitch, and was now what they would call easy prey.

Lucky just sat inside his single cell, his head leaned back against the graffiti-covered wall. He tried to figure out where things went wrong for him. He thought about his ex-girlfriend and daughter, also hiding somewhere safely.

Lucky kept his family business to himself. No one in the police department knew about them, he made sure to keep their identity a secret. Hurting a cop's family was high on a criminal's wish list. Lucky was starting to have second thoughts about his decision to come forward.

He stood up and began pacing back and forth in that tiny cell. "What did I get myself into? They're going to kill me for sure," he kept repeating to himself.

He sat down and tried to relax his mind. He leaned his head back against the wall again and reminisced about his past, his childhood. Reflecting on his painful past had always helped him get through any issues he was dealing with in the present.

Donald was born and raised in the South Bronx. An only child, his mother, Dawn Gibson, was a Southern lady, born and raised in New Orleans up until she was seven years old. That's when her family moved up to New York.

Dawn met Lucky's father when she was sixteen years old. Four months later, she noticed her stomach was getting bigger, and she was dealing with morning sickness. She was devastated. She didn't tell her sex partner until she was six months pregnant. Right after she told him, he got up, got dressed, and walked out. Dawn never saw Lucky's father again. From that day on, she never looked back.

Young Donald was a witness to his mother's suffering, and he made himself a promise to help her out as best as he could. All she'd ever wanted for him was a good education. He made it through elementary and junior high school unfazed. He was an honor roll student and was loved by his peers because he wasn't a follower. Everyone considered him a leader.

By the time he reached high school, the smooth-sailing ride was over. Not having a father figure started catching up to him.

Donald was into girls heavily. Popular and good-looking, girls were throwing themselves at him. There were some questions he thought his mother couldn't answer. He needed a male's advice. He wanted to know how to handle them, and he didn't want to listen to his friends.

His mother had always said, "Leave those fast girls alone. They're nothing but trouble." But, in reality, Donald wanted the attention. The word *sex* was now in his vocabulary, and he wasn't waiting until his prom to lose his virginity.

He had sex for the first time after a home game with a cheerleader he really liked. She was his girl for three weeks, until the next one threw him some new pussy. He kept switching girls as they came. If his mother had any idea he was having sex with so many different girls, she would have had a heart attack.

He maintained a 3.9 average through high school. He lost his love for karate and grew a passion for football and basketball. He played safety for his school football team and shooting guard for the basketball team, breaking several school records. His senior year he ran for school president and won. All the faculty members wanted him to get into politics, while the coaches were arguing about which sport he should play in college. Everybody wanted to make a decision for him, but he stunned everyone with his decision to attend a community college and join the police academy.

No one understood why he would join the academy with such a bright sport career ahead of him. No one but his mother. She knew Donald grew a passion for his community and wanted to help turn his neighborhood around.

He'd joined the academy in hopes of having other African Americans follow his lead. The police department had an image of only nerds and rednecks in its ranks. He figured once the public noticed a basketball and football star had joined the force, it would bring better qualified applicants. And he was right.

Everything was on track when things took a turn for the worse. The summer right before he was to start college, Dawn was involved in a very bad car accident. While she was driving home from her second job around 2:30 in the morning, she was involved in a head-on collision with a pickup truck. The other driver fell asleep behind the wheel. By the time Donald reached the hospital, his mother was pronounced dead. He didn't even get a chance to say good-bye to her. Her last words were a voice mail she left him:

"Okay, baby, don't you forget dinner is in the microwave. Mommy will be home late. I love you."

Donald changed after his mother died. He never made it to college that year. He was lucky his mother had a $150,000 life insurance policy, with which he was able to pay off bills and survive for the following eighteen months in isolation with no problem. For an entire year and a half, he basically blocked the world out and only went outside his house like an inmate, an hour a day.

Donald had blocked the world out, but he didn't shut down his mind or body. He kept exercising them both and grew physically stronger and mentally tougher, working out at least five hours a day. He was growing muscles he didn't even know existed.

He read all the "survival" books, and would actually live out the drills in them, sometimes starving himself for a few days. He was trying to become a superhero cop. He restarted his karate training and learned how to live in the dark, and for four months didn't turn any light on at the house and kept all the blinds down.

Lucky woke out of his daze when the district attorney, wanting to prepare him for the bombs the defense team would throw at him, came by to see him.

"Listen, Lucky, get ready to talk about your whole past. If you have any secrets, they are about to get exposed on that stand. Matthew will do everything in his power to damage your credibility, trust me. The important thing to remember here is your poise. Stay cool, calm, and collected under his attack. If you lose your cool in front of the jury, you could damage our case. Are you following me?"

"Yeah, I hear you. I'm ready. It's not like I'm lying. I can handle Matthew, don't worry."

"Well, we got five minutes. Good luck. I will talk to you after court."

"That's funny, Mr. Johnson. As soon as court is over, I'm going back in the hole I crawled out of. You won't see me anymore."

"You just can't disappear again. We could protect you, Donald. Give us a chance. We may need you again."

"We got five minutes before court begins, right? We don't have the time to talk about this bullshit right now. My decision is made. Thank you, but no, thank you."

"Have it your way," Johnson shot back and left the cell.

Lucky's hands started sweating. He sat back down on the metal bed and placed his hands over his head. He didn't have a clue on what to expect once he took the stand.

When the bailiff called his name, his heart dropped. He knew it was time to face the music one last time.

Chapter Four

Cross-Examination

This time when Lucky entered the courtroom, he didn't take his time. He walked straight to the stand and was sworn in. "Counsel, you can cross-examine the witness when you are ready."

"Thank you, Your Honor," Matthew replied.

Tyler Matthew walked toward Donald and stared him right in his eyes, hoping to intimidate the former detective, but Lucky wasn't fazed by the staredown. He held his ground until the fancy defense lawyer looked away.

Tyler Matthew first got his license twenty-five years ago as a public defender. He became famous when he was able to get all charges dropped against Al "The Stallion" Soprano in one of the biggest Mafia cases to hit NY in the '80s. He even won a civil lawsuit against the city. Ever since that case, he had been defending high-profile clients who could afford his rate, which was anywhere from $5,000 plus, an hour.

"Donald, can you please state for the court and jury your last employer."

"You mean who I worked for?"

"Correct. You do remember your last employer, right?"

"For the past fifteen years I've worked for the New York Police Department."

"Are you aware of the brotherhood code in the police department?"

"What brotherhood?" Lucky asked, confused.

"Testifying against one of your own is against the brotherhood."

"I object, Your Honor!" Johnson interrupted.

"Withdrawn, Your Honor. Lucky, today you made some accusations in this courtroom. You have implicated my clients' involvement in all sorts of criminal activities. It is my job to make sure those accusations are nothing but the truth. How old are you?"

"I'm thirty-eight years old."

"Are you a family man?"

"No, I'm not. My job didn't permit me to have a family. I worked too many hours."

"But, all three of your partners, they have a family. I don't see why you couldn't. Any reason as to why?"

"I object, Your Honor. His questions are irrelevant to the case."

"Your Honor, I'm just trying to see if Mr. Gibson is a credible witness. I'm trying to establish his character, that's all," Matthew shot back.

"Overruled. Counsel, I hope you are going somewhere with this. You are running on thin ice."

"Thank you, Your Honor. I understand. Please continue, Mr. Gibson."

"I understand my partners are all married, but trust me, you don't want to use them as examples or role models. They are horrible husbands and fathers. They have all committed adultery. The clients you are defending loved having sex in our department. It didn't matter where—in the police car, holding cell, right on their desk. You name it, they did it." Lucky chuckled.

"But you still haven't answered my question. Why are you avoiding answering me? Why don't you have a family?"

"I don't want a family, and I don't need a family. When my partner was killed in the line of duty, I had to call his wife and tell her about the murder. I wouldn't want my wife to receive a call like that. That's why I avoided a family. I still dated females. I just stayed away from serious relationships."

"You don't have any kids?"

"No."

Matthew paused and walked back to his desk.

Lucky took a deep breath, hoping they didn't know about his daughter. He poured himself a glass of water. He knew he was in an awkward situation, but he kept his composure because the jury was still watching him.

"Donald, you know you are under oath. Once you make a statement, it becomes a record of the courts."

"I understand."

"Let's go back to the M&M case for a second. You stated you couldn't comprehend why Money Mike was let off the hook and his members received short sentences. Could it have been because of you?"

"What? Are you serious?" Lucky shouted back. "I did what I was told to do. I did my job."

Mr. Johnson caught Lucky's attention from his chair and hand signaled him to calm down.

"Did they tell you to go around killing rivals?" Matthew asked.

"As an undercover detective, you have to play whatever roles you need to in order to keep their trust and to stay alive. That's nothing new. We killed if we had to, just to stay in character."

"You still didn't answer my question. Did you kill rival members with the fella you call Thirty-eight?"

"I object, Your Honor. He's leading my witness."

"Overruled. C'mon, Mr. Johnson, you know you can lead in cross-examination."

Lucky, looking for help, was hoping Johnson's objection didn't get overruled. Matthew had him trapped against the wall.

"We are all waiting for your answer, Mr. Gibson."

"Yes."

Lucky knew his credibility was shot. Even the body language of a few jurors changed a bit.

"Is it true that some of your wiretaps also included your voice in the background?"

"Of course, they did. They were strapped on my chest. You could hear my heartbeat."

"Mr. Gibson, let me refresh your memory."

"I object, Your Honor. Where are these wiretaps? There could be anything on those tapes."

"I agree. Sustained. Counsel, don't talk about mysterious wiretaps in my courtroom. Unless you are submitting new evidence, please proceed."

"Is it true your captain approached you about your conduct during the investigation?"

"No, he never approached me about my conduct. He patted me on the back and told me to keep my mouth shut."

"He wanted you to keep your mouth shut about what?"

"They didn't want me to talk about my involvement with M&M. They thought my behavior was a bit much."

"Over the edge, you think?" Matthew asked with a friendly smile, hoping Lucky would bite.

"I guess a little too much."

"I just asked you if you were approached by your captain about your behavior and you said no."

"No, I didn't. I thought you were referring to IA, Internal Affairs."

Lucky's credibility took another hit. Perry's family was all sitting on the edge on their seats. They knew Lucky was messing up, and that was hurting their case.

"I warned you earlier that you are under oath. Secretary, read back for the records."

"Counsel," she said. "'Is it true your captain approached you about your conduct during the investigation?'

"Witness. 'No, he never approached me about my conduct. He patted me on the back and told me to keep my mouth shut.'"

"Mr. Gibson, how can we trust anything that's coming out your mouth is the truth? In the past few minutes, we all have witnessed you change your testimony. Were charges dropped against M&M because your wiretaps also incriminated the police department?"

"No, I don't agree. I was asked to do what's necessary to bring down M&M. I acted as a gangster, only to build the trust I needed to shut down their operation. My behavior wasn't a mystery. It was necessary to perform at a maximum level."

Matthew walked right up to the jury, and without looking at Lucky, facing the jury and smiling the whole time, he said, "Mr. Gibson, today you could go to jail for perjury. Did you know that? You have lied to us all," Matthew spread his arms like wings.

Johnson jumped in, hoping to save Lucky from himself. "I object, Your Honor. He is bashing my witness."

"Overruled."

"Earlier in your testimony, you stated you don't have any children, Donald. Again, were you lying?"

"I object, Your Honor!"

"Withdrawn." Matthew walked toward Lucky. "Is it true you have a pretty little daughter?"

Lucky just sat there. Once he heard the word *daughter*, he automatically assumed the worst, that maybe they got to her. No one knew about his baby girl, so for Matthew to bring it up meant he knew something.

After this trial he was going have to move his daughter to a new house. He was stuck in a tough situation. He didn't want to admit he lied again and hurt this case even more. He assumed the defense had some type of paperwork to prove he was the father, but he took his chances anyway.

The judge snapped, "Mr. Gibson, please answer the counsel!"

"No, I don't have a daughter. I have a god-daughter, who I haven't seen in years."

"Is that your final answer?"

"I object, Your Honor. Counsel is delaying this case in hopes he could trap my witness in his own words. It is obvious to the court the defense is hoping for a miracle mistake."

"Sustained. Counsel, let's speed things up. We are not here on a paternity case. We would need a DNA test, and we don't have time."

"I understand, Your Honor. I was trying to prove to the jury that Donald Gibson has no credibility."

Matthew walked back to his table and consulted with his team about the next step. They were hoping to keep pushing and hurting his credibility.

Right before the judge banged his gavel, Matthew jumped up from the chair and continued his questioning.

"Mr. Gibson, you stated you accepted bribes from criminals and important businessmen, correct?"

"Yes, I did. Personally, from criminals only. The business-men always dealt with my captain."

"If you weren't present in those meetings, how can you accuse my clients of making under-the-table deals?"

"I always waited in the other room while these meetings took place. Once the deals were made, I was always given a black garbage bag filled with money."

"But you never heard the bribes. You are only assuming."

"I don't know the details of the negotiation, you are right, but if my cut is one hundred thousand, that's more than assuming."

"Donald, for how long have you been snorting cocaine?"

"Maybe five years. I was working on a case, and in order to join their organization, I had to snort cocaine. Only problem is, after that, I became addicted."

"So you are an addict?"

Johnson jumped in again. "I object, Your Honor!"

"Withdrawn. Do you have a problem with cocaine, Mr. Gibson?"

"No, I've been clean since I left the force. Cocaine became a part of our job. We would snort every day, before we hit the streets. As a matter of fact, we snorted all day long, but those days are behind me."

"On the night in question, how much drinking and cocaine did you do before the shooting took place?"

"I don't recall how much cocaine, but it was a lot. Maybe three grams."

"You snorted three grams of cocaine?"

"Not just me. Between all four of us, we used about three grams, and we all had about three to four shots of vodka."

"Is it safe to say that maybe you were too high to remember what you saw?"

"No, it's not. I clearly remember what I saw."

"But you were high and drunk, yet you want us, the jury, and the court of law to believe an ex-dirty cop and former drug addict. Sitting over there, we have three honest cops, fathers, and husbands. Why are you trying to sabotage their careers and families?"

"What about Perry's family? Who's thinking about them?" Lucky stood up as he replied. Matthew finally got to him. "Listen, I know what happened that night. We killed an innocent man for no reason, and now we are hiding behind our badge, this city, and the law."

"Mr. Gibson, if you don't sit back down, I will hold you in contempt!" the judge yelled at him. "Are we clear?"

"Yes, we are clear," Lucky said as he sat back down.

By this time, everyone in the courtroom, including the judge, was losing a little patience. Matthew was trying his best to avoid asking the main questions he should be asking.

The judge said, "Mr. Matthew, please get on with your case, so we could move to closing arguments by tomorrow morning."

"Mr. Gibson, didn't you shoot your gun that night as well?"

"No, I never drew my gun from the holster."

"All of my clients testified you were the first one to shoot back. Remember, you are still under oath."

"I never drew my gun, and I never shot it. There were no shell casings found on the scene that matched my gun. Those three officers over there killed Perry out of pure hatred. 'Another dead, Black criminal. Who cares?'—Those were the words my captain used that night."

Again, the courtroom exploded. This time, some even rushed the three officers charged. They'd had enough and couldn't hold back their anger. The extra court officers available were able to control the crowd rapidly, but not before Steve "Loose Cannon" got hit with a chair across his back that threw him to the ground, but he was okay.

The judge banged his gavel and adjourned court until the following week. He then made his way out of the ruckus and ran straight into his chambers.

Lucky didn't want any part of the rumble. He made his way back into the holding cell, more concerned about disappearing again.

Meanwhile, the police officers on the scene were slapping handcuffs on anyone that moved or supported the Coleman family. It was like something out of the movies.

It took about forty-five minutes to finally get the courthouse under control. Those who weren't arrested were sitting in their seats not knowing what to do next, shocked at the way things turned out.

Lucky had some quick words with the DA.

"Listen, Lucky," Johnson said in a soft, worrying tone. "They're going to try to move this case to another county, maybe upstate or Westchester. If we continue, I expect a hung jury. The judge will give me a date to hear the closing argument, but I guarantee that day will never come. They don't want a deadlocked jury. This case will get moved, especially after the ruckus that just took place in the court."

"There's nothing you could do to stop it? C'mon, brother, this is the time to step up. You sound like you giving up," Lucky shot back in disbelief.

"Giving up? Listen, I worked my ass off for this case. I believe your story. I know they killed that poor kid for no apparent reason. Since this case started, I have noticed the loopholes in our great government. I'm getting pressure from the fuckin' mayor to plea-bargain down to a misdemeanor."

"What? That's only a twelve-month sentence. They'll be out in six months."

"I know, Lucky. I'm glad you came forward. You sure you don't want to hang around a little longer? We could really use your help."

"Man the fuck up. They are testing you to see how far you will go. If you show fear to take chances or risk everything you have, they will own you. I can't hang around. I now have a hit on my head for stepping on that stand. I won't disappear quietly—I could promise you that."

Before the district attorney could reply, Lucky was already heading for the door. Once he heard about the case being moved, he automatically knew the charges were going to get reduced or maybe even dropped. He made his way outside the courthouse and disappeared into the downtown Manhattan crowd.

There was nothing Johnson could have said to keep Lucky around, but Johnson had a funny feeling he wouldn't be too far away either.

Outside the courtroom, Perry's mother was getting ready to speak to reporters, while her husband, and Perry's wife and son stood by her side.

Chapter Five

The Phone Call

Laura took a deep breath when she saw there were over thirty media personnel waiting for her on the front steps of the Supreme Court, where many celebrities had held their press conferences. Laura dreamed about this moment. This would be her first shot at redemption, closure. She knew the world was watching. She wanted to make sure she kept her composure and chose her words wisely. The last thing she wanted to do was come off as a hateful woman who had a vendetta with the entire police department.

"Today, we learned the truth about what really happened to my son," she said. "We heard it from one of the officers who was present when the shooting took place. He testified against his former partners, and finally painted a picture for us. Now we know what happened that night.

"Since the first day my son was murdered, I was told by everyone, the mayor, police commissioner, and even you guys, the media, that my son had a weapon. I didn't raise him to shoot people. I'm not saying I'm a better mother than any woman, or that Perry is a better son than anyone's, but the portrait you guys painted of my son was untrue. Today, it was a blessing to hear Donald Gibson come clean and tell the truth to the world. I know my son didn't shoot at the police officers. He didn't even own a gun. He made one mistake when he was a juvenile with some school friends, but since then, he has blossomed as a respected, positive man.

"At today's hearing I was shocked to hear the racist language coming from other police officers who were showing their support. It's sad that we still face racism, like we are still in the fifties and sixties. I hope today's ruckus doesn't dilute the jury's decision when it's time to hand down the verdict. These animals must pay for what they did to Perry, his family, his wife, and son. A guilty verdict won't bring him back, but at least he will be able to rest in peace.

"I'm curious now to see what you guys will print in the papers tomorrow. I hope one of you apologize for jumping to conclusions and defaming my son's name. That's all I have to say right now. Any other questions, our family lawyer will answer them for you. Have a good day."

As Mrs. Coleman, her husband, Kim, and little Perry walked down the steps of the courthouse, reporters followed them, hoping for one more statement. They all quietly jumped in a black Lincoln Town Car and drove away.

While in the car, Laura leaned back, closed her eyes, and exhaled. She was hoping when she woke up, her baby Perry would still be alive, and this would all be one big nightmare. On their ride back home, they kept hearing a phone ring.

"I know I'm not going crazy. Can someone please answer their phone?" Perry Sr. said.

"I hear it, too, honey. Excuse me, driver. Is that your phone?"

"No, Mrs. Coleman, that's not my cell phone ringing. I have mine on silent."

They all looked puzzled and confused and started searching for this cell phone. Perry Sr. was riding shotgun and didn't see anything in the front.

Kim reached under her seat and pulled out a black RAZR, still ringing. "I found the phone. It's ringing. Should I answer it?" Kim asked.

"Wait, not yet!" Laura shot back in a scared tone.

"Someone left it here because they want to communicate with us," Kim argued. She flipped the phone open and answered the call. She had a gut feeling the caller had information to provide.

"Hello?"

"Put Mrs. Coleman on the phone, please."

"Who is this?" Kim replied, looking over her shoulders. She knew whoever was on the line was watching them, because they knew she wasn't Laura.

"Listen, I need to speak to Mrs. Coleman. Please pass her the phone."

Kim attempted to pass the phone to Laura, but she didn't want to take it. The past few weeks all kinds of nutheads had been calling her. She was tired of the harassment.

Her husband had to encourage her to take the call. "Go ahead, honey. Speak to them. See what they want. The minute they say anything crazy, just hang up."

"Okay." She pulled the phone close to her mouth. "Hello?"

"Mrs. Coleman, no matter what you do, please don't say my name until we hang up."

"Who is this?"

"Mrs. Coleman, it's me, Donald Gibson, the cop who just testified."

"I don't understand why you are calling me."

"Just listen. First, I want to apologize for what happened to your son. You have my deepest sympathy and condolences. I'm calling you because I wanted to warn you about a few things. If I know my partners, they already bugged your car and house. They know I would be contacting you guys, so in other words, they are listening. However, they can't hear me. That's why you can't repeat what you hear. Are you following me, Mrs. Coleman?"

"Yes." Laura sat up on her seat.

Perry Sr. was getting a little concerned about the conversation. By her body language, he knew she was uncomfortable, but not frightened. He held back from grabbing the phone.

"Okay, listen, I have some bad news. The defense is going to try to file a motion to move the trial to another county. That's going to hurt your case, if they approve the motion. Let's meet. I have something to give you. Meet me tomorrow morning in Central Park. You know how to get there?"

"Yes."

"Let's meet at nine in the morning on 110th Street and Fifth Avenue. When you get off the phone, I want you to say out loud my name, and a fake address where we're meeting. Good day, Mrs. Laura. I will see you in the morning. Oh, before I forget, remember, you are being watched. I would say, at least a ninety percent chance, you are. I would come up with other ways to communicate without making it obvious. Good-bye, Mrs. Coleman."

"Wait, I don't—"

"Shhhh. I will answer anything you want to know when we meet. Are you coming?"

Laura had to take a deep breath. She grabbed her husband's hand, squeezed it, inhaled, and said, "Yes," like she signed her life away. She exhaled and leaned back in her seat.

Perry Sr. was very concerned. "Honey, you okay? Can you hear me, sweetheart? Who was that on the phone?"

Laura just sat there for a good two to three minutes in dead silence. She knew her husband and Kim were both talking, but she couldn't hear a thing. Finally, she snapped out of it and told them what Lucky said.

"You won't believe who was on the other end of that phone."

They both asked, "Who?"

"That was Donald Gibson. He said he wants to meet and hand me some evidence that would help our case."

"You mean to tell me that was Donald and he wants to meet? It doesn't sound right, baby. What the fuck is going on here?"

"I don't know, but I guess we will soon find out."

Perry Sr. pointed his finger at his wife. He looked like he had the devil in his eyes.

Even Kim sat back and held Li'l P tight on her lap. She'd never seen him act this way. The stress of this whole ordeal had to be wearing him down.

"Listen, woman, we are not meeting with that cop. You heard the things he said in that courtroom. He's a murderer. Who knows what kind of trick he's trying to pull?"

Kim jumped in. "I think he's right, Mrs. Coleman. You might want to think about it."

"Think about what? My baby is gone." Her voice started cracking. "This man called me and said he has something to give us. Plus, I have some questions of my own. We are meeting tomorrow morning at nine, at Penn Station on Thirty-fourth Street."

"You never listen to me, woman. You are not going alone. I'm coming with you."

"I'm not going," Kim quickly added. "You guys could just fill me in later."

They all sat quietly for the rest of the ride.

Laura thought about different communication strategies.

Lucky's hunches were right. Captain, Loose, and Speedy were determined to capture him. They'd hired their own surveillance crew, two brothers who called themselves "The Watcherz." Their names were Hack and Little Hack, and their rap sheet could stretch a mile. They were the best underground hackers in the game. Their specialty was tracking people down and hacking into systems. They'd made millions helping the mob locate witnesses. It was rumored they hit a bank for about twenty million, right from their living room, and just by hitting the enter key on their keyboard. That was before they both got busted and served over twelve years apiece in federal prison.

The Watcherz were back in business after they had been paroled, but they kept a low profile. They didn't take those high-paying jobs, because they wanted to stay under the radar.

Until Captain Tuna approached them about the job of tracking down Lucky. Their mission was to find him and the whereabouts of his daughter. The captain wanted Lucky and everything related to him dead.

They bugged the Lincoln Town Car the first day of trial and struck gold. As soon as they heard Laura say Lucky was on the other line, the captain was contacted on his cell phone.

"Who the fuck is this? It better be good. I'm in no fuckin' mood."

"We got Lucky," said Hack.

Tuna's attitude did a three-sixty. "You did what? Great job. I'll be right over."

As soon as Tuna pressed the END button on his cell phone, he speed-dialed Loose.

"Cap, what's up?"

"The Watcherz, they found our boy."

"You're shitting me!" Loose yelled back.

"Find Speedy and meet me at the spot in forty-five minutes."

The spot was an old, beat-up apartment building on 102nd Street and Lexington Avenue with five floors, each floor with a four-bedroom apartment. Tuna's uncle owned the building. He rented the fourth and fifth floors to Tuna for his operation, he lived on the third floor, and the second and first floors were rented out to only family members. The fifth floor had nothing but state-of-the-art surveillance equipment, most of it illegal.

The fourth floor was basically a bachelor's pad/safe house. One room on the fourth floor kept all the money, guns, and drugs. Only the captain knew the combination to the safe. Speedy and Loose Cannon arrived at the spot early so they waited in the car until Tuna pulled up. Then they all went in together. They sat down, cracked open a few beers, and listened to the tape, evil smiles on their faces.

"We finally got this muthafucka, Cap. I'm going to cut his fuckin' tongue out!" Loose yelled.

"I knew he would slip up. Good job, boys. Now find his daughter," Cap said to the Watcherz. "We got a lot of work to do. The meeting is tomorrow morning, and it's going to be a madhouse in Penn Station. He picked a good location, but his ass is still fried."

"Wait a minute, Cap. Play the tape one more time," Speedy requested.

"We already know the drop. What else we need?"

"You see, Cap, that's the problem right there. Everything is too easy. Lucky is a lot smarter than that. We all know that."

After listening to the tape again, Speedy stood up and paced the room back and forth. He knew something was funny about the location. He asked The Watcherz if it was possible to pick up the conversation on the cell phone. They nodded their heads and asked for fifteen to twenty minutes.

The captain and Loose were starting to see Speedy's point.

Within three minutes, The Watcherz had the cell phone conversation playing through the speakers:

"Okay, listen, I have some bad news. The defense is going to try to file a motion to move the trial to another county. That's going to hurt your case, if they approve the motion. Let's meet. I have something to give you. Meet me tomorrow morning in Central Park. You know how to get there?"

"Yes."

"Let's meet at nine in the morning on 110th Street and Fifth Avenue. Good day, Mrs. Laura."

"Damn, Speedy! You a bad son of a bitch," Loose said. "That was a great pickup. We would have been at Penn Station like assholes, while the real meeting is taking place in Central Park."

The room got quiet after they heard the real meeting location. Everyone was in a daze, thinking about tomorrow morning. Lucky had almost fooled them, but Speedy was on point. They quickly started getting ready.

They all had been waiting for this day since the night Perry Coleman was killed and Lucky disappeared. They'd searched for him all throughout the city. They had a million-dollar bounty on his head. No one knew his whereabouts. That's why they were so nervous when he'd showed up in court.

The captain started pulling out different maps of Central Park. Loose and Speedy cleaned and loaded all their guns like they were being deployed to Iraq.

This was the day they would get payback on a disloyal member.

The Watcherz were back on the computer, looking for the second targets while the Cap, Speedy, and Loose went down to the fourth floor to celebrate. These officers didn't care that they were each facing murder charges, they still partied hard. They'd stopped going to strip clubs, so they called strippers to the apartment. These NYC police officers were living and acting like gangsters, legal thugs.

While they were snorting coke, taking shots of vodka, and getting lap dances, someone else was busy preparing for the meeting.

It was one o'clock in the morning, and Lucky didn't plan on sleeping. He also set up his own spot like his former partners. His equipment wasn't as fancy and expensive, but good enough.

He'd bought a house in the Bronx, in the Pelham Bay area, a three-floor house he shared with Diamond, a twenty-three-year-old woman. Everything was under this girl's name. Her real name was Tracey Sanders, and she was a runaway from Alabama. She'd come to the Big Apple six years ago at seventeen.

As soon as she stepped off the bus, a pimp snatched her up and had her turning tricks that same day. She was working for only six months the night Lucky bumped into her. He was coming out of the strip club in Hunts Points when she walked by and offered him a blowjob.

"Hey, big guy, would you like for me to suck your dick?"

Lucky looked around to make sure she was talking to him. His dick was already hard from all the lap dances.

"Hell yeah. How much is it going to cost me, baby?"

"For you, forty dollars, but if you get a room, I will suck and fuck you for seventy-five. You could even go inside my tight ass."

At that point, it wasn't hard to convince him. They started walking to Lucky's car and headed to a nearby run-down motel called Crown Inn, right off the Bruckner Expressway. Diamond was hot, even at a young age. She was five-six, with long, black, silky hair, caramel complexion, and juicy lips. Her body was right and tight for a young thing. Her baby face and pretty, chinky eyes made her desirable to any man. Her ass was big enough, and her tits were perfect.

Lucky had a feeling she was young, but he also thought she was old enough to get fucked. He knew he was paying for the sex, but he still felt special being with such a gorgeous girl.

When they got in the room, he told her, "Go ahead, baby girl. Jump in the shower. I want you fresh, baby girl, but please get undressed in front of me."

"I hope you know we are wearing a condom, so do it really matter how fresh I am?" Diamond quickly asked.

"Of course, we are. I just don't want to smell the streets on you. Go ahead, take your clothes off."

"Okay, but turn the lights off. I'm shy. You could leave the bathroom light on, but turn this one off," she said, walking toward the light switch.

She was hesitant about taking her clothes off with the lights on. Being the detective he was, he sensed something was wrong. *Why would a pretty girl with a body like that be so self-conscious about how she looked?* He played it cool and told her it was okay.

Right after she dropped her panties, he quickly jumped up and flicked the light on. Her beautiful, young, tender body was covered with bruises. Her pimp apparently loved beating on her. Once Lucky saw the marks, it blew his high. His dick went soft, and he thought about his own daughter.

Long story short, he took her in that night, and she'd been living with him ever since. Three days after he took Diamond in, he went back to Hunts Point in the Bronx, where he found and killed her pimp.

Lucky treated Diamond like a woman from that day on. He took care of her and offered her a place to stay. All she had to do was maintain his house and not tell anyone about him or where they lived. She basically became his student, studying his every move. She became so good at it, she even committed crimes with him.

Diamond was his eyes and ears in the streets. He transformed her into a new woman. First, they became best friends, then partners, which led to them falling in love with each other. It wasn't until her twenty-first birthday that they finally had sexual relations; that's how much respect and love Lucky had for her.

She was the one who'd planted the phone in the Colemans' car, distracting the driver with her sexy self. She would also be the one who would be watching the cops in the morning in Central Park. She was a rider, and since Lucky saved her life, she owed it to him and did what he asked without hesitation.

While Lucky was plotting in the basement, Diamond was in the kitchen fixing a late-night meal. It was going on two in the morning, and she was in there fixing fried chicken, French fries, and bisques.

That's why he loved that young tender. When she came downstairs with the food, she gave him the boost he needed.

For a moment, he was sitting there spaced out. When Diamond came downstairs, he snapped out of it and started eating like a beast.

"Damn, nigga! Slow down. Save some for the homeless." She laughed.

"Thanks, baby, I needed this right here."

"I know." Diamond leaned forward and kissed his greasy lips.

As Lucky ate, Diamond browsed through his paperwork on the table, catching up on the latest.

Fifteen minutes later, Lucky was back on his feet, ready to finalize the plan. "Diamond, everything on your end is ready to go?"

"Yes, baby."

"Good girl. Well, take your pretty ass to sleep. You got about three to four hours. We're leaving at six-thirty in the morning."

"Okay, baby. Don't worry too much. We got this. The plan is perfect. Just come to bed for dessert."

"Not right now. Pussy is the last thing I need. No distractions. You know better than that. When we get back, we could do something special. Whatever you want."

"Sounds good. I'll see you in a few hours."

As soon as she went back upstairs, Lucky got back to work, going over all the details. He wondered how hard his former partners were working. Little did Lucky know, his former partners were all drunk and passed out. However, The Watcherz were still up, trying to get closer to the little girl.

Chapter Six

The Meeting

When the clock hit nine in the morning, no one was at the Penn Station location but uptown, on 110th Street near Central Park. It was the moment of truth. The action was about to kick off.

The captain and Loose were both hiding in the bushes inside the park and had a clear view of the street, where Speedy was parked in an all-black surveillance van.

Speedy noticed the Coleman car pulling up. He reached for the radio and called his boys. "Hey, fellas, Elvis is in the building. They are parking as we speak."

"Which car? The red Chrysler parking behind the green truck?" the captain asked.

"Affirmative."

"Perfect. They parked right in front of us. We will be able to see Lucky when he approaches the car," the captain radioed back.

Diamond, watching from the rooftop on 111th Street, also saw the Colemans' car. She sent the signal to Lucky that the target had just arrived.

The Colemans were nervous as hell, not knowing what to expect. Perry Sr. kept looking at his wife with a face that didn't need words.

Laura was now regretting the idea. She was seconds away from telling her husband to drive away, until she saw someone approaching.

That's when Speedy got back on the radio. "Here we go, boys. The mouse is coming right at you guys. He's wearing a black jacket and blue Yankee hat. I can't tell if it's Lucky, but he's built just like him. That's him, fellas, it has to be."

"We see him, Speedy," the Cap fired back.

"Let's just rush him now!" Loose yelled.

"Are you crazy? Right in front of the Colemans? We finally have a visual. We are going to sit here and follow him then kill him. Understand?" the captain whispered in an angry tone. He wanted to make sure Loose, who had a tendency to not follow directions, understood his orders.

"We clear. I just hate that double-crossing bitch."

As they watched Lucky walk up to the car, his back was toward them.

"Hey, Speedy, he has his back toward us, we can't see the transaction. He's going to give her something. Keep your eyes open. We'll follow Lucky, you follow the Colemans and retrieve whatever he gives them."

"How in the world can I retrieve the property, Cap?"

"I don't know. Think of something. Call your cousin over at the Thirty-first Precinct. He's blue and white. Have him pull them over or something."

"Cap, I just saw the drop. He passed her what looked like a CD jewel case. There must be a disk inside. He's walking away now, and I just heard the Colemans' car engine start up. I will follow the car, and you take care of Lucky. Cut out his dirty tongue."

"With pleasure, trust me," Loose shot back, not letting Captain Tuna respond.

Tuna and Loose started following Lucky down Fifth Avenue.

Diamond was looking for them and finally spotted them when they jumped out of the bushes. That's when she ran down the six flights of stairs, but by the time she hit the street level, with the heavy traffic going down Fifth Avenue and a lot of people walking the streets, Tuna and Loose were out of her sight.

The captain decided to follow as far as they could before they made their move. They were getting restless as they were already approaching 103rd Street.

"Look, Cap, he's turning into Central Park."

"I see him." The Cap reached for the radio. "Speedy, Lucky turned into the park. We are making our move now. Make sure you get that CD."

"Understood," he radioed back.

By Lucky turning into the park, it made it easier for Tuna and Loose to catch up to him. They began running. Loose was running with his gun out in his hand. When they made their turn, they started shooting.

The sound of gunfire had everyone running and screaming, making it look like a scene out of *Grand Theft Auto*.

Even Diamond's heart paused and skipped a beat when she heard the gunshots. She started running faster toward the shooting.

After about eight to ten shots, the captain wanted to leave, but Loose thought otherwise. "Hold on, Cap, I have to make sure he doesn't survive this one. We don't call him Lucky for nothing." He ran up to the body, which was motionless in a pool of blood. He kicked the body on the back. "What the fuck! Who in the fuck is that?" he yelled.

When Tuna saw Loose's reaction, he ran toward him. It wasn't Lucky, and they both were tripping the fuck out.

"Let's go. C'mon, Loose, let's get the hell out of here," Tuna said, pulling him.

They disappeared through the bushes before the cops showed up.

Diamond made her way to the scene and radioed Lucky. "You were right, baby, these muthafuckas want you dead in a bad way. They just killed my boy in broad daylight in Central Park. Anyway, handle your end, and I will see you tonight. Remember, you made me a promise. I will be waiting for you."

"Cool." He laughed. "Anyway, I'm sneaking into the Colemans' crib right now. I will hit you later. And I didn't forget about my dessert."

The Colemans owned a beautiful, four-bedroom house in Astoria, Queens. Kim and Little Perry were the only ones home. Kim had just put Perry to sleep and was in the living room watching television.

Lucky was standing about fifteen feet behind her, and she had no idea he was there. He was stuck because he couldn't figure out a way of approaching without scaring the shit out of her.

He decided to sneak up on her and place his hand on her mouth, to prevent her from screaming. "Kim, it's me, Lucky, Detective Gibson from court."

Kim struggled at first until she heard his voice and name.

"I came here to talk," he said as he removed his hand from her mouth.

"What in the hell are you doing here? They left to go meet you."

"Listen, this was a setup all along, I wanted to talk to you. I don't have a lot of time to explain. Can we talk in the laundry room?"

"Laundry room? Why there?" Kim looked at him up and down suspiciously.

"This house is bugged. With the washer and dryer on, they won't be able to hear our conversation."

"Okay, follow me."

As he followed her to the laundry room, The Watcherz were on the phone calling the captain. At first he couldn't answer because he was on the radio with Speedy, who'd told him the Colemans were at a restaurant eating.

When the captain finally answered the phone, he almost caught a heart attack when he got off.

"Who was that on the phone?" Loose asked.

"The Watcherz. They confirmed Lucky is at the Colemans' house right now speaking with Kim."

"Let's go then. We need to hurry up."

"Loose, they live in Queens. It's going to take like an hour to get there."

"Yeah, but maybe he thinks he has two hours. It's worth the shot. Call Speedy. Tell him to meet us there."

By the time they were on their way to Queens, Lucky was already fifteen minutes deep into his conversation with Kim. She had tears in her eyes hearing the story all over again.

"I'm sorry, Kim. Perry didn't do nothing that night but reach for his cell phone. Anyway, in the basement you will find a white envelope I left with helpful evidence against these police officers. Wait a day or two before touching it or telling anyone about it."

"Why are you giving it to me and not the courts?"

"Listen carefully. You are going to have to explain it to the Colemans. They are going to move this trial to another county, basically an all-white county. That way, they get an all-white jury."

"What? They can't do that, right?" a shocked Kim asked.

"You can say it's written in stone."

Kim started breaking down. She couldn't believe her husband was murdered and the people responsible would get away with it.

Lucky knew he didn't have time to sit there and console her. "I'm sorry, I wish I could do more. Tell the Colemans to move forward with a civil case. You guys will be better off getting money from the City than a guilty verdict. The evidence I left, if you use it in the case, you will lose it. Trust me, it will disappear. Remember, your attorney is the district attorney for the City of New York. He's getting all kinds of pressure from politicians."

"I really don't understand everything you're saying to me. Wait for Laura and her husband to get home."

"Kim, you are not paying attention. You have to be strong. The City will do everything in their power to make this criminal case go away. They don't care if they have to pay money. They will offer to settle."

"So, that's the way it is? All my baby gets is money, no justice?"

"Unfortunately, that's the way it is here in this corrupt city. It doesn't matter that you have all these Black politicians and these big-name African American organizations backing you guys up. It's all propaganda. Just listen to what I'm saying— Do it my way, and at least you will be financially set. Just think about what I said. I'm leaving now. I will be in contact again, but you will never see me in a courtroom. Oh, and tell the Colemans they deserve the gift."

"What gift?"

"You will see when they get home. Just tell them it was from me."

"You are leaving just like that? What if we need you to testify again?"

"I left you enough evidence. You don't need me anymore. And, to answer your question, no, I won't testify. Good-bye, Kim, and take care of little man, and again, I'm sorry."

"Wait. Before you leave, did he say anything?"

"Who did?" Lucky replied, looking puzzled.

"Perry, what were his last words?" Kim asked, hoping Lucky would say what she wanted to hear.

"I'm sorry, Kim. By the time I reached him, he was gone."

"That's okay, Donald. We also appreciate you coming forward and placing your life on the line to tell the truth. We thank you so much. We knew in our hearts he didn't shoot at you guys first."

Lucky gave her a hug, threw his black hoodie over his head, and he disappeared again.

The only image the Watcherz obtained was Lucky's backside leaving out the back door.

While the Cap and Loose were still stuck in Manhattan traffic, Lucky was making his way back to the Bronx.

Lucky arrived back at the house and quickly realized something was wrong with Diamond. "What's wrong, girl? Everything went perfect today. We executed the plan. Why the long face?"

"Perfect? What about Larry?"

"Who in the fuck is Larry?"

"I can't believe you right now." She got up and walked away from Lucky.

"C'mon, tell me what's wrong. Come here," he said, grabbing her hand. "Where you going?"

"He was twenty-three years old. Larry was the mark I used as your stunt double, remember? He was killed today."

Lucky felt like a bag of shit, only because he wasn't more sensitive toward Diamond's feelings. To him, Larry's death was just another body, but to her, he was something more. She committed the mistake of falling for the mark. He picked up on her emotions quickly, and instead of flipping and coming down hard on her, he played his part.

"Listen, on some real shit, my bad. I was hyped, caught up in the moment because, you know, things went well. You are right. We lost someone who put his life on the line for us."

"Wait," Diamond said, interrupting Lucky. "He put his life on the line for us without knowing he did."

"You're right. These muthafuckas really want me dead. Hey, listen, girl, you know a mark is a mark. We knew, whoever we picked, we were gambling their life away. I see you felt for the mark."

"No, no, Daddy, I didn't," she said, frightened.

"It's okay. You felt for the mark in some shape or form, and you didn't want to see him dead. We all go through that. All I'm saying is, don't get caught up. Emotions in this game are a no-no. You could lose yourself in guilt and never find your sanity again. Let's just relax for the rest of the day. Call up the Chinese spot and order us some food. I got a few bootlegs we could watch tonight, before we get it on."

"So you're not mad at me?"

"Not at all, baby."

Lucky gave her a hug and kissed her on the forehead. "I'll be downstairs until the food gets here." And down to the basement he went. He wanted to check the surveillance cameras around his neighborhood.

Lucky had installed ten cameras in a three-block radius. To sneak into his house, you needed a few 007 agents. It was safe to say he was one paranoid individual. On the day he became a cop, paranoia became second nature.

Lucky was also able to pick up and hear any conversation within eight hundred feet of his house. He wanted to make sure no one followed him home. After returning from every trip, he would always spend at least thirty minutes reviewing footage and looking for anything suspicious. He had ten different camera views, all on a fifty-inch monitor. He would lean back on his chair and watch the streets like a nighthawk, hoping to see his partners or any idiot who wanted to die.

Lucky's former partners were all back at Tuna's spot, scratching their heads at the events that took place before them. They were mad and they kept throwing the blame around at each other. They'd thought for certain they had Lucky, especially when they picked up the cell phone conversation, but they didn't know he was actually setting them up.

"This fuckin' filthy nigger is getting on my last fuckin' nerves," Loose said.

"I agree. We need to find him, and I mean like yesterday," the captain added.

The Watcherz stopped their search for the little girl and refocused their attention on Lucky. Meanwhile, Speedy wanted to know exactly what Lucky had given the Colemans.

"Cap, we need to break into the Colemans'," Speedy said. "I know he left something at their house."

"Calm down. There's no need to worry. Whatever evidence they present in court, we will make disappear. I'm not worried at all."

"But we don't know what he gave them," Speedy shot back.

The captain stood quiet for a few seconds and realized Speedy was making sense, but he was too stubborn to admit Speedy was right. He quickly switched the conversation.

"What we need is a bigger team and a trap to bring the rat out of his hole."

"But who can we trust in the force?" Loose asked.

Speedy looked confused as well.

"We are going to have to reach outside of the force on this one. We need maybe two to three more bodies. Us three, we can't cover the whole city. With all the heat this case is catching, no one in the force would dare do anything stupid. We need to think, and come up with names."

"So now we are employing street criminals to join our movement? Are we giving them guns, too? I don't like this idea, Captain," Speedy said.

"That's why I'm the captain and you're not. Don't start questioning my tactics now. We have no choice but to reach out. We are not going to ask any asshole in the streets with a criminal record to help us. We are reaching out to professionals, maybe out-of-state help."

Loose and Speedy were starting to see the direction of the plan. They all sat on a black plush sofa and went into thinking mode.

While they were thinking, the Watcherz were having a difficult time on their end of the job. They were so frustrated, it got to the point where they started slapping each other. The two brothers were weird like that.

Speedy had to run between them to calm the situation. After about five minutes of struggling to get them to calm down, he ended up slapping both of them. Speedy wasn't known for having a temper, but Lucky had him stressed out.

The captain got up. "What the fuck is wrong with you, Speedy? Go home and come back tomorrow when your mind is right. You are not the only one going through it. We can't let this nigger win. This trial is bigger than us. We can't let this boy win."

"My bad, Cap. I will see you in the morning. Loose, see ya."

Loose walked Speedy downstairs, laughing his ass off the whole way. He thought it was funny that Speedy had slapped the brothers.

As they went downstairs, Tuna asked The Watcherz what happened.

"When Lucky went in the house, he went straight to the laundry room, and we couldn't pick up the conversation, so we don't have any visual or sounds," Hack said.

That was bad news for the captain. He was hoping they'd at least picked up some type of sound. Tuna was now stressed himself, and he needed a relief. He got on the phone and called up his usual spot.

"Thank you for calling The Candy Shop."

"Hey, Dimples. What's up? This is Tuna."

"Hey, baby. How are you doing?"

"I had better days."

"Well, you called the right place. The Candy Shop carries all flavors. You want the usual, baby?"

"Surprise me tonight. Remember, I don't like caramel or chocolate flavor."

"Don't worry. I know how you like them. Give me about an hour."

Tuna hung up the phone and noticed Loose wasn't back yet, which seemed weird. He quickly reached for his Glock and clicked off the safety. He walked toward the front door of the apartment, which was cracked, but saw no sign of his friend. Tuna's heart was pounding as he slowly walked up to the door. He managed to open the door with his foot while both hands were holding the gun.

When he reached the front door, he looked around and still didn't see Loose. He started walking down the steps, not knowing what to expect. He was shitting his pants. What if Lucky got to both Loose Cannon and Speedy, and now he was in the building trying to get him?

Tuna was able to make it all the way down to the first floor without any signs of Loose Cannon. As he approached the front door of the building, he could see the shadow of someone leaning their back against the front door. Tuna couldn't make who it was, but as he got close, he was able to hear Loose Cannon's voice.

"What? You want more? C'mon, you think you tough. Bring it."

Once Tuna heard that, he ran and opened the door as fast as he could and pointed the gun at whoever was fucking with Loose. Tuna scared his friend, catching him off guard, and Loose jumped on Tuna. In the struggle Tuna's black 9 mm Glock went off, and they both fell on the ground. Tuna didn't know if he shot his best friend or not.

Tuna quickly jumped up and started checking him for gunshot wounds. He couldn't find any and didn't see any blood. He then looked up to see who he was arguing with. It turned out, he was play-fighting with a ten-year-old boy.

After thoroughly searching Loose, they both looked at each other thinking it was impossible for that bullet to have missed him. Loose got up and told the kid to run home before the cops came.

"Damn, Loose! God didn't want you tonight. You are blessed, my brother."

"Cap, why in the hell did you jump out like that?"

"I don't know. You took too long to come up, so I came down. I crept up on the door, and that's when I heard you say, 'You want more?' so I didn't want to take any chance."

"Lucky got us all fucked up in the head. What if the kid got shot? Let's go upstairs and relax. You need to call The Candy Shop."

"I'm already two steps ahead of you. They should be here in like forty minutes. Go upstairs. I'm waiting for the uniforms to show up."

"No, Cap, come on. Don't wait. We don't need the attention."

"You right. Fuck that! Let's go get ready for the girls. I told Dimples to surprise us with a new flavor."

"You told her no chocolate or caramel, right?"

"They already know."

They went upstairs, took showers, and got dressed like they were going out to one of the hottest clubs in the city. The captain walked to the back, toward the safe house room. Ten minutes later, he came out with about eight grams of cocaine, a few pills of ecstasy, and seven thousand dollars, mostly singles and five-dollar bills, for the girls.

These above-the-law cops were living like kingpins, spending thousands on a daily basis, and killing with no mercy. And instead of playing it low-key until the trial was over, they were still committing crimes and partying like rock stars.

While the corrupt cops were partying, Lucky and Diamond were sleeping. They had watched a few movies and fucked each other's brains out.

The Colemans were still up and confused about what took place. They were supposed to meet Lucky, but instead met a stranger, who passed them a CD. When they opened the CD case, there was no disk, just a note ordering them to eat at a certain restaurant. They were hoping Lucky was going to show up. After a few hours, they decided to leave the restaurant and head home.

When they arrived home, Perry Sr. needed to get something out of the trunk of his car. That's when he noticed a big black duffel bag. He called his wife over. "Laura, did you put this black bag in the trunk?"

She walked over and looked at it, "No."

When they opened the bag, they couldn't believe their eyes. It was filled with money. They didn't know how much, but they quickly closed it and agreed to keep it a secret between them. They went inside the house and acted like they never saw the money.

Kim wasted no time approaching and handing them a four-page letter. She wrote everything Lucky said word for word. Everything, except what he left in the basement. The Colemans took turns reading the letter right in the living room. Now they knew who left them the money in the car, but they weren't surprised.

Kim was looking around the living room, searching for the camera. She couldn't stand being watched. She knew they were watching them read the letter.

The Watcherz desperately tried to zoom in on the letter, but they couldn't get a good angle. They even tried reading the Colemans' lips, but were unsuccessful as well. They knew Kim wrote about her meeting with Lucky.

After the Colemans finished reading the letter, Kim burned it with a smile, knowing whoever was watching would be upset by her actions. Once again, she was right. The Watcherz were pissed.

The Colemans were getting ready for another long night. No one could sleep, not after going through the type of day they'd gone through. Laura and her husband were in the same bed together, but their thoughts were miles apart. Perry Sr. was relying on his belief in God to get him through this, while on the other hand, Laura wanted those pigs killed.

"Honey," she said in a cracking, low voice.

"Yes, sweetheart."

"How in the hell did we get into this? First, we lost our baby. Now we're losing our privacy. I have so much hatred for those police officers."

"I really wish I had an answer for you, sweetheart. I been asking God why this has happened to our family myself, but I'm still looking for the answer. I don't understand how my son, who was unarmed, was gunned down like an animal," a choked-up Perry Sr. said.

"Honey, I've been asking God the same questions myself. I'm starting to question my beliefs. We are a good family. This is not supposed to be happening to us," she said as she sat up on the bed.

"I'm questioning my faith as well. I'm trying to stay strong, but it's hard. I wasn't there to protect him, but I will fight his death till the end," he said, also sitting up.

"I can't live like this anymore, Perry, knowing they are watching us. I can't sleep, use the bathroom, or change my clothes. I've had enough." Laura jumped out of bed.

"It's almost one o'clock in the morning, Laura. Why are you picking up the phone? Who are you calling?"

"I'm calling up the minister and our civil lawyer. They told me to call whenever I needed them, and that's what I'm doing."

Laura threw on her robe and walked down to the kitchen for a cup of coffee while she dialed the minister's number. After the fifth ring, he finally answered the phone.

"Who is this?" Minister Al Muhammad said in a angry, sleepy voice.

"I'm sorry to bother you. This is Laura, Laura Coleman."

"Laura, my goodness! What time is it? What's wrong? I'm listening."

"We need help. I think we are being watched. No, we are one hundred percent sure we are being watched. Our house is bugged."

"What? Excuse me, come again?" Minister Muhammad quickly got on his feet. "Listen, Laura, I will send a few FOIs by your house."

"That would be great, but I'm more concerned about our house being bugged."

"Don't worry. I'm sending someone who specializes in surveillance technology. He will find anything. It will take him less than an hour to sweep your house for bugs. I will be on my way after I make all these phone calls. We need to act now because, if your house is bugged and we wait, they will find a way to clean their mess."

"Okay, I understand."

"Don't let anyone in your home. I don't care who it is. I will get there as fast as I can. FOI will be there guarding the premises until I arrive. Remember, don't let anyone in until I get there, not even my security."

When Laura hung up the phone, she was nervous. She didn't know what she'd started. She just sat in silence with her head down.

Perry Sr. walked in the kitchen and hugged his wife. "Are you okay, sweetheart?"

"Yes, I'm fine. The minister is on his way, and he's bringing us a bunch of security."

Perry Sr. started laughing. "That's why I married you. You are a determined woman. I love you, baby."

As the Colemans continued talking in their kitchen, waiting for the minister, the Watcherz had called Tuna on his cell a few times, but he was not picking up. They'd also tried calling Loose Cannon, but his phone was turned off and going straight to voice mail.

Hack walked down to the fourth floor and knocked on the door repeatedly. He even banged on the door, but still no answer. All he heard was the loud music playing in the background. He went back upstairs and told his brother. They didn't know what to do.

They decided to call Speedy, but he was no help. He was still upset and didn't want to hear about Lucky or the Colemans. They continued watching the house, not knowing what to do.

When the minister arrived, he brought a few friends with him. They swept the house and cars and found five cameras in all with built-in speakers.

The Watcherz lost both audio and video. They were fucked. All the monitors went pitch-black.

The Colemans were shaken to see so many cameras. By this time, Kim and Li'l Perry were also up and shocked to see all the commotion.

The minister walked over to consult the family. "Laura, I'm glad you called me. I have with me one of my top lieutenants. He's an ex-Navy SEAL. He quickly identified those surveillance gadgets were not property of the NYPD. They look more federal, or bought in the black market."

"We already know who's responsible," she shot back.

"You do. Who then?" a puzzled Muhammad asked.

"Those dirty cops who killed my son. They were keeping an eye and ear on us, fearing that the other cop who turned on them was helping our case."

"And you are one hundred percent sure about this?"

"You don't even want to know what we've been through in the last twenty-four hours. Donald 'Lucky' Gibson himself told us. He was the one who tipped us off about the cameras."

"What else did he say?"

"He told us there was going to be a hung jury."

The minister was in a state of shock. Not surprise, but shock. He couldn't believe the government was about to let those cops get away with murder. He preached every day about a better day to come, but this mess he was facing was setting those days back by a few years.

"Okay, look, I'm going to make a few phone calls. I have some powerful friends in the force who could verify if this stakeout is legit. I'm also calling up members of my board. We are going to organize a rally in memory of Perry. We are going to march down by One Police Plaza. We need to show White America we will no longer take it. We will get a lot of media attention, which we need to fight the case from moving to another county. That can not happen."

"That sounds good, a parade for my child. He would love that," Laura said.

"Now, we need to talk about your safety. Are you guys willing to relocate until the trial is over?"

"Nope, that's not an option!" Perry Sr. fired.

"This is our home. We are not letting these dirty cops run us away from our home," Laura added.

"I completely understand. In that case, I'm leaving four members from my personal security team. The lieutenant is also a personal friend of mine. Brother Noble, he will stay as well. But, before we move forward, let's get one thing clear. I need to know everything. No matter how small or big, I need to know everything. Anyone else have anything they would like to add?"

Everyone got quiet for a few seconds.

The Colemans didn't bother telling the minister about the money in the car that Lucky gave them.

Kim was in a daze, thinking about the package Lucky left. She didn't know if she should say something and didn't see any harm in telling him about it. "Wait, I have something," she said.

Shocked she was withholding information from them as well, the Colemans quickly looked at her.

"What is it?" Minister Muhammad asked.

"Lucky said he would get in touch with us again."

"When? How soon?" he asked.

"He didn't say."

"He didn't say, huh. Well, we'll have to wait and see," Minister Muhammad replied, knowing Kim was hiding information.

"Oh, before I forget, you guys need to get ready. I have a reporter coming in about an hour to run this story. I guarantee you the mayor and police commissioner will bang their heads against the wall a few times. I will shake the city with this report. Hopefully it will work in our favor."

"That's the thing, Minister, but what if it backfires and hurts our chances in court?" Laura asked.

"I doubt it will. We clearly have foul play, and you guys should not be under surveillance like criminals. This is unacceptable, and we will take action. I don't care if we have to march from City Hall all the way down to Washington, D.C. We need to show our true character as a nation."

Chapter Seven

The Media

When Channel 5 News first came on at five o'clock in the morning, they reported the story on the early show. The news station titled the breaking news, "An Illegal Government Home Invasion." The news reporter stated they would go live with an exclusive interview with the Colemans at eight o'clock in the morning right from their home, along with Minister Al Muhammad, and their civil lawyer, Joseph Anderson.

The breaking news was the rush-hour gossip in all of the city's public transportation. Everyone wanted to know what happened and who was responsible for the invasion of privacy. New Yorkers were very concerned. No one knew what was going on, but rumors were already circulating through the grapevine. Some were saying the Colemans' house was broken into by a warrant squad looking for evidence that would damage Perry's reputation. Others were saying the Colemans were being watched by the federal government as a precaution.

People couldn't wait until the exclusive interview at eight o'clock. New Yorkers crammed into every businessplace with a TV. Some didn't care they were running late for work. They were not leaving their house until the interview was over. This case was real important to the people of NY. At this point, it didn't matter the color or gender of those involved. New Yorkers had had enough. A few were even calling for the resignation of the mayor and police commissioner.

Back at Captain Tuna's place, the Watcherz were still waiting to hear from Tuna or Loose. Around seven forty-five in the morning, Speedy zoomed in through the front door.

"Oh my God! Did you guys see the news? Where's the captain and Loose?"

"They are still on the fourth floor. They had a party, and the girls are still in there. We tried calling and knocking on the front door, but we didn't get an answer. We called you last night as well, but you slammed the phone on my ear."

Speedy raced downstairs and started banging on the door as hard as he could. He couldn't believe their whole operation was just shut down and the captain and Loose were in there celebrating like it was New Year's.

After about thirty seconds of banging, Loose Cannon finally opened the door. "Speedy, what the fuck is wrong with you? Why are you banging on the door so early? Where the fuck is your key?"

"Where's the captain? We have a fuckin' situation upstairs that needs immediate attention. Tell the bitches the party is over, and meet me upstairs in five minutes."

Speedy looked at Loose then looked at the naked girls passed out on the floor. He just walked away in disgust.

Loose knew it was a serious situation.

The captain woke up when he heard Speedy's loud voice. He turned over and asked what happened.

"I don't know, Cap, but we better get upstairs in five minutes before he comes back down here. He also said get rid of the girls."

"Get rid of the girls? They could wait down here. I'm not sending these pretty bitches back today. I'm paying for another night."

"I don't blame you. I had the time of my life last night, but I think you should get rid of them. I got a funny feeling we won't have time. You should have seen his eyes. I haven't seen him that spooked since our rookie years."

The captain was shocked to hear Loose agree with Speedy. He knew it was serious, so he told the girls to leave. They slowly made their way upstairs.

Speedy was waiting for them at the top of the staircase. "Hurry. We only got two minutes before showtime."

They both looked at each other, not knowing what to expect. When they entered the apartment, Tuna quickly noticed all the monitors were blank. The power was on, but the screens were pitch-black.

"Why are the monitors blank? What the fuck is going on? Why are you guys sitting in front of the TV?" Tuna asked Speedy and the Watcherz.

"The Watcherz tried calling you last night. They even banged on the door. Pull up a seat, the both of you. Watch the news and see why those monitors are blank. Laura Coleman has an exclusive interview coming up."

"What!" the captain yelled.

"They are calling it 'the home invasion,' or some shit like that."

"This can't be fuckin' happening right now!" Tuna yelled as he got up and threw a metal stool right through one of the big-screen monitors worth ten thousand dollars.

Loose tried to spit a few words out, but Tuna quickly rejected him.

"Shut the fuck up! Not right now! This right here, gentlemen, this interview, is about to send our asses to jail. I don't need to see the interview. If the monitors are blank, and the news is calling it a home invasion, then the Black bitch must have found our cameras."

"Let's hear what she has to say first. Once she finishes her interview, we will know what they're working with. Then we could figure out a plan. We're in this together," Speedy said, walking up and embracing his boss.

"I'm calm. Turn the TV up, and someone please find me a beer. Better yet, some fuckin' vodka. I got a feeling this interview will be a historic disaster for us, but a celebration for all niggers. I will bet you one million dollars that fuckin' scumbag, Minister Al Muhammad, is planning a rally."

"Shhhh! It's on, Cap. Here we go," Speedy said, his eyes glued to the TV screen.

Everyone was quiet and sitting still, except Tuna, who was the only one standing. He was about to watch an interview that would almost guarantee a guilty verdict in his court case. His heart was pounding, and his knees were shaking. The anticipation would have given any man a heart attack. They weren't the only ones watching. The whole New York City was. Plus, it was being broadcast via Internet as well.

**

Lucky was also up watching from his bed, sipping coffee, a smirk on his face. As the interview was about to start, he shook Diamond awake.

"Get up, baby. C'mon before you miss it. Get up."

"I'm up. My eyes are open. Turn the volume up," she replied in a low, grumpy voice

"Good morning, my name is Destine Diaz from WBZT Channel Five News. Today, I have an exclusive interview with the mother of Perry Coleman. Perry was gunned down by three New York detectives. We have some new disturbing allegations made by the Colemans' family lawyer, alleging that the their house and vehicles were illegally bugged by surveillance cameras and listening devices. Hear for yourself as we roll the tape."

The media did an excellent job in attracting the public attention through fear. This was the way to sell ratings and newspapers, coming up with catchy titles that would attract attention. By using words like *illegal* and *invasion*, the media sparked the attention they needed. The media still couldn't be trusted, but it couldn't be ignored either. The media's best attribute was their backstabbing motives and sneaky ways. All they cared about was ratings, but many felt they were still manipulated by politics.

Five seconds after the reporter said roll the tape, TV screens across the tri-state area went blank for three to four seconds, and then the weather guy came on with the forecast. While Blacks and Hispanics already knew the deal, a lot of White people didn't and were puzzled.

Meanwhile, the captain, Loose, and Speedy were all celebrating and whipping the shit out of their asses. They knew they were still in deep trouble, but happy the media didn't air the interview.

Once the mayor got word of the interview, he called up Eric Macintosh, the station's CEO, and his golfing buddy.

"Hello," Eric said, on the way to his office.

"It's me, Ralph."

"Good morning, Mr. Mayor. To what do I owe the pleasure of you calling early this morning?"

"I need a favor, and I need it in ten minutes."

"Let me guess. This has to do with the interview airing at eight in the morning?"

"You know about it and you're letting it air?"

"Calm down, old friend. I received about four phone calls already. You know I don't screen every report. But don't worry, I already made some phones calls, and it won't air."

"Thank you. I owe you one."

"You bet you do."

"Damn, Captain! We are untouchable. Once these charges get dropped, I'll bet you, we all will get promotions. I love being a cop, I love it," Loose said.

"Let's not get too excited. I'm pretty sure a lot more heat is coming our way," Speedy said.

"Don't worry. They will do what they always do—yell and yell. Loose is right. Once these charges are dropped, things will get better."

All three of them went down to the fourth floor. They wanted to relax and wait for the call. They knew the commissioner would either call or request a sit-down.

While they went downstairs, The Watcherz resumed their hunt for Lucky.

Lucky was in his bedroom doing exercises. He wasn't surprised that the network pulled the interview. Two corrupt moguls, the media and the government, pulled another fast one on the community. Lucky had bigger issues to worry about. His identity was back at risk once he showed his face in that courtroom.

He turned the TV off and continued working out, listening to music, and acting as nothing happened. He couldn't be rattled.

The real drama was taking place back at the Coleman residence, where Minister Muhammad quickly started making calls and trying to set up a press conference with independent outlets.

"I can't believe what we all just witnessed. White America just made a mockery of us. Brother Perry and Sister Laura, I apologize for this pain not going away. It just keeps pounding harder and harder. In the name of Allah, we will get justice, by all means," the minister preached.

"Well, I don't care who or which God, Allah, Jesus, Jah, whomever. We need closure, and it seems like we won't find it," Laura said.

"I understand, Sister. That's why we won't stop. We can't quit. At the press conference, we will tell the truth to the city. Trust me, the people want to know. Several media outlets will show up. Are you ready to start fighting back?" Minister Muhammad extended his hand to her.

She grabbed his hand and told him, "Yes, I'm ready."

When 10:00 a.m. came around, there were at least eight media outlets outside the Coleman residence. Laura, Perry, Kim, and the minister were all standing on the porch.

Laura took the center stage and told the world about the hidden cameras and microphones found in their home and cars. "We don't know how long the government has been watching us, but we discovered these devices last night. Donald 'Lucky' Gibson made us aware of the hidden show taking place in my home."

Reporters quickly began hounding Laura with questions, but Minister Muhammad stood up and said, "Please, ladies and gentlemen, one at a time, or your questions will go unanswered. We are here to talk. We will get to everyone's questions, but please, one at a time."

"Laura, hi. My name is Angela Stile. I'm with BETV Channel Twenty News. Did you just say Donald Gibson, the police officer who testified in court, made you aware of the surveillance taking place in your home?"

"Yes, that is correct."

"Laura, hi. Channel Four NBZ Prime Time. Let me ask you this—Are you sure the government is behind this?"

"Donald stated, the police officers who are on trial for killing my son are the same ones watching us."

"So it's not the Government, but these three police officers, correct?" the reporter shot back.

"Let me jump in here," the minister said. "When Laura called me out of my bed and told me about the hidden cameras, I called in my very own friend, an ex-Navy SEAL who, for over ten years, specialized in surveillance tactics. He indicated the gadgets were top-of-the-line equipment. If these three cops are responsible, then they must be receiving federal help because the equipment we found is very expensive in the black market."

"So you don't know who's behind it?" another reporter asked.

"No, we don't. That's why we called this press conference. We wanted to share this with all New Yorkers and let them know how your privacy could be invaded. We are not pointing fingers, but these three officers and the police department are on the top of our list of suspects. We will launch our own investigation."

After a few more rounds of questioning the Colemans realized the media was out there trying to downplay the involvement of the government and police department. Minister Muhammad picked up on the media's intention and ended the press conference without warning. He had his FOI security escort everyone off the Colemans' front lawn.

Inside the house, Laura was having a nervous breakdown. The poor lady had had enough. Her baby boy got killed by police officers drunk and high off cocaine, and the whole system was against her. Now the media, which she thought was her only hope of spreading the truth, was turning against her as well. She was on the floor, kicking and yelling like a four-year-old child.

"Why? Why, Jesus? You don't need him up there. I need him. Please, bring my baby back. Why did You have to take him? Take me instead. I lived my life already."

Kim attempted to console Laura, but Perry Sr. stopped her.

"Let her be. Just let her be. This is the first time she has cried like this since our son was murdered. Just let her get it out of her system."

Kim held her ground but couldn't stand there and watch. She grabbed little Perry and went upstairs. Minister Muhammad and his people walked to the kitchen area.

Once Perry Sr. noticed everyone was gone, he approached his wife. "Just let it out, baby. I'm right here when you're ready for comfort."

Laura looked up at her husband, wiped her eyes, and hugged him like it was her last hug.

"I just want my baby back, that's all. I want him back."

"Come here, sweetheart," Perry said as he hugged his wife.

They both sat on their sofa crying together, rocking back and forth. They asked the minister to leave because they were tired and wanted to be left alone.

The minister left a few bodyguards behind before leaving. Then Laura and Perry Sr. went upstairs to their bedroom to catch up on their rest. The rest of the day went pretty quiet, which was exactly how they wanted it to be.

The captain, Loose Cannon, and Speedy kept it quiet for the night as well. For the first time ever, they finally realized they needed to keep a low profile.

The next morning, Diamond went out to the front door to pick up the paper, routine for her every morning around seven. She would brew coffee and get the newspaper. Lucky would head down to the basement and go over his video footage from the night before.

This morning was a little different. Diamond was shocked when she saw the front page. She quickly ran down to the basement, calling out Lucky's name. "Baby, you are not going to believe this. Here, check the front page of the newspaper."

Lucky grabbed the paper and stared at Diamond for a few seconds. He was hoping he could read her eyes before looking at the paper. He couldn't read her eyes, but knew by her facial expression it was bad. When he finally looked at it, he laughed.

"Those dirty muthafuckas," he said, laughing.

"That's all you have to say, Lucky? I don't understand."

"There's nothing I could do about this. Now it's time to think about leaving. This will bring a lot of pressure our way. As a matter of fact, let me finish watching these tapes from last night. You start packing your shit."

"But, Lucky."

"But nothing."

Diamond walked away upset. She didn't understand why Lucky wasn't upset about his face being on the front page of the most popular paper in the city. The headline read: *NYPD ISSUES WARRANT FOR LUCKY'S ARREST IN CONNECTION WITH BUGGING THE COLEMANS' RESIDENCE.*

Diamond went upstairs to pack, but she turned on the TV first. Lucky's face was on every channel. She turned the TV off in disgust and started packing. Things were moving too fast for Diamond. She sat on the edge of the bed to catch her breath. She was scared to death. She knew her life would be in jeopardy if she left with Lucky.

Actually, for the first time ever, she thought about staying behind and leaving him. But her love for him was too strong, and she wasn't about to let anything get in the way of her man. Whenever she was in doubt about her love for him, she always thought about the first night she'd met him and how he saved her life. Not only did he save her life, he gave her hope and a new beginning. He'd always treated her like a lady, and she knew he was in love with her. She also respected the fact that he waited until she was twenty-one years old to have sex. She didn't care about the age difference between them. They were in love with each other, so it was a no-brainer. She decided to roll with him. She didn't even know why she second-guessed herself.

An hour later, Lucky went upstairs. "Hey, baby, we are leaving in thirty minutes."

Lucky went back down and started to work out the final details for his new plan. With his face now being exposed, his privacy was next. Even though Lucky kept a private profile, he was sure one of his neighbors got a good look at him in the past. That's why he knew he needed to leave as soon as possible. He knew this day was coming, so he was prepared.

This was the risk he took by testifying for the government. He didn't know why he had trusted the government in the first place. He already knew they didn't protect witnesses.

Lucky had a disguise locked away in a suitcase. He didn't change his look too much, just adding a mustache, beard, and pair of run-down reading glasses, giving him the appearance of a nerd or a washed-up teacher that read every book in the world.

He called Diamond to get her opinion on his makeover. "Baby girl, come down to the basement for a quick minute."

"What is it?" she hollered back. "I'm still packing."

"Get your ass down here! Stop asking questions."

Lucky could hear Diamond stomping on each step on her way down. He knew she was still upset about having to leave, but he didn't care. He didn't let his emotions make his decisions.

When Diamond made it down to the basement, she took one look at Lucky and burst out laughing. "What the hell is that on your face? You look like bin Laden."

"Bin Laden? Don't play with me, girl." Lucky started laughing, too.

"Is this your new disguise, honey?"

"Yes. What do you think? Can I get away with it?"

"Since I know it's you, it's hard for me to give you an honest answer. But the disguise looks real. The facial hair is believable."

After a few more jokes, Diamond went back upstairs to finish packing.

Lucky started pulling out folder after folder from his safe. He placed them in a suitcase, along with all his computer software. He wanted to make sure he didn't leave any evidence that would link to him. He destroyed all three of his computer hard drives and grabbed his keys.

Diamond was done packing, and they headed out the door. "Where are we going? And why are we only taking clothes?"

"I have another apartment in Jersey City. Actually, a condo."

"A condo? You have a condo, and I don't know anything about it?"

"Baby, it's all part of the plan. Now hurry up. Let's get out of here. We will talk once we're in the car."

As soon as Lucky locked the door to his house and turned around, an SUV with tinted windows made an abrupt stop right in front of his house. Diamond ran for cover, while Lucky dropped his bags and reached for his .40 Glock sitting on his hip.

Both front doors opened on the SUV, and a Spanish man and woman jumped out screaming at each other. Lucky didn't see any weapons on them, so he didn't shoot, but he was pointing the gun right at them.

The Spanish couple was so busy arguing, they never noticed Lucky pointing a gun. Lucky also realized these two were not assassins, just a drunk couple fighting, so he called for Diamond, and they both jumped in his black Expedition and sped away, not waiting for the couple to stop arguing and get back in their truck.

"That was a close one, baby," Diamond said, exhaling.

Chapter Eight

Corrupt City

By the time Lucky reached his New Jersey condo, Diamond was asleep in the car. He drove around the block a few times, checking out the scenery. Lucky didn't have cameras around the area, so he didn't know what to expect. After about a good half-hour of driving around, he finally decided to wake up Diamond. He parked, and they went inside.

The condo was a beautiful two-bedroom loft with a view of New York City. The exterior wasn't impressive, but no one would have guessed the building was filled with luxury lofts. When he unlocked the front door, Diamond lost it.

"This is a beautiful place, Lucky. Wow! Are we going to live here? I want to stay here, baby, please. But I can't believe you never slept in here before. How come you never told me about this place?"

"You know how I am. I always have a trick up my sleeve. I bought this condo because I knew this day was coming. I always have a plan B. Shit, at this rate, I need a plan C and D."

Diamond walked around the condo, touching and feeling every piece of furniture.

While Diamond was fawning over the beautiful condo, Lucky quickly started mapping out the surveillance equipment he needed. He loved the view from his living room and balcony because it was easier to set up cameras. He turned on the news, and they wouldn't stop mentioning his name or showing his face. With a fifty-thousand-dollar reward on his head, a lot of people would be looking for him. He knew his house in the Bronx would be in the news soon, especially with the large reward. Lucky didn't want to waste anymore time. He grabbed one of his bags and pulled out all his folders.

Diamond walked over and started looking through them. "What's in these folders? You have guarded them more than your money."

"This here is the plan of all plans. This is how I'm going to turn this city upside down. Three years before the Perry shooting and about five days after Tango was murdered, I decided to bug my own crew. For three fuckin' years, I wore wires and sometimes a video camera, and I recorded all our dirty deeds. You wouldn't believe what I have on tape, and the pictures I have in my possession."

"So no one hired you? You did this on your own? That's crazy, Lucky. Why risk your life?"

"When Tango was murdered, our cover was blown, and our backup showed up after the ambulance. I had a gut feeling someone in the crew gave us away. I didn't trust them, so I recorded their every move. I knew one day I would need everything in this folder to show the world how corrupt New York City police really are." Lucky opened up some of the folders.

Diamond couldn't believe her eyes. Lucky had pictures of politicians having sex and using drugs in hotel rooms with high-class escorts, and of high-ranking priests naked with little boys from their choir. He even had a picture of the mayor leaving a Hampton villa with an escort girl. Lucky also had evidence where they'd framed criminals for crimes they hadn't done.

"I don't understand. Why would you frame criminals for crimes they did?"

"No, baby, we framed them for crimes we did, not them. But since they were already convicted felons, no one cared."

"But why frame criminals?"

"Because it was easy. Sometimes we were hired to kill. We didn't want another open unsolved murder, so we solved the case by framing a convicted felon."

"Wow! That's fucked up, Lucky. How about these pictures? How did you get them?"

"Those are all cases I worked either alone or with my team. The escort agency was a real high-class organization. These weren't cheap whores. An average date will run you at least two thousand dollars. That was just a date. We are talking at least five thousand for oral, and fifteen for a sleepover."

"Get the fuck out of here. They were charging five grand just for head?" Diamond had a quick flashback about her days on the streets. The most she ever got from a trick was a hundred and fifty dollars, and that included everything.

"For real, girl. Some of these senators were spending around twenty thousand on just one date. These pigs were getting penthouse suites at five-star hotels and only staying two to three hours in those muthafuckas. They were blowing serious money."

"What about these filthy preachers touching little boys?"

"They all received slaps on the wrist. We reported those sick bastards. We weren't about to defend or help child molesters. But our great judicial system didn't think they deserved jail time. Some of these bastards were allowed back in their churches to resume their positions."

"I can't believe they let these sick people go. What? Pictures of them naked with little boys wasn't sufficient evidence?"

"I guess not. You can't trust this government. I'm not trying to justify my actions, but once I saw how dirty everyone else was, I joined the party. That's why I kept these pictures to protect myself, just in case I needed to blackmail myself out of trouble. I have politicians, state attorneys, the police commissioner, and the list goes on."

"Whatever happened to the whorehouse? How come they weren't charged with anything?"

"They paid us a lot of money. I don't know how much in total, but I was given sixty thousand dollars to keep my mouth shut. Before we destroyed all the evidence, I kept a few pieces as well. But that's not all I have. I also have a list of bogus corporations and non-profit organizations that our city officials used to launder money. Shit, I even know a few election campaigns that were funded by the Italian mob and a couple of cartels out of Mexico and Panama. And let's not forget the tapes I left with the Colemans."

"So why not go public with it right now and clear your name?"

"Baby girl, are you not paying attention? We are on the run because I came forward about a murder. Imagine if I accuse the mayor of this city of adultery, and the police commissioner of money laundering and murder. Do you really think that's a good idea? I'm leaving these papers and files with you. All things in life have a right place and time. They will get theirs, if my plan goes accordingly."

"Why are you leaving it with me? Here we go with this shit again."

"What shit?"

"You are leaving. I already know the rules. If something was to happen to you, you want me to make sure these files go public, right?"

"Something like that, but why the big attitude if you know the routine?" Lucky asked in an angry tone.

"When are you leaving?" she asked, tearing up.

"I don't know, but not soon. It all depends on the amount of heat I'm under. I'm staying indoors as long as I can. I don't want you to wait until I'm gone to mail out these folders. I want you to head to the post office in the morning."

"Oh, well, that's good to hear," she replied with a big smile.

Lucky and Diamond talked for a few more minutes then he gave her a list with names and addresses and specific instruction on how to mail each folder. It was a simple plan, and he felt confident she didn't need the pep talk.

Diamond still curious and wanting to find out more, kept flipping through the files, and each one seemed worse than the other. She discovered some graphic pictures of fatally shot victims.

"Who are these dead people?"

"Witnesses we got rid of for the DA."

"Damn! How corrupt is this city?"

"Listen, I personally took care of witnesses in five major drug and murder cases. I did a lot of dirty work that I'm not proud of. That's why I want to mail this information to the lawyers of each of those cases, and I want the truth to come out. They want to fuck with me? Well, they made a big mistake. I know I'm throwing myself in a deeper hole, but I won't go down alone or without a fight."

"This is a little too crazy for me. I see why you want me to stay away."

"Sweetheart, you wouldn't believe the things I learned in the NYPD. I was taught how to racially profile the minority. We had quotas we had to meet, and they were all targeted toward African Americans and Latinos. We used to get bigger bonuses. It was unreal. I remember a partner of mine was fired because he arrested a White man who was smoking weed in the streets. Our captain, at that time, was upset at my partner because he didn't give him a fine or a warning, never mind that our holding cells were full of arrestees picked up for jaywalking, and beating the fare on the New York subway. It was a double standard rule. I remember we used to laugh at all the complaints we received for illegal searches. We used to shred those reports. No one cared. They trained us how to profile, so all complaints were irrelevant."

"Damn, Lucky! So it's really true? Cops profile Blacks and Hispanics?"

"It wasn't written in stone, but it was code among cops. It was hard for me because I'm Black, and here I am, harassing my own people. They brainwashed me to the point where I thought it was right to disrespect my own kind. I thought my paycheck was more important than my pride. I did so many of my people wrong. There were nights when we went on gun missions. Our job was to bring in as many guns and suspects as we could. We didn't care if we witnessed a drug deal in front of us. Our mission was to bring in guns. We would drive around and jump out on whoever was standing on the block. We'd search them illegally, and we were destined to find either drugs or a gun. If we didn't find either, we would harass them until they told us where to find suspects with guns. I remember one time I framed a seventeen-year-old kid."

"What do you mean by *frame*?"

"Well, one night we were out on our gun mission for like three to four hours and we didn't find any guns. Every time we jumped out on suspects, they were only carrying drugs. We would take the drugs from them, and if it was a large amount, we used to resell the drugs to other drug dealers. We were parked in the Bronx, by Yankee Stadium. It was going on two

in the morning, and we were all upset and tired. I jumped out
on this kid who was coming from a party. He was scared to
death when he saw me approach him with my gun drawn.

"This little punk, instead of following my orders, started
back-talking to me and calling me every name in the book. I
threw his little ass on the floor and put my knee on the back
of his neck. His tough talk quickly turned into screams for
mercy. Two transit police officers heard his big mouth, and
they quickly came up running from the subway. They noticed
I was a detective by the color wristband I was wearing. They
asked me if I needed help, and I told them yeah. I got off the
suspect and told the officers I witnessed him removing some
drugs from his pockets and stuffing them in his drawers right
before he was going to enter the subway. I gave the officers
some drugs, and they quickly arrested the teen. I felt bad, but
the little muthafucka should have stood quiet."

"That's fucked up, Lucky. I can't believe you were out there
like that."

"It came with the job. I agree with you, I was a scumbag,
but at the time, I didn't see anything wrong. Truth be told,
we really removed a lot guns and reduced crime by profiling
our suspects. People could complain all they wanted, but the
fact still remained that nine times out of ten when we did
profile our suspect, we were right. They were either carrying a
weapon or had drugs in their possession. Hey, listen, we didn't
go around harassing working-class people. We harassed those
who we saw on the street corners every day and night. If you
are walking down the streets with your pants hanging down
your ass, hat turned backward, and visible tattoos around
your body, expect to get harassed by police."

"I could understand what you mean, but you know there are
a lot of followers in the hood. Just because they fit the profile
doesn't mean they are criminals. But looking at your folder,
I see a lot of criminals who should get life for what they've
done. Why not go after them? Why only go after the Blacks
and Hispanics?"

"I'm going to give you another reason. Because they are
poor. We know ninety percent of our charges would stick
because they can't afford lawyers or hush money. We went

after the bigger fish that you see in those folders, but not to arrest them. We went after them so we could blackmail them and suck their bank accounts dry. We made millions off these pricks. My police duties changed after I joined Captain Tuna's team, and I became an aggressive businessman."

"What really made you realize you needed to change? I don't believe it was just the death of Perry Coleman."

"You know me so well, baby girl. It was a mixture of things, but the main reason was my mother. I wasn't raised this way, and it started to catch up to me. Since my mother passed away, I've always promised I would make her happy in heaven. But once I got a taste of that fast money, it blinded my common sense. The night Perry was killed, that was the final sign, my wake-up call. I knew in my heart I had to step up and come clean, not just about the murder, but also about the dirt I did as a police officer. That's the reason all the folders are set up. I would be able to help a lot of suspects that we arrested and tampered with their cases. I'm risking my life, because real talk, I have enough money put away to disappear. I don't have to do this. I didn't need to come back and testify, but I won't be able to live with myself if I didn't. Remember, the information inside these folders will also incriminate me as well."

"I understand, baby, and that's why I fell in love with you. You are determined and a go-getter. I will never judge you, but it was just a little shocking to hear about your behavior as a police officer. I'm starting to understand why you don't want me to come along. Just make sure you bring your ass back in one piece."

"I promise."

Diamond logged on the Internet to search for restaurants that delivered, and Lucky went back to work, organizing all the folders and stacking them away in a box. They decided to call it a night, and it was only 7:00 p.m. By the time the food arrived, they both had already taken showers and were ready to eat and go to sleep. Diamond fell asleep right after she ate, while Lucky stayed up and watched ESPN until he fell asleep.

Back in the Bronx, there was a twenty-man SWAT team posted all around his house, hate in their eyes. They felt like Lucky had betrayed their brotherhood. They were hesitant to enter, only because of the surveillance cameras they found around the area. They knew the equipment belonged to Lucky. They figured he was inside watching and waiting with all sorts of guns and explosive devices. Once the snipers were in position, the captain of the squad called for tear gas.

Four members ran up to the house and threw eight tear gas bombs through the front window of the house. They waited two minutes before entering. A total of ten were ordered to storm in and kick in the front door. The cops entered the house with only one thing on their mind—Kill Lucky and anyone else in the house.

Twenty minutes later, they realized Lucky wasn't home, that he had destroyed all his computers. When the officer in charge was informed of the bad news, he had to call it in and report the mission a failure.

By the officer calling it in, the Watcherz picked up on the call and alerted his boss. When Captain Tuna got the call, he rounded up his squad, and they headed up to the Bronx location as fast as they could.

Speedy was still confused about why they were rushing if Lucky wasn't there. "Cap, I don't understand why we are rushing," he said.

"I know they reported no sign of Lucky, but we could still find evidence that might help us. Nobody knows him like we do. Maybe a picture or a postcard could help us."

"Okay, now I understand."

"And knowing that muthafucka, he may be still hiding in that house in a secret wall, on some Batman shit," Loose Cannon added.

"You right." the captain said. "Lucky may still be there."

While they rushed to the house, Lucky was off his bed and watching the cops walk through his house. He left one little camera in his basement, a silent alarm attached to it. He was sitting on the edge of his bed laughing because the cops were trying to figure out a way to save his burned computers.

Lucky's laugh and facial expression changed when he saw his former partners walk into the picture. They had just arrived and quickly received permission to take over the crime scene. Leaving that one camera gave Lucky a big break.

Once Lucky saw the Watcherz in his basement packing up his burned computers, he realized his former partners had hired them to track him down.

After the Watcherz packed up the computers, Lucky realized his captain was holding a picture frame. Lucky didn't have the capabilities of zooming in, so he couldn't see the picture the captain was holding. It was bugging him so much, he wanted to drive up to the Bronx.

The captain knew what he was doing. Loose Cannon and Speedy kept asking him why he was holding that same picture frame. The captain walked back upstairs and called Speedy and Loose up with him.

"Listen, I got a funny feeling that Lucky is watching us. If I know him like I do, he has a camera somewhere in that basement, so I figure I'd throw him off by holding this picture frame."

"Smart move, boss," Speedy said.

They all headed back down to the basement to finish up their walk-through. They wanted to make sure they looked through everything before leaving the scene.

Loose Cannon kept whispering stuff into the captain's ear, but he wasn't saying anything. He was just adding to the suspense.

Lucky kept asking himself out loud, "What the hell are they talking about now?"

The captain played along with Loose Cannon's idea, so he also whispered back in his ear. They all pointed at the picture frame as they left the house, leaving Lucky wondering what was really in that picture.

When his former partners were outside, they were hoping their little plan worked, and that Lucky would come out of hiding.

By this time, the media was already outside the house and had reported in the news that Lucky made a last-minute blazing escape as a twenty-member SWAT team ambushed his residence.

Lucky went and woke Diamond out of her sleep and started asking questions about the pictures they had around the house.

"Slow down, Lucky. I can't understand you. Can you at least let me get up and rub my eyes?"

"No, I can't. Focus because this is serious. Listen to what I'm asking you. How many pictures we had hanging up at the old house?"

"Why?"

"Just answer the fuckin' question. How many fuckin' pictures?"

"I don't know, not many. I think four. Yeah, only four. The rest were just hanging up for decorations."

"Are you sure only four?"

"Yes, I'm sure, and I have all four packed in one of my suitcases. Why? What's going on?"

Lucky then switched the channel on the TV and let Diamond watch the news for herself. When she noticed police cars and camera crew in front of their old house, she realized why Lucky was nervous.

She got up from the bed and went into the kitchen, where Lucky was heating up some leftovers. "Lucky, what happened? Are you okay?"

"Yeah, I'm good. The alarm I set up back at the house woke me up. These clowns came at full force, and it looked like they were hunting to kill. I was only able to leave one camera, so I had limited vision, but I noticed my old partners were at the house as well. My captain kept holding this picture frame, but I couldn't clearly see the picture. That's why I was asking how many pictures in total we had at the house."

"What color was the frame he was holding?"

"I don't know. Everything was black and white."

"I know for sure I got all four picture frames we had up."

"I believe you. Maybe they were bluffing because they thought I was watching. Plus, I also noticed they had the two best underground hackers in the game with them. These two brothers call themselves The Watcherz. They are the best in the business. I remember the FBI once employed them to help locate some of the most wanted criminals in the country. They could find anybody."

"For real, I see they really want to find you, baby. What are we going to do?"

"For right now, I just have to wait. I know they are hoping I come out of hiding, but they will need a better tactic than just a picture frame. My only fear is that they find my daughter and her mother. I have done a real good job of hiding their identity."

"You really have, because I barely know anything about them. Hopefully they are bluffing with the picture frame."

"I need to be sure they're bluffing. I'm going to have to hit the city tomorrow and get a closer look at their operation."

"How are you going to do that? You just said they are using the picture frame as bait to get you out of hiding. Don't you think that's a bad idea? Just wait a day or two. You don't even know where they are located, so how can you look for them?"

"You're right, but I know where the Watcherz grew up. I figure I could go around their old neighborhood and see what kind of information I could get on them."

"I don't know, Lucky. It sounds risky, but you make the final call. In my opinion, we should stick with the plan of mailing out these folders and sitting back and let everything else unfold."

Lucky knew Diamond was right, so they went back to the bedroom and watched some more TV.

Meanwhile, Captain Tuna was busy back at his place. He was hoping the Watcherz could get some type of information out of those burnt computers. The Watcherz tried for six to seven hours but couldn't retrieve anything.

The captain began screaming at the two brothers. "How in the world are you guys the best in the world, but yet, no sign of Lucky, and now you can't get anything out these computers? Am I wasting my fuckin' money? Let me know. Either you guys find Lucky, or I'm going to put a bullet through each of your heads. Do I make myself clear?"

They didn't answer, but by the look in their eyes, they knew the captain wasn't playing. The Watcherz got back to work and promised the captain they would find Lucky.

While they went back to work, the captain went down to the fourth floor to make some phone calls. He figured they needed a bigger team to catch Lucky and kill him. He called his cousin Floyd from Florida, who was dirty himself when he was employed as a cop in Florida. Now he ran his own bail bond and bounty hunting business.

"Floyd, it's me, your cousin Tuna."

Floyd was surprised to hear from his cousin, but not stunned. "Tuna? Captain Tuna from NY?"

"Yes, from NY."

"Cousin Tuna, I haven't heard from you in a long time. I guess you are calling me for another mission. It's been like ten years since the last time you called me and asked for help. I knew this day would come. What's up?"

"Well, we can't talk over the phone. Let's meet."

"I'm not going to say no. Just let me know when do you need me up there, and how many men you need."

"I knew I could count on you, Floyd. I need at least four extra bodies. I need some real good people. Our target is a specialist. I will leave it at that. I will fill you in once you are here. I need you up here ASAP."

"Give me about three days, I'm up there."

Captain Tuna was excited about the extra help coming up. He quickly called Loose and Speedy and told them about the new hired help. Speedy didn't sound too happy, but Loose Cannon was excited. He knew his captain had war on his mind.

Chapter Nine

The Manhunt

Within two days, Floyd was in the city with three of his best men. They didn't know the details of the mission or who Captain Tuna was, but they were in New York with Floyd, ready to put in work. The captain sent Speedy to pick up the new squad. When the captain and Floyd saw each other, it was a family reunion moment. They embraced each other like brothers.

"Damn! Ten years. Come here, you bum," Tuna said.

"It feels more like twenty years," Floyd replied, hugging his cousin. "I really missed you, Floyd."

"Okay, enough with the bitch talk. Let's get down to business." Tuna asked Floyd to follow him upstairs to his office. He took him to the fifth floor, where The Watcherz were busy at work. Floyd was impressed with all the high-tech equipment.

"I like what I see, little cousin. I see you have done really good for yourself, but I have to ask . . ."

"Ask what?"

"I'm sorry to switch topics, but I have to ask. Was the kid armed?"

Tuna took a deep breath. "No, he wasn't. I wish I could really take that day back, you know. But I can't."

"Hey, listen, you don't have to explain nothing to me. I know it was a mistake. Fuck the public and their opinion. They don't understand the risk of being a police officer, especially in New York. They don't think about the lives you saved by removing guns and drugs off the streets. What's the latest on the trial?"

"It's looking good, but we have a major issue. That's why I called you up here."

"I'm all ears," Floyd said as he pulled up a chair.

"Well, our ex-partner testified against us, and he didn't hold back on the stand. He told it all like a little girl, and raised a lot of eyebrows in the department. Even after we win this case, the heat will still be on us."

"Okay, so let's find and kill him!" Floyd yelled.

"Listen, I want him dead, but he's good at what he does, and we can't find him. By the time we found his house, he was long gone."

"His house? Wait a minute, you guys know where he lived? That's perfect. Let's go. Show us the house."

"We already checked the house. There's nothing there. If it wasn't for the burned equipment we found in the basement, you would have never known he lived there."

"No disrespect, little cousin, but my squad makes a real good living finding the unfound. Let's go back downstairs so I can introduce you to my team."

The Cap agreed, and they both went back downstairs.

It didn't take long for everyone to get accustomed to each other. When they walked back in the apartment, all the fellas were drinking beers and talking football.

"Okay, listen up. Loose, turn the music down. Hey, fellas, listen. For those who don't know, my name is Captain Tuna, and this is my team. Speedy, he would chase down and catch anyone. He's one hell of an officer. He's our forensic guru. He's the one who keeps us on our toes and makes sure we follow our plans. If it wasn't for him, I wouldn't be standing here today talking. I would be in a federal prison, serving life for all the shit I've done."

The room exploded with laughter.

"Then we got Loose Cannon. The name speaks for itself. It doesn't take much to set him off. Long story short, he's been my right-hand man for almost fifteen years. The 'Cleanup Guy' is his other nickname."

Tuna turned toward Loose and Speedy. "Listen here. I got some out-of-town boys to help us with our situation. My cousin Floyd will do the honor of introducing his boys, but it looks like you guys know each other already."

"What's up? Like Tuna said, my name is Floyd, and this is my team. That's Country, Ace, and Chucky. We are the best bounty hunters in the state of Florida. We hunt muthafuckas down. No one could hide from us. Their work speaks for itself. I'm not too big in telling stories. We just put in work. My boys and I are up here to help find this little bitch and rip his mouth off. Tuna was telling me you know where he lived. I need to get my crew in there and check out the premises again."

"No problem. Speedy will take two of your guys up there," Tuna said.

The captain sent Speedy, Ace, and Country back to research Lucky's house. He was hoping Floyd was right and was able to find new clues to hunt down the traitor. The captain wanted his cousin to give out more info about his team. He wanted to trust him enough to not question their skills, but he had to ask just to make sure.

"Hey, Floyd, while we're waiting around, tell me a little about your team."

"Sure, no problem. We got Ace, who's my best man on the team. His nickname is 'Hound Dog.' He's able to track down anyone. It doesn't matter where or how. He once was able to track down one of Florida's most wanted criminals.

"Then we got Country. He's the only member who tries his best to follow the rules. He was born and raised in Louisiana. He moved to Florida when he was twenty-five years old. He joined the police force, and that's when I first met him. Country had assisted me in tracking down a homicide fugitive. Country is the guy that will break every bone in your body from just one punch.

"Now Chucky, he's another Loose Cannon. He lives on a short fuse and doesn't care about the law. If it was up to him, he will shoot and kill each fugitive we captured. He didn't care how big or small the case was, he wanted blood every time. He is one racist muthafucka too. He hates every race. He's the only one who was never a police officer. Is that enough information? I'm ready for a drink."

"Ha! I'm ready for one, too, and yes, that's enough information. Let me get some entertainment for us."

The Cap was up to his old tricks again. He got on the phone and called up The Candy Shop and placed an order for four girls. Within forty-five minutes, they were partying with naked call girls and high off a mixture of drugs. It was hard to tell which lifestyle they preferred, because these cops loved the gangster life.

Speedy, Ace, and Country were back at Lucky's house searching every inch. As soon as they walked in the house, Ace was examining every piece of furniture, even smelling some of it.

Speedy was looking at him like he was crazy. He called Country over to smell one of Lucky's pillows in the master bedroom, and they both agreed on the fragrance. It was a woman's perfume, for sure.

They went around smelling other linens, curtains, sofas, and even the closet. They identified the same smell all over the house. They now realized Lucky had a female sidekick. This was the break they were looking for. Until now, they'd thought Lucky was a loner. Speedy was really impressed with how quickly they figured out he had a female sidekick.

Speedy went outside to speak to some of Lucky's neighbors, while Ace and Country kept searching. When they reached the basement, they triggered the alarm.

Meanwhile Lucky was watching these new faces rumble through his basement. He was puzzled, but it quickly hit him. His old partners were desperate and had hired more outside help.

As Ace and Country looked through the basement, Speedy was yelling their name out loud. They quickly ran upstairs to see what Speedy found or wanted.

"Wait a second. Before I tell you what I just heard, let me ask you a question first. Did you just come up from the basement?"

"Yes, we did."

"Shit! Fuck!" Speedy yelled.

"What happened? We weren't supposed to enter his basement?" Country asked.

"No, but it's my fault for not mentioning it. We believe Lucky has a camera set up in the basement, so if you guys went down there, he now knows how you look. If I know him like I think I do, he's on the Bureau's database right now trying to type-match your identity."

"Aw, man, we didn't know," Ace replied. "But seeing our faces may bring him out of the dark."

"Yeah, maybe, but anyway, I was calling you guys because one of his neighbors spilled the beans on his female friend. He said he knew there was foul play involved. She seemed so young, young enough to be his daughter. He said she went to the same diner every day to pick up lunch. He gave me the name of the diner, which is right up the street."

"Well, let's go over there and see if they have any kind of surveillance that may help us identify this mysterious, good-smelling female. Country, you stay here and see what else you can find. Check their garbage too," Ace said.

When they reached the diner, they went in and noticed a security camera. They smiled. The Italian restaurant was full of customers, so they didn't want to make a scene.

Speedy approached the hostess, flashed his badge, and requested the manager. When the manager introduced himself, Speedy asked him to step outside.

"Okay, what's going on here? Why are we outside? And who's that?" the manager asked, pointing at Ace.

"Okay, listen," Speedy said, "you are not in trouble. What's your name?"

"Sergio."

"Look, Sergio, we just have a few questions. I know you watch the news. Two blocks from here lives a very dangerous man, and I'm stunned that no one has seen his face around here. So let me ask you. Has he ever eaten at this diner?" he asked, holding up a picture of Lucky.

"Yes, he has, but a long time ago. Maybe two years before all this media frenzy."

"Two years ago. Are you sure?"

"Yes, I'm positive."

"What about this pretty little lady, about five, three? From what I hear, she has an awesome body. She came in here every day for lunch. Do you know who I'm referring to? Do you know her?"

"You mean, Chanel. Yes, I know her. What about her?"

"We think she was connected to the rogue cop we're after."

"Are you sure? She said the lunch was for her ill father."

"Well, I'm sorry to break the news to you, buddy. Pretty lady is a criminal. Anyway, we noticed you have a camera. I'm going to need some footage with . . . What's her name again? Chanel, right?"

"I don't know her name. I just always called her Chanel because that's the name of the perfume she wears. As far as the tapes, I'm going to have to wait until the owner gets here."

Ace removed his sunglasses and removed the toothpick from his mouth. He walked up to Sergio and got about eight to ten inches from his face. "Listen, unlike my partner, I don't have the fuckin' patience. You have about three minutes before I whip my gun out and turn your brain into fuckin' meatballs."

Sergio froze when he saw Ace reach under his shirt and grab his shiny chrome 9 mm.

Speedy gave Ace a small shove and got in between Ace and Sergio. "Sergio, please hurry up with the tapes. Don't make my partner upset. You don't want to see him upset."

Sergio was already shitting in his pants, so he didn't even need Speedy to convince him. "I will be right back with those tapes. Give me two minutes."

Speedy and Ace were laughing their asses off when Sergio walked away. They couldn't believe he fell for that old good cop, bad cop trick.

A few minutes later, Sergio walked out and handed them a DVD.

"What the fuck is this?" Speedy asked.

"It's a DVD. I downloaded about six months' worth of surveillance."

"You better not be fuckin' with us. I have a laptop right in the car. I hope I don't have to come back."

Sergio ran back in the restaurant, happy to be alive.

Speedy and Ace walked back to Lucky's house. They both went straight to the car and popped in the DVD, and Sergio was on the money. He gave them six months worth of footage, and the DVD program was user-friendly. All they had to do was type in a date and time, and the clip would pop up. Every time they punched in 12:30 on a weekday, the same pretty girl everyone kept talking about appeared. The only bad thing was, she always had on shades and a big hat, so she didn't give them much to work with. They knew that was Lucky's sidekick.

Speedy called out, "Captain, I finally got some good news."

"Speedy, spit it out."

"We found his sidekick, and she's a girl."

"That's perfect. Bring that bitch over to the apartment right now."

"No, Captain, not in the physical form, but we have some footage on her."

"Just bring what you have. How are the new boys working out?"

"They are perfect. Nothing fake about them. I will be there in thirty minutes or so."

The captain got off the phone and continued the party.

Speedy and Ace walked back in the house to look for Country. When they found him, they asked him if he'd found anything else.

"Yes, I found the camera in the basement. I know where it's located."

"You do? Let's take it down," Ace said.

"No, leave the camera alone. Let's get back to the apartment and re-group."

Speedy grew balls and was calling the shots on this run. While they were walking back to the car, he thought of something.

"Wait, hold up. Ace, grab my laptop, and let's all go back down to the basement. I got a plan."

"I think I already know," Ace said, grabbing the notebook.

They all went back down to the basement, and Speedy opened the laptop.

Lucky jumped off his sofa, curious as to what Speedy was up to. "What are you doing, Speedy? What do you got there?" he said to himself.

Lucky wasn't surprised that they'd found the camera. He was wondering what took them so long to find it in the first place. However, he was on his feet, eyes glued to the monitor, as he waited in anticipation. He knew his former partner wasn't bluffing.

When Speedy flipped the laptop around, Lucky saw video footage with someone in it that resembled Diamond. He sat up, turned his monitor off, and laughed. Instead of getting nervous because of the new footage, he just brushed it off and got ready for his next plan. He calmly called Diamond in the room and made her aware of the footage Speedy had.

"Listen, we need to bounce. No, let me rephrase that. I need you to bounce because they are getting too close. This is getting too dangerous, and I'm not trying to lose you, baby."

"Where the fuck is this coming from now?"

"Come here, baby."

Lucky hugged her for two minutes. In that two-minute span, he thought about the first day he'd met her outside the strip club. He would have never thought they would be in this position, where he would actually fall in love with her.

It had started out as some quick head, and now they were living together. It was tough in the beginning, especially not having sex. It took a lot for him to hold back and not touch her beautiful body.

But Lucky thought it was always harder for Diamond. Taking sex away from a prostitute was like taking dope away from a fiend, who'd go through long, sweaty nights of withdrawal. Lucky always felt it was important to gain Diamond's trust and respect. So he reformed her into a new woman, and that's how their bond was forged.

He remembered their first month together. He knew she was sneaking around her old way, looking for her pimp. She was hoping he was still alive and could take her back. He understood her issues, and instead of flipping out on her, he kept it to himself. It took about four months to get her to realize that her old lifestyle was a deadly way to make money.

When she finally realized Lucky's true intentions, she started to fall in love with him as well. At first, what Lucky was doing for her was no different than what any pimp would do, providing shelter, clothing, and food. That was the reason why she didn't feel comfortable at first. She thought Lucky was some pervert looking to turn her into his sex slave.

But as time went by, she began to learn who he was, and his passion for respecting a woman, which Lucky learned from his mother. Their relationship was rocky the first year as they grew to learn each other's ways, but after that, it was smooth sailing.

While Diamond was hugging him back, she also had some flashbacks about the first time they'd met, and about her family. She wondered if her family ever missed her. She had two younger sisters, and all three were treated horribly.

After she'd made those accusations against her father, everyone turned their back on her. She ran away because she thought they would be happier without her. She'd once read a story in the newspaper about young girls making a good living in New York City by being high-end hookers, so she bought a bus ticket, only packed her sexy garments, and never looked back. Every now and then, she would wonder about them, if they missed her.

When she jumped off the Greyhound bus in Time Square, she had high hopes of being a famous call girl, but she ended up sucking dicks in alleys and fucking in elevators to make a living.

Diamond, to this day, felt like God sent Lucky to save her life. She always thought she was blessed, having such a great man on her side. She had been through hell since birth and thought maybe God sent her an angel. At first, she didn't trust him. He was too honest. To her, all men were liars and cheaters, but he proved her wrong.

While they were hugging, Diamond was crying and shaking because she knew the day had arrived. Lucky was leaving her behind, and there was a big chance she would never see him again.

"Okay, baby, I'm going to let you get back to work. Call me when you're ready for me to hear the next move, daddy."

"That's my baby. I love that attitude. It's good for your health to always think positive. I'm going to be as safe as possible and make sure I come back in one piece."

Once Diamond left the room, he turned his monitor back on and saw a piece of paper with a telephone number written on it that Speedy left for him to call. Lucky turned off the monitor and turned on some music to help him relax and think. His next move had to be clever, but he was tired of running. He just wanted to get this over with and face off with his old partners. He knew in order for him to even think about resting anywhere in peace, they all had to be killed. Lucky wouldn't be satisfied if they each received a life sentence. Death was the only resolution. He was also aware that his former partners felt the same way.

When Speedy and the others returned to the spot and gave Tuna the tape, they were celebrating like they'd found Lucky. All they had was footage, but to them it was a small victory. They'd finally caught him slipping.

Tuna was really excited. He quickly gave The Watcherz the DVD, so they could get to work. "Shit, we need to find this girl," he yelled out loud.

"What about the media?" Floyd suggested.

"What about them?"

"They could show her face on every news channel there is," Floyd added.

"Cap, he's right. What other choice do we have? We need to find Lucky as soon as possible. This girl could lead us right to him," Speedy added.

"I don't want the media involved. It will attract heat for us as well. Let's keep this information to ourselves until we figure out what to do. Maybe by then the Watcherz will find her real identity. I don't even want Lucky to know about this new video."

"It's too late for that, Captain," Speedy added in a low-toned voice.

"What do you mean, it's too late for that?"

"Well, Cap, I thought it would be a good idea to show Lucky we had his girl, so we went down to the basement and showed him footage of his girlfriend through his camera."

"You did what? How stupid can you be, Speedy? You basically showed him our hand. You never reveal your hand."

"I thought maybe by showing him the footage, he would come out of hiding. I'm now realizing it was a dumb idea. I'm sorry."

The captain was pissed. He couldn't believe his most loyal cop disobeyed a direct order of staying away from the basement.

While the captain was chewing Speedy's ass off, his cell phone started ringing. He picked up.

"Hello, Captain. This is the commissioner. What's the latest on this scumbag? Did you locate his whereabouts?"

"No, Mr. Fratt, but we have a lead on his new girlfriend. We only have footage of who she is, but we still haven't identified her. We don't have a clear shot of her face."

"Send me the footage, and I will have the media take care of the rest. Somebody will come forward with some information."

"I don't think that would be a good idea."

The commissioner interrupted Tuna. "I didn't ask you to send me the footage. I'm giving you a direct order. Listen, you are not at liberty to make choices. Do we understand each other?"

"Yes, I will send over the footage as soon as I hang up the phone."

"Okay, listen, I will give you a few days to identify her before I turn the video over to the media."

"That's all I need, a few more days."

"Another thing, Captain, let me remind you that you need to cool down this heat. Hurry up and find this scumbag."

After the captain hung up the phone, he turned to his crew and said, "Listen, fellas, this is my show. I'm sailing the boat. If any of you guys make a decision without consulting with me first, that would be your ass."

The captain was still in fumes about Speedy's decision to show Lucky what they were working with. He'd dodged a bullet when the commissioner gave him a few more days to identify Lucky's female friend, but five minutes after the commissioner got off the phone, he called right back and told the captain he needed the tape ASAP.

"I thought you were giving me a few days," Tuna said.

"I changed my mind. You need help in this case, and the media has always been our friend in tracking down criminals."

"I have everything under control, Mr. Fratt."

"Do you really? Again, have the DVD in my office before the day is over."

The captain was pissed the fuck off. There was nothing he could do to stop the footage from hitting the media. He sent Speedy downtown to meet the commissioner and hand him the footage.

By the ten o'clock news, images of Lucky's sidekick were all over the news and Internet. Since the media had little information to work with, they started getting creative with the title of each story. Some stations called her "The Rogue Cop Lover," others called her, "The Young, Pretty, and Dangerous Girl."

The police department released a statement that she was wanted, though they didn't have any evidence to charge Diamond with a crime, and considered her armed and dangerous.

Once Lucky noticed all the news channels broadcasting the story, he knew it was time to panic. He had to find a way to disconnect Diamond, who walked in the room and asked him about his plans, from all this drama.

"We are in a tough situation here," he said. "The last thing I wanted was for you to get hurt. Now you are wanted by the NYPD. You should hear the names they're calling you."

"But they don't know who I am. Fuck them! They can't find us."

"Listen, Diamond, I think it will be best if we just separate, period, end of discussion."

"What part of 'I'm rolling with you' don't you understand? I'm wanted by the law. You can't leave me now."

"I don't know if you are ready, and for the record, I'm not going to leave you, girl. What's wrong with you? I'm going to try to clean your name up first. I'm going to paint the picture that I kidnapped you. Once they learn that you're a runaway girl, they will believe our story, and you should be good after that. The only bad thing about my plan is, they will try to reunite you with your family."

"No! I won't be good after that. I will be good right here with you. But, whatever, you are the shot caller. I just want you to know that I hate your plan," she said right before walking away from him.

Lucky called Diamond at least three times, but she never acknowledged him or came back in the room. He could hear her crying in the other room, so he just left her alone. This decision was hard on him as well, but he felt like it was the best decision because he didn't want her to get hurt. The burden would be too much for him to handle. A little leery about his plan, he was, hoping Diamond didn't fold on him.

Lucky made an anonymous call to the Twenty-eighth Precinct on 124th Street and Eighth Avenue and informed them that the girl all over TV would turn herself in tomorrow morning. He also called one of his old contacts from the local newspaper and told him the made-up story, knowing the reporter would run his mouth.

By the time the morning came around, the story was all over the city paper that "The Rogue Cop Lover" was turning herself in. The story mentioned that Diamond was being held against her will.

Now, the pressure to capture Lucky was high on the police department's list. The media was doing a good job in creating this hate against Lucky. Already considered a rogue cop, Lucky was going to face additional charges of kidnapping and, because it was believed he had snatched her before she was eighteen years old, endangering the life of a minor.

Lucky called the Twenty-eighth Precinct around one-thirty and told them the girl would arrive at two o'clock in the afternoon.

The Watcherz heard the call on the police scanner and notified Tuna. He thought Lucky was smart by having her dropped on the same day the Colemans had a protest march taking place downtown, putting a strain on limited police resources. There wouldn't be enough cops around to capture him.

"I got your ass now," Tuna said to himself. "You can't fool us."

Tuna quickly got the boys together and set up a surveillance watch all around 123rd and 124th streets, waiting for Lucky to show up. They figured this would be a perfect opportunity to get close to him.

It was now going on two o'clock in the afternoon, and still no signs of him or the girl. They weren't buying the whole kidnapping theory, but they didn't care. He was their target, not the girl.

Lucky was present but watching from 122nd Street, from the inside of an abandoned building. He knew his former partners were hiding and watching as well.

"Captain, I believe that's her walking up to the front now," Speedy radioed in.

"I see her. Black shirt and white pants, right?"

"Affirmative."

Speedy, Ace, and Tuna kept their eyes on the girl, while Loose, Country, Chucky, and Floyd were searching the perimeter for Lucky. Ace and Speedy were on the roof with sniper rifles, waiting on the signal that Lucky had been spotted, so they could take him out, but they couldn't find him.

The captain was getting a bit overzealous looking at the girl. He yelled into his radio, "C'mon, fellas, find this muthafucka! I know he's out here somewhere. The bitch is standing right outside the precinct for a reason. It must be a signal she's giving him. Please, someone find this nigger, and do something before it's too late."

A few seconds later, two loud shots were fired, both hitting Diamond. One hit her in the head, and the other, in her chest, slamming her beautiful body against a parked police cruiser. The gunfire sent the streets of Harlem into chaos, with people running and screaming all over the streets.

Ever since the 9/11 terrorist attacks, New Yorkers have been real sensitive to any type of loud noises. When the people heard the loud shots and saw a body on the ground, they didn't know what to think. Not to mention, it was right in front of a police station. Some thought there was a maniac inside the station killing people, or maybe another cop went crazy and shot an innocent bystander.

The captain was furious about what just took place. He radioed his troops. "Who just took that shot?"

No one answered him.

"Didn't I make myself clear about making decisions without me? Who in the fuck took that shot?"

Everyone radioed back in and confirmed they didn't take the shot, but the captain didn't believe them. They all re-grouped and went back to the apartment.

Ace and Speedy were being blamed because they were the ones with the sniper guns, but Loose Cannon and Chucky were also nearby and didn't need a rifle to take her out.

Everyone in the van was blaming each other. The friction got so bad, even Tuna and Floyd got into it.

"Floyd, I hope one of your boys didn't cross the line."

"It sounds more like one of your boys. You need better control of your team, Tuna."

"The hell, I do. Well, once the autopsy is done, we will know who shot her. Till then, I don't trust anyone in this van. I cannot fuckin' believe it. This will bring more heat our way. Why in the world would I want to kill her in front of the police station?"

As they drove home, you could tell everyone was scared about what could happen next. Everyone started looking at each other, looking for the smallest clues, so they could blame the individual.

The only one who wasn't scared was Loose Cannon, who actually had a smirk on his face the whole ride back. The captain feared he was the only one who could have pulled the trigger but didn't want to pull his card in front of the team. He planned to pull him to the side, once they got back to the apartment.

The captain's only fear was the local newspaper. He knew Lucky had already contacted them and spread the word he was going to turn her in, but once they found out she got shot in front of the police station, the accusations would start flying all over, and of course, Tuna and his team would get blamed. He couldn't afford any more charges or complaints against him, especially since they were all suspended. He also knew once the organizers for the Colemans' protest heard about the shooting, they would use it as fuel for their movement.

Chapter Ten

The Protest Rally

It was going on three o'clock, and City Hall was jam-packed with protesters eager to vent their frustrations. The rumors were correct. Minister Muhammad had arranged a huge rally in support of the Colemans and their tragedy.

Everyone was gathered around One Police Plaza, and they were going to march all the way to City Hall. A small stage with six seats was set up right in front of the police plaza, four for the Colemans, one for Minister Muhammad, and one for their civil lawyer, Joseph Anderson.

As three o'clock approached, the stage was still empty. People were too busy shouting out rants to notice the time. The city already knew that the girl Lucky had kidnapped was supposed to turn herself in. Now word started spreading through the crowd that she was shot dead in front of the police station.

Around three-fifteen, the Colemans, Muhammad, and Joseph finally reached the stage. The protesters exploded in cheers. The city really wanted to show them how supportive they were of them. There were at least 6,500 people out there ready to protest and singing as loud as they could the words of the late great Bob Marley's "No Justice, No Peace."

Minister Muhammad approached the mic and raised both hands, signaling the crowd to calm down. "Good afternoon, New Yorkers. Today we show the unity of this great city. Today we show we've had enough, and that we won't take it anymore."

The crowd erupted in cheers.

"Today marks a day of change. As I stand before you and I look among you, I see a nation of all colors. I see a city of all ethnicities, which means we as a city stand as one. Today is the day we destroy racism and sexism. I hope the world is watching because, America, this is how you begin a change . . . by uniting as one."

There was more applause from the crowd.

"Behind me, I have a family who's living in a twenty-four-hour nightmare. A family who has been hit with a tragedy that destroyed their peace of mind. This family . . . Laura, can you please step forward?"

The crowd exploded in support of Laura because of the strength she had shown throughout the ordeal.

"Laura, can you please stand next to me and bear witness to this beautiful sight? These New Yorkers, most of whom are strangers, have now become your new family. They are here to fight the war with you. Am I right, New York?"

Once again, the protesters went nuts and started singing again.

Laura, amazed at the amount of people who came out to support her only child, couldn't stop the tears from running down her face. It took her a few minutes to speak, and while she stood there mesmerized, the crowd's roar grew louder by the second.

"Good afternoon, everyone," she said, her voice cracking. "I first want to thank all of you who showed up today looking for answers to a better way of life. As we all know, we are here because three police officers opened fire on my son, killing him for no apparent reason. They destroyed not only our lives, but the future life of his son." Laura pointed at little Perry, who was sitting on his mother's lap. "These police officers got a slap on the wrist for their crimes. But they have the opportunity to go home and kiss their wives and play with their children, not my son. I'm not blaming the entire police department, but when you have the police commissioner and the mayor saying this shooting was justified, it leaves me no choice but to attack the department as a whole.

"My son"—Laura paused and let a few more tears out—"my son was a great husband and father. He didn't deserve this. My son was an innocent city taxpayer who woke up every day to earn his living and provide for his family. I will no longer get the opportunity to speak to, or even touch him. I understand he committed one little error as a juvenile, but who among us is perfect?

"My husband and I worked hard to buy our first home. We worked hard and prayed every day that we would have a normal life. When Perry was six years old, he always talked about joining the army to fight for this country, like his grandfather and two uncles. Perry always dreamed big. Throughout his school years, he maintained a 3.7 grade point average. He loved playing sports and his band. Oh, boy, I could still hear those drums. He played his drums every night for about a good six years. He drove us crazy, but that was his drive, and we never discouraged him. I can't recall ever having to attend his school and hear negative things about him, even after he was arrested. Mostly, all his high school teachers were there to support him, because they all knew he made a silly mistake.

"I remember I used to go to bed happy every night because I felt confident that I raised a great young man. That was until I received that awful phone call that I can't seem to erase from my head. When I first heard that my son was shot and killed because he pulled a gun out on undercover cops, I knew for sure they were lying and were trying to cover another unjustifiable police shooting. That's why I was relieved to hear that my son never had a gun on him and he was indeed murdered by racist cops.

"If we continue to let these trigger-happy cops run our streets, soon all of our babies will be dead. This could have happened to any one of us. I won't stop until justice is served. I won't stop until those police officers are stripped of their badges and thrown in jail. I won't stop until I receive an apology from the mayor. I want to thank everyone who came out." Laura threw her fist up in the air and yelled, "No justice, no peace!"

The protesters all joined Laura and sang those famous words. Laura's speech had angered a few protesters because they felt her pain, and they began fighting with a few cops there to keep the peace. They were quickly arrested, but the message was clear—New Yorkers had had enough.

Minister Muhammad walked back to the mic. "Listen," he said, "I have some bad news to report. Today, while we are here in downtown Manhattan fighting for our rights, I have just been informed that a young female has been shot in front of a police precinct in Harlem. I can't confirm who killed her, and at this moment the police don't have any suspect or leads. Today, Officer Donald Gibson was turning her in, and she gets assassinated on the doorsteps of a police precinct. Something doesn't smell right. And that's why we are here today, because we are tired of it."

The minister didn't know his words would ignite a riot. Protesters started picking fights with all the officers present.

The officers were already looking for an excuse to shut down the rally, and now the people were providing one for them. They began pepper-spraying as many protesters as they could.

Meanwhile, Minister Muhammad was yelling on the mic, trying to restore order. He knew the rally would get shut down if they continued to act in this manner. "Please, calm down. Don't give the police a reason to shut us down. This is exactly what they want us to do. Please, calm down!"

Most of the crowd listened to the minister and stopped, but others kept fighting with the officers.

Ten minutes into the melee, about one hundred more cops showed up to the scene. They restored order amongst the wild bunch, handcuffing every idiot who was causing a disturbance. A few police officers were hurt in the process, but there was no way the NYPD was going to lose control of the situation.

Twenty minutes later, after order was restored, the crowd turned its attention back to the podium, because Kim had made her way toward the mic to address the supporters. She was the only one who had been silent throughout the ordeal. Everyone was eager to finally hear her voice and feel her pain.

"Hello, everyone," she said nervously. "I want to thank everyone who showed up today, and please stop the fighting. Please, no more violence. This is why we are all here today. To stop the violence. We need to lead by example. I know my silence has shocked certain individuals, but I can't explain how I'm feeling. I know I'm supposed to be strong, but how strong can I be when little Perry keeps asking for his"—All of a sudden, Kim fainted right in the middle of her speech.

Laura quickly ran to her aid and began fanning her face. Since there were ambulances present, attending to some of the officers and protesters who were hurt during the melee, Kim quickly received medical attention. She was rushed to a nearby hospital, the Colemans and little Perry accompanying her.

The crowd was stunned. Some were in tears because they could relate to her. Minister Muhammad approached the mic, at a loss for words himself. He'd never used words like *quitting* or *giving up*, but for the first time ever, he had to cancel his protest.

"I guess we were too concerned with making a stand that we forgot to help the one who really needed our support. However, on a positive note, I want to let everyone know that Kim is conscious in the ambulance, so that's a good sign. We are going to have to cancel this rally, but the battle is not over. I hope America is listening. We the people declare war on the government. No justice, no peace!"

As the minister walked away from the podium, some cheered, but others, a lot of frustration built up inside, were upset because they still wanted to march. But without the minister or the Colemans present, it felt like a lost cause.

About an hour after the ambulance left with Kim and the Colemans, the streets were cleared, and everyone rushed back home to watch the news, eager to catch up on the latest events in Harlem.

The police department was puzzled, because Lucky was supposed to turn her in. So how could she get shot right in front of the police station? The media wanted to blame Lucky but didn't have proof. The autopsy would give them a better idea, but everyone had to wait a few days for that.

It was a circus outside the police station. Mayor Gulliano and Commissioner Fratt were slow to respond to the shooting, only because they were downtown, overlooking the rally. Once they arrived at the police station in Harlem, the small crowd outside started shouting out negative remarks toward the both of them.

"Take control of the city, you coward!"

"Stop letting the trigger-happy cops run through our city!"

A White male yelled, "Once the pigs start killing White people, then you will care!"

Both the mayor and commissioner, ignoring every comment thrown their way, made it through the hostile crowd. Their facial expressions said it all. They were hurt by what the people of the city were saying. The small crowd outside consisted of not just African Americans and Latinos, but White people as well.

When the mayor finally made it inside, he quickly demanded a meeting with both the sergeant and the captain on duty. They entered one of the interrogation rooms, along with the commissioner.

The mayor was upset and didn't waste any time letting it be known. "Before I start, please state both your names."

"My name is Sergeant Michael Spinks."

"And I'm Captain Brett Roots. I've been in the force for—"

"Did I fuckin' ask how long you have been a cop? I just asked for your name. Now, listen carefully. I'm going to ask another question and please just answer it. I'm not interested in your favorite color. I didn't come here to spark a friendly conversation. Got it?"

Both officers nodded in agreement, too scared to even say yes.

"What the fuck happened today? Who shot this poor girl?" The mayor pointed at Sergeant Spinks.

"We still don't know. We're one hundred percent sure it didn't come from inside this precinct. We are waiting on the autopsy report, and we are hoping the ballistics will provide us with a lead."

"Let me get this clear. She was supposed to be turned in today, right?" the mayor asked.

"Correct."

"So who shot the girl? If you had to give me an answer, whether right or wrong, who do you think shot the girl?"

"Honestly, Mr. Mayor, I don't know," Spinks said.

"How about you, talk a lot?" he asked Captain Roots.

"Whoever did it wanted to bring more negative attention to our city and department. If you ask me, one of the thousands of supporters for the Coleman family could have pulled the trigger, just to add fuel to the fire."

"We have a serious situation on our hands. I will expedite the autopsy report and have it up in an hour or two. Meanwhile, I have to go back outside and face these reporters and get my ass chewed in front of these live cameras. I want you two to interview each uniform in here privately and find out what they know."

The mayor went outside alone and faced the wrath, answering every question as best he could, making it clear that, to his knowledge, it wasn't a police shooting, and that the investigation was still ongoing.

"Today, not far from where I'm standing, a young lady was shot. This young lady was allegedly kidnapped by a former detective named Donald Gibson. There are still a lot of unanswered questions, and at this moment, we don't have any leads or suspects. We are trying to iron out all the facts about this case."

"Mr. Mayor, was she killed by a police officer?"

"I can't confirm nor deny that at this moment."

"Mr. Mayor, then who shot her?"

"Again, we are investigating the situation as we speak. We are waiting for an autopsy and a ballistics test on some fragments left behind from the two bullets that entered her body."

"But an autopsy could take a few days," another reporter commented.

"Because of the magnitude of the situation and how this could somehow be connected to another high-profile case, we are making a few exceptions. We should have one in a few hours."

"This other case you are referring to, is it the one involving Perry Coleman who was gunned down by police officers?"

"Well, at this moment, we are focusing our attention on the death of a young lady. We are looking for answers, and I'm confident those answers will arrive quite rapidly. I stand behind this great city, and also the brave men who risk their lives every day and night. Police officers are not bad people. In fact, wearing the badge is one of the greatest honors."

The mayor was getting annoyed by the questions being asked. Right before another reporter was about to ask a question, he noticed Richard Claiborne, a spokesperson for his office. To quickly get out of the situation, he said, "Well, if you guys need more answers, Mr. Richard Claiborne is the guy to ask."

As the reporters all rushed him, the mayor was able to get back inside.

Forty-five minutes later the autopsy was done, and the information was related to the mayor. The two bullets matched a unique rifle that wasn't due to hit the market for another two years. The FNAR .308 rifle guaranteed at least a mile of accuracy.

No one in the police station had ever heard of such a weapon, except the commissioner. He knew he'd heard of that gun before but couldn't remember from where. They put a call out on the radio asking for help.

The Watcherz heard it and quickly contacted Tuna.

When Tuna got the call, he gathered all the troops back in the apartment and related the news.

"Listen, fellas, we just got word what kind of rifle was used to kill the girl. I know it wasn't one of ours, so I apologize."

Everyone looked relieved, no one wanting friction among the team, usually the first sign of a sinking ship.

"I know everyone is happy to hear the good news," Tuna said. "But now it really throws a wrench in it. If we didn't kill that girl, and Lucky didn't, then who shot her?"

"How we know Lucky didn't kill her himself?" Floyd asked.

"That's not his style. I think maybe there's a third party involved," Tuna replied.

That was the question of the day. Who shot Diamond?

As Tuna was about to talk to the crew about a new plan, the Watcherz called him upstairs to take a call.

Tuna went upstairs, grabbed the phone, and didn't bother to ask who it was. He already knew the commissioner was on the other line. "Hello, Mr. Commissioner."

"Oh, it's not the commissioner, you bitch! Surprise! It's your worst nightmare."

"Lucky, you got some nerve calling me here." Tuna snapped his fingers at the Watcherz, so they could start a trace.

"I see you got yourself some hired guns from out of town. You think I don't remember you mentioning your cousin Floyd from Florida? He's one of the best bounty hunters in the state, so you say. How the fuck is he the best, and you still don't know where I am?"

"Don't worry about me. You need to worry about yourself, and what will happen when we do catch you. Trust me, one day you will run out of luck, Lucky."

"Ha! Ha! I know that's what you're wishing for."

"You will slip up. Just like we found your little girlfriend, we will find you. Talking about your little girlfriend, whatever happened to her? I heard she never turned herself in. What a shame."

"Fuck you! This will come back to haunt you. Remember the Jersey job? And, for the record, I know you didn't pull the trigger—You don't have the balls."

"You know I have the balls to pull the trigger. I don't even know why you would question my actions."

"I know you didn't shoot her."

"How you know, Lucky? Please enlighten me," he said, looking at the Watcherz, wondering why they hadn't located Lucky's signal yet.

"Because I killed her. I couldn't take the risk of her talking. I pulled the fuckin' trigger, and I'm coming after you next, bitch!" Lucky slammed the phone down.

Tuna pulled the phone away from his ear and looked at it in disbelief. Lucky had caught him off guard with the call. He didn't understand why he would kill her. That was out of character for him, but it made sense. What really puzzled him was the mentioning of the Jersey job. He didn't see the connection.

As the captain was about to leave the apartment, the phone rang again. He turned around, ran back, and answered the phone.

"Listen, when I catch you, fuckin' little rat, I'm going to rip your fuckin' heart out!"

"This is not one of your little playmates on the line."

Tuna tried to clear up his voice when he realized it wasn't Lucky on the line. "This is Captain Youngstown. How can I help you?"

"Please, Tuna, cut the crap. It's the commissioner. Is this line secure?"

"Yes, sir."

"Remember that job I wanted you to take care of for me in New Jersey?"

"Which job?" Tuna asked, playing dumb.

"You know, when we hit those gunrunners and we kept five assault rifles for ourselves. Remember those weapons? I can't recall the names."

"I think I remember that job. But, boss, why are we talking about the Jersey job, anyway?"

"The girl that got killed in Harlem today was assassinated by slugs that were fired by one of those rifles."

Tuna went silent on the line, finally figuring out why Lucky had said this would haunt him.

"Tuna, please explain how that could happen when I specifically told you to destroy those weapons. This could land us in some serious boiling water, and if my name comes up even as a rumor, I'm throwing you under the bus. Got it?"

"I understand, but let me explain. Lucky is behind this. He killed the girl in Harlem. It's a ploy to set up my unit. He must have kept one of the rifles."

"Lucky killed the girl? It makes sense, but I'm going to need proof he pulled the trigger. But how in the world can he have kept one of those when I asked them to be destroyed?"

"I thought they were. He's usually the guy who destroyed all the evidence. I didn't know he kept one. Let me ask you this. Why do I need to prove it? I know no one from my squad pulled the trigger."

"Please, Captain . . . just like you told me all five rifles were destroyed. I'm not taking anymore chances with your reckless unit. I need proof. You better hurry up and get this Lucky situation under control ASAP. Your career and life depend on it."

"How easy we forget. You hired my reckless unit on many occasions to handle your dirty deeds. Now you can't believe a word coming out of my mouth. I know for a fact he killed the girl. I have him on tape, confessing the murder."

"If you have him confessing on tape, that's perfect. Let's release it to the press."

"Didn't you say you don't want your name to surface near this case? If we release the tape, it will open the possibility."

"You're right. Just handle the situation. Remember, you owe it to us. We're doing everything possible on our end to make the Coleman case disappear. Good-bye. I'm hanging up."

Tuna walked back downstairs and gave a brief update on what just took place. The team couldn't believe Lucky was responsible for pulling the trigger, but they weren't surprised.

Floyd, for the first time, realized why his cousin was having such a hard time with Lucky. "I see why you need help catching this son of a bitch. He's a monster, for him to kill that girl in front of a police station, with a gun that could implicate the police commissioner of this city. This is one slick animal. We need to take him down like the dog he is."

"I couldn't agree more. That's why we need to be a lot better at whatever we are doing. We need to pay attention to every little detail, go with your hunches," the captain pleaded.

After Lucky got off the phone with Tuna, he sat on his chair and leaned back, mentally exhausted. His thoughts were getting him dizzy. These last few weeks had been the most intense in his whole life. He needed a few minutes of quiet time, so he sat there for a good seven to eight minutes in complete silence. You would have thought he knew yoga and was meditating. Lucky snapped out of his daze when he heard the sound of a flushing toilet. He sat up.

Diamond came out of the bathroom. "So what happened, baby? Did they buy your story?" she asked.

"Yeah, I know they did. The plan is now in motion. In tomorrow's headline, I will be wanted for murder. They will find a way to blame me. But at least this time I really did commit the crime. You were in that bathroom a long time. Did you wash your hands, stinky?"

"Don't play with me. You know I did."

Lucky was trying to soften her up before he dropped the bomb on her. It was time for them to separate. It was time for her to disappear.

"Baby girl, we need to talk. You definitely have to skip town. There is no way we can be seen together. This shit here is way past dangerous."

"Trust me, daddy, I'll never question your word again. After what you pulled off today, I'm amazed. I don't know how you think of shit like this. You're a fuckin' genius."

"What do you mean, girl?"

"This whole setup thing between you and Sergio. You have been working on this for a long time. How did you know they would go in the restaurant and ask about me?"

"That's why I became a cop. It's a gift of mine. They fell into a trap. It's like I'm psychic. I'm always thinking of a way to outsmart my opponent. Anyway, I know the heat will be getting closer. I need you gone by the morning. Pick up a hundred thousand dollars from the storage spot. Your Honda Accord is still parked there, so take your keys. While you are in there, look for a shoebox that has the word *cemetery* written across it."

"Cemetery?"

"That's right, *cemetery*. Pay attention. Inside, you will find a red envelope with an address written on a piece of paper, and keys to a town house I own in Glen Burnie, Maryland."

"Glen what? Come on, Maryland? Are you serious?"

"Didn't you just say you wouldn't question my words?"

"Okay, okay, I've just never heard of it before."

"It's nice and quiet. Trust me, you will love it. When you arrive there, get familiar with the area. That will be our new home. There's a telephone number on there. The person on the other line, he will take care of all your paperwork."

"Paperwork?"

"Yes, baby girl. You know, a driver's license, social security card, and a job if you want one. You will have a new life and identity. You get a chance to start all over."

"A new job and identity, huh. I see what you're doing. Lucky, you are never coming back. You think I'm stupid?"

"C'mon, baby, you can't think like that. Honestly, the chances of me surviving are real slim."

"So then leave with me. We have enough money to disappear. You must have over two million dollars in that storage. Please say yes. Let's just go."

"I can't. If I don't kill them, I will be running forever. They won't rest until I'm dead, either. I'm coming down there, baby. Don't worry. Let me take care of business and eliminate these fools. The folders haven't even hit the fan yet. It sounds like fun, but—"

"I know, I know. It's too dangerous."

"Oh, you're being smart? Come here, girl," Lucky said as he grabbed her. "You know I love you, right? I just want you to go down there and become a free woman. It's time for you to shine." Lucky hugged her for a few minutes. He knew she was crying.

Diamond was so in love with Lucky, he probably didn't realize how much. They got in bed, and she quickly started to please her man.

After hours of sex, Lucky was still up thinking about his next move. He'd already sent out all the packages. All he could do now was fall back. Lucky expected the federal government to get involved. He was lying in his bed, playing his plan over and over in his head, while Diamond rested on his chest. He kissed her on the forehead and whispered, "Don't worry, baby. Soon all this will be over."

"I'm more worried about you, daddy."

The next morning they both jumped in the shower. Diamond was trying to enjoy every last moment with him. While in the shower, she decided to fuck her man one last time. She moved the shower head toward the wall because she didn't want to get her hair wet. She dropped to her knees and began to slowly kiss on Lucky's balls, jerking him off with one hand, and rubbing his buffed chest with the other. Once Lucky was hard like a rock, she began to jerk him a little faster.

Lucky leaned back against the wall and enjoyed the show. Diamond then started to suck and kiss the tip of his dick while she looked up at him. Her eyes alone almost made him cum.

He looked down at her and placed his hands on her face, one on either side, and slowly pushed his dick in and out of her mouth. Every five or six strokes, he would go deeper and deeper.

After a good five minutes of mouth-fucking, Diamond broke loose and started to suck him off exactly the way he liked it. She would go as deep as she could while jerking it then switch to no-hands and begin her deep-throat magic.

Lucky's knees buckled, ass cheeks got tight, and he wasn't even about to climax. That's how good she could blow. Diamond never gave him head without swallowing his cream, which never took long. She was Lucky's personal "Superhead."

After he came, he flipped around and started finger-popping her to get the pussy ready. He always started slow, ignoring her cries about fucking her hard.

Diamond spread her ass cheeks apart with her hands and said, "Fuck me, baby. I want it right now. Kill this pussy!"

Lucky granted Diamond her wish, placing the tip in her pussy, enough to get her excited. Right before she opened her mouth to ask him to fuck her, he rammed his dick in her, and she let out a scream that almost burst his eardrum. He ignored her yells and continued ramming her pussyhole. Diamond was screaming for more, and that's what she received. Lucky knew he was going to miss her great pussy, so he was up for the challenge of killing it.

They got out of the shower and moved the party back to the bed. Diamond got on top and started riding his dick slowly. Every eight to ten strokes, she would jump off and suck his dick then jump back on. She was riding so hard, she was making her ass clap. Then she started shaking and squeezing her tits. She was climaxing, multiple times too, her eyes rolling to the back of her head. After she came, she jumped off and sucked all her pussy juices off his dick.

Lucky then flipped her on the bed and got on top. He bent back both her legs around her neck and began to eat her out. Diamond always thought he did tongue exercises well. He had one strong tongue. He would press it against her clit and move it side to side, up and down, as quickly as he could. He always drove her crazy when he did that, and she climaxed a few more times.

She grabbed him by his head, pulled him up, and started kissing and licking all her juices from around his lips and chin. She whispered in his ear, "Daddy, I got my legs cocked back, what are you waiting for? Break this pussy in half."

Diamond dirty talk was his Red Bull. He slid his dick back in her wet pussy and started to pound her out. A good thirty minutes later, they were both laying across the bed out of breath.

"I'm going to miss you, daddy."

"I will, too, baby girl."

"Let me jump back in the shower. I need to hit the road."

As she jumped back in the shower, he quickly turned on the news and logged on the Internet. He wanted to see if any new developing stories hit the press.

Lucky was laughing at some of the articles he was reading online. He said to himself, "You think the shooting shook up the city? Wait until these envelopes hit the press."

Fifteen minutes later, Diamond came out of the shower. While she got dressed, Lucky called up a taxi to take her to the storage facility. They hugged and kissed each other for a few moments.

Lucky wiped her tears and told her, "No worries. I will make it back safe. Stop crying. You have a long day ahead of you. Stay focused. Now is the time to be strong. Remember your training. This is the time when you need to apply your skills and survive. You feel me, baby girl?"

"I guess so. I know I will be all right. I just hope I see you again," she said as she walked out the door.

Lucky stood by the front door and watched her walk down the hallway and catch the elevator. He felt bad about lying to her. He closed his front door and leaned against it, thinking about all the good times he'd had with her. He wanted to open the door and chase after her, but he couldn't find the strength to go against his ego, his pride.

He didn't have any plans of heading down to Glen Burnie and reuniting with Diamond. The house and the money he gave her were his buyout. He could only hope she didn't break down when she realized the truth. In his heart, he knew it was better for her to start a new life without him. He didn't want to keep holding her back. She was beautiful, young, smart, and a perfect female to marry. He didn't want to ruin her future.

What really made him change his mind was when he looked through the scope and killed that girl in front of the precinct. Right before he'd pulled the trigger, he envisioned Diamond's face. That scared him, and it was the sign he needed.

He leaned off the door and walked to his bedroom. The guilt was starting to wear off. He knew he did the right thing and wasn't about to beat himself over his decision. Plus, Lucky thought it would be a better idea to hide and live with his baby mother and daughter. He would always love Diamond, but when it came to his daughter, it was a no-brainer. He decided to work out and then rest, which usually helped to ease his mind.

A day later, Lucky was still depressed. He sat on the edge of his bed, and for the first time since the night Perry got killed, he caught an itch. An itch to snort cocaine.

Lucky quickly jumped off his bed and began to slap his head with both hands. He was trying to prevent those demons from recurring. This was the mental war the addicts talked about all the time. The war on drugs was a lifelong battle. The itch to relapse would come again and again.

Lucky was going through one of his withdrawals. He wanted to find a quick solution to help the pain fade away, and coke used to be that quick fix. He paced back and forth in his living room for about two hours, sweat pouring down his face. The only thing that saved him from snorting was, there wasn't any cocaine in his presence. For the moment, he won the battle and was able to refocus on the task at hand. It wasn't an easy recovery, but at least he was able to snap out of the hypnosis.

He went in the kitchen, grabbed a box of Apple Jacks cereal, milk, a spoon, and a bowl. He went back to his room and turned on the TV. He didn't get a chance to pour the milk in the bowl before the TV got his attention. It seemed those envelopes were starting to hit their destinations. The news was reporting that there were numerous reports that lawyers defending different high-profile cases were receiving new evidence that could clear their clients of all charges.

Chapter Eleven

The Shake-up

"*Good morning, everyone. This is Angela Stile, for BETV Channel Twenty News. This morning, we are receiving numerous reports about different lawyers receiving packages through the mail with evidence that will prove their clients' innocence. We are hearing that some of the evidence will prove their clients were set up by the NYPD. Unconfirmed reports are implicating the same officers involved in the shooting that killed Perry Coleman. We will have more on this story as it develops. Again, we have, I believe, three envelopes sent in total. This is Angela Stile, for BETV Channel Twenty News.*"

Lucky forgot all about his Apple Jacks and began to get dressed. His next plan was in motion, and he had a lot of work ahead of him. He had to stop thinking about Diamond and get focused before he became the next murder victim.

While Lucky was getting dressed, his old partners were shitting bricks. All stunned and shocked, they couldn't believe what they'd just heard on the TV. The captain and Loose looked at each other because they knew all the foul activities they'd done. If only 10 percent of their dirt was publicized, they could ruin the NYPD's image forever.

"This son of a bitch, who in the hell does he think he is?" Tuna yelled.

"Captain, I know Lucky is behind this. This muthafucka never destroyed any of the evidence. What are we going to do now?"

Loose didn't like the look in his captain's eyes. He hadn't seen that look in years. The captain quietly escorted everyone out and sent them down to the fourth floor, everyone except Loose. And, of course, the Watcherz, they were always on the computer.

"What's up, boss? Why you kicked them out? What's going on? I don't like that look. Talk to me."

"Loose, I'm getting sick and tired of me finding out new information via the news, radio, or third party, but never from my own goddamn team." Tuna turned toward the Watcherz. "Why in the fuck am I paying you guys all this money and you are never close to providing anything? You guys can't find your own dicks!"

Loose tried to calm Tuna down because he knew where it was leading. He was about to take out his frustrations on the two brothers. He pushed Tuna away from the brothers, but he didn't realize Tuna walked in the kitchen and grabbed a Louisville Slugger he kept by the refrigerator.

The Watcherz turned back around and went back to work. They never once noticed where Tuna went, and never saw him creeping.

Loose noticed, but he did nothing. He wasn't the type to stop too many fights.

Tuna got in a Barry Bonds stance and swung the bat as hard as he could. He hit Hack first, and as he was falling on the floor unconscious, Little Hack turned to his left to try to grab his brother before hitting the floor. When Little Hack looked up to Tuna to ask why he hit his brother, Tuna hit him across his face, breaking his nose and knocking out all his front teeth. As they both were on the floor bleeding, Tuna kicked both brothers across the face and head.

"You two muthafuckas think I'm stupid! I'm paying all this money for shit! How you like me now, bitch?" Tuna yelled as he kept hitting both brothers.

After three or four more hits, Loose finally decided to grab Tuna and take the bat away. He looked over at the Watcherz. He knew one of them was dead. The other one was shaking like he'd caught a seizure. Loose walked over and gave him one more shot over his head. He hit him so hard, blood spattered all over his clothing. It looked like a scene out of the movie *Saw*.

After he made sure both brothers were dead, he kicked one of them in the ass and said, "Ha! Ha! You should have done your job, asshole!"

Speedy grew suspicious when Tuna asked everyone to leave. That only meant his partners were plotting on deadly violence. He didn't wait downstairs like the others. He didn't like being left out. He headed upstairs to see what was taking them so long to come downstairs. When he opened the door, he expected to seen Tuna and Loose working on new tactics, but he saw the Watcherz lying in a pool of blood.

"What in the world happened here?" Speedy yelled. "Please tell me they are not fuckin' dead, please."

"I'm sorry, Speedy. The captain lost it and took it out on them. They took too long in finding Lucky. The captain is in the bathroom. If I was you, I wouldn't go in there. Well, at least not right now."

"You know what? You are one crazy, psycho cop. How the fuck you let this happen?"

"Watch yourself there, Speedy boy."

"I don't have to watch shit. I can't believe you guys. Right now, we have all this heat on our backs, and you want to add two more murders? We are so fucked! I'm out of here. I'm not going down for this bullshit."

"Wait a second. What the fuck you mean, you are not going down for this shit?" Loose got in front of Speedy and blocked his way. "You starting to sound like Lucky. What are you trying to imply?"

Speedy pushed Loose out of the way so hard, it caused him to bump the back of his head against the wall. Loose rushed Speedy, tackling him to the floor. He stood over him and began to punch him, hitting him across his face.

Floyd got in between them. Curious like Speedy, he had come up to find out the latest updates. He was also shocked to see all the blood in the room.

"What the fuck is going on here? You two are partners. Why in the hell would you want to hurt each other? What the fuck is wrong with you two? Where is Tuna? And can someone explain why there are two dead bodies in this apartment that were not here just twenty minutes ago?"

Tuna came out of the bathroom, dazed out in his own world. He didn't know about the fight.

"Tuna, wake the fuck up and snap out of it! Someone, anybody, please talk and explain what is going on."

Tuna didn't respond, and Loose was too frustrated to talk. He still wanted to fight.

"I will explain what the fuck is going on." Speedy wiped the blood coming down his nose. "We are all going to jail, what's going on. My captain and his sidekick just bought us a first-class ticket to the big house."

"Shut the fuck up, Speedy!"

Floyd held Loose as he tried to rush Speedy. "Hey, cousin, speak up. What the fuck is going on?"

Tuna finally broke his silence. He looked at his cousin and said, "We are all fucked. What can I say? This muthafuckin' nigger beat us at our own game."

"C'mon, cousin, I never heard of you quitting before. What is wrong with you? Get a grip. We could find a way to still catch this son of a bitch. I will have Ace and Country clean up this mess in here, and no one will ever know the Watcherz were ever in this apartment. But let's not give up."

"Floyd, didn't you see what we saw on TV? Lucky sent evidence to lawyers that will prove we framed their clients. I could see the headlines now. They will eat us alive. We'll need a miracle to get out of this one," Speedy said.

While Tuna and Floyd moved over to a corner of the apartment to have a private conversation, the rest of the crew began cleaning up the mess.

Ace and Country picked up the bodies and threw them in the tub. Within an hour, both bodies were chopped up in little pieces, and all the blood drained.

Chucky and Loose began cleaning up the blood and wiping down all the computers. Speedy locked himself in the bathroom and was cleaning his face.

Loose knocked on the bathroom door. "Speedy, open up. We need to talk."

Speedy wanted to blow him off, but he opened the door. "What's up, Loose?"

"Hey, listen, my bad. I didn't mean to call you a snitch. Right now, my state of mind is all fucked up. I hope you could accept my apology."

Speedy thought, *What apology?* But coming from Loose, the most stubborn human on this planet, it meant a lot to him.

"Don't sweat it, bro. Brothers fight all the time. We need to get back to business and figure out how we're going to avoid jail," he said, embracing his partner.

It was only 10:30 in the morning, and the day was just beginning to unfold, but there was already so much drama for one day.

Floyd took his crew back down to the fourth floor while Tuna spoke to Loose and Speedy about their next move.

"Okay, we are in deep shit, and I'm sure I will get a call in a few minutes to come in the office and explain these recent events. The commissioner already came down my throat about not getting rid of those guns from the New Jersey job, so I'm sure he will chew me a new asshole. Do you guys have any suggestion or ideas?"

No one answered, a clear signal they were all clueless about their next move, or maybe they didn't believe in their boss anymore. They both saw how dazed Tuna was through the drama.

Tuna picked up on their lack of enthusiasm. "Don't tell me you two are losing your faith in this team. C'mon, we're in this together. This will be the worst time to fuckin' quit on me."

"Boss, things are not looking good, and I can't go to jail. My wife and kids, they need me."

"I have to agree with Speedy on this one. I'm not going to jail. They will have to kill me first. Another thing, boss, I never saw you freeze up until today."

"What the fuck you mean? C'mon, Loose, you know me better than that. I'm just in a state of shock. I don't want to go to jail, either. We should have killed him, like Tango."

"What do you mean, you should have killed him as well? Are you saying Tango's murder was our call?"

Tuna tried to downplay his comment, but it was too late.

Speedy started to yell at both Tuna and Loose. "How in the world can you guys kill your own brother? I could understand why we want to erase Lucky. But Tango, why?"

"Tango was working with Internal Affairs. We got word from an insider over at IA. You know our source over at IA is legit. We had to take care of him quickly," Tuna explained.

"I still can't believe it. Tango was a snitch? C'mon, did you guys ever really confront him about it? I don't understand why you guys kept a secret from me, but we call ourselves brothers. I'm out of here. I'll call you guys later. I'm going home to play with my kids. Given the current events, I don't have a lot of time on my side."

Speedy caught them off guard, wanting to leave, but Tuna allowed him to leave without any argument.

Loose Cannon wasn't happy. "Speedy, remember, we are in this together."

Speedy didn't look back. He just walked out the front door and went home. He was disgusted with his partners and didn't feel comfortable around them anymore.

The first thing that came out of Tuna's mouth when Speedy left was, "I hope we don't have to get rid of him too."

"Just give me the word, Captain, and he's a goner."

"Let's just watch him for a few days and let's make sure he doesn't do anything stupid," Tuna said.

Tuna and Loose joined the rest of the crew down on the fourth floor. They told everyone that Speedy left to take care of some personal family issues.

Going on noon, they decided to watch the news and see the latest on the envelopes Lucky was sending out. When they turned on the news, a reporter was talking about an alleged report of the commissioner's involvement in corruption. Before the reporter finished her story, Tuna's cell started ringing.

"Hello?" a dumbfounded Tuna said, knowing it was Commissioner Fratt on the other line.

"Hello? That's all you have to say. I know you are watching the news. I need to see you ASAP. Meet me at the village. Do you still remember the apartment?"

"Yes, I do."

"And hurry up and get here, and come alone."

Before Tuna could answer, Fratt hung up the phone on him. Tuna told everybody he would be back in a few hours.

Before he left by the front door, Floyd said to him, "Hey, listen, cousin, I was talking to my crew, and we all decided that this will be the end of the road for us."

"What the fuck do you mean, the end of the road?"

"We are all going back to Florida. We were under the impression you had this situation under control, and you don't. We are out of territory, and it looks like the heat is about to broil. I can't continue to risk my crew's freedom with unorganized tactics."

"Hey, coward, if you want to leave then go ahead. I thought blood was thicker than water, but I see you have your new family to worry about. Thanks for coming, and fuck you very much!"

Tuna left furious. His team was falling apart like a music group, and now family was moving away as far as they could from him. After Tuna left, Loose Cannon tried to explain what was happening.

But Floyd didn't want to hear it. "Save it," he said. "We're all leaving."

They all drank a few beers and continued watching the different reports surfacing on the local news channel.

Lucky was also watching from a local coffee house. With his disguise, he blended in perfectly with everybody else in New Jersey. No one knew they were sitting right next to the most wanted person in New York's history. He wanted to catch Destine's report because he'd mailed her a package as well, with graphic pictures of a priest sexually molesting little boys.

"Good afternoon. This is Destine Diaz for Channel Five News. We are here to bring the latest on these mysterious packages. We believe there are a total of five. Four were mailed to lawyers, and one was mailed to me. I have specifics, but they are sickening, graphic pictures of little boys getting sexually molested.

We have unconfirmed reports that the man in those pictures is none other than Cardinal Joseph King III, the same priest who performed the marriage vows for the mayor and his wife. According to the letter I received along with the pictures, this mysterious informant is indicating that Joseph King III was never prosecuted because of his political friends. Again, these are uncon-firmed reports. We are waiting on official word from Police Plaza and the district attorney's office."

Lucky was smiling from cheek to cheek, happy to hear Destine speak about the envelopes. He knew he'd picked the right reporter. She wasn't scared of the controversy. He ordered another cup of coffee and continued to listen to her report.

Lucky wasn't the only one listening. The people in New Jersey were also eager to hear the story, being closest to all the madness.

The Colemans were hoping some new evidence would pop up to help their son's case against the city. Laura was sitting on the edge of her seat, watching the news.

"Laura, sweetheart, sit back please. Let's just hear what the young lady has to say," Perry Sr. said.

"I'm just praying for a little help from God. I think we deserve it, baby. We need the help."

"I agree, but let's just watch the news and see what else they got. If the same cops are involved, this will help our case to some degree. It will prove how corrupt those officers are."

"You're right, baby. Oh, the commercials are over. Be quiet. Let's see what else she has to say," Laura was on the edge of her seat again.

"Welcome back. This is Destine Diaz, Channel Five News. We have new information on those other four fold-ers. I don't know if some of you guys remember, but about seven years ago Rell Davis was charged and convicted of double murder. He was sentenced to double life sentences without the possibility of parole. Rell pleaded innocence throughout the whole trial, claiming he was framed. Rell has also had two appeals denied. Well, today his lawyer, Nicholas McCarthy, confirmed he received a package with evidence that Rell Davis was not the shooter the night Connie and Rodger Newton were gunned down while they slept in their Hampton mansion. We will have more information on this one as it develops.

"The other package was sent to the lawyer of Juan "Pito" Medina, a convicted drug kingpin who was sentenced to life in prison without parole. His lawyer, Edwin Gustavo, has stated he also has concrete evidence, which includes photos and conversations, proving his client was set up as well.

"Then there is the case involving a family in the Bronx, where a father was gunned down when police mistakenly raided the wrong house.

"And finally I remind viewers of our earlier report this morning about Police Commissioner Brandon Fratt. These stories have the whole city disturbed and disappointed.

"This is Destine Diaz. We now turn it over to traffic."

Laura and her husband were sitting with their mouths open. They couldn't believe the reports they'd just heard.

While they were discussing the latest news report, Kim walked in the living room and was asking what all the fuss was about, and they told her what they'd just heard.

She thought it was time to tell them about the package Lucky left behind. "Well, I have a confession of my own. Remember the day Lucky came by the house?"

"Yes," they both said.

"Well, he left a package behind as well."

"What? Why did you take so long in telling us? I'm surprised at you," Laura said.

"I'm sorry, but I was told not to say anything until the trial was over. I'm sorry, Laura. I hope you can forgive me."

"It's okay, baby. I just don't know why he wouldn't want us to see it until after the trial."

"He said, if we bring it up during the trial, the evidence would disappear. He wanted us to wait until the civil case was in progress. I think he was just looking out for us and making sure the City pays for what they did to Perry."

"Honey, I think I understand his logic behind keeping this a secret from us. Let's not come down hard on her. Let's just see what he left behind and take it from there. Kim, please bring us the package."

While Kim went to get the package, Laura and Perry Sr. waited in suspense. They wanted to know what he'd left behind, but they were also scared. When Kim returned and placed the package on the coffee table, they all stared at it. They knew whatever was inside could place their lives in even more danger.

Laura reached for it and began to rip it open.

There was a computer disc along with a note. The note said that the CD contained a conversation between his former partners the night after Perry was gunned down. The CD was sufficient evidence to implicate Loose Cannon and Speedy.

They placed the CD in their computer and turned up the speakers. They heard the cops discuss how it was a brilliant idea to get the gun out of the car, shoot out the windows, and place it on her son.

They all began to cry when they heard the captain say, *"Good thing we keep that gun with us at all times. The press bought the story about that little nigger carrying a gun and shooting at us first."*

Laura stopped the CD from playing and asked her husband, "What are we going to do now? Should we call Minister Muhammad?" She had to pinch him to get his attention. "Honey, I'm talking to you. What are we going to do?"

"I don't know, baby. I just heard a trigger-happy cop make a racist remark about my son and also implicate himself. So Lucky was telling the truth. Not that I didn't believe him, but this certifies his side of the story."

"So, Who should we call? is my question, babe."

"I don't know. Kim said Lucky didn't want us to bring this evidence up in court, he wanted us to wait until the civil case. I don't know, baby. I really don't know who to trust. Remember how they pulled the plug last time we went public?"

While the Colemans contemplated their next move, city officials were scratching their heads over a way to respond. Lucky not only blew the whistle on his former partner, he blew the whistle on the city that never sleeps, the mecca of entertainment. New York City had earned a new name, "Corrupt City."

Donald "Lucky" Gibson was now officially the number one enemy, but not to the people, because they loved the fact that he had the guts to come forward and expose the truth. The City was real concerned about the allegations against the commissioner and Cardinal Joseph King III had caught the attention of both the Republican and Democratic parties, and there was going to be a discussion on it in a City Hall meeting in two days.

Even the President of the United States of America made a comment on his weekly radio show, stating:

"It saddens me to hear the negative attention the great city of New York is getting. I don't know all the facts, but I'm gathering there are allegations of corruption and murder. I will be visiting the city soon, meet with both parties, and address exactly what's going on. I could understand the concerns my fellow New Yorkers are expressing about police brutality, but also as the President of this nation, I must also listen and see all the facts before I make judgment. We all know I cleaned up corruption in the White House, so if we indeed are experiencing corruption, we will clean it up and return the glory back to the City of New York."

When Lucky heard the playback audio on the news about the president coming to New York, that really shook him up. He knew he was going to shock the city, but he had no idea the whole country was also going to pay attention to all the drama.

He quickly headed to the supermarket and spent close to five hundred dollars on groceries. He figured the next few weeks he would have to stay indoors because soon the FBI would also be looking for him.

When Captain Tuna met up with the commissioner, he was shocked to see two gentlemen in suits there with him. He thought for a second the commissioner had called Internal Affairs on him. He was wrong.

"I'm glad you finally joined us. Please have a seat."

"I didn't know you were having company over. What's this all about, Brandon?"

"Well, first it's *Commissioner* Brandon. Address me correctly. I took the liberty of inviting two of my friends from the Bureau. Please meet federal agents William Kuntz and John Pillar."

"What the fuck are they doing here? You know we don't deal with the feds. I'm surprised, Commissioner Brandon. Don't set me up like this. At least give me a warning first."

"You mean like you warned me about all this shit coming out through the media?"

"You know I didn't know what was coming. I was also surprised."

"You shouldn't be. I specifically told you to personally destroy all the evidence, not let some fuckin' monkey do it. You no longer have the situation under control. Agents Kuntz and Pillar will help you find Lucky."

"Fuck you! And fuck both of these pigs! Working with the feds is like working with Internal Affairs. I'm not doing it. We will find Lucky and shut his mouth up once and for all." Tuna got up and headed for the door.

Tuna didn't like that the commissioner tried to corner him like a fucking rat. He was going to leave without shaking his friend's hand. He'd just about had it with all his friends trying to turn on him now that the heat was on. He wasn't an idiot. He knew the commissioner was trying to figure out a way to escape the allegations, which meant Tuna and his team would have to take the fall.

Right before Tuna reached the front door of the apartment, Kuntz said, "Tuna, we know where Lucky's daughter lives."

Tuna stopped, turned around, and looked at him up and down, trying to make sure Kuntz wasn't pulling his tail. "You do. Where?"

"We will share this information with you if you let us help you catch him. And, for the record, our Bureau is not aware we are here to help. We're here because our good friend Brandon, excuse me, *Commissioner* Brandon, asked for our help."

That changed the whole ballgame. Tuna knew those agents were there to help find Lucky and kill him. He agreed and told them to drive back with him to meet Speedy and Loose Cannon. He said, "I need to warn both of you guys now. They won't accept this new partnership peacefully, but once they hear you guys know where his daughter is located, they'll change their minds."

Chapter Twelve

www.thesmokygun.com

The next day, after those mysterious envelopes hit the media, more concrete evidence was starting to surface via the Internet. The public had a better idea of what was going on and so far, the rumors were turning out to be true. Also, according to a few reliable sources, those envelopes came from Donald "Lucky" Gibson himself. In total, five envelopes were sent, and all five, along with a few pictures, were posted on a Web site called www.thesmokygun.com.

This Web site specialized in exposing high-profile cases. They were the first ones to post the video of an R&B singer pissing on little girls. They'd also posted all the mugshots of every time a celebrity was arrested. The Web site had a breakdown of each envelope.

Envelope #1: The State vs. Rell Davis:
Rell was charged and sentenced for a double murder and received a life sentence for each murder. Rell has maintained his innocence since day one. He was convicted of killing Rodger and Connie Newton.

Rell, a convicted felon, lost his case before the trial even started. The DA's job was easy on this one because of all the bogus evidence pointing at Rell. Nicholas McCarthy, his lawyer, held a press conference and stated that Rell was expected to be released from jail within days and he said his client is 100 percent certain he will sue the City and police department for the injustice against him. There were already rumors circulating that the City, not wanting to drag out this embarrassment in court has already reached out to Nicholas McCarthy about a settlement.

Envelope #2: The State vs. Juan "Pito" Medina.
He was charged with kingpin charges and received life without possibility of parole. Pito's case played with heavy

rotation in the media as well. A high-profile gangster who partied with all the major superstars and politicians, you would always find him in the front row of any sports arena, concert, or award show. Pito had it all—good looks, money, and power.

If he didn't have felonies on his record, he could easily run for a Senate seat. There were rumors for years that he had cops on his payroll. Pito claimed those drugs found in his backyard were not his.

He also claimed over $3 million was stolen by the police, but those allegations were dismissed in trial. Pito also accused the cops of extortion for all the protection money he was forced to pay over the years. In fact, he was the first one to go public about Captain Tuna and his rogue team terrorizing the city. Those allegations of corruption were also dismissed at his trial. No one believed a two-time felon, whose nine-to-five was to run a drug cartel in Harlem.

Envelope #3: The State vs. The Wiggins Family.

In 1999, the Street Crime Unit was working on an anonymous tip about a two-family house in the Bronx that was selling guns at wholesale prices. At the time, Officer Tuna only had two years' experience with S.C.U. They raided this house at four o'clock in the morning.

Inside lived an African American family of six, two parents, three kids, and an uncle that lived in the basement. Instead of staking out the house to make sure there were guns inside, they pressured the judge to sign off on a search warrant without any concrete evidence. Only thirty-six hours went by between receiving the tip and the actual raid.

When the front door of the Wiggins' house flew open and the agents marched in yelling, "Get on the floor," with their guns drawn, all hell broke loose.

The Wiggins were caught off guard, so of course the father, Joe Wiggins, and his brother Jonathan put up a fight. Joe didn't know what was going on, and he briefly fought off two agents, knocking them down to the ground. Once Joe heard his wife and kids yelling, he stopped throwing punches and ran toward them.

The agents didn't allow him to reach his family. Joe ignored the officers' plea to freeze, so they shot him three times in the back, killing him in front of his family. The officer claimed Joe was running to retrieve a weapon, which was never found.

Meanwhile, Uncle Jonathan was still fighting, even after he realized they were agents. Two minutes into the struggle and one minute after Joe was shot, Jonathan was shot as well in his lower abdomen, the bullet rupturing his spine, and paralyzing him for life.

After the smoke cleared, they realized they must have raided the wrong house, because they didn't find any drugs or guns. This case went under the radar for years. No one had ever heard of this incident before, not until Lucky brought it to the media's attention. The reason for the silence was because the City of New York had paid an undisclosed seven-figure settlement to the Wiggins.

Envelope #4: The State vs. Cardinal Joseph King III:

This case was sensitive and went under the radar just like the Wiggins' case. The cardinal was the same priest who'd married the mayor and his wife, and the one, after the 9/11 attacks, to organize so many relief programs, generating millions in funds for those financially handicapped after the attacks.

He ran a film company that produced child pornography. There were video clips of the cardinal performing sexual acts with little boys who appeared to be no more than nine and ten years old. Grown men were penetrating the rectums of little boys and recording everything. They went through about twenty-five videos and witnessed about thirty-five different kids being molested.

Captain Tuna and his crew were not about to protect a child molester, so they decided to expose the cardinal, instead of extorting him. They arrested him and pressed charges. A week after pressing charges against the cardinal, he was out on only $30,000 bail. The city was shocked, but they didn't rush to judge.

Envelope #5:

This package was the most dangerous one because now he was implicating the top cop in New York. Commissioner Brandon Fratt had started out as a trooper in New Jersey, where he learned to profile African Americans. When he worked the New Jersey Turnpike, that's all he pulled over, African American drivers. Years later, he transferred to the NYPD when his uncle became a chief.

Brandon, at twenty-seven, was made one of the youngest captains in the force. Five years later, he was running an elite squad called "Operation DG," which stood for drugs and guns. Their job was to lock up drug dealers and get the guns off the streets. Brandon handpicked his squad, and his first choice was then Officer William "Tuna" Youngstown.

Operation DG didn't help reduce crime and murder, they helped increase the numbers. That's how dirty this unit was. They were working with drug dealers like Pito, helping them move kilos of cocaine all around New York City. When Operation DG made arrests, they usually would lock up low-end criminals and then frame them with bigger crimes. This process kept the heat off their back from the mayor, and more money coming in from the criminals who paid for protection.

Since Lucky wasn't around at that time, the only evidence he had was recorded conversations between Tuna and Brandon.

Tuna had always credited Brandon for showing him the ropes and how to make millions of untaxed money. Lucky was able to provide certain files to the media, showing Brandon's signature on at least five different house deeds, two of them million-dollar condos. This was excluding the $1.2 million house he currently lived in with his wife and children. Commissioner Brandon also ran a non-profit organization called "The Future Is Now," a non-profit venture to help kids with special needs.

In the three years the company has been in existence, he has raised over $15 million dollars. Lucky provided documents of an overseas account with Brandon Fratt's signatures on deposit slips. There were over ten deposits totaling $15 millions dollars. The documents also showed a history of withdrawals, and for the past five years, he had spent over $7 million dollars in houses, cars, and lucrative vacations. In 1994, he co-owned a construction company that did all the major projects in Brooklyn.

His company was given a hundred-million-dollar contract to renovate public schools in Brooklyn. Out of more than sixty public schools, only about twenty were renovated, while another fifteen or so received new computers and books. In total, maybe forty million was used for the schools. The rest of the money was used to buy residents out of their home in order to start building these big department stores in the neighborhood and build big hotels in downtown Brooklyn.

According to Lucky, Brandon Fratt was the mastermind behind their unit. Captain Tuna ran everything through him first, and the commissioner was always the first one to get paid. The commissioner has already gone on record and denied all accusations.

Thesmokygun.com would like to thank everyone who read this article about the five envelopes. Our information comes from a reliable source down in City Hall. We are not responsible or liable for any suit, due to this third party information we received.

Chapter Thirteen

Lucky's Daughter

Tuna arrived with both agents at the apartment, so he could introduce them to his partners. Loose and Speedy didn't overreact like he thought they would. They understood that if Tuna was introducing them, they were legit and in it for the same reasons.

"Fellas, these two brothers are law enforcement, but they are feds. They are here to help us. The commissioner recommended them. They know where Lucky's daughter lives."

"For real?" Loose said. "So what are we waiting for. Let's go find her."

"I agree with Loose. Let's go find her. If they are working with us, then let's do it. Floyd and his boys already left. We need all the help we can get," Speedy added.

They gathered around the living room and listened to the information the agents had to share. They knew, by finding Lucky's daughter, this nightmare would go away. They would force Lucky to get in front of a camera and tell all of New York and America that he basically made up everything to frame his former employers because he was upset over his salary.

"Okay. So, Agent Kuntz, where is Lucky hiding his daughter?" Tuna asked.

"We have a P.O. box address up in Cape Cod, Massachusetts. This is the address that came up on some old hospital document. We ran Donald Gibson's name through the hospital database for the entire United States of America."

"But how do we know this is Lucky's daughter? There could be hundreds of Donald Gibsons," Speedy added.

"You are right, but there were only three Donald Gibsons in the force, and only one of them is African American. Donald used his police medical insurance to pay for the birth of his daughter. The birth certificate also gives us the name of both his daughter and the mother. His daughter's name is Tamika Freefall, and the mother's name is Tasha Freefall. Their last known address is a P.O. box in Cape Cod."

"Wow! That's some slick shit. I would have never thought about searching birth certificates and shit. I guess we are heading up to Cape Cod, right, boss?" Loose Cannon asked.

"Yes, we are, but we have to be smart. Loose, you and one of the agents go check this address out and bring back the little bitch. I'm sure they're still up there hiding."

"We have to be extremely smart. Tasha must be an expert in hiding because, besides the P.O. box address, we can't find anything else on them. It's possible they changed their names and their looks as well," Agent Kuntz added.

"You are right, but at least we know where to search. It shouldn't be hard to find a nigger in Cape Cod," Tuna added.

They all laughed.

"Boss, I think we should let Lucky know we're heading to Cape Cod. This will put fear in his heart and make him go out there as well. We could kill two birds with one stone."

They all thought it was a great idea.

About an hour later, after getting all the details worked out for their mission, Commissioner Brandon called Tuna's cell to express his frustrations.

"We are running out of fuckin' time. Find this nigger, and end it before we all go to jail for life. Now I have to get the feds off my ass. The DA is still gathering evidence, so we might have a slim chance of getting away clean from this mess. But you need to kill this son of a bitch. Got it?" He ended the call without letting him respond.

"Listen, Speedy, call our people down at the newspaper and make up a tip," Tuna ordered.

"What kind of a tip?"

"Come up with a story about how you received a call from a hotel employee and that those three police officers accused of killing that Black kid just checked in. Tell them that they can't name the hotel, but it's located in Cape Cod. Tell them to make sure they mention that all three police officers checked in, even though only Loose is going out there."

"That's a smart idea. You know Lucky will be watching the news, once he hears about us being in Cape Cod, he will shit in his pants. He will know we know about his daughter's whereabouts," Speedy added.

When the six o'clock news came on, the first story were those five envelopes. They were still the hot topic, and everyone had an opinion about the whole ordeal.

"Good evening. My name is Barbara Water, Channel Five News. Tonight, we have more details about those five envelopes. We all know they came from former police officer, Donald Gibson, who not long ago took the stand against his former partners for the murder of Perry Coleman. These allegations are not only shaking the streets, but they also have members of Congress scratching their heads. Every criminal from every corner is support-ing Rell Davis and Juan "Pito" Medina. The city streets are feeling their pain about being wrongfully accused and imprisoned."

"Meanwhile, a new trial date has not been set. The DA's office is still deciding whether or not they should move the case to another county."

"Did you hear that, honey?" Laura asked.

"I sure did. They're still undecided about moving the case to another county. I'm sure these recent reports will help us more than hurt us."

Lucky was watching the news as well, smiling. He was looking around the living room, missing Diamond's presence. Usually, around this time, she would feed Lucky whatever he wanted.

He finally got off the sofa and was about to make a sandwich when he heard the breaking news theme song come on. He quickly sat back down to listen.

"This is Barbara Water again. We have breaking news coming out of Queens, New York. The family of Perry Coleman, who was killed by the NYPD, also received what's believed to be a tape. A tape sent by, you guessed it, Lucky. On this tape, the Colemans are saying the three officers are heard talking about shooting, and implicating themselves. They won't allow the media to hear the tape, but they will let the district attorney hear it. They are set to head downtown tomorrow morning for a meeting. This is what Laura Coleman said, the mother of Perry Coleman."

"Good evening. A tape was brought to our attention by detective Donald 'Lucky' Gibson. Bless his heart for caring and making sure justice is served to these animals hiding behind a badge. On this tape, the officers are thanking each other for a cover-up. They call my son the N-word. At least now I can sleep at night knowing my son never pointed a gun at those officers. That's all for now. I want to thank New York for their continued love and support."

Lucky, at first, was upset that the Colemans went public with the evidence, but then he actually believed it was a perfect move. Due to all the recent allegations against the City, now was the perfect time to hit them where it hurt.

Lucky refocused his attention on the TV when he heard the news reporter say they were attempting to reach the three officers who were on trial, to see if they had any comments about all the allegations.

"We have tried to make several phone calls to their residences, but we've received no answer. However, through a reliable source, we hear the officers are in Cape Cod, fishing, but fishing for what?"

Lucky froze when he heard Barbara Water mention Cape Cod. The first thing that came to his mind was his daughter. "Fuck! They must know where Tamika lives."

He grabbed a few pieces of clothing and packed up his Expedition. Then he drove to his storage on Gun Hill Road in the Bronx.

One of Lucky's best friends, Divine, ran the storage facility, Put-It-Away, and Lucky was a silent partner. They were smart enough to invest their money after the armored truck heist they'd pulled a few years back. He had hired Divine and his two muscles, Pee-Wee and Blood. They made over ten million off the heist, eight million in bonds and two in cash.

The storage facility was really a front. Divine ran a business called Street Secrets. He let high-profile criminals store their money, drugs, and weapons, whatever they wanted. With Lucky's protection and intel, the storage was a successful business. Divine played the roll of banker, offering lockboxes with a 100 percent matching insurance policy. He ran a legit business, too. About 75 percent of the storage units belonged to regular customers, so they were able to keep the IRS and cops off them.

Divine and Lucky had one rule. They only did business with high rollers. There were times they were holding over $100 million in cash and a few tons of cocaine. They were making a lot of money, so Lucky had a state-of-the-art alarm installed, custom designed for the entire property. They went with technology, instead of armed guards, which would have made customers suspicious.

When Lucky arrived, Divine knew it was war.

"Yo, fam. Wat's good? Everything a'ight? You look like you about to start a war. Let me get my shit, too."

"Not on this one, Dee. I have to go alone. I think these pigs know where Tamika lives. It's going to get ugly. I need you here, just in case."

"Just in case? What you mean, dog?"

"Just in case something happens to me, you could continue running the business."

"C'mon, you sound crazy. I'm ready to die for you, hood. You took me out the streets. I'm still criminal-minded all day, but you got me off the block. I owe you, family. I'm not scared to die, not if I'm riding with you." Divine hugged his childhood friend.

"Damn, nigga! You tryin' to make me cry? Don't worry. I'm coming back. I just want you to hold shit down while I'm gone."

"I got you, but I just wanna let you know I'm not feeling all these moves you're making on your own. You know I'm here, twenty-four/seven for you. You should have came by and scoop me up, my dude."

"My bad, but that's what I been trying to say all along. I need to do this alone. Get the minivan ready."

"And you takin' the minivan? Now I know you about to start a war."

They both laughed as they walked to the back of the business. Lucky headed to his unit, while Divine went to load up the all-white minivan with all kinds of weapons.

Right before Lucky jumped in the van with limo-tinted windows, he turned to Divine and said, "Don't worry. God, I will be back."

"You better! Watch your ass out there, and don't sleep on no one, not even baby mom. It's been a while since you seen them," Divine said.

They once again embraced.

Lucky turned the van on and began his trip. He ignored that last comment by Divine. There was no way Tasha could betray him. It was only about a five- to six-hour drive. Lucky figured he could make it four and a half. He started off doing close to ninety miles per hour. He didn't care about any troopers or his own safety. The thought of any harm to his daughter took precedence over common sense.

After three hours of driving like a maniac, he started to realize he needed to slow down a bit. Long drives always made his mind wander, and he started thinking about Tasha and how they'd met.

He always felt she was a perfect match, a love at first sight for sure. She was also a gym rat, one of the many things they had in common. She loved working out and keeping her body in shape. She worked as a bartender in two of the hottest clubs at the time, Club Limelight and the Palladium. Tasha also took a lot of self-defense courses. Being a female bartender in New York City wasn't an easy task. Every night, she was either cursing or fighting a drunken jerk off her. She had to be on the defense at all times.

Tasha was five-four, caramel complexion with hazel eyes, had a flat stomach, and a nice juicy peach on her backside. No stretch marks or bumps, skin real silky, Lucky always thought she bathed in milk. Customers, both men and women, would always come on to her, looking for one-night stands.

Lucky always partied at the Palladium, and from afar, he had a big crush on her. He would always order from different bartenders because he didn't want her to remember his face and think he was a stalker. He wanted to wait until the perfect moment to make his move and ask her out.

One night, there was a stabbing after the club closed, and Lucky and Tango were two of few officers at the scene trying to calm down the rowdy partygoers. Lucky noticed two drunks harassing a young lady. As he got closer, he noticed it was the bartender. He didn't have to intervene, though. Tasha kicked them both in the nuts and slapped one of them with her purse while she maced the other. Tasha noticed Lucky approaching, and was about to spray him, until she saw the badge hanging from his neck. Lucky always remembered that day. It was the first day Tasha lay in his arms.

They dated for about six months before they moved in together. It didn't take long for her to realize his dirty laundry in the streets. She often asked him to stop before he lost his job or his life, but Lucky didn't take her advice at the time. He was making too much money. Instead of losing his life or job, he lost his first love.

Tasha knew it was over before she got pregnant. They had a long conversation about their next move. She wanted an abortion, he didn't. Tasha thought it was worth believing his words. After Tamika was born, Lucky indeed began slowing down, but was still playing with the devil's cards. Tasha didn't like it, but she didn't complain.

One morning, Tasha found him passed out on the floor of their driveway, car still running. Lucky had cocaine smeared all over his nose and mouth. That morning she decided it was time to leave, and leave him for good. When she went to turn off the car, she found an open box of condoms, two of them missing.

Tasha was more devastated about the drugs than his sleeping around. She had no idea he was snorting cocaine. She left him there on the floor, packed up a few things, and left with Tamika.

When Lucky woke up, he was on the floor with the sun beaming. He went inside and found a letter on the kitchen table. Tasha kept it short and sweet.

Lucky, you are a drug addict, a cheat, and a criminal. I'm moving into the summer house in Cape Cod. You know how to find us and send money. Don't you dare

show up unless that life you are currently living has one hundred percent disappeared out of your system, no ifs, ands, or buts.
   Tasha

Lucky snapped out of his daze, his eyes watery. He couldn't believe he let Tasha and Tamika walk out of his life. He still didn't know why he'd waited this long to finally reach out to them. All he could hope for was for a new chance. He was ready to settle down and become a real family man.

For the past few years, the only communication he had with his daughter was through a P.O. Box address. Every holiday and birthday he would send cards and gifts. Every six months he would send money. Lucky even helped in changing their identities with fake but legit birth certificates and Social Security cards. He even gave Tasha a new driver's license with the new address in Cape Cod.

About two years ago, the last time he actually spoke to Tasha over the phone, she gave him an address at the time and told him, if he ever decided to come up there, to stop by that address first.

When Lucky finally reached his exit, he became real excited. He was about to see his little girl. The long drive was helpful to him because not for one minute did he think about his old partners.

Lucky pulled up to the address and was taken by surprise at the look of the old house. He had to double-check the address a few times. It was the correct house. He just didn't believe someone lived in it. He walked up to the front door and rang the bell three times.

"Why are you ringing my bell this late, Sonny?"

"Tasha gave me this address. She said you have a place for me."

"Oh, yes, yes. You must be her cousin. She told me when the Army discharged you, you would stop by. C'mon in and let me show you to your new room. By the way, my name is Mrs. Rosie. Did you just arrive today?"

"Yes, I did. I really want to thank you for helping. I promise I won't stay long. I just need a few days."

"Don't worry, honey. You can stay as long as you want. Tasha left some things for you about a week ago. I guess she knew you were coming."

After the old lady left the room, Lucky quickly looked through the stuff she left him and found two handguns and pictures of their new looks and names. He laughed out loud when he saw the guns but then refocused his attention to the pictures. They didn't change much. Only their hair looked different. Lucky could tell Tasha had some facial surgery, but she still looked the same.

Tasha's new name was Luz, and Tamika's was Jessica. For a few minutes, he choked up looking at the pictures of Tamika, now twelve years old. The last time he saw her, she was six going on seven. He felt bad about the choice he made. He promised, after all this drama was over with, he was going to build that relationship back with Tamika.

Lucky lay on the bed, backtracking his past, trying to figure out where he slipped up, and how could they have found his girls. He knew he must have made a mistake somewhere, but his mind went blank. He couldn't remember anything.

He got up and looked out the window to help his mind wander. That didn't help. All he saw was trees and birds. He felt like an inmate looking out his tiny window in a state prison. He wasn't used to the quiet, laid-back atmosphere.

Lucky had to wait until the morning for Mrs. Rosie to notify Tasha. Mrs. Rosie didn't own a phone, so she never asked for anyone's phone number.

Lucky couldn't take the suspense of waiting all night, so he sat on the edge of his bed in frustration and began talking to himself. "Fuck! I feel like a prisoner. I need a drink or two to help my mind relax."

He opened the door to his bedroom and peeked out to see if he saw the old lady. He wanted to ask where the closest liquor store was, or if she had any liquor in the house. He heard what sounded like pots and pans banging against the sink. He figured she must be downstairs washing dishes, so he went downstairs.

He called her name out loud to not surprise her when he approached. "Mrs. Rosie, is you downstairs in the kitchen?"

"Yes, Sonny, I am."

"Do you know where I could purchase some liquor, or even beers?"

"It's almost midnight. Nothing is open this late, but I have a few bottles of whiskey in the basement that belonged to my husband. You could go down there and pick what you like."

"Oh, no, I don't want to impose or use your husband's liquor."

"Sonny, you are not imposing. My husband won't mind. He's been dead for eight years. Go on downstairs and pick what you like. I also have some leftovers in the refrigerator."

Lucky couldn't believe how nice this old lady was.

He was wondering how Tasha met her. He figured she must have been Tamika's babysitter when she was younger or something. When he finally reached the basement, there were so many bottles of liquor, he thought Rosie's husband must have died of liver poison. He'd never heard of the whiskey before and figured it was just some Cape Cod brand. He didn't care. He grabbed a bottle and went back upstairs.

Before he went to his room, he asked Mrs. Rosie, "Mrs. Rosie, if you don't mind me asking, what kind of whiskey is this? I have never heard of it before."

"It's homemade whiskey. My husband and his friend used to make it and sell it. I have to warn you, it's very strong. It will burn a hole in your throat," she said, laughing.

"I was wondering why there were so many bottles downstairs, but now it makes sense. Can I ask you another question? How did you and my cousin meet?"

"Actually, your cousin responded to an ad I left in the local grocery store. I was watching her little girl. She's the most precious girl I have ever met. It's a shame her father was never around. After a few years, we became family. She spent a lot of time in this house. She loved the quiet. Well, it's way past my bedtime. I have to get up in a few hours. I'm sorry, Sonny. I'm going to sleep. Make yourself at home."

"Thank you for everything, Mrs. Rosie. Good night."

As Lucky went back to his room, he cracked open that whiskey bottle and put his lips on it faster than a two-dollar hooker. Lucky had been drinking for over twenty years, so he wasn't scared of homemade liquor. He was ready for the challenge.

As soon as he took a big shot of the whiskey, he spat everything out. He started coughing so hard and loud, Mrs. Rosie was laughing at him.

"I told you, Sonny, it will burn a hole in your throat."

Lucky was on the floor holding his neck, still coughing and tearing up. It took him a good fifteen seconds to regain his composure, but then he caught a head rush for another fifteen seconds.

He wiped the tear off his eyes and looked at the bottle. "What the fuck is this? I can't believe these red-necks drink this shit out here." He closed the bottle and took it back downstairs. He didn't even want the bottle in the room.

While walking back upstairs, still banging his chest, trying to clear up his system, he decided to try to go to sleep. He got back in bed and started thinking about Diamond, wondering how she was. He knew she was lonely, but okay, because she wasn't a homebody type of female. She would find something to keep herself entertained.

Lucky felt bad about the whole situation. She was the one to get a raw deal. He was never going back to her. That's why he gave her so much money and the house. It was a hard decision, but a man couldn't choose another woman over his family. Lucky understood Diamond was deeply in love with him, and he only hoped she didn't take it too hard and tried to hurt herself. He sat back up on his bed, experiencing one of the longest nights of his life.

Right after getting Diamond out of his head, he started thinking about Tamika. He could remember the first day she was born. He'd kissed her on the forehead and promised he would protect her for life. He broke that promise, and now he needed to make it up big-time, because of his drug abuse.

Once he finally saw her in the morning, he knew it was going to be an awkward reunion. A lot of years had passed, but they wouldn't have time to catch up right away because he was going to have to tell them about the danger they were in, and about possibly relocating.

When the morning sunlight hit the glass window and the reflection glared off his face, Lucky woke up. He didn't know at what time he'd passed out, but he was happy it was morning. It felt like a Christmas morning.

He washed up, got dressed, and waited for Mrs. Rosie to return. Around ten in the morning, she returned but had a long face.

"Is everything okay?"

"Tasha never showed up. I waited for two hours, and she never showed. That's not like her."

"Maybe she was tired and never got out of bed," Lucky said, hoping that was the case.

"It's still not like her."

Lucky couldn't hold back and play Mr. Nice Guy anymore. "Mrs. Rosie, let me have the address where you were supposed to meet her. If you have her home address, that would be better. Any information would be helpful."

"I'm sorry. I don't know her home address. We were going to meet at Joe's Diner for our usual breakfast meeting. I'm telling you, something is not right. If you want the address to Joe's Diner, here is their card. It has the address on it."

"Thank you."

Lucky entered the address in his GPS system and headed out the door. He wasn't about to sit back, knowing his old partners were out there and Tasha was missing.

While driving, he was so nervous, he couldn't stop shaking, and his heart was pounding in his chest. It was about a fifteen-minute drive, and he drove with caution, looking inside every car he passed. The pounding in his heart felt more like a stampede.

He wanted to stay positive, but it was hard to. He kept saying to himself, "If you touch my little girl, I'm going to kill your whole family."

Lucky noticed the Joe's Diner sign was getting closer. He pulled up to the restaurant, drove around the parking lot first, and didn't see Tasha's car. Mrs. Rosie told him she drove a green truck, but didn't know the make of the car. Lucky thought, *Maybe she got the colors confused,* so he parked down the street and walked to the diner.

He went in, glanced around the dining area, and didn't see anyone who resembled Tasha or Tamika. He asked one of the waitresses if she knew where the post office was located.

The waitress pointed out the window. "It's right across the street, mister."

Lucky thought quickly and asked for a table. "Well, since I'm already here, I might as well eat something."

Lucky was able to get a seat right by the window. He figured he would sit there until Tasha showed up. He ordered three pancakes, scrambled eggs, and a beef sausage. He was starving.

After eating his meal and drinking three cups of coffee, he noticed this one car had been parked in the same spot for the past hour. What was odd was, the driver had been sitting there for almost an hour with his engine running. At first, Lucky thought the driver was waiting for someone, but he thought it was crazy to keep your car running so long.

"Shit, not even getaway cars keep the shit running that long. But who's the suit in that car? I'm going to have to take a closer look. Something is not right," he said to himself.

He signaled for the young, pretty blond waitress to bring his bill.

"Here you go, mister. Thank you for coming to Joe's. Come again."

"I sure will come whenever I'm in town."

"Oh, you from out of town, too. Are you with John?"

"I'm sorry. Who?"

"With John. Him." She pointed outside to the car Lucky was about to check out.

"No, I'm not with him, but between us, he's been there for like thirty minutes," he said, trying to bait her into giving up more info.

"Thirty minutes, yeah, right. More like all morning. When I came in this morning, they were parked there. There were two of them this morning, but now I just see one."

Lucky gave her a fifty-dollar bill and told her dumb ass to keep the change.

Then it hit him. "They must know about the P.O. Box address." Lucky walked past the car on the driver's side, close enough to see that the car doors were unlocked. When he walked back, he noticed John was barely keeping his eyes open. They must have been there all night.

Lucky moved in quickly. He went around the passenger side, opened the door, jumped in, and pressed the barrel of his gun against his face.

"What the fuck is going on here? I'm a federal agent. You sure you want to kill me?"

"A federal agent? Get the fuck out of here. Why are you watching the post office? Did Captain Tuna from New York send you here? If he did, then you a dirty agent."

Agent John tried to play it cool. "No, I'm just waiting for my wife to come out the postal office."

"Bullshit! You think I don't know you been here since eight o'clock in the morning? Where is your partner? Who else came out here with you?"

"Again, I don't know what you're talking about. I'm here waiting for my—"

Lucky cocked back his gun. "Go ahead and say you are waiting for your wife again. Go ahead and say it."

John froze like a statue. He knew he was dealing with someone who would pull the trigger. "Okay, yes, you're right, Tuna sent us out here, but I came out here by myself."

Lucky pistol-whipped John and split open his head, and blood splattered all over the steering wheel and dashboard.

"I'm going to ask you one last time. Who else came here with you, and where are they at? Are they inside?"

"Okay, okay, I'm sorry. Don't hit or shoot me."

"I won't if you tell me what I want to know."

"I came out here with Loose Cannon."

"Loose Cannon? Where is he at?" Lucky's heart started pounding again when he heard that name. His aggression level went sky-high. He grabbed John by his collar and raised his gun to strike him again, but John started talking.

"He's inside the post office, watching the boxes. We know about your P.O. Box."

"Put the car in drive and go around the back of this diner," Lucky ordered.

As soon as they pulled around and parked, Lucky began pistol-whipping him until he was unconscious. Blood was pouring out of his skull like a faucet. Lucky left him alive, but with a chance of bleeding to death if help didn't find him quickly. He didn't care if he was a federal agent. Dirty is dirty. He cleaned the blood off his gun, put it back on his hip, and fixed himself up. He looked around the parking lot to make sure no one was watching before exiting the car.

Lucky wasn't going to waste time and wait for Loose Cannon to come out of the post office. He was going inside to kill him. He started walking toward the front door, his mind already set on shooting on sight and disappearing.

As Lucky was walking up the steps of the post office, out came Loose Cannon. This was the one confrontation where you couldn't pick a winner, because neither was afraid to die. They both hated each other's guts, so killing the other was not going to be a problem. It was like one of those old cowboy movies. Whoever drew first and shot would survive another day.

As both men approached each other, Loose saw right through the fake disguise and knew it was Lucky.

Lucky saw he was mad, drew his weapon, and pointed at Loose Cannon, who also had his weapon drawn, but was pointing at the head of a hostage.

Downtown Cape Cod went hysterical once someone yelled, "Gun!"

People were running and screaming all over the place.

Lucky thought Loose made a dumb move by grabbing a hostage. "What the fuck are you doing? I don't care about any goddamn hostage."

"Well, you dumb son of a nigger! Take a closer look at who I'm holding!"

Lucky, for a quick second, took his eyes off him and looked at the hostage. It was Tasha. He couldn't believe it at first, until he heard her voice.

"Donald, I'm sorry, baby."

Lucky quickly refocused his attention back on Loose Cannon and tightened his grip on the gun.

As Loose was walking forward, Lucky was backing down the steps, not losing his focus or aim. Loose started to yell different shit at him about dropping his gun, but Lucky couldn't hear him. He was spaced out, thinking about his days at the academy, where he won all those awards for his precise shooting.

He aimed, saw an opening, and fired one shot. As the bullet left the barrel, Lucky heard both of them scream before the bullet knocked them to the ground. He ran toward them, hoping he hit the right target.

Tasha was lying stiff on the ground, and Loose was still moving. Lucky thought the worst, that maybe he shot his baby girl. He walked up to Loose Cannon and shot him twice in the head before even checking to see if Tasha was all right.

He then dropped to his knees and flipped Tasha over. She was bleeding from her head. There was blood everywhere. Lucky was in tears, and he could hear the sirens coming. He sat there rocking Tasha back and forth. He didn't care about the sirens.

"Baby, are you going to rock me to death or help me get up?" Tasha said as she gained consciousness.

"Baby, you're okay. I thought I lost you for a second." He looked down at Tasha, and she looked right back at him.

When he'd first shot Loose Cannon, the impact of the shot slammed both bodies hard to the concrete. Tasha landed headfirst, explaining the blood.

Lucky jumped to his feet and quickly attended to her. "Wow! Baby, you bumped your head pretty hard."

"Yes, I'm still a little dizzy, but I could manage. We need to hurry up and get out of here."

"I'm parked over there," Lucky said, pointing up the streets to his van.

"Let's take my car, Donald. Plus, I know the way around here."

Within thirty seconds, they were in the car and speeding through some back roads.

As Tasha was driving, Lucky was thinking about the shot he just took. He kept visualizing Loose Cannon lying there with his head split.

They finally pulled up to Tasha's house, and he snapped out of his daze.

"Where is Tamika? Is she inside?"

"No, she's at Mom's house."

"Mom's house? Your mother lives out here too? I thought you guys didn't have a good relationship."

"Why you think I begged you to buy a summer house in Cape Cod? Both my parents were living out here. After my father died, our relationship grew to the next level."

"Wait a minute. Mrs. Rosie, that's really your mother, right?"

"Yes, that's her. How you knew?"

Lucky started laughing out loud.

"That's a good one. Wow! Good cover-up. I thought it was kind of funny because I saw a few pictures around the house. But when Mrs. Rosie mentioned she was babysitting, I just thought this lonely old lady treated my daughter as one of hers. It never hit me that that was actually her grandmother. I can't believe I couldn't see right through it."

While they made their way inside the house, Tasha said, "Donald, we need to talk. I know we don't have time, but baby, I need you to sit down and listen."

"Oh-oh."

"Don't be silly," she said, laughing.

"Okay, I know you're trying to be serious, so let me sit down. But if you are about to tell me about other men, please save it. I'm not tripping."

"Boyyee, sit down! I don't want to talk about other men. I want to speak to you about you. Right now, I have to make a decision to hit the road with you and relocate, or tell you, 'Fuck you! Keep it going.'"

"Wow! It's like that?"

"Yes, it's like that. You haven't been around for a long time. For years, I had to lie to our daughter defending you. That way she didn't grow up hating you. I held all that anger and pain inside, and I raised us a great little girl. I figure, why ruin her happiness just because I'm not happy?"

"Baby, I never wanted to hurt you."

"But you did, Donald, you did. Let me finish, please. Just listen. I want you to understand that a lot of things I did for you were because I loved you, not because I wanted to do them. I hope you understand the difference."

"Tasha, listen, I'm willing to do anything to have my girls back in my life, especially Tamika. I just have to take care of some things first before I could give you my full commitment. I'm a new man, but I just have to clean up a little more laundry."

"Are you referring to all the stuff I been reading about you and your former partners on the Internet? I'm assuming the guy you killed today was one of them."

"So you know?"

"Of course, I knew. That's why I went by my mother's house and fixed your room up, I knew you were coming. You took so long, I thought maybe, they . . ."

"What? That they killed me?"

"Something like that. It got to the point I was checking the Internet every day to see what else you did. That way, I knew you were alive. What took you so long to come? And who's this female partner the media keeps saying you have working with you?"

"You can't trust the media. I don't have any partners. I can't trust anyone anymore. I shook the city up, huh?"

"You sure did, but now what?"

"I don't know, but please let's grab what you need. I want to see my daughter. It's been almost seven years now."

"Baby, please don't waste my time. These past seven years were tough, but they were quiet. Do you promise not to fuck that up? Do you swear on your mother's grave you are giving up your old ways for good?"

"I swear on my mother's grave, baby. I'm sorry. I was the one who made the wrong choice. I will work hard to gain the trust and respect back. I haven't used drugs in almost two years, since the night Perry Coleman was killed. I'm focused. I have found peace in my life. I just have to close a few more chapters before I close this old book of mine."

As they were packing, Lucky was smiling because he was able to dodge the bullet about Diamond.

Within twenty minutes, Tasha had all the belongings she needed, and they hit the road. She parked her truck in the garage and drove her '02 Chevy Impala.

Lucky was impressed with the way she carried herself, always keeping a backup plan. He remembered why he fell in love with her. As they got closer to her mother's house, he began to get nervous. He didn't know how Tamika would react to seeing her father for the first time in seven years.

"Tasha, how you think she will react once she sees me?"

"Oh, don't worry about that. I made sure she always respected you. You will actually make her day with your presence. She is always asking about you."

When they pulled up to Mrs. Rosie's house, Lucky almost caught a nervous breakdown. He knew Tasha just said everything was going to be all right, but he still was a little leery.

As soon as Lucky walked in, Tamika ran toward him. "Daddy, Daddy, you're finally home. I missed you so much, Daddy."

"Hey, baby. I missed you so much. Look at you. You have grown so much."

"Are you here to stay?"

"Yes, baby. Daddy will be around a lot more."

They spent about twenty minutes hugging and talking to each other. Even Tasha and Mrs. Rosie teared up watching them bond.

Tamika went back to the kitchen to finish helping her grandmother fix dinner.

Lucky walked over as well. "Mrs. Rosie?"

"My real name is Angela. You can call me Angie or Angela. Please, no *Mrs.* in front of it."

"Angela, again thank you. I'm sorry we had to meet like this."

"That's okay. My daughter explained everything years ago. I understand. She said one day you will be back, and here you are. But I see you have some drama to take care of."

Before Lucky could answer, Tasha ran back in the kitchen and asked Lucky to come and watch the news.

Chapter Fourteen

Headline:
Two NY Cops Found Dead in Cape Cod

"Good evening. My name is Robert McClouss, for BETV Channel Twenty News. We are live in downtown Cape Cod in front of the United States Post Office. Today, we are here to report that two New York police officers, one of them a federal agent, were found dead. According to reports, one of the officers is named Steve Stanley, currently on trial for shooting an unarmed African American in New York City. The other officer's name, at this moment, is still not available, but our sources are confirming he was a federal employee.

"According to witness statements, Officer Steve grabbed an unidentified woman by her arm and forced her outside. The lady kept screaming for him to let her go. When Officer Steve made it outside, he was confronted by another unidentified African American male. The African American male and the officer both were pointing their guns at each other. We have another witness' statement that alleged she saw the officer point the gun to the woman's head, and that's when the African American male shot him and got away with the unidentified female.

"The other officer was found dead in a black Caprice across the street in the parking lot behind Joe's Diner. There are still a lot of questions to be answered here. We are still waiting for an official statement from the police department. This is Robert McClouss, for BETV Channel Twenty News, reporting live from downtown Cape Cod."

"Lucky, I thought you said you didn't kill the federal agent?" Tasha asked.

"I thought he was still alive. I guess he didn't make it. I only pistol-whipped him a few times. But fuck him, anyway. They were up here to try to kill or kidnap Tamika. Let's not forget that."

"But wouldn't you get in more trouble if a federal agent pops up dead?"

"Yes, I would, but by the same token, this is a dirty federal agent, and the government doesn't protect or support dirty agents. They will realize he was corrupt because he had no business out here in the first place."

Back in New York, Captain Tuna was going ballistic over the death of one of his best friends. Speedy and Agent Kuntz tried numerous times to calm him down, but they couldn't. Tuna was tearing up everything in sight. He even took a few swings at both of them.

"Get the fuck off me! Don't you two realize what just happened here? Two of our brothers were just murdered. We are in deep shit, and we still don't have a clue where Lucky is located. I'm sure he will disappear along with his whole family."

"Tuna, one of my agents was killed too. I'm going to be in deeper shit myself, but we need to stick together and figure a way out of this mess."

"You know what, Agent Kuntz? Go fuck yourself! And get the hell out of my apartment! This all happened because of you. You were the one who made us aware of the whereabouts of Lucky's daughter. This is why I don't like working with the feds. Our business is over. You go deal with your superiors, and I will handle mine."

"C'mon, Tuna, we need to stick together."

"Work together how? You see how they released Loose Cannon's name in the media, but not your boy John. They startin' to protect him already. My guess is the feds will come up with a story about how John's murder wasn't related to the shooting between Loose and Lucky. Please, get the hell out of here now. I have to call the commissioner."

William Kuntz tried to plead his case, but he realized Tuna was under too much stress, so he left the apartment.

Speedy and Tuna were clueless on their next move. Lucky did enough damage to ruin not only their lives, but also the commissioner and a few high-ranking officials. Tuna kept delaying his call to the commissioner. He needed a break and was praying for a miracle.

Speedy, on the other hand, knew they were doomed. There was no coming back from this mess. And with Loose out of the picture, Tuna would most likely fold under pressure and maybe start cooperating to save his butt. Speedy already knew the commissioner wasn't going down on his own, but with so much evidence out in the public about all the dirt they each did, cooperation wouldn't help too much. Their key to freedom was capturing Lucky, and at this point, that was like hitting the lotto. They had their opportunity in Cape Cod, but once again, Lucky outsmarted them.

Tuna sat back on the couch and broke down in tears. He couldn't hold it back anymore. His best friend was just murdered, and his boss had been exposed because of him. Tuna knew he would end up in jail, or maybe even dead. That was enough to break down any man.

Speedy didn't have time to sit back and mourn. "Captain, do you think the commissioner will turn his back on us to save his ass?"

"Yes, I do. He already told me he will flip the script on me and my crew."

"Captain, I will be back later."

"For a second, I was about to call you a coward for trying to leave, but I'm about to go home myself. First, I have to call Loose's wife and go over funeral arrangements. Damn! I can't fuckin' believe he caught Loose Cannon off guard like that," a tearing Tuna said.

Speedy and Tuna embraced like it was the last time they were going to see each other as free men.

After Speedy left, Tuna started to empty the money out of his stash house. There was a little over two hundred thousand dollars in cash, and about another fifty thousand in drugs in the safe room.

While he was packing up his money and destroying the drugs, his cell phone started ringing. He didn't want to answer the call and hear the commissioner run his mouth about how he fucked up, but the phone continued ringing. He looked at the caller ID, and saw it was a restricted call. He finally answered.

"Hello, this is Tuna. Who is this?"

"I'm sorry about your loss."

"Who in the fuck is this? Is that you, you piece of shit?"

"I'm coming for you next. I know where you're staying. If you a man, you would wait for me. If you a coward, then I guess I will catch you another time."

Tuna didn't know if he was bluffing or not. He knew Loose would never talk, but he wasn't sure about John. "Whatever. You don't know where I am."

"I know you in Spanish Harlem. Let me guess—You're at your old-ass uncle's building. You're forgetting I know everything about you. Once that stupid agent said somewhere on Lexington Avenue in Spanish Harlem, I figured out the rest."

"You want me to wait for you? C'mon, you cocksucker! I'm tired of chasing you."

"I will be there in twenty minutes, bitch." Lucky hung up the phone laughing. He was still at Angela's house in Cape Cod and just wanted to let Tuna know he knew where he was at.

On the other hand, Tuna took the threat seriously. He called Speedy's cell phone, but it went straight to voice mail. He had no choice but to call the commissioner.

"About time you fuckin' call me. What the fuck happened out there?"

"I don't really know. I sent Loose with one of the agents, and somehow Lucky outsmarted them and got to them first."

"Damn, Tuna! Who are we really dealing with here? He's like a RoboCop or something. Why didn't we make him the golden boy of our team?"

"Remember, sir, he's Black."

"I know, but damn, I didn't know he was this good. We should have promoted or killed him back when we first saw his potential. Now look at how he's destroying us one by one. We will never find him."

"He just called right before I called you. He said he knows I'm on 102nd Street and Lexington Avenue, and that he would be here in twenty minutes. I need some help. I'm here by myself. Speedy left and went home."

"I will have people over there in ten to fifteen minutes. You just hold on tight. Do you have weapons there?"

"Yes, I'm well armed. Hurry up and get me out of here."

Tuna hung up the phone then grabbed his money and went up to the fifth floor. He went in the closet and pulled out a loaded AK-47 and two hand grenades. He leaned back against the kitchen wall, from where he could watch both the front door and the windows connected to the fire escape. Those are the only two places where Lucky could enter through.

Tuna was sweating, and his hands were shaking. He kept switching to a different aiming position every ten seconds until help arrived. His cell phone started ringing again, and it was the commissioner.

"I hope you have good news. I'm sweating up here like a little bitch."

"Calm down. They're outside. There are three of them, and they're sweeping the area. Hold your position for a few more minutes."

"Okay, hurry up."

"Wait five minutes and come downstairs. Once you see them, you will recognize who they are. Remember, five more minutes."

"I got it. Five minutes."

Tuna started to feel a lot better knowing he wasn't alone. He put the AK and the grenades back in the closet and pulled out his 9 mm Glock. He grabbed his bag full of money and drugs, and proceeded to go downstairs. He took his time, stopping and looking around at every step, aiming his gun everywhere. He didn't trust Lucky. He was good at sneaking up on people.

He finally made it downstairs and opened his front door. He walked outside and noticed who the commissioner sent. He'd called the mob and got him some Italian help.

Tuna quickly ran to the car they were standing by, jumped in, and told them to hurry up and drive away. He kept looking back, making sure no one was following them. The Italians drove him to a secret apartment, where he could relax while all the heat on him died down. They drove to the Bronx, Little Italy off Fordham Road.

When Tuna arrived, the commissioner was there waiting for him, looking like a hot mess. The recent allegations against the police force were breaking him down mentally and physically.

"Brandon, are you okay?" Tuna quickly asked. "You don't look good."

"Of course, I don't look good. By tomorrow morning, the headline will be another blow to the police department and City Hall. I'm almost positive they will reopen the Cardinal case. I'm not really worried about myself. I will be okay and beat these charges. But this won't help the case against you and Perry Coleman. And I'm hearing they're about to release both Rell Davis and Juan 'Pito' Medina."

Tuna shot back, "Are you serious? They can't."

"They will. That means they believe Lucky and the evidence backing up his claims. That also means, at the end of the day, I will lose my job. The media is already talking about who's going to replace me."

"I'm sorry, boss, but we can't quit. We need to find this pig and somehow flip this whole thing around on him. We need to look into his past and find something sentimental besides his daughter. There has to be something we could find. I remember, when we were after M&M, he got close with that gangbanger name Thirty-eight. We all thought Lucky had turned his back on us for him. I know for a fact Thirty-eight will definitely bring Lucky out of hiding."

"So where is Thirty-eight? How can we find him?" Commissioner Fratt asked.

"I don't know, but I know I can find him a lot quicker than Lucky."

"Okay, that's our last resort. I have some people who might be able to help you find him."

"I got this one, trust me. I will find him. People like him don't leave their neighborhoods."

"Just give me till the morning, Tuna. I'll have someone for you. Meanwhile, get comfortable and relax. We have a long night ahead of us."

They decided to talk about different scenarios and strategies.

Meanwhile, Lucky was sitting at Angela's kitchen table, going over a few last-minute details. First, they needed to discuss where they were going to next, because Cape Cod was no longer safe.

"Okay, Tasha, you tell me where you want to go, sweetheart."

"Atlanta. A friend of mine lives there. Actually we used to work together. I visited her last year, and I love it out there."

"Atlanta, that's not a bad choice. Call your people and tell them to get you plugged in with a realtor, because we are on our way."

"Are you for real, baby? We are moving to Atlanta? Thank you so much. I thought you wouldn't go for Atlanta."

"Baby, it's all about you and Tamika. If that's where you want to live, then let's do it."

Tasha, jumping up and down like a little girl, went to tell her mother the great news.

Everyone was excited about moving to Atlanta. Tasha made reservations with a villa company, and they put a four-bedroom villa on hold for sixty days while they get settled in Atlanta.

While the girls were packing, Lucky was outside sitting on the porch thinking about Diamond and how much he was really missing her. He only hoped she was safe and didn't grow to hate him. In his heart, he knew he did the right thing, but he knew he was wrong for the way he played it.

For a quick second, he thought about disappearing and never showing his face ever. He thought he had done enough damage. But there was another side of him that couldn't let him quit until he killed both Speedy and Tuna.

Tasha came outside looking for him. "What's up, baby? Why are you out here by yourself? What's on your mind?"

"I'm just thinking. I want to stop and just stay in Atlanta and never show my face again, but then I still have business I need to close. I don't know what to do."

"Well, baby, I think you should close those open businesses, and do it now. That way they don't haunt you forever. We will wait for you. We waited seven years. What's another few weeks? It's in God's hand. If destiny wants us together, I will see you again."

They both sat there in silence for about thirty minutes, until Tamika came outside and asked her mother for something to eat. Tasha went in, and Lucky stayed out there until everyone finished eating.

They loaded up Tasha's car and hit the road. Lucky even left his van parked by the diner. There was nothing in that car that would connect anything back to him, except the New York license plate.

Tasha barely spent any of the money Lucky sent her, and so she had over a hundred thousand dollars saved up. It was about a twenty-five-hour drive to Atlanta, so Lucky had plenty of time to think about his next move. He was still undecided.

While Tasha and Lucky drove through the night, Tuna was up himself, thinking about his future. He wasn't sure if he would be around any longer. At this point, there were only two choices—getting killed or going to prison. He didn't like either one.

Tuna didn't sleep at all. He couldn't wait for the morning news to come on. He wanted to know what the latest news was. He wasn't the only one. Everyone was waiting for Destine Diaz's report.

When the morning came around, the commissioner was right about the media. They were hanging the police department and blaming them for everything that had occurred.

"Good morning. It's Destine Diaz, Channel Five News. I have the latest update on the two New York officers killed in Cape Cod. We know for sure one of the officers was Steve Stanley, better known as Loose Cannon, who was currently on trial for the murder of Perry Coleman. We still haven't received any information as to why he was in Cape Cod. While on bail and on trial, you need permission to leave the state. We are still investigating to see if that permission was filed or even granted.

"The other officer was a federal agent, and his name has still not been released. The federal government doesn't release the identity of their employees, but they are confirming one of their own was found dead. He was found across the street from the post office behind a diner, beaten to death with a blunt object. The feds are denying any involvement or connection to the standoff between Officer Steve Stanley and another unidentified African American male, in which another woman was taken hostage. Despite their denial, the evidence doesn't look good. There are witnesses putting both Steve and this federal agent inside the same car parked across from the post office for hours. Post office cameras show Steve Stanley inside, watching the area where the P.O. boxes are located. One could only speculate about the woman Stanley was after, and about that unidentified male who confronted Stanley as he stepped outside. We will have more on this story as it unfolds.

"At five o'clock today, we'll also have more updates about those five folders that Officer Donald Gibson sent us. I have updates on the releases of two inmates, and more on the cardinal. I might also have an update on Perry Coleman's case and trial. This is Destine Diaz, Channel Five News."

Tuna sat there in disarray, on the verge of insanity. For a quick second, he thought about cocking back his gun and blowing off his head. He really gave it a serious thought. Losing Loose, his right-hand man, was a hard pill to swallow.

Commissioner Fratt returned from the store with the newspaper. On the cover of one, there was a picture of a police station and the caption "Corrupt City."

"Tuna, look at this. This is just cruel. After all we've done for this city, this is how they treat me over one lousy mistake or allegation? Listen, I have someone coming down this afternoon to help you find Thirty-eight," he said.

"I don't need help. I know the area. I'll be back before noon. I'll call you if I find him."

"Are you sure?"

"Positive. We don't have time to wait until this afternoon. You sit tight and stay away from these papers. Don't believe what you read."

Tuna snatched away all the newspapers he bought and threw them in a large black garbage bag. He got dressed, took the trash out, and headed for the projects. He jumped on the Bronx River Parkway, merged onto the Bruckner, until he reached Third Avenue, and then he parked.

He decided to walk around and try to get a closer look. Tuna was unshaved, and his clothes were not ironed, so he figured he would blend in. He looked like just a poor White man living in the projects or a crackhead.

He started walking and realized things had changed since they shutdown M&M. He noticed a lot of freelance dealers. A few years back, only one gang was allowed in the projects, not multiple associations. As Tuna was walking around, this young kid was signaling for him to come his way.

When he got closer, the kid said to him, "What's up, White boy? What you need?"

"What you got? I just came home yesterday. I'm used to buying trays."

He laughed. "Trays? Damn! That's old-school. Get in the building. I got you."

Tuna followed the kid in the lobby of the building, where there were two of his friends. It was ten o'clock in the morning on a school day, and three seventeen-year-old kids were pushing crack and smoking weed.

"Hey, you. White boy here just came home. He's looking for trays," the young hustler said.

His two friends started laughing, and Tuna played along, laughing with them.

"How much time you did, White boy?"

"About ten years."

"Damn! At least you're home now. Anyway, enough fuckin' talking. Let's get down to business. I got dimes, big fat rocks for you. Since I like you, three for twenty-five. We family."

"Sounds great. I'll take the three. Man, I remember when M&M used to run this shit here. That's when I used to fuck with that dope."

"Oh, you remember M&M? Well, they all dead now. The last living member, what was his name? It was after a gun. Oh, yeah, Thirty-eight. He was killed last year. He was trying to run shit like the olds days, but too many muthafuckas in the hood own guns. You can't boss people around anymore. Anyway, here you go, White boy. Now, get the fuck outta here. You fuckin' up my swagger."

Tuna, disappointed to hear that Thirty-eight was killed last year, walked away upset. He smashed up the crack he'd just bought, jumped back in his car, and headed back to Little Italy. He was going to call the commissioner, but he figured he would rather tell him face-to-face.

When he arrived back at the house and told Brandon that Thirty-eight was killed last year, Tuna was surprised he wasn't upset.

"Don't worry about Thirty-eight, Tuna. I have better news. You wouldn't believe the phone call I received an hour ago. I need you to come with me downtown Manhattan. We have a tip about one of Lucky's hideouts."

"About fuckin' time. Give me a few minutes to wash up and change my clothes."

Tuna was excited to hear about the tip. Hopefully they could find and kill Lucky once and for all.

A lot of New Yorkers were calling on the federal government to help restructure the system and clean the dirt. City Hall had major concerns about rioting. So the federal and the state governments were coming up with a strategy to build a working relationship in order to climb out of the hole Lucky threw them in.

The governor of New York, Andrew Silver, was overseeing the crisis, and he wasn't a happy camper. He hated dirty cops more than criminals. He visited Gracie Mansion for a quick lunch with the mayor.

"Good afternoon, Governor. Welcome. Please have a seat."

"Thank you. I'm sorry I have to visit to discuss bad news, but our jobs are always taking us to unwanted territory. Anyway, how are you holding up?"

"I'm fine. I'm just fine, Andrew. No need to worry. Let's eat. I'm hungry."

"Cut the bullshit, Ralph. What the fuck is going on here? You think I don't know about Donald Gibson? How come you can't kill one little rat?"

"It sounds easy, but this son of a gun is one hell of a rat."

"Was that a joke? Please, tell me that was a joke. Listen, I've been ordered to come down here and clean house. As we stand right now, so far your name is clean. But the commissioner, he's done. I need you to name his replacement in twenty-four hours."

"I can't do that."

"I'm not asking. You either take care of the situation, or your ass is gone, too. Brandon is done. Ask him to resign, and tell him we'll still pay his salary for the remainder of his term. The decision has been made."

"Yes, I got it, but I need more time."

"You have one week. Where do we stand with this Lucky guy you can't catch?"

"We have one more lead to follow. Hopefully, that will help us get closer. But we know that was him in Cape Cod who killed our two men."

"Okay, keep me posted. I want him dead. We don't need him alive."

"We were thinking of capturing him."

"We don't need him at all in order to win this city back. For us to succeed, we have to be honest. We'll admit these crimes, take the hit, and repair from there. The commissioner and those dirty cops will have to take the fall. You have a choice to make—fall with them, or stay afloat and return this city back to its glory."

The mayor had a lot to think about. The governor was telling him to turn his back on one of his good friends. It was a hard decision, but not a tough one. At the end of the day, the mayor understood looking out for self was always the better option.

Governor Silver excused himself because he had a 1:00 p.m. press conference with the media.

"I have to go now. You take care, and for the next few days—no, weeks—you and I are going to be the best of friends. I know we represent different parties, but we have to put our differences aside through this outcry."

After the governor left the mansion, the mayor was dumb-founded. He didn't know what to do. He felt bad about having to fire his friend.

***

While Brandon and Tuna were driving downtown, Brandon's cell phone started ringing. He didn't recognize the number.

"Who is this? This is a private line."

"It's me, Ralph."

"I'm sorry about that, sir. How are you doing? Right now, we're following up on that lead. We're getting closer. I think we finally got him."

"That's great, but I called you because I need to speak to you about something else. Can you stop by?"

"I don't have the time right now. What is it, Ralph? I've known you a long time, brother. Talk to me. What's wrong?"

"The governor just left my office at the mansion, and a decision has been made to replace you."

"What! Replace me? C'mon, Ralph, this is not my fault. I'm about to deliver Lucky. Give me one more chance," Brandon begged.

"I'm sorry. The decision has been made, and it was made before he came to my house. They're going to say you resigned because you don't want to cause any more distractions. You'll still get your salary for the rest of your term, along with all your perks."

"This is bullshit, Ralph. I don't get perks in jail. What about these charges against me?"

"Listen, Brandon, I have to go. I will talk to you soon. Take care. They're giving you a week. Make something happen." The mayor hung up the phone.

Brandon looked at his cell phone in disbelief.

Tuna was eager to hear what happened. "What happened, Commish? What did he say?"

"Don't call me Commissioner anymore. My name is Brandon. The mayor said a decision was made, and I have to resign."

"Aw fuck! We're doomed. You know what that means, right? They're going to let us take the fall."

"Ralph is a good friend of mine. We started in the academy together. He wouldn't double-cross me."

"I hate to be the one to break it to you, Brandon, but Ralph just fucked us."

It was getting closer to one in the afternoon, and the governor's press conference was about to begin.

"Good afternoon. I'm here today to promise one thing, a new beginning. I promise to rebuild this police department and gain the trust of this city again. I know, the past few weeks, we have dealt with great turmoil. Our police department has come under scrutiny because of allegations of corruption. I'm here to clean it up, but I can't do it alone. I will need a favor from this great city, just one favor. I need a little patience.

"I'm going to make a few announcements. I'm not taking any questions, not today. I just want to let my fellow New Yorkers know that we are not sitting back and accepting any more damaging allegations. We will get rid of the poison and move forward. Those officers and city officials who acted unlawfully will have their date in court. I'm not just moving my lips. I'm a man of my word.

"I have also granted the release of two young men who were wrongly accused and jailed for many, many years. I'm referring to Rell Davis and Juan Medina. All charges against Rell Davis will be dropped, and Juan Medina will receive a new trial. I have a meeting with District Attorney Johnson in regard to the Perry Coleman case. The rumors that the trial was getting moved to another county were just rumors.

"We have some other things to further investigate, which I will comment on at a later date. I also want to look into this Wiggins family incident and revisit all the evidence against the cardinal. But, most importantly, we need to capture former officer Donald Gibson and bring him to justice as well. I'm officially placing Donald on the top of the list of the most wanted criminals in New York. I do understand the courageous act he is displaying, but let's not forget he also incriminated himself. We also have reason to believe he was behind the shooting in Cape Cod.

"I want to thank everyone who came out. I will hold another press conference soon, when I will answer questions and concerns, but right now I have a ton of work waiting for me."

After the governor's press conference, the City of New York, for the first time in a long time, felt there was hope in the air. They believed their governor was genuine and spoke from the heart, not a scripted message.

When Brandon and Tuna heard the press conference on the car radio, they were devastated, and so was every other cop in the city. They felt betrayed.

"Damn! Did the governor screw us live on TV?" Tuna asked.

"I think he just did. We're on our own. We have two choices, run or face the music."

"How much time are we looking at? It can't be much. I think we should still find Lucky and have him confess. That will help us a lot. I don't like the idea of running. At least in jail I will get a chance to see my family," Tuna said.

"I really don't know. I'm forty-eight years old. I'm too old to go to jail. If I'm thrown in jail for these charges, once I make bail, I'm hitting splitsville."

They both started laughing, but they both knew they were screwed. Tuna kept thinking about his family. He knew his wife had to be hysterical back at the house if she saw the press conference.

Brandon kept his poker face on as well, but he knew his only option to escape was suicide. That's what he meant by splitsville. His last hope was the tip about Lucky. Once he heard the new intel, he would make his decision then about whether to face the music or the barrel of his gun.

The Colemans were excited when they heard the press conference. They started thinking, maybe they would get justice for their son's murder. To hear the governor say it live on television that the location for the new trial would not change gave them some relief. They were all in tears.

"Thank God," Laura said. "Our prayers have been answered."

While all this drama was taking place in New York, Lucky was still driving down I-95 on his way to Atlanta, Georgia. He had no clue any of this was going on. He told Tasha to pull out his laptop and see if she could get a signal for the Internet.

"Why do you want the Internet? You are driving, babe."

"I know, but I want you to check the news to see what else they're saying about the shooting. I'm sure they're blaming everything on me. I was waiting for Tamika to fall asleep."

"Boy, you never stop working," she said as she was logging on.

To their surprise, they couldn't believe all that had taken place in the past few hours. They first played back Destine Diaz's news report from the morning news, and then they heard the governor's press conference.

"Damn! I don't think I need to go back and show my face. It looks like they believe everything I sent. My plan worked to perfection."

"So does that mean you're not leaving us?"

"Well, I still have to go up to New York, but only to empty out my storage unit."

"Can you just forget about whatever is up there? I have enough money to buy us a house and maybe start our own little business."

"Sweetheart, we're talking close to five million dollars. I'm not walking away from that. But, don't worry, it will be an in-and-out situation. I'm not grabbing anything else, just the money. I'm even leaving my truck behind."

"Okay, I understand. I wouldn't leave five million dollars behind either. But, baby, can you just wait a few days? Maybe a week or two? We have enough money to rent the villa until we're ready to buy. You don't need to run up there right now. Let the heat cool down. You heard the governor say they've made you the number one most wanted criminal in New York."

"Baby, I don't want to wait. I want to close this part of my life. This type of situation will haunt us forever. I don't want to settle in Atlanta then have to move again. Once we get to Atlanta, I will chill for a few hours, catch my rest, and then I'm off to New York."

"That's too quick. You're going to need more than a few hours of rest. I understand you need to get up there as soon as possible, but please get some rest."

"My bad. I'm just hyped. This kind of drama excites me. They're falling right into my trap. I'm glad to hear the Perry trial won't be moved. You are right, baby. I will get my rest before I bounce. As a matter of fact, let me start now. I'm pulling over at the next exit, and we'll switch spots. You could drive through Maryland and Virginia."

"I might as well drive the rest of the way. You are so crazy, boy. I don't have any problems with driving, I know you're tired."

Chapter Fifteen

The Final Tip

Tuna and Brandon were just arriving downtown, to Fifty-ninth Street and Third Avenue.

Brandon made a five-second phone call. All he said was, "I'm outside." He turned to Tuna. "I just called my second cousin's son. He was the one who called me about the new tip on Lucky."

"You trust our future on your kid cousin? You can't be serious."

"Let's just hear what he has to say. His job is to answer incoming calls off the crime tip hotline. He gets the information before we do."

"Well, I hope we're not wasting our fuckin' time."

They waited for about five minutes for Brandon's little cousin, Roy Fratt, who appeared to be very nervous when he showed up.

Brandon made the introductions. "This is Tuna. Tuna, this is my little cousin, Roy." They shook hands.

"Okay, listen, Brandon, let's walk up two blocks to McDonald's."

"Sure. No problem, kid. You look nervous. Are you okay?"

"Yeah, I'm just a little shaken up, that's all. Let's hurry before someone from my job sees me talking to you."

"I understand, but I hope you're not wasting my time."

As they walked two blocks to the McDonald's, Tuna and Roy made small talk about the Yankees and the Mets. Tuna was trying to help Roy relax. When they arrived inside, they all headed straight to the bathroom.

After checking to make sure no one was inside, Tuna placed his left foot by the door to block anyone from entering.

"Okay, Roy, what do you have for me?" Brandon asked.

"Last night I received a call about a storage unit in the Bronx that is used by kingpins to hide drugs and money. At first, I was going to ignore the call, but when they mentioned that Donald Gibson is a silent partner, I sat up on my seat and took down all the information. Here is the recorded conversation on disc, as well as the tipster's name and phone number."

Tuna and Brandon couldn't believe how easily this information just fell on their lap.

"Little cousin, this is fuckin' great. The whole conversation is on this tape?"

"Good job, Roy," Tuna added.

"There's more shit on that tape that you need to hear. Well, fellas, this is the end of the road for me. Bathroom meeting is over," a confident Roy said.

Tuna and Brandon waited a few seconds before walking out after Roy. They almost ran back to the car. They couldn't wait to play the CD and hear the call.

As they were walking, a white van with dark-tinted windows pulled up beside them. The side door opened, and two armed men with M16 rifles jumped out, wearing SWAT team patches on their arms and federal badges hanging from their necks.

Tuna and Brandon didn't have time to react or reach for their weapons, but they were relieved it was FBI and not Lucky. Tuna and Brandon were forced in to the van and ordered to sit still. The two armed men sat behind them, aiming their rifles. The men drove toward First Avenue and jumped on the FDR north toward Spanish Harlem.

While they were driving, Tuna asked, "Where are we going? And are you really the feds?"

One of the armed men tapped Tuna with the barrel of his gun and told him to shut up.

When Tuna turned around to ask why he needed to shut up, the armed officer cocked back his weapon. "I'm not going to repeat myself. Please, shut the fuck up."

"C'mon, Tuna, just turn around and listen to their commands," Brandon told him. "If they wanted us dead, we would be."

After a ten-minute drive, they arrived on 100th Street and First Avenue. The driver parked the van, and the passenger up front, the only one wearing a three-piece suit, turned around and started speaking.

"My name is Special Agent, but everyone calls me Mr. Asshole. Personally, I'd rather play with my dog's shit than to work with dirty cops. We were ordered to help you eliminate the target. Hand over the CD, and let's see what this tip is all about."

"How the fuck you know about the CD? And why the fuck you couldn't just introduce yourself? What's up with the whole kidnapping scenario?" an angry Tuna asked.

"We've been following you ever since the Cape Cod shooting. When one of our agents gets murdered, we move quickly, unlike the NYPD. The kidnapping thing was just for fun."

"Hey, listen, asshole, enough with the insults and jokes," Tuna shot back.

"Just hand over the CD, sit back and relax, and see why we are the FBI."

Brandon handed the CD to them and asked if he could talk to Tuna outside the van. At first, Mr. Asshole was hesitant, but since he had the CD in his hand, he figured there was no risk, so he agreed.

Brandon just wanted to make sure Tuna understood his options. "Listen, Tuna, I know you're used to running your own team and being in charge, but right now, today, you no longer have that luxury. We're in no position to be turning down help. I hate working with the FBI, but they have the manpower and connections to capture him a lot quicker. Let's get back in this van and remember our number one target is Lucky, not Mr. Asshole."

"Okay, I understand where you coming from."

When they went back in the van, Mr. Asshole said, "Hey, listen, let's start over. My name is Fred McCarthy, not Mr. Asshole, although I could be one at times. I will be honest. I don't want to be here working on this mission, but I am. So let's make the best of it. Let's get this muthafucka and cut his head off. By the way, where is your other partner?"

"Now we are talking. Hey, no worries. I understand why you don't want to be here. Right now, I'm at your mercy. The commissioner too. All the help will be greatly appreciated. Speedy, he's at home, depressed. I will call him after we listen to the tape and bring him up to speed."

Lucky was getting ready to leave for New York. He didn't listen to his own advice about resting. He kissed his daughter and told her, "I love you, baby girl. Keep taking care of your mommy for me. I will be right back."

"Are you sure, Daddy?" Tamika replied. "Please come back."

Lucky turned to Tasha and kissed and hugged her as well. "I will see you real soon, sweetheart. Trust me, nothing will happen to me. I will be in and out."

"You promise?"

"Yes, baby, I promise. Get with your friend and start looking at houses."

As Lucky was driving up to New York in Tasha's car, he kept thinking about his last conversation with Tasha. It was almost exactly like the one he had with Diamond. He'd lied to Diamond, but he wasn't lying to Tasha.

He started thinking about Diamond and how much he missed her. He was thinking about stopping by to visit her in Maryland on his way up to New York. He wanted to, but he knew that was a bad idea. If he stopped and visited, she would try to keep him there for a few days, which he didn't have to spare. He had a lot of hours to debate on whether to stop by the house or not.

Diamond was the type of broad any man would want to marry. It was just so hard to walk away from a lady with a full package.

Lucky rarely second-guessed himself, but the more he thought about Diamond, the harder his dick got. That's when he realized it was all a sex thing. He loved how she fucked and fed him, but he needed more. And that's where Tasha came in the picture. He refocused himself and started thinking about the mission ahead. He was going to need help.

Once he touched New York, he would stop by and holler at Divine and his two boys. He always liked how they operated. He thought it was finally time to give them another shot.

After a few hours went by, Lucky was hitting North Carolina. Those thoughts about visiting Diamond were coming back to his head. He was able to keep shaking them off, but he decided on his way back to Atlanta he would stop by to see her and also come clean about his decision.

As Lucky was driving up, his old partners were regrouping at a new hideout in the Bronx. Captain Tuna called Speedy and gave him the address. When Speedy arrived, he didn't know what was going on.

"Speedy, I'm glad you made it. My name is Special Agent Fred McCarthy, and we are with the FBI."

"I could see that, but what the fuck is going on here?"

"I will let your captain explain."

"They are here to help us find Lucky."

"But didn't the last two agents we met also imply they were here to help? Now, Loose Cannon is dead."

"Speedy, these guys are not dirty. We have a recording. A call came in where a caller told us about a storage facility in the Bronx where they believe Lucky is storing his money. We finally got him, Speedy. We finally got him. We have the address, but we were waiting for you to arrive. Are you okay? Two days ago you couldn't stomach this shit anymore. I need to know if I can still trust you with my life."

"Hell yeah, I'm okay. I'm back, Captain. Can I hear the tape and make sure it's not another setup? Remember how he fooled us in Central Park?"

"You're right, Speedy. I was so caught up in the moment, I forgot how he fooled us before. C'mon, let's go to the other room and play back the CD."

Speedy was still very skeptical about the whole tip. Knowing Lucky, he was just setting them up once again. He went into the room with his mind already made up. He sat down next to Tuna and listened.

"Thank you for calling crime tips. My name is Roy Fratt. How can I help you?"

"Hello. My name is Diamond. I have some information for those cops that are on trial for shooting the unarmed Black kid."

"Okay, Diamond, I'm familiar with the case. What kind of information do you have?"

"Well, the kind that can help you find Donald 'Lucky' Gibson. He keeps his money in a storage facility in the Bronx, actually off Gun Hill Road, called Put-It-Away. Lucky is a silent partner, and the owner is one of his childhood friends."

"How can we make sure you're not pulling my leg? We get all kinds of calls coming in through here."

"I'm not lying. I'm the girl that everyone thought was shot and killed in front of that police station in Harlem. That was all a setup. If you want to find Lucky, then watch the storage facility. He will pop up. He has a few million dollars hidden in there. In fact, all types of high-profile drug lords stash their money and drugs at this location."

"Okay. I will pass this information over. In the meantime, do you have a callback number?"

"Yes, it's 347-555-1212. My real name is Tracey Sanders. Please call me back because I'm going to need protection. I'm on my way to New York."

"Can I ask why you are coming forward with all this information?"

"Let me ask you something first, Roy. Do you have a wife or a girlfriend that you love?"

"Yes, I do. I've been married for five years now."

"Well, always treat her right. You don't have to be loyal, just treat her right. Don't ever lie or misguide her because one day she will wake up and smell the bullshit. This mutha-fucka thinks I'm stupid. He buys me a house in some hick-ass town and gives me all this money. I know why. Because he's not coming back. He abandoned me. Payback is a bitch."

"Point well taken. Well, I'm glad you called. Lucky is number one on the most wanted list. I will have someone call you back to arrange protection."

"Thank you."

Tuna got up and turned the CD player off. He said, "So, Speedy, talk to me. Is it legit?"

"Wow! I don't know, but it sounds real. I guess the only way to really tell if she's telling the truth is to, one, check out the storage place, and two, run her name. She said Tracey Sanders. Also, did anyone try calling the number she left?"

"We tried calling, but she gave us a bogus number," Tuna replied.

"Why a bogus number? That's a red flag. Let's run her name through the system. Check the national database for runaways, and let's see what comes up. We need some background on this girl. It sounds like she's emotionally distressed."

"Damn! I have to hand it to you guys. I'm looking at real police work. I guess all the media drama is overshadowing some good police officers," Special Agent Fred said. "I'm really impressed on the chemistry you guys have."

"Are you shitting me, Fred?" Tuna shot back. "You just gave us a compliment. Well, let's not dance just yet. Let's go watch this storage facility and see what we come up with."

All the men agreed and decided to wait until after hours. They figured, if the place was a drug safe house, most of their activities would be at night.

As they were planning their operation, additional charges surrounding the Rell Davis case were filed against Captain Tuna, Speedy, and Lucky. The DA was able to receive a rapid indictment, and warrants for their arrest were issued.

The mayor called Brandon up. "Hey, my friend, have you heard the latest?" he asked.

"No, I haven't, but by the tone of your voice, I know it's not good."

"New warrants have been issued for Tuna and Speedy. Where are you?"

"I'm following on this hot tip on Lucky. We finally got him. He was the one who killed the girl in front of the precinct. But his luck has finally run out because we know about his stash house."

"Sounds good. Let them handle it. I need to see you. We need to talk more about your resignation."

Brandon got off the phone, upset. He didn't even bother sharing what Ralph had said about the new charges, not wanting to further stress them out right before a stakeout.

"Hey, listen, you guys are going to have to handle the mission without me. I have to meet with the mayor."

Speedy and Tuna understood. They drove around the perimeter a few times and noticed two things that struck them as odd. There were two high-tech cameras covering the front and back, and the storage facility looked old and in need of a few repairs.

Tuna parked two blocks down. "Speedy, why would a shitty place need surveillance? I don't understand."

"I don't either. Now I'm thinking Diamond's story is legit. Let's stay here. I can see the front. I don't want to get any closer, not with those cameras."

They sat there for two hours and didn't see or hear a thing. Tuna was getting a little impatient and wanted to get a closer look.

"Captain, you know a stakeout is unpredictable. We've only been here for two hours. Go ahead and get some shut-eye. I got it from here."

"Speedy, now that we're alone, I want to share a few things. Loose Cannon was like a son to me. I didn't mean to shut you guys out the way I did. I still can't believe he's gone, but it was nothing personal."

"I can't believe he's gone, either. We had our differences, but he was one hell of a cop and partner. There was no one more loyal than him. I miss him a lot. Let's mourn at another time. This is not a great location to start crying."

"You're right. I just needed to say that to you. Also, I'm sorry you didn't know about Tango. We had to kill him. Tango was working with Internal Affairs."

"Captain, please get your shut-eye and let's stay focused."

As Speedy and Tuna continued to watch the storage facility throughout the night, Lucky was entering Washington, D.C. Only about four hours away, he figured he would drive straight to the storage and pick up his truck. Plus, he wanted to holler at Divine about closing this final chapter of his life. He needed ready-to-die soldiers, and Divine and his boys were perfect.

Unaware of the new charges brought against him, Lucky was only thinking about one thing—killing Tuna and Speedy.

As it was getting into the morning hours, the newspaper was starting to circulate, and of course, they were bashing the commissioner and his dirty unit. New Yorkers were shocked to see the number of charges filed. Charges were also brought against the cardinal for child pornography, child prostitution, and child molestation. New Yorkers were also waiting to hear the latest on the Perry Coleman trial. In fact, there were rumors that a plea deal would be offered.

Around five o'clock in the morning, Lucky was pissed the fuck off as he sat in traffic on the New Jersey Turnpike. He didn't understand why.

Tuna and Speedy were still watching the storage facility when Special Agent Fred showed up. "What's the status?" Fred asked. "Any movement inside?"

"Nothing. A Cadillac Escalade showed up about an hour ago. That must be Lucky's friend who owns the place. So, right now, we know for sure there are two bodies inside."

"Two bodies?" Fred asked.

"Yes, when we drove through the front, we saw someone sitting by the front desk. Since the Escalade got here, we haven't seen anyone else exit."

"Got it. Well, I'm here. I'm going to make my way toward the roof across the street and see if I can get a visual," Fred announced.

Before Fred could exit the van, they all noticed headlights approaching.

"Okay, here we go. Who is that driving by?" Speedy asked, referring to Lucky, who'd just passed their car.

Lucky instantly knew they were watching the storage place. The windows on the minivan were tinted, so he couldn't see inside. He didn't know if those were cops watching him personally, or maybe one of their customers. Lucky had no choice but to enter the storage unit. He only had a 9 mm on him. If he got pulled over, he would be a sitting duck. He couldn't start a war with a handgun. At least inside he had an arsenal of guns.

When Lucky drove by, Speedy said, "Look at the license plates on the car. They're from Massachusetts. That has to be Lucky returning from Cape Cod. If he goes inside, then we know that's him. Call for backup."

"Backup? We're on our own here," Tuna replied.

"Well, then fuck it. Once he goes inside, we make our move," Fred said.

"But, Captain, if that is Lucky, then he knew we were cops when he drove by. I doubt he would stop and go inside," Speedy added.

Lucky made the left turn and drove into the storage facility. He knew something was wrong because Divine came out the office and greeted him as he exited the car.

"Lucky, what are you doing here?" Divine asked nervously.

"Why? What's wrong? Is this about the cops parked down the street? How in the fuck they know about this spot? Who is snitching? is the million-dollar question."

"I don't know who's talking, but Pee-Wee picked the pigs up on the camera. He said they circled the block twice and parked. About an hour ago, another cop got in the minivan."

"So there are three men. That's great news. They can't call for backup because they've been suspended from the force. If I know Tuna like I do, he will make his move in a few minutes. Let's get our guns ready. Lock up all the rooms and doors, and let's head to the roof."

While Lucky and Divine headed upstairs to the roof, Pee-Wee remained downstairs watching the front door, two shiny chrome 40-calibers sitting on his hip, both clips full. Plus, he had a box full of bullets sitting right next to him. His job was to make sure no one came in the door. Pee-Wee sat on a chair about twenty-five feet from the front door, aiming a 12-round street sweeper shotgun. He was going to blow off the first head he saw creeping through the front door.

Pee-Wee wasn't just your average graveyard worker. He was one of Divine's main hitmen, and a ride-or-die soldier. His brother Blood was out of town in South Philly. Pee-Wee wouldn't have any hesitation killing cops, especially the dirty ones who killed Perry Coleman.

Lucky and Divine were on the roof watching the van. Divine was looking through the scope of a high-powered rifle. He couldn't see if anyone was in the van.

Lucky, holding the same rifle as Divine, kept running from one side of the roof to the other, looking for movement, but couldn't see anything.

"Dee, do you see anyone in the van? Because I don't see any movement. These muthafuckas are up to something. Stay on your toes and watch everything," he yelled at Divine.

"I'm watching. I don't see any of these muthafuckas. Radio down to Pee-Wee and ask him."

"Pee-Wee, you see anything?" Lucky asked in a low tone.

"It's all clear down here. I can't see shit," he replied.

Lucky and Divine were a bit confused. How could they exit the van so quickly?

Divine kept a close look at the van, hoping to get a little visual of anything so he could blow it to pieces. It got to the point where he was getting frustrated and losing focus.

As he was about to call Lucky over, he noticed the red dot on the side of Lucky's head. He yelled, "Lucky, duck down!"

Lucky didn't hesitate, and just dropped to the ground.

Two loud shots went off.

As Divine was running toward Lucky, more shots were fired.

Special Agent Fred, who came up as a marksman in the federal government, was across the street on the roof of an apartment building. For him to get back behind a rifle and look through that scope again was natural.

Divine reached Lucky and realized he'd cheated death. Lucky wasn't shot or grazed. He'd either ducked super fast, or Fred was a bit rusty and didn't know how to shoot.

Divine helped Lucky get up off the floor, and they ran for cover.

"There's someone on the roof across the street shooting," Divine said.

"I see him. Let's split. You go that way and cause a distraction, and I will pop up and knock him the fuck off. That muthafucka tried to push my wig back, Dee."

"You sure you know his location? Don't have me run out there and get shot and killed," a nervous Divine said.

"Have I ever let you down before? On the count of three, I need you to run like bullets are chasing. All I need is three to five seconds to take him out. You ready?"

"Yeah, I'm ready, dog. Let's do this," a more confident Divine said.

Before Lucky could count to three, they heard more shots.

"Wait, Dee," Lucky quickly said. "He's shooting at us. Don't run out right now."

"It sounds like the shots are coming from downstairs. We need to get down there and help Pee-Wee out."

Just as Divine said that, they heard more shots, many more than the first round.

Divine added, "Damn! We need to hurry up and help Pee-Wee. It sounds like they're using high-powered rifles."

"I hear you, Dee, but we first have to take out the marksman on the roof."

"With all the commotion going on, I doubt he's not distracted already. We don't have time to wait. I'm making my move now. Get ready and take this pig out."

"Hold on, Dee, we need to make sure he didn't move his location."

"Hold on? C'mon, Lucky, we need to get back inside, dog. Get ready on my three, all right?" Divine said, looking into Lucky's eyes.

"On your three," Lucky said as he gripped his rifle.

After Divine counted to three and made a dash for the roof exit, Lucky jumped up and aimed his rifle, hoping his target didn't move.

When Fred saw Divine make a run for it, he opened fired, not realizing Lucky had spotted him.

Lucky didn't hesitate to pull the trigger, letting off two shots as he watched through the scope. His shots ripped through the body of Special Agent Fred McCarthy, one bullet penetrating the left side of his neck, the other bullet entering through his chin and exiting through his cheekbone. Fred hit the floor and was dead on arrival.

Once Lucky saw his target fall, he then turned and started running toward the staircase, only to trip over Divine's motionless body.

Divine was shot twice in the head and was drowning in his own blood. He'd only taken a few steps before Fred shot him down like a dog.

Lucky was so focused on his target, he didn't realize his boy since junior high school, his partner, and brother he never had, was shot and killed.

"Oh, shit, no! Oh, hell no! C'mon, Divine, I need you to get the fuck up!" Lucky kept yelling as he kicked Divine's lifeless body.

Lucky knew Divine, pieces of his brain hanging out his bullet wounds, was dead, and he just didn't want to accept it. He dropped down to his knees and held Divine's hand.

"Wake up, bro. It's not your time. Wake up!"

As bad as Lucky wanted to pay back his old partners, he didn't want to lose those close to him. For a quick minute, he almost lost it while he was on his knees staring at yet another dead body.

Lucky snapped out of his daze when he heard more gunfire coming from the first floor. He quickly turned around and started heading toward the staircase to help out Pee-Wee.

Right before he reached the stairs, another option opened up for him. Instead of running down the staircase and blazing his rifle like a wild cowboy, he could just jump onto the next roof, a getaway. He leaned against the wall and thought for a second. He explored his options—jump to the next roof, or run down and help Pee-Wee on a suicide mission.

Lucky remembered he'd made a promise to Tamika that he would be back. He was still undecided, as he heard gunfire being exchanged in the background.

As soon as he started hearing sirens, he went with option B, jumping to the next roof, and disappeared within seconds. Leaving Pee-Wee behind wasn't as difficult. That wasn't his boy. He only knew him through Divine. Lucky felt bad, but there was no way the two of them were going to win the war. He wasn't a coward or scared to die. He just wasn't prepared to die at that particular moment.

Pee-Wee fought every step of the way. He kept looking at the staircase and was wondering why Lucky or Divine didn't return. He thought maybe they were shot dead on the roof by snipers. He panicked and ran back to the stash room, grabbed two gallons of gasoline, and began emptying them all over the first floor. He figured he could start a fire, burn down the place, and hide in the stash room for a few days.

As Pee-Wee was running around the first floor and pouring gasoline all over, more cops were arriving at the scene. He was outnumbered a hundred to one.

An officer yelled on the bullhorn, "Donald Gibson, you have fifteen seconds to come out with your hands in the air. If you fail to comply, we will be forced to use deadly force!"

Pee-Wee became even more nervous once he heard them call him Lucky. He began to sweat heavily. One of the gallons slipped out of his hand, and when it hit the floor, gasoline splashed on his pants. "Shit! I got gas over my new fuckin' jeans."

He wiped himself off and ran to the office. He looked at the surveillance monitors, and all he saw was cops outside with heavy artillery. He only had about five seconds to start the fire and lock himself in. He disabled the security system, so the sprinklers wouldn't come on, and grabbed a book of matches out of the office.

After Pee-Wee had sparked a few matches, the flames grew fast, and the fire began to get closer to him, like it was chasing him. He started running toward the stash room, but the fire caught up to him first. Within seconds, his whole body caught on fire.

Instead of running into the human safe, he ran and jumped out the first-floor window, banging his head on the concrete and losing consciousness. The force of landing actually helped put out some of the fire.

A few officers ran toward him with blankets and patted his body with them until all the flames were put out. Pee-Wee's body was burned so badly, they all assumed it was Lucky.

Tuna and Speedy were standing over Pee-Wee's body, convinced it was Lucky, but they wanted DNA proof just to make sure.

Everyone present was pronouncing Pee-Wee dead, until one of the medics yelled, "I found a pulse."

They gently rolled his body onto a stretcher and rushed him into the waiting ambulance, where the paramedics began working on his burned up body, hoping to keep him alive until they arrived at Montefiore Hospital.

When the ambulance pulled off, the fire department was asking officers on the scene to move away from the burning building. By now, the entire storage facility was up in flames. Firefighters didn't waste any time in containing the fire, not wanting it to spread to other buildings.

While the fire was being contained, so were Tuna and Speedy. They didn't resist the warrants for their arrest because, with Lucky in custody, they were satisfied.

Chapter Sixteen

Where Is Lucky?

"*Good evening. This is Destine Diaz reporting live from downtown, in front of One Police Plaza. We are waiting on a press conference where we believe both Commissioner Fratt and Mayor Gulliano will address the city. According to our sources, early this morning, around two o'clock, gunfire erupted in the Gun Hill area of the Bronx. Our sources tell us that Donald Gibson and a childhood friend owned a storage facility called Put-It-Away. Police officers believed that this was Lucky's hideout. When they tried to serve a warrant, they were fired upon.*

"*At this moment, it is still unclear who discharged their weapons first. However, according to the police department, Captain William 'Tuna' Youngstown, Jeffrey 'Speedy' Winston, and Donald 'Lucky' Gibson are all in custody. There is also confirmation of two dead bodies found at the scene, one in the burned-up building, and another across the street, believed to be that of another FBI agent. This is where the story becomes very confusing, so we will wait until we have further information on the identity of these two victims.*

"*Donald Gibson is in the hospital with third-degree burns all over his body and in a coma clinging to life. Captain William and Detective Jeffrey, both on suspension, shouldn't have been close to any gun battles. What happened next is what Commissioner Fratt is going to explain to us all. Did the city serve an illegal warrant that turned deadly, leaving yet another federal agent dead? Who burned Lucky? Was he found burned before his arrest, or was he burned while handcuffed? Donald drew a hefty list of enemies amongst the force when he testified. This is Destine Diaz, Channel Five News.*"

Destine's report sent chills throughout the millions of viewers watching, the most popular reaction being, "Oh, shit."

They were all shocked to hear that Lucky was burned and was lying in a coma. Lucky was hated among the police community, but not in the streets. New Yorkers grew to love him for his heroism. They couldn't wait to hear the commissioner's press conference.

The Colemans were in tears after they heard about Lucky's situation. If it wasn't for him, they would have never received any kind of justice for their son. They owed a great deal of gratitude and respect for his actions.

"Okay, sweetheart, turn the volume up. The press conference is about to start," Laura said to her husband. They sat there holding hands, hoping to hear Lucky would survive.

Right before Commissioner Fratt was about to start his press conference, the mayor's spokesperson, Richard Claiborne, came out first.

"I'm here today on behalf of Mayor Ralph Gulliano. I have a few updates, and I will answer a few questions."

"So are you saying neither Commissioner Fratt nor Mayor Gulliano will be speaking tonight?" one reporter asked.

"That is correct. Trust me, they both wanted to be here and speak. They are still currently in the middle of the investigation. Please hold your questions until after my statement. First, let me clarify one thing. We have not confirmed that's Donald Gibson in a coma. I know you guys read the papers this morning, and it quoted that Donald Gibson has been captured. The unidentified male victim was badly burned. The details of his wounds are too graphic to explain. We are still investigating the whole ordeal that took place this morning. We are questioning the officers involved and in contact with the federal government. Tomorrow afternoon, we will hold another press conference when Commissioner Fratt will have full details."

"So now the burn victim in a coma is not Donald Gibson? Did you guys get the DNA results?"

"The blood test was inconclusive," Richard replied.

"What about dental?" the sharp reporter shot right back.

Richard ignored the reporter. *"Next question."*

"Any new charges been filed for the two suspended officers at the scene discharging their weapons?"

"I can't discuss that at this time. Next question."

"What about Perry Coleman's trial?"

"I can't discuss that, either. Listen, guys, the investigation is ongoing. I promise by tomorrow we will have more information. I just wanted to come out here and give a brief update. The answers you are looking for, I don't have at this moment. I want to thank everyone who came out. Have a good night."

Richard left that podium like he was taking part in a hundred-yard dash competition. He did a great job of dodging all the bullets the press fired at him.

The governor paid another visit to the mayor to talk, and hopefully bring closure to the nightmare that was destroying the image of the police force. The mayor wasn't surprised to see him, but he was shocked. He thought maybe he would get a phone call, not a face-to-face talk.

"Ralph, we need to talk and strategize."

"I agree."

"What's the latest on Donald Gibson?"

"We still can't prove that's him in a coma. There's no way we could go out there and say we have Donald Gibson in custody," Mayor Gulliano declared.

"I understand, but we can't say it's not him, either."

Ralph understood what he was trying to say, but then he noticed his private line flashing. He knew it was Richard calling, so he pressed the speaker button, to allow the governor to hear as well.

"This is the mayor."

"Good evening, sir. It's Richard. I just wanted to inform you that the burned victim at the hospital didn't make it. He died about five minutes ago."

"Damn! We don't need another dead body. Are you sure?"

"Correct, but this actually helps us, sir."

"How does it help us, Richard? Please, enlighten me."

"Now we can perform a full autopsy. With the victim still alive and in a coma, we were limited. I'm on my way to the hospital now. I have a forensic team meeting me there. I will call you once we are done."

"Sounds great."

After getting off the phone with Richard, Mayor Gulliano was a bit more relaxed.

Governor Silver popped the question. "What are we going to do with those two dirty cops?"

"What do you mean? They have suffered enough. Captain William and Detective Jeffrey both are facing murder charges already. You want me to file more charges? Let's not forget, two FBI agents popped up dead as well, which means we all have dirty laundry."

"I understand the great deal of respect you have for them, but they still broke laws. I will make sure additional charges are filed against them."

"You see, Andrew, this is where we clash. You think you could bring your ass down from Albany and run my city. Stop disrespecting me in that manner. I will handle the situation."

"Let's stay focused. I'm not here to see whose dick is bigger. We should start thinking of plan B, just in case Lucky is still out there," Governor Silver shot back, ignoring Ralph's invite to a verbal match.

Governor Silver and Mayor Gulliano hated each other's guts, but they had no choice but to work together. Andrew decided to hang around until Richard called back.

While they spent the next forty-five minutes discussing strategies, Ralph's private line rang again. It was Richard.

"Boss, the dead body is not Donald Gibson."

"Are you positive?"

"Yes, the body was identified as Dwayne "Pee-Wee" Mooks, a career criminal. His rap sheet includes a few gun charges and manslaughter charges. He's a known associate of the other dead body we found, that of Bernard "Divine" Dooley, another career criminal. He's one of Donald's closest friends. His name is on the lease for that property."

"Great job. Anything else?"

"No, sir. I will start on the paperwork and get everything ready for the press conference tomorrow. Should I let the media know that Lucky was never in a coma? If we don't say it, the information will leak."

"You are right, but make sure you make them aware that the two dead bodies were dangerous criminals and associates of Donald. Make sure you smear the storage facility. It was a place where criminals hid drugs, guns, and money. Donald was a partner and provided protection and confidential police information. Tomorrow, when I read the morning paper or see the news, I don't want to hear or see any different," he said as he hung up the phone.

"So we have ourselves a big problem," Governor Silver said.

"Why? Because if he's still alive, we will catch him."

"You sound like a broken record, Ralph. I can't keep trusting you with the integrity of the city."

The governor picked up his cell phone and called Internal Affairs. He walked away from Ralph and spent about two minutes on the phone with IA.

When he returned, Ralph quickly questioned him. "Who was that?"

"Internal Affairs."

"Didn't I just finish telling you, I will handle the situation? Why are you pissing on my backyard? I have it under control. I can understand the concerns, and I welcome your help. But, please understand, I run this city, and you are standing in my house."

Ralph picked up his cell phone and called Richard back.

"Richard, I have another assignment for you. This requires your immediate attention."

"No problem, sir. What is it?"

"I want you to head down to Central Booking and advise both the captain and the detective to keep their mouth shut when IA approaches them. Got that?"

"Internal Affairs? Why? What happened?"

"There is no time to ask questions. Please head down to Central Booking and call me after you speak to them."

The mayor hung up the phone, and turned toward Andrew.

"You see, you're not the only one who could pick up the phone and make things happen."

"There's nothing you could do to stop IA. Those officers will be questioned, and they will be questioned now. Please don't obstruct a pending investigation. This could get you in trouble."

"Was that a threat?"

"I don't make threats, Mr. Mayor, I make promises. Get in the way of this investigation, and I will come after you."

Mayor Gulliano laughed. "Come after me? Well, I would like to see you try it. Since you like giving out promises, let me give you one. I promise IA won't interview the captain or the detective tonight."

"Is that right?"

"Keep ignoring me when I say I run this city. Now, will you excuse me? I have work that needs to be done."

"Are you kicking me out?"

"No, I will never do that. You kicked yourself out."

The mayor didn't walk the governor out, and so he left shocked and upset. Andrew couldn't believe the level of disrespect displayed by the mayor. Andrew thought he was being nice, not taking over the whole investigation when he'd first arrived, but since the mayor wasn't willing to cooperate, he changed his mind. By the morning, he was going to meet with a select House committee to have the federal government replace certain divisions in their police department, such as homicide and narcotics. The governor was also going to bring in his own special unit to run the streets and hunt down Donald Gibson.

The mayor called the commissioner once Andrew left.

"Brandon, we have major issues. The dead victim at the hospital is not your guy."

"Yes, I know."

"You know, so what's next? The governor just left here highly upset, but not before calling Internal Affairs."

"Internal Affairs? Damn! This is now getting uglier by the day. Can you stop them from interviewing my guys?"

"Maybe for a day or two. That will give you enough time to go in there and see them before IA does. You have about twelve hours. The press conference has been changed to tomorrow around noon. Hopefully, you will have some good news for me, because so far, you keep coming up empty. I will speak to you tomorrow. Oh, let me remind you again. I'm not taking the fall for this mess. You and your wild goons are on your own." Ralph hung up the phone and didn't give Brandon the opportunity to respond.

Brandon knew he was in deep hot water, especially now since two dead FBI agents had popped up. The federal government would demand answers. Brandon was clueless on his next move, but he wasn't about to turn his back on his two officers in custody. His main concern was getting them released and reunited with their families.

He wanted to go home and catch some rest, but with all the drama going on, he couldn't afford any sleep. He headed down to Central Booking to see Captain Tuna and Detective Speedy. When he arrived there, he noticed Richard Claiborne had also just arrived. He approached his car.

"Richard, what's up? Are you here to see my boys?"

"Yes. The mayor sent me down here to make sure I see them before IA gets ahold of them."

"Right. Well, you go interview Speedy, and I will go see the captain. Just tell him to keep his mouth shut no matter what. I will handle everything."

"Okay," Richard replied.

Commissioner Fratt went inside to see Captain William.

"Didn't I fuckin' tell you not to add any more heat? What the fuck happened out there?"

"I'm sorry, boss, but shouldn't we be celebrating? We finally caught him."

"Oh, you want to celebrate, Tuna? Well, let me be the first one to stomp on your parade—Lucky is still alive. The only thing you caught was more charges."

"What? Get the fuck out of here! Then who was that?"

"I don't know. I just wanted to come down and let you know that he's still out there roaming the streets. Now Internal Affairs are on the way to see you and Speedy. Why would you work with another FBI agent? One was already murdered. Now we have two dead agents, and their blood is on your hands."

"Man, what do we have to do to catch this son of a bitch? Remember the girl that was shot in front of the police station? Well, that wasn't the girl we were looking for. Lucky set all that up. The real girl, her name is Tracey 'Diamond' Sanders. She was the one who told us about the storage facility. She also gave us this address in New Jersey where Lucky owns a condo under a different name."

"Where is this Diamond girl right now?"

"We don't know. After she gave up Lucky, we offered her protection, but she declined."

"Why did she give up Lucky? You think they set this all up?" Commissioner Fratt asked.

"No, she was pretty upset and mentioned something about payback for leaving her."

"Well, give me the address, and I will send a police squad to watch the condo."

"Brandon, you can't send regular cops or detectives to watch the address. Lucky is too smart for that. Look for outside help on this one. This will be the last lead we have on him. After what happened this morning, I'm assuming he will disappear forever."

"I understand. In the meantime, you make sure you keep your mouth shut when IA shows up."

"You don't have to worry about that. The one we have to worry about is Speedy. A few days ago he was talking about how he couldn't take this anymore."

"Do you think he will run his mouth?"

"More like killing himself, but if he doesn't commit suicide, he will most likely open his mouth and try to strike a deal."

"Okay, I will keep my ears open. Trust me, if he starts talking, I will be one of the first ones to know about it. Right now, just worry about yourself. I will work on getting you released."

Commissioner Fratt called Mayor Gulliano.

"It's me, Brandon. I just finished seeing Captain Tuna, and to be honest, I think he finally has lost it, my good friend."

"What do you mean?" the mayor asked curiously.

"He just doesn't look right. I looked into his eyes, and I could see he's tired of all this drama. I'm not second-guessing if we should even help him out. He just doesn't look right, boss."

"Well, we can't leave him in jail. Once we get him out, we'll just provide the proper help he needs to get by. Remember, he also lost one of his best friends. Sitting in a cell gives you a lot of time to think. What about the other detective?"

"I didn't see him. I let Richard interview him. When I finished with Tuna, I left out. I have to follow up on this tip he gave me. I have to find this witness who told them about the storage facility. She has to have more information."

"Okay. Don't forget tomorrow we have a press conference. I will need as much information about the whereabouts of this son of a bitch who is turning our city upside down. Once the city reads the papers, and they know that Lucky was never captured, I'm afraid we may have a riot on our hands."

"According to Tuna, the witness that's cooperating said Lucky owns a condo in New Jersey. We have an address. I'm already sending over two detectives. Hopefully, the tables turn our way, and we run into some luck."

"Keep me updated. Also, a new trial date has been set for the murder of Perry Coleman. The district attorney is willing to work out a deal, but I'm hearing they won't go for manslaughter charges. We're looking at murder one."

"Murder charges? I think I'm going to pay the DA a visit and remind him what side he should be on. I need at least the captain charged with manslaughter."

"I will see what I can do, but he will have to be released through bail. I will call the judge when we get off the phone. But, Brandon, I need some hard-core evidence to damage Lucky's credibility. Find me something."

"Thank you, Ralph. I'll call you when I get to New Jersey. What if we don't find Lucky before the press conference? Can you cancel it?"

"Not again. We're both going to have to face the music. We could still blame him for everything, even in the murder trial. I will come up with a strategy. Plus, I'll find new lawyers. Anyway, we'll speak about that later. Hurry up and call me as soon as you find anything."

After Brandon hung up with the mayor, he called up two detectives from the Seventy-sixth Precinct in Brooklyn. The same precinct where an African American male was raped by police officers in a holding cell. Some of the most corrupt officers worked out of there.

Brandon needed detectives he could trust, and the first two that came to mind were detectives Sean Lee and Mark White.

Those two were similar to Captain Tuna and his crew, but they didn't work in multiple divisions. They were only homicide detectives. They would do whatever it took to solve a murder case.

Brandon called Mark's cell phone. After it rang about six times, Mark finally picked up.

"Commissioner, what's up? This better be good. Tell me how much first, or I'm hanging up."

"Twenty thousand," he quickly shouted.

"I'm about to click this red button on my cell," Mark replied, raising his voice in disappointment.

"Maybe forty thousand, if you could agree to my terms."

"Now I'm listening." Mark jumped off the bed and started to get dressed, while holding the phone with one hand.

"It's about Donald 'Lucky' Gibson."

"I was wondering when you was going to call me."

"Well, I'm calling you now. I have an address in New Jersey I need you to check out. It's out of our jurisdiction. Are you available?"

"I'm almost dressed. What are the terms?"

"Well, if you capture him and keep him alive, we will give you forty thousand dollars, if you kill him, then only twenty."

"That sounds fair."

"I need you to call Sean."

"Wait a minute, if Sean has to come, then we need to double the price tag."

"Not a problem. I will double the pay. Just catch the son of a bitch," Brandon said while cutting Mark off.

"I will call Sean now. Give me the address. I will see you in New Jersey."

About an hour later, Brandon and his two new dirty detectives were across the street from Lucky's condo, and there were no signs of him anywhere. They waited until about nine in the morning before they called off the stakeout. They didn't see any reason to waste time in one location.

"Listen, fellas, I will make it an even one hundred thousand dollars, that's fifty apiece, if you could catch this rat by noon today," Brandon said, a desperate look in his eyes.

"Are you serious, Brandon?" Mark said. "Please stop fuckin' with us."

"For a hundred thousand dollars, we will not only find him, but we will hunt down every person related to him."

"We need to speak to the witness who told you about this location. Where is she?

"No problem. I'll write the address down. She gave us a bogus phone number. Hopefully, this address is legit, but it's in Maryland. You won't have time. I have a press conference at noon. I need him located by then."

"So, we are fucked. We need more time. Plus, if you want us to head down to Maryland, we're going to need more money. I think you're leading us to a dead end."

"You might be right. I just need him found and caught. The hundred-thousand-dollar offer stands, if you guys could catch him. That includes going down to Maryland. Anyways, thanks for coming out. I'll send five thousand for the trouble. I'll be in touch."

"Cool. Thanks for the money. We will think about it. Maybe only one of us will go."

Brandon left and headed to Manhattan to his apartment in the city. He wanted to jump in the shower and get ready for the most difficult press conference of his entire police career. He was about to face the press with no answers as to the whereabouts of Lucky and what exactly took place in the Bronx that left three people dead, including an FBI agent.

He didn't even bother calling up the mayor. He headed straight to the apartment, took a shower, and threw on one of his better suits, hoping to at least buy a little sympathy from the public. He headed down to One Police Plaza where the press conference was taking place.

He picked up his phone and finally called up the mayor. "Ralph, it's me."

"I know it's you. Where the hell have you been? What's the latest? You better have some great news. I have the feds crawling up my ass."

"I'm sorry, boss. I still don't have anything."

"What! Are you serious? I sometimes wonder if I hired the right man for the position. You are really disappointing me.

This kind of nonsense should have never escalated. Where are you now?"

"I'm on my way to One Police Plaza after I stop and get something to eat."

"Well, I'll be there at noon. I'll see you then. Make sure you call Richard when you arrive to go over your speech."

"What speech? I thought I was just going to answer a few questions."

"Just call Richard."

Mayor Gulliano hung up in disgust and mumbled to himself, "A few will burn with you. Let's see." He made a few more phone calls before getting dressed to head downtown. It was going on eleven o'clock. He was running late and didn't care, not wanting to be on the podium in the first place.

By eleven-thirty, a half hour from the press conference, the streets were crowded with reporters and news vans. Everyone was desperate for answers as to what was going on. When reporters didn't even have a clue, it usually meant corruption was involved. All the files and evidence so far had been labeled top secret. There were reporters from several states and foreign countries present. The press was eager; so were the few hundred protesters who were out there singing that Marley tune once again, "No Justice, No Peace."

Commissioner Brandon and the mayor's spokesperson, Richard Claiborne, were both in a conference room, rehearsing the prepared statement while they waited for the mayor. It was going on twelve-fifteen, and no sign of Ralph Gulliano yet.

"Okay, I don't know where Ralph is, but we need to start this press conference before we have a riot," Richard said as he looked out the window. "I see a lot of angry protesters out there."

"Are you sure we should start without the mayor?" a nervous Commissioner Fratt asked.

Before Richard could answer, the mayor walked through the door. "I'm sorry I'm late. Are we ready?" he asked the both of them.

"I'm ready," Brandon quickly responded, happy to see Ralph. He thought maybe the mayor had bailed out on him.

"Well, let's go downstairs, face the city, and let's hope God helps us all."

As all three men walked down the hallway and made their way outside, they noticed everyone they walked past was looking at them like they were criminals. They were all shocked because those were people in uniforms who were turning up their nose. When they reached outside and were up on the podium, the whole crowd went silent. You could hear a mouse pissing on cotton. That's how quiet it was.

Brandon made his way toward the microphone. It was only about twenty feet from him, but it seemed like it took him almost three minutes to reach it. He cleared his throat.

"Good afternoon, New York. Today I come, my friends, with a few updates that may be positive or negative. I'm not going to stand here and fool with the people of this great city. I will never insult your intelligence. I understand in the recent weeks, a lot of allegations, eyebrow-raising accusations, were made public against the great police force that protects our freedom. These allegations couldn't come at a worse time. We are still dealing with the murder trial against the police department where Perry Coleman was killed. I also have an update on that trial as well, but I first want to speak on what I think everyone wants to hear about.

"Yesterday, around one or two in the morning, Captain William Youngstown and Detective Jeffrey Winston were following up on a lead. They were told Donald 'Lucky' Gibson was hiding in a storage facility, which, by the way, according to our sources, was used by kingpins to store large quantities of drugs, guns, and money. These two officers, who are currently on suspension, acted on their own to watch the facility in hopes of catching Donald Gibson. Their plan backfired. They were hoping they could at least catch Donald and retrofire the embarrassment they've been put through.

"When the officers approached the establishment after witnessing Donald Gibson himself walking in, they were met by flying bullets. The officers fired back, and as they retreated, they called it in and waited for backup. In regards to the dead agent we found on the roof, we are still investigating what role he played as we piece this puzzle. We indeed have two other dead civilians, both of whom are career criminals.

"I know the number one question everyone is asking. The answer is no, Donald 'Lucky' Gibson has not been captured. But I do have a message, Lucky. I know you are out there watching. I will guarantee this. Your luck will run out one day. Trust me, old friend."

Bang!

Commissioner Fratt's head jerked back so hard, it almost touched his back. A bullet entered between his eyes, blowing off the back of his head. The force of the bullet knocked him off his feet, and he landed about five feet from the microphone. He was dead before he hit the ground.

All the TV channels went blank, either switching to the weatherman or the sports anchor. But it was already too late. Commissioner Brandon Fratt's assassination was just carried live on national TV.

Chapter Seventeen

Who Killed the Commissioner?

It was going on seven in the morning when Sergio heard loud bangs on his front door. When he finally woke up, got out of bed, and looked through the peephole, he saw a scary-faced, out-of-breath Lucky standing on the other side of his door. He looked like a crackhead outside of his connect's door, waiting for that hit. At first, Sergio was a bit skeptical about opening his front door. He hadn't seen Lucky since the day before he'd testified in court. Sergio had helped Lucky set up that video swap in that Italian restaurant in the Bronx when his former partners were looking for him and his girl. He was the one who told the detective he called her Chanel because that was her fragrance of choice.

Sergio knew it was bad news, but Lucky had been like a father to him, giving him all the tools he needed to survive on the streets. Sergio did a lot of hits and robberies for Lucky and was basically his dirty hands. Since Lucky was a police officer, he couldn't go around killing people, so he would send Sergio to handle it all. Sergio trusted him with his life. And Lucky had no other place to run to apart from his young protégé.

Sergio couldn't leave him standing out there in distress, so he opened the door.

A fatigued Lucky quickly rushed inside and yelled, "Hurry up! Shut the door, Sergio, and keep the lights off!"

"Okay, but what the fuck is going on?" a now scared Sergio asked.

"How in the fuck did they know about the storage facility? Who in the fuck is snitching? Everything is over, Sergio. These muthafuckas almost killed me," Lucky said as he paced back and forth in the living room. He'd escaped a near-death situation on the rooftop of his storage facility in the Bronx.

"Just calm down and tell me what happened. You need something to drink? Who tried to kill you?"

"Man, these last few days have been hell, and it's only getting worse by the second. Every time I turn around, it seems like my life is in danger. I should have never fuckin' testified. People always want you to say the truth, but in the end, it will always backfire on you. I would be considered untrustworthy in the court of public opinion. I'm tagged with bad luck for life."

"I saw the news about those two dead cops in Cape Cod a few days ago. Once I saw one of your ex-partners' faces, I knew that was you. I can't believe you killed him at the steps of the post office building."

"Those muthafuckas were up there trying to kill my daughter and her mother. I couldn't let that happen. You know how I feel about my family."

"But what the fuck happened at the storage facility? Why did you come back to the Bronx?" a curious Sergio asked.

"I don't know. It all happened so fast. After Cape Cod, I went down to Atlanta. I dropped the family off and came back to finish what I started. When I pulled up to the storage facility and noticed police were watching the spot, like an idiot, I still pulled over and stopped."

Sergio was surprised to hear him make a mistake like that. "So why didn't you keep going?"

"I don't know that, either. I figured, if I go in, I would at least be able to get bigger guns and kill those bastards. Maybe I should have kept going. Don't matter now. I went in, and that's when all hell broke loose. Divine and Pee-Wee were inside. They already knew about the stakeout. They were watching the cops on our cameras. We just loaded up the weapons and got ready for war."

Lucky paused and thought about his good friend getting his head blown off right in front of him on the rooftop. This was the first time he had a chance to mourn his friend.

Sergio picked up on his mood swing. "What's wrong?"

"Divine, he didn't make it."

"Get the fuck out of here! Are you serious? I'm sorry to hear that. I know how close you two were." Sergio embraced him.

"Yeah, they got Divine. We went up to the roof together, and a sniper shot him right in front of me. I was able to locate the sniper, and I took him out. When I was about to go back downstairs and alert Pee-Wee, I heard more gunfire. I ran toward the edge, looked down from the roof, and there were cops all over, so I decided to bounce."

"Shit. I don't blame you. Who do you think snitched about the spot? Maybe it was one of your clients."

"I doubt it. None of the clients knew about my involvement. They all dealt with Divine directly. All they knew was that Divine had friends in the police department, but no one knew it was me. Well, at least, to my knowledge."

Lucky sipped on the tall glass of orange juice Sergio gave him and just sat back and exhaled. He couldn't get over the bad feeling of leaving Pee-Wee like that. He knew in his heart he was wrong. Lucky knew if he hadn't run, he wouldn't be sitting in Sergio's living room.

As Lucky sat there trying to clear his head, Sergio tapped him on the shoulder. "Look, Lucky, the news is talking about the shooting."

They both sat there and heard Destine Diaz's report. Lucky was shocked to see his storage facility on fire. He assumed the cops set the fire to trap and kill him. The news report freaked them out when Destine said Lucky was now in police custody, suffering severe third-degree burns and lying in a coma.

"Wow! These bastards are getting desperate. How in the fuck am I in custody? I wonder what slick move they are trying to pull now."

"They can't be serious. How can they claim you in custody when you're sitting on my damn couch? What are you going to do, Lucky?"

"The media may be hyping the story. That burned-up body laying in a coma has to be Pee-Wee. The cops may think it's me, but once the DNA comes back, they will realize I'm still out here. I need to get to Diamond down in Maryland."

"She's in Maryland? How are you going to get down there? There's too much heat on you."

"All I need is a car."

"Done. How about money? You have any on you? Do you need more?"

"I'm straight. I left Diamond with enough. But I still have to go back to that storage facility."

"Are you crazy? For what?"

"I still have a lot of money and drugs hidden in an underground fireproof safe. Once our clients see this footage about the fire, I'm sure they'll be hunting for me as well."

"Well, just let me know what you need me to do. Anything for you."

"I'm going to need you to go in the storage facility and get my money. I only trust you. We may have to wait a few days, a week or so, but we have to move fast."

"Cool. I'm ready. Just let me know. Hey, Donald, I need to speak to you."

Lucky quickly became suspicious when Sergio addressed him by his government name. He placed his left arm around Sergio, and with his right, he gripped his 9 mm parked on his hip.

"What's going on, Sergio?" Lucky asked, praying he wasn't the snitch. "You haven't called me *Donald* in a long time."

"This is going to be my last ride."

"Your last ride?" Lucky removed his hand from the gun, relieved that Sergio wasn't about to reveal anything that would cost him his life.

"I'm homesick. My family in Venezuela needs me."

"Venezuela? I thought you were Dominican." Lucky laughed. "That's cool. I understand. I'm glad you been as loyal as you have been. Once you help me get my money, I will throw in a bonus for you. I love you like the son I never had."

Sergio laughed. "You don't have to, but I'll take it."

They both started laughing.

Lucky sat back on the sofa and tried to continue to laugh, but he couldn't. Not after the night he had. He was beat. If it wasn't for Sergio's presence, he would have broken down like a little bitch. In less than a month, he had killed four people, witnessed his best friends get murdered, lost his operation, had to push away Diamond, reunited with his daughter, and almost lost his life. He was starting to feel like he had worn out his name. Maybe he wasn't so lucky, after all.

Sergio picked up on his daze. "Lucky? Yo, what's up? Snap out of it. You need to start thinking of your next move."

Lucky didn't respond to Sergio's call. He just sat there motionless. He should have listened to Tasha and waited a few days in Atlanta before coming back to New York. That was when he realized he needed to call her.

"Serg, I need a quick favor. I need you to run down the street to a pay phone and call this number. Ask for Tasha and tell her I'm alive and I'm not in custody as they claim. Tell her I will call her soon."

"No problem," Sergio replied as he headed toward his bedroom to change his clothes.

Lucky figured Tasha must have heard about him being in custody and lying in a coma. He wanted to make sure she didn't have a panic attack.

While Sergio was gone, the demons reemerged. Lucky was getting that old itch, that call of freedom. He started snooping around the apartment, looking for Sergio's coke stash. At that particular moment, he didn't care about the twelve-step program. He needed to escape reality. He was growing frustrated with all the current drama. Drugs would be the only answer to his call for help.

Lucky kept coming up with every excuse in the book, just to find a way to break his sobriety. The longer Sergio took, the closer Lucky got to meeting the devil.

About five minutes later, Lucky quickly ran to the sofa when he heard Sergio's keys.

When Sergio walked in, Lucky stood up and asked, "So what happened? What did she say?"

"I can't repeat everything she said, but she was pretty upset. She was happy to hear you were alive, but, man, she let me have it like I was you."

Lucky laughed. "I'm sorry you had to hear that. She begged me not to come up here. She sensed something was going to happen. Again, my bad, but thank you for relating the info."

"It's all good," Sergio replied.

"Hey, listen, you still party?"

Sergio paused and looked into Lucky's eyes. He couldn't believe what he'd just heard. "I'm sorry. Can you come again?"

"You heard me. Do you still party?"

"C'mon, you don't want to go back down that road. I know things have been crazy, but let's smoke some weed or something."

"Sergio, I just need one line. That's all I'm asking for, one line, partner. I have a ton of shit on my mind, and I can't function like this. I need to relax."

"I don't have any in the house, but I could have it here in thirty minutes," Sergio lied, not wanting anything to do with Lucky's self-destruction.

"Fuck it! Never mind. I don't want any visitors. I guess it's not meant to be. I'm just going to try to get some rest and wait to hear what the commissioner has to say in his press conference tomorrow. I'm going to stick around until then before I bounce down to Maryland."

"That's cool," Sergio said, relieved. "You can stay as long as you want."

Sergio was glad he was able to get Lucky to stop thinking about his old habit. He basically saved him from relapsing. He'd witnessed firsthand the way drug abuse was destroying Lucky's life. Right before the Coleman shooting, Lucky was doing badly, sniffing at least five grams a day. The more he sniffed, the more corrupt he became.

While Lucky lay on the sofa with his eyes closed, Sergio went into his room to get dressed. As he was walking out, he tapped Lucky on his shoulder.

"Hey, man, I have to step out and handle a few things and stop by my girl house."

"Okay, that's cool. I'll be right on this sofa. Around what time you are coming back?"

"Around midnight."

"Damn! That long? Well, bring me something to eat."

"Ha! Ha! Diamond is not around to cook, huh? Well, there's food in the kitchen. Don't wait up. I got this little PYT, and she can fuck for hours."

Lucky waved at him and turned back around to try and continue sleeping.

Two hours later, all he kept doing was tossing and turning back and forth on the sofa. He couldn't stop thinking about what had happened a few hours earlier. The ghosts were haunting him. He could still hear Divine's voice in his head. He kept replaying that last moment when he got shot in the head.

Lucky got off the sofa and started doing push-ups, sets of fifty. Forty minutes and three hundred push-ups later, he stopped, feeling good. Dripping with sweat, he jumped in the shower. He figured a nice, hot shower would help him relax and maybe catch some rest, which he needed.

After a half hour in the shower, Lucky came out feeling like a new man. He'd hand-washed his boxers and undershirt, so he came out with just the towel wrapped around his waist. He figured his clothes would air-dry before Sergio got home.

Lucky lay back down on the sofa and closed his eyes. After a few minutes he felt himself dozing off, but every time he was about to knock out, the sound of gunshots kept waking him up and making him jump. He couldn't shake it off.

He stood on his feet and headed toward Sergio's bedroom. He thought maybe lying on his bed would be better. He didn't want to disrespect him and sleep naked, so he looked in his closet and found a robe. When he removed the robe from the hanger, it accidentally knocked down a few shoe boxes. And that was when Lucky noticed Sergio had lied to him. He found at least a half a kilo, maybe more, hidden in his closet. He wasn't upset. He knew why Sergio had lied, and that was understandable.

Lucky quickly put everything back together and closed the closet door, acting like he didn't see the drugs. He threw the robe on and jumped on Sergio's bed.

He was upset at himself for not thinking about sleeping in Sergio's bed earlier. The bed was the most comfortable bed he'd ever lain on. So comfortable, it was impossible to have nightmares. As he lay there, he started thinking about Tamika and her beautiful smile. He kept rewinding her voice in his head, to help him relax. Before he knew it, he was passed out cold and snoring like an old, fat guy.

About a good four to six hours later, around eight o'clock, Lucky woke up. He couldn't believe he had slept for that long.

Feeling hungry, he walked to the kitchen and made himself a sandwich.

As he sat at the table, eating, he thought about Diamond, the love of his life. He was hoping he didn't make a mistake by letting her move down to Maryland on her own. He was happy he was going to see her again. Just then, Tasha, his baby mother, popped up in his thoughts.

It was all downhill after that. His happy thoughts didn't last long. He wanted to return home and reunite with his baby girl and live a normal life. The pressure was on, and he felt like he was hauling a ton with every step he took.

Lucky thought about the coke. He tried to fight the thoughts away. He thought about his twelve-step program. He tried to recite the steps in his head, but all he could think about was white lines and the skies. He tried to remember the motivational speeches his sponsor had preached to him, but he couldn't. Addiction was winning the battle.

Lucky was backed into a corner. It was easy for him to stay sober when he wasn't around the drug. He sat down on the sofa, thinking about the Ziploc filled with raw, uncut coca. He quickly stood back up and started walking to the kitchen. Then he made a sharp right down the hallway and entered Sergio's room.

As he reached for the closet door to hit the stash, out of nowhere his daughter, Tamika, popped in his head. He jumped back and landed on Sergio's bed. "What the fuck am I doing?" he asked himself.

As he sat on the bed, flashes of his daughter's innocent face kept running through his mind. He couldn't relapse, for her sake. He walked out of Sergio's room and sat on the sofa and tried to watch a movie.

It didn't take long for thoughts about his partner's death to resurface. Divine was his childhood friend and business partner. He couldn't accept his death, and he blamed only himself. A lot of people were dying around him, and it was fucking with his head. For a second, Lucky thought he was going crazy. He stood up and said, "Man, fuck this!" He walked back into Sergio's closet, grabbed a Ziploc filled with cocaine, and headed back to the kitchen table.

He reached in the Ziploc, grabbed a handful of coke, and threw it on the glass tabletop. He stared at it for at least twenty minutes, fighting the demon within. His body wanted to do it, but his mind was putting up a good fight, but not for long.

Lucky dropped his face in the cocaine like Tony Montana in *Scarface*, sniffing and eating it like a savage. After a few seconds of nonstop action, he leaned his head back and let the high take him over.

Because Lucky had been clean for so long, his body didn't know how to react. He grabbed his head in hopes that it would make the room stop spinning. When he leaned forward, he noticed blood dripping from his nose. He tried to get up and quickly fell back down. He couldn't walk a straight line. The floor felt like an escalator.

He stumbled his way back to the bathroom, knocking lamps over and pictures off Sergio's nightstand. When he reached the bathroom and looked in the mirror, he got spooked. Instead of seeing his reflection, all he saw was blood. That was when he punched the mirror, shattering it instantly.

With blood pouring from his knuckles, Lucky began yelling out loud, "C'mon, muthafucka! C'mon!" He was throwing wild punches into the air. He ran out of the bathroom and closed the door behind him, thinking he was locking the demons in the bathroom.

Instead of him just lying back down on the sofa, he went back to the kitchen table and jammed another mountain of cocaine up his nose. He didn't care about the blood dripping down his nose and lips. His main concern was what was going up his nose. He paused to catch his breath and slapped his body back down on the sofa. He was wasted, incoherent.

Sergio's beautiful white robe was now filled with bloodstains from both Lucky's nose and fist. Lucky's only hope was for Sergio to walk in and save his life. Unknown to Lucky, though, Sergio's girlfriend wasn't letting him go until the morning. He was going to have to ride the nightmare out alone, the whole night.

As he lay on the sofa, trying to let his new high sink in, all he thought about was bullets and dead bodies. He thought about running in a police station and killing everyone. He jumped up and began laughing out loud. "I'm going to get my revenge!" He closed the bloody robe, threw on his shoes, grabbed his rifle, and left.

It was going on almost midnight when Lucky left, wearing nothing but his shoes and a robe. There was no way he would make it far without someone calling 9-1-1 and reporting a maniac running naked, armed with a rifle. He was really testing his luck with that stunt.

The next morning, around eleven o'clock, Sergio walked in his front door and realized something was off when he didn't see Lucky on his sofa. He reached for his gun and slowly started walking around his own house like a burglar. He noticed blood on the floor that led to his bedroom. When he looked in his kitchen, he saw the drugs on his table. He put his gun away, figuring Lucky had found his stash, but he couldn't understand why there was blood everywhere.

He walked into his bedroom calling out, "Lucky? Lucky, you back here, man? Please don't tell me you did what I think you did."

Sergio was shocked to see his room ransacked and Lucky missing. He went to check the bathroom, where he saw the bloody, broken mirror. He knew something was wrong. He ran out his front door and went outside to look for Lucky.

After a good twenty-minute search and coming up empty, Sergio returned home in hopes that Lucky was waiting for him. When he made it back to his apartment and saw no sign of Lucky, he thought the worst.

He looked at his watch and noticed it was going on noon, so he turned his TV on. He didn't want to miss the commissioner's press conference. As he sat there listening to one of the city's most corrupt officials, the unexpected happened. The commissioner was assassinated in the middle of his speech.

Sergio quickly jumped back and placed his right hand over his mouth. He thought maybe he was dreaming because what he'd just witnessed only happened in the movies. He turned the TV off and started walking back and forth in his living room, repeating to himself, "Lucky, where are you?" Sergio's fear was that Lucky was the triggerman.

About five minutes went by and Sergio was still pacing back and forth in his living room. He was puzzled and didn't know what to think. Was Lucky capable of pulling off such a hit?

An hour went by, and still no sign of Lucky. Sergio spent about half an hour cleaning up the mess Lucky left behind. He ran to the front door when he heard someone knocking, and looked through the peephole, hoping it was Lucky, but it was Roc, one of the neighborhood kids.

He opened the door. "What's good, Roc? Remember, I don't sell weed anymore."

"Man, fuck da bud. I went up to da roof to roll one an' celebrate the death of da top pig, and I found this big-ass rifle up there. Can I hide it in here? Momdukes be flippin'."

"Let me see that gun." Sergio quickly noticed it was the same rifle Lucky had had with him. "Where you said you found this gun at?"

"On the roof. Don't even try to say dis gat is yours. I found it first, son."

"Nigga, shut up!" Sergio almost bitch-slapped Roc. He thought maybe he had something to do with Lucky's disappearance. "This gun belongs to my boy. Show me where you found it at."

When they reached the roof, Roc pointed to where he'd found it. "Right dere, fam. It was right dere."

"Okay, you could leave now."

"What about my—"

"Roc, the fuckin' gun is not yours. Bounce!" He waited as Roc took his time to leave.

Roc wanted to say something slick back but knew that even though Sergio looked like a slouch, he was far from one.

Once Roc left, Sergio began looking around on the roof. The large roof had a tall wall that hid the boiler and water tank.

To his surprise, he found Lucky in a sitting position, leaning back on the water tank. Sergio couldn't believe his eyes. Lucky was naked and using a bloody robe as his sheet. Sergio thought he was unconscious. He ran up to him and got on his knees and shook him awake.

After a few shakes, Lucky came to it. His eyes were open, but he was still a bit woozy.

"Lucky, c'mon, wake up. Let's go back in my apartment," Sergio said as he helped him off the floor.

When they finally made it back to the apartment, Sergio locked his door and windows. He was scared to death.

Lucky was still out of it, but slowly getting back to normal. "What's going on, Sergio? What time is it? The commissioner should be coming on soon with his speech."

"Are you serious? You really don't know what happened?" Sergio asked in shock.

"Seriously. I mean, I don't know how I passed out on the roof. I mean, I know how, but I don't know what the fuck you are talking about," a confused Lucky answered.

Sergio turned his TV on and turned the volume up as high as he could.

Lucky turned toward the TV, and within seconds, he was in disbelief. "Tell me I didn't see what I just saw. Did someone just assassinate Commissioner Fratt?"

"Someone? You sure it wasn't you?"

"It wasn't me, Sergio. I was on the roof, passed out. I don't remember shit. That couldn't have been me."

"It doesn't matter now. They are going to pin this on you, regardless. You exposed corruption in the entire city and cost them millions in lawsuits. They will either kill you or lock you away for life. We need to get you down to Maryland as soon as possible."

"Sergio, you have to believe me."

"Lucky, I don't know what to believe. You wasn't here when I came home. You left the apartment, coked out of your mind. You don't even remember what happened yourself, not to mention you up in my place in the process."

"I'm sorry," Lucky shot back. He refocused on the issue at hand. "Sergio, how in the fuck I'm going to get out of the city? All the tolls and bridges will be locked down."

"I have an idea."

"What's good, Sergio? Give me something good."

"Dress up like a woman. I have a costume right here. Don't ask how or why I have it. What do you think?"

"Ha! I like it. Let's do it. I want to leave right now, anyway. This will be perfect."

Lucky wasn't in a position to question his manhood at that moment. Asking him to dress up like a woman a few weeks ago would have gotten Sergio a black eye. He actually thought it was a brilliant idea. He jumped in the shower and got dressed.

Sergio helped him with the makeup, which made Lucky feel uncomfortable.

"Hey, man, you a fag?"

"C'mon, you know me, Lucky. Relax. You know I'm not gay."

"Then you need to explain the costume," Lucky said, backing away from him.

"You think I'm fuckin' gay? Hell no! While you been away in rehab and hiding, I started my own enterprise. I was hired to do a few jobs, and that costume came in handy."

Lucky looked at him up and down. He couldn't do anything but believe Sergio was telling the truth. "My bad. I still had to ask and be sure." He continued to let Sergio apply makeup on him and fix his wig.

Twenty minutes later, Sergio had Lucky looking like a believable woman. He gave him ten thousand dollars, the keys to the car, and a cell phone.

"Call me as soon as you touch Maryland and get with Diamond. I'll figure out a way to get in the storage facility."

"A'ight, cool, but don't go in the storage without speaking to me first. Good looking out for coming through, kid."

"You are like a father to me. Hurry up. Get out of here and be safe."

They embraced each other for a few seconds, both ready to cry, but they held their emotions. They knew it might be the last time they would ever see each other.

"Hey, before I leave, I'm sorry for going through your shit and messing up the crib."

"Don't worry about it."

Lucky grabbed a small black bag and went out the door. He jumped in the car and got on the Cross Bronx Expressway, headed toward the George Washington Bridge. The expressway was stop and go, so it took Lucky a little over an hour to get close to the bridge.

As he got closer, he realized what was causing the delay—checkpoints on every lane. Lucky even noticed dogs going into people's backseats and trunks. *Shit! The dogs would sniff the guns, for sure.*

As Lucky pulled up, he lowered his window and acted dumbfounded, his heart pounding harder in his chest. He didn't want to mess up his rehearsed female voice. "Hello. OMG, what's going on? Did we just have another terror attack?"

"No, miss lady. The commissioner was shot today, and we're looking for the suspect."

"Well, as you can see, I'm traveling alone on my way to visit my mother in New Jersey. Go ahead and search the car."

"I already see you're alone, and I don't need to search the inside of your car, but please pop the trunk, let me look inside, and then you are good to go."

As soon as the officer said "Pop the trunk," Lucky thought about hitting the gas, but it sounded like the cop just wanted to take a peep inside. He hit the button, and the trunk opened automatically.

"Thank you for your kindness, ma'am." As the officer walked toward the back of the car, he called for his partner to bring the dog.

Lucky's heart dropped when the other officer ran over with the dog.

After the two cops spoke for a few seconds, one of them walked back over to the car. "Okay, ma'am, my partner doesn't see the need to have the dog sniff your car. You're free to go."

Lucky thanked the officer and drove off.

Chapter Eighteen

Chaos in the Streets of New York

About an hour after the commissioner was assassinated in front of hundreds of reporters and millions watching live on TV, New Yorkers panicked and began rioting. They didn't know if Lucky was dead or alive, and didn't think it was him.

Many were running and yelling, "We are under attack!"

It was hard for New Yorkers to ever forget 9/11, many still feeling like al-Qaeda would attack again. And the heavy police presence and helicopters didn't help at all, either.

All across the five boroughs, the looters were outnumbering the law. In Brooklyn, there were reports that five officers had been shot, one fatally.

The mayor's office was chaotic, with every phone line ringing. Ralph Gulliano was on the phone with the secretary of defense, Hilda Canton. He was begging for the National Guard to step in and help with the riot. New York was sinking at a fast pace and needed national help.

"We need help down here," an out-of-breath Ralph said. "We have the entire city running wild, and five police officers already have been shot."

"Okay, Mayor, calm down. The president has agreed, and help is on the way. We're dispatching troops from Fort Hamilton now, and we have more coming from Fort Dix, New Jersey. You do your best until help arrives. General Edgar Thomas will contact you."

"Thank you, and please thank the president for me."

"You can thank him yourself. He will be in New York tomorrow to debrief you."

Ralph hung up the phone. "Fuck me!" he yelled out loud. He was happy to hear about the help but worried about the president's visit. The mayor went in his boardroom, where he met with lead detectives from all divisions across all five boroughs. When he entered the room, he was quickly attacked with questions.

"Who killed the commissioner?"

"What are we all doing here?"

"Calm down, everyone. Right now, our prime suspect is Lucky, but we still don't have any concrete evidence that he pulled the trigger. At first we thought we'd captured him and he was in a coma. This backstabber is still on the lam, and he's our suspect until further notice. We will hold a press conference and blame it on him until we hear otherwise. I need everyone in this room to work around the clock and come up with leads. I need to know what kind of weapon was used to kill Brandon. I just got word military help is on the way, and the president will be here tomorrow. I need some fucking leads on the gun and Lucky's whereabouts before the big guy gets here. Now please, everyone, stop listening and sitting on your ass. Hit those streets and get some answers. I have a riot on my hands, and we need to stop it ASAP."

After they all left the boardroom, the mayor stood in there for about another minute before he left. He wanted to catch his breath and pray to God he could stop the riot before the president arrived.

He headed downstairs to meet with his team of secret agents and the SWAT team. They gave him a bulletproof vest as he entered a military Humvee. He wanted to drive around and see with his own eyes what was going on. He was disappointed to see New Yorkers destroying the city.

Most businesses, some in flames, had their front windows busted in. Every car parked in the street was destroyed, some with pipe bombs. At that particular moment, he felt ashamed to be called a mayor.

After about three hours of driving, the mayor got the call that General Edgar Thomas was already in the city. They agreed to meet on Thirtieth Street and Eleventh Avenue.

The general arrived by helicopter. The mayor was surprised at the quick response, but he was happy. He needed the experienced personnel. He didn't have any experience in handling a riot.

When the mayor came out of the Humvee to greet the general, he was shut down.

"How are you doing, General? I'm Mayor—"

"I know who you are. You're the asshole who can't run his city quietly! I'm in New Jersey, training the finest men for combat before they deploy to Iraq. I don't want to be here, but since I am, let's get straight to the point. I have three thousand soldiers on their way, and we don't have time to waste."

"So you know my police commissioner was assassinated, and now the city has gone mad and they are running wild in the streets?"

"Don't worry. I will restore order. My men should be here shortly. Please alert your police department to arm their men with rubber bullets and Tasers. When we hit the streets, we are sweeping through them, and we are hitting every idiot who doesn't obey. Make sure the media is out there with us. Once word gets out we are shooting everyone with rubber bullets, we should have order restored by the morning."

The mayor waited a few seconds to respond. He wanted to make sure he understood the general clearly.

"Let me get this right. You want to run through my city with three thousand troops shooting rubber bullets?"

"Affirmative. Any problems, take it up with the president tomorrow."

They all entered the Humvee and headed back down to One Police Plaza to regroup and strategize on a plan to regain control of the city. When they arrived, the governor joined the team, and they worked rigorously.

After reviewing the little bit of facts they had, they decided to divide the troops up. They sent nine hundred troops each to Brooklyn, the Bronx, and Harlem, two hundred and fifty to Queens, and fifty to Staten Island. Queens and Staten Island were the only two boroughs where the disturbance was at a minimum and not a major threat.

While the soldiers were deploying to different boroughs, the mayor grabbed the governor's arm and pulled him to the side. "Are you sure this is the right decision? We're about to hit the streets and just start shooting people. Also, do we need those water cannon tanks?"

"They are only rubber bullets. We don't have a choice," the governor fired back.

"I still think it's the wrong move. I pray God helps us all," the mayor said.

They walked back toward the general and entered one of the many water cannon tanks.

Both the mayor and governor had concerned looks on their faces. Hearing the loud screams of the people made them both think they might be making a mistake.

The general picked up on their weakness and tried to lift their spirits. "I don't know why the long faces, gentlemen. In a few hours you will have control of the streets again."

"I just hope those rubber bullets don't kill anyone."

"Don't worry. They won't. Get ya tail out ya asses!"

They didn't respond to the general's remarks, as they kept looking out the window in disbelief. When they reached Delancey Street, it was a mess, with most of the stores in flames or broken into. And people were running out of stores with stolen merchandise.

At first the rowdy crowd was hesitant to obey the military warning to stop rioting and return home, but once the rubber bullets started flying, they all scatted like roaches. As hard as it was for the mayor and governor to admit, the general's plan looked like it was working.

Within three hours they were able to mobilize most of downtown Manhattan, but Times Square was a different story. The beautiful lights were now dimmed, and the place was in flames, with thousands of people running around, destroying everything in sight.

"General, when are we going to use these damn water cannons?" the mayor yelled.

"You must have read my mind. I'm giving the order now." The general looked at the mayor and grinned slightly. He finally grew balls, he thought.

As the two hundred and fifty pounds of pressured water was fired into the crowd, folks dropped to the ground like flies. The mayor's worries were gone as he saw the crowd running away in fear. The mayor asked the general for an update on the troops in the other boroughs.

Five minutes later, the general told the mayor, "Well, the troops in Harlem are experiencing difficulties. The urban community is fighting back with real bullets, and a few soldiers were injured, but none fatally. As far as Brooklyn, they're still experiencing major issues as well. Three more police officers have been killed, over a dozen soldiers were shot, and three were burned severely. We have about ten civilians confirmed dead."

"What the fuck! How did that happen?" the mayor asked.

"Listen, I can't provide details. I'm just giving you an update. These civilians are shooting at my troops."

"I thought we were only using rubber bullets. How did the civilians get killed?"

"Mayor, c'mon, our troopers are discharging rubber bullets, but since civilians are using live ammo, we have to return fire as well. But, according to my intel, not all fatalities were caused by gunfire. You should consider most of these civilians lucky."

"Lucky? Please, General, don't you ever say that word in my presence."

As the general was about to respond, the governor jumped in. "General, the guy possibly responsible for the assassination of the commissioner goes by the name of Lucky. He is also responsible for starting this riot."

"I understand. Well, when all this is over, if you need my assistance in capturing this Lucky character, just give me a call. Anyway, let's get back to work. That way we can head up to Harlem as soon as possible and help the other troops."

Lucky had caught the city by surprise, and so far he was winning and getting away with everything.

As they headed up to Harlem, the mayor started thinking about Lucky. He couldn't help it. He was actually thinking like a man who had been through a twenty-round fight with Mike Tyson. He was drained and couldn't come up with any new strategies to capture him. He decided he was going to follow up on the general's offer to help catch Lucky. He knew the longer they took in restoring the peace, the farther away Lucky was getting. He wanted to end this before the morning. That way he could find out who killed his commissioner.

When they arrived in Harlem, they saw that the situation was under control. There were still a few idiots running around, but the threat had been eliminated. It didn't take the Harlem residents long to realize they weren't going to beat the army.

The mayor called Richard on his cell phone. "Hey, where do we stand with Lucky's apprehension?"

"Nothing yet. We shut down all the bridges and tunnels. No one can come in or out, and we are searching every suspicious car."

"At what time did you shut everything down?"

"Right after the soldiers came in. Why?"

"Maybe he slipped through before the shutdown."

"That's not possible. Right after the assassination, we were already checking every car, bus, and truck before the shutdown."

"If he's still in New York, his ass is mine. Meet me back at One Police Plaza."

"Okay. You sound like everything is under control. Did the general's plan work?"

"Yes, ninety percent of the riot has been stopped. We had a few civilian casualties and more police officers that were shot and killed."

After the mayor hung up the phone, he turned around and shook hands with the general. He'd doubted him at first, but his plan worked. The mayor and the governor jumped out of the tank and got in a waiting black Suburban. They wanted to get back to work on capturing Lucky as quickly as possible.

On their way downtown, the governor asked, "Do you really think Lucky is capable of pulling off a stunt like that?"

"Yes, I do. After what took place at the storage facility, I'm sure he knows we are gunning for him. He just wanted to strike first. I'm not surprised at all."

The rest of the fifteen-minute drive downtown was silent as both men were in their own world, thinking about their next move. The mayor was worried about the president's visit, and meanwhile the governor was going through the list of candidates to replace the mayor.

***

Lucky was frustrated and puzzled. Because of traffic, it took him seven hours to get to Maryland, when it should have taken only three to four. What really had him stressed was the fact that he was dressed like a woman, making the whole ride uncomfortable.

Lucky was ready for a nice shower and a home-cooked meal when he pulled up to the house in Maryland. But he didn't see Diamond's car, and the house looked like it was abandoned.

Automatically, he knew something was wrong. He was going to keep driving, but then he remembered he was dressed up like a woman. He parked and got out of the car. Folks in the neighborhood would think he was just looking at the house with plans of buying it.

He walked up to the house, and his suspicion was on point. Diamond had never made it to the house.

He walked back to his car and sat there for a few minutes to think about his next move. He was worried for Diamond. He wondered what had happened to her, if was she still alive. He leaned his head back and closed his eyes, and the tears almost dropped down his cheek. Lucky didn't know where to turn. He needed to check into a hotel, but he couldn't use his ID.

He drove down Robert Crain Highway and stopped at the first gas station. He went in the bathroom, which to his luck was coed. He ripped off the costume and washed the makeup off his face. When he was done, he asked the gas attendant for the nearest mall.

He grabbed his black bag after parking the car because he didn't intend to use the car again.

Five minutes later, Lucky was walking through Marley Station Mall in Glen Burnie, walking around looking for a female victim, planning to get her drunk so she could use her ID for a hotel room.

After a ten-minute walk, he found his victim. He saw two girls walking out of Victoria's Secret. The fat, ugly girl was holding a large bag, and the pretty, petite girl was holding a small bag. Lucky thought it should have been the other way around because big girls shouldn't shop in Victoria's Secret.

He approached the two girls. "Excuse me, sweet ladies." He turned to the pretty girl. "Can I ask why you are only holding a little bitty bag?"

The two girls were a bit annoyed by Lucky's interruption, but when they got a good look at him and they saw his biceps, they both were mesmerized.

"I didn't see anything I liked in there."

"What's your name, love?"

"My name is Janay, and that's my friend Peaches. What's your name?"

"My name is Donald. Tell your friend Peaches you will be right back."

"Peaches rolls with me everywhere," Janay said.

"Listen, baby girl, I just want to go back in Victoria's Secret and pick out a few things I would love to see you in. Don't worry about the price. I got it."

Janay went silent. She didn't know what to say. No man had ever approached her the way Lucky just did. Plus, she wasn't honest about why she was only holding a small bag. She just didn't have the funds.

Peaches tapped her on the arm. "You better go on with that man, girl. I will see you later. Call me."

After Janay and Lucky walked in Victoria's Secret, they were quickly told they had about thirty minutes until closing time.

"Listen, baby girl, go grab whatever you want. My favorite color is red."

"Is that right? I love red, too. I see we have some things in common."

"That's why I approached you. How about after we shop, we go get a few drinks and find out how much in common we have?"

She licked her lips. "Sounds like a plan."

Lucky knew he had her from the way she was looking him up and down. After Janay picked up a few outfits, perfumes, and body mist, she was ready to go.

"That's all you want, baby? We still have about ten more minutes before they close."

"I'm good. I'm ready for some drinks, though."

As they left the store, Lucky put his hands around her and asked, "Where can we eat and drink around here?"

"Where you from? I know you not from Maryland. You have a New York accent."

Lucky laughed. "Is it that obvious?"

"Yes, it is, but I love it. It's a turn-on," a flirty Janay said.

"Let's hurry up and get these drinks in our system. That way you could tell me what else turns you on."

They both looked at each other seductively, like they were ready to rip each other's clothes off.

Janay thought quickly and said, "I'm parked by the front. Where is your car?"

"Let's go in your car, sweetie. My brother dropped me off while he handled his business. I was shopping for an outfit. He's taking me out to a club."

"Oh, word? What club?"

"I think it's called Love. It's in D.C."

"Yeah, I've been there. You will love it."

"I heard. I didn't even find an outfit. I'll just wear something I brought with me. I was going to call a cab, until I seen your pretty face."

"Awww, so sweet. I'm assuming a cab is a taxi, right?"

"What do y'all call them out here? Just *taxi?*"

"We just call them *taxi*. In Baltimore they call them *hacks*."

"Hacks? I'm not going to ask. Anyway, we're in your town, so you pick the spot where we are going."

"In Maryland, we are known for our crabs. Do you eat crabs?"

"Yeah, I do. I love seafood."

As they walked to Janay's car, Lucky was surprised to see she was pushing a red 2005 Ford F-150.

"Damn, girl! I would have never thought you was pushing a truck. You look more like a Honda Civic type of girl."

They both laughed as they got in the truck and made their way out of the parking lot, headed to Romano's, an Italian restaurant known for their crab cakes and mixed drinks.

When they arrived, they had to wait about twenty minutes to get seated. Lucky didn't want to sit by the bar because of the TVs nearby. He didn't want to risk his face appearing on the screen. They waited by the front door and took the chance to get to know each other.

"Tell me about you," Lucky said as he got close to Janay. He had to work fast to get her to a hotel.

"Well, I'm single, and I work full-time, no kids, and I like to have fun. How about you, daddy? What do you do?"

"I'm a street dude, and I do street things to survive."

"I kind of figured that, the way you were balling at the mall. I thought you were either a street hustler or a ballplayer, but your face doesn't look familiar, so I knew you must have been a street hustler."

They both started laughing again.

Lucky also learned something new about Janay. She was a gold digger.

They were finally called to be seated, and right off the bat, Lucky ordered two double shots of Hennessy and two Long Island iced teas.

"How you know I like Henny?" she asked, a smirk on her face.

"Reading a person is a gift of mine, but if you would like something else, that would be fine, too."

"Henny is fine, but Long Islands I rarely drink because they get me too horny."

"Oh, word? Then I should cancel the Henny and tell the waiter to keep the Long Islands coming."

Janay started laughing, but Lucky was dead serious.

About an hour and eight drinks later, Lucky and Janay were all over each other like a married couple. They were both drunk, so they were ready to fuck each other's brains out.

Lucky ordered two more shots of Henny and whispered in Janay's ear, "After we finish these two last drinks, let's get out of here. I'm ready to taste you."

"I thought you would never ask," Janay replied, squeezing his big biceps.

"Where is the nearest hotel?"

"Hotel? We could just go to my house," she replied while kissing him.

"I think a hotel would be better. I would feel more comfortable. I don't want any of your old boyfriends popping up."

"You're silly, but there's a Holiday Inn right down Ritchie Highway."

"Let's go then."

They both got up after finishing their drinks and headed back to Janay's truck. It took only about five minutes to reach the hotel. When they reached the front, Lucky gave her two hundred dollars and told her to book a suite.

When they got in the room, it was on like game time as soon as they entered. Lucky jumped on her and started ripping her clothes off. At first he'd just wanted to use her for her ID and to book a room, but after spending time with her, he realized he really wanted to fuck her. He didn't even give her time to change into the red Vicky Secret she picked out. They were too drunk to remember it. They just wanted to have hot, steamy sex.

After about two hours of licking, sucking, slapping, fucking, hair pulling, and choking, Janay lay on the bed like a beaten slave. Lucky had rocked her world and put her ass to sleep.

That was all Lucky was waiting for. He wanted to go downstairs and log on to the Internet. He'd been in the dark on what was going on in New York since he'd left. Janay had done exactly what he wanted her to do—get his mind off things—but now he needed to get back on point.

He walked up to the counter in the lobby, where a young lady sat half asleep. He told her his room number and asked to pay for another night. He knew the sleepy worker wouldn't ask for ID.

He then logged on to the Internet and couldn't believe his eyes. The pictures alone told the story, but Lucky still decided to click on one of the reports. He was shocked to read about the military sweeping through the streets, using rubber bullets and water cannons. He also read that thousands were hospitalized and arrested. Even a few police officers and civilians were killed. Though everything he read was disturbing, he was pleased to read that the mayor had control of at least 90 percent of the city.

Lucky was no innocent angel. He knew that. But some of the articles he read were hurtful. The media kept hinting that he was responsible for the assassination and igniting a riot.

Lucky was pissed at himself for sniffing all that coke and passing out. He hated the fact that he couldn't remember what happened that night. He wanted to believe he didn't pull the trigger, even though he knew he was capable of pulling it off.

After spending about thirty minutes browsing the Net, he went back up to the room and saw Janay sitting up on the bed, looking sad.

"What's wrong, baby girl?"

"Nothing now," she replied, her whole mood switching and a smile on her face.

"You thought I left, right? What kind of dudes you fuck with out here? I went to use the Internet."

"I'm not going to lie. I thought you bounced on me. But what kind of thug logs on to the Internet?"

"An organized thug, baby."

Lucky jumped back in the bed, and they went for a quick round two.

Janay had to be at work early, and it was going on four in the morning. Around four-thirty, she decided it was time to bounce. "Daddy, I have to leave. I have to be at work in, like, four hours. When can I see you again?"

"I'll be back real soon. I got your number. I will keep in touch."

"Sounds like a plan. I'll call you when I get my lunch break."

They kissed for five more minutes, Janay jerking him off all the while. She got his dick rock hard again and decided to give him a quick blow. She really sucked the shit out his dick. She wanted to make sure all he thought about was her and her skills.

After a long ten minutes of vacuum service, Lucky came all in her mouth, and Janay didn't miss a beat. She kept sucking until the last drop of cum was in her mouth and down her throat, swallowing like a veteran.

Lucky walked her to the door. He slapped her on her ass and said, "Baby girl, I will be thinking about you all day."

After Janay left, Lucky turned on the TV and browsed through the news channels. To his surprise, his face was all over the screen, along with the riots. It almost felt like he was still in New York, with all the coverage he was receiving. That made him nervous because he'd clearly shown his face when he walked through the mall and when he was eating at the restaurant. He figured he would just stay in the hotel room for his entire stay. Meanwhile, he would have to figure out a way to reach Tasha down in Atlanta. He was now regretting that he'd tossed the woman's costume at the gas station.

While he was lying on the bed, he thought about Diamond and wondered where the hell she was at. It didn't make sense. Why would she run away?

Lucky thought about numerous scenarios. He thought she either went back to Hunts Point in the Bronx to look for her pimp or she went back home. Both scenarios seemed dumb, but that old saying came to his head. *You could never turn a ho into a housewife*. Lucky laughed out loud and said, "Especially not a recovering hooker. They're liable to make you lose everything and make you fall flat on your face."

Lucky quickly got serious. He jumped off the bed, dropped down to his knees, spread his arms like wings, and began to ask, "Why?"

He asked the question a few more times and then started insulting himself. "How can you be so stupid? You dumb, pussy-whipped bastard!"

It finally hit him that Diamond had set him up. He started punching the walls until his fists began to bleed again. The wounds from breaking Sergio's mirror were still fresh, so blood started flowing rather quickly. Lucky was mad at himself because it took him so long to realize where the knife in his back came from.

He calmly sat on the edge of the bed and rubbed his head. The feeling was almost like the day when his mother died in that horrible car accident. Diamond meant everything to him. He did lie and deceive her, but he would have never double-crossed her. What she did was unforgivable. She obviously wanted him dead and out of the picture.

Lucky was more concerned about her motives and why she fucked him. He felt like he'd been played by his own student.

With Captain Tuna and Speedy still in jail, and a dead commissioner, Lucky had a new mouse to chase. Diamond became his number one target. He still couldn't get over the way she'd crossed him. *You got me, bitch, but please don't let me find you. Please don't,* he thought to himself.

As the morning went on, he kept watching TV, trying to get things off his head, but he couldn't. Around nine in the morning he decided to finally try and get some sleep. He made it a point to stay away from watching the news channels, so he watched ESPN. He didn't want to hear anything else about the riots or the assassination. By nine-thirty, he was knocked out cold.

Chapter Nineteen

The Day after the Riots

By ten in the morning, there were numerous news reports hitting all the TV outlets, newspapers, and the Internet, basically still reporting about the aftermath. Everyone was giving the mayor praise for how quickly he defused the riot and got things back in order. At first, city officials were a bit skeptical, especially with the military enforcement and their shoot-first strategy. They thought there were going to be a lot more casualties. Regardless, it was going to cost the city millions of dollars to repair the damage caused by the riot.

A lot of hardworking folks lost their lifelong dreams right before their eyes. It was sad to see so many businesses destroyed. New Yorkers were so upset and caught up in the drama, they didn't realize they were destroying the same stores where they shopped for groceries and household needs. The same stores they would go into with their children and buy school clothes and medicines. The same restaurants they would have family dinner nights at. All of those community stores where you were known by your first name when you entered were the first to be destroyed.

No one ran up in a courthouse and tore that place up, or in a police station and slapped a few police officers for their corrupt behavior, two places where the major corruption was taking place. New Yorkers felt the need to destroy their own communities. Now, instead of just walking down the streets for some eggs and bread, they had to walk for miles in search of a grocery store that was open. New Yorkers started to feel like fools.

And now, instead of supporting Lucky, the whispers around the city were loud and clear. Lucky was to blame for everything.

Just then Destine Diaz's report was about to come on with the latest update.

"Good morning, New York. Today I have to be honest. I really don't feel too proud to be a New Yorker. My drive to work this morning was heartbreaking. Tears were flowing as I was driving. I couldn't believe my eyes. I'm still not over the fact that our police commissioner was assassinated during live taping.

"I know we all want to believe Lucky is responsible for the assassination, but we have not yet heard an official statement from the NYPD. I also want to salute our great mayor and governor for their courage. They actually were out in the streets of New York helping our military troops cease the riot. I also want to thank the many New Yorkers who volunteered their time to help clean the streets this morning. We have a long road ahead of us, and the only way to recover from this tragedy is by working as a whole. We need to show the rest of the world that New York always has been and always will be one of the greatest cities in the world.

"The president is in town, and he's meeting with both the mayor and the governor. I'm sure they will come up with a formula that will rapidly help us recover. There will be a private press conference scheduled right after the meeting with the president. Only two cameras will be allowed to record and broadcast, no reporters. One of those cameras will be one of ours. Once we have a confirmed time, we will broadcast the press conference. Until then, please let's refocus our attention on rebuilding. Destine Diaz, Channel Five, broadcasting live from One Police Plaza."

Most of the city agreed with Destine's statement about rebuilding its image. City officials had major issues on their hands. They were still dealing with the aftermath of the commissioner's assassination, they still had two of their own locked in Central Booking, facing numerous felonies, Lucky was still unaccounted for, and now he had become one of the fiercest sought-after felons in New York's history.

The government and police department, still embarrassed after they realized Lucky was never in a coma, wanted to capture him in the worst way. Lucky's name was being mentioned in the same breath as bin Laden's.

Lucky's testimony had helped the prosecution build a strong case against the city and police department, and the cops on trial were going to get charged with Coleman's death, destroying the city's good image.

Those five envelopes Lucky had mailed out to the press and lawyers were going to cost the city more millions. The city was facing two major lawsuits for the unlawful arrest and incarceration from the Rell Davis and Juan "Pito" Medina case. The scandal with Cardinal Joseph King III was causing major embarrassment for the church community. New York went from the city of big dreams to one big nightmare.

The recovery process looked like it was going to take years. But then something happened. About thirty minutes after Destine's report, New Yorkers made it their business to speed up the process, and thousands of volunteers hit the streets and began cleaning up, with people of different ethnic backgrounds pitching in—blue-collar workers, Wall Street stockbrokers, and even street-corner hustlers.

While the city was hard at work, Mayor Ralph Gulliano was a nervous wreck because he was going to have his one-on-one with the president in ten minutes. After their initial meeting, he would allow the governor to come in while they strategized on their next move, which was now a federal matter.

When it finally came time to meet President Bernard Osama, the mayor almost pissed his pants. First, the Secret Service came in his office and looked around for about fifteen minutes, making sure there were no hidden cameras.

The president walked in with his million-dollar smile. "How are you doing, Mayor Gulliano?" He extended his hand to greet the mayor.

"I'm doing okay, I guess. It's an honor to be speaking to you, sir," the mayor said as he shook his hand, smiling and acting like a little groupie. "Please, sit down, Mr. President. Can I get you some tea, sir?"

"No, thanks. Let's get down to business. I don't have time to waste."

"Where do you want me to begin? Because, if you want to hear the story from the beginning, it's going to take some time," the mayor said in fear, hoping he didn't offend the president.

"You're right. Just tell me what I need to know and what else you need. I've been informed the military support was a success. What leads do we have on this former cop you guys keep calling Lucky? Do we have facts he actually pulled the trigger yesterday?"

"You are correct, Mr. President. The military presence helped out tremendously. We were able to stop the riot and gain control. Right now, we have no leads on who killed the commissioner, and Lucky hasn't been seen since we raided his storage facility a few days ago."

"Wait a minute. Are you saying no leads and no Lucky?"

"That is correct, sir."

"No wonder the city of New York lost its morals and self-dignity. The people don't feel comfortable following a government with no sense of direction. I'm embarrassed to even be sitting here having this conversation. I'm still trying to figure out a way to stop the war in Iraq and bring our troops home. I don't have the time or the manpower to spare to help fix your problems. Are we clear?" The president asked just to make sure the mayor was paying attention.

"Yes, we are clear, sir," the mayor quickly responded.

"I know the governor is working closely with my office in providing federal help, but I'm going to bring in two agents, ex-Navy SEAL guys, from Washington D.C. They will catch Lucky for you. They are arriving as we speak. I expect my guys to be brought up to speed on everything. With regards to rebuilding New York, don't worry about the cost. FEMA will take care of it. We won't drop the ball like we did in New Orleans. New York is one of the greatest cities on this planet. I want this rebuilding process expedited."

"With all due respect, Mr. President, we don't need any more wild cowboys running around looking for Lucky. We tried that, and it was unsuccessful."

"I understand your concerns, but quite frankly, you are in no position to reject any help. This is bigger than you and I.

Don't you see the message we are sending across the world? We can't tolerate assassinations live on TV. What's next? A mayor? Governor? Or even the goddamn president?" the president said, raising his voice and heading toward the door. "This meeting is over. Mrs. Canton will be in contact. I expect full details on your progress. I want this situation taken care of or that's your ass. Have a good day, Mr. Mayor."

The mayor just sat there, frightened like a little kid after his father just finished yelling at him.

As soon as the president left, the governor ran in. "What happened in here? The president didn't look happy," the governor said.

"Everything I expected. It started out nice and calmly, but then he started talking about what if they assassinated us as well, two ex-Navy SEAL guys are coming to help, live TV assassination. I mean, all kinds of crazy shit, and also my ass is on the line. I have a few more days to catch Lucky, because the world is watching."

"What? Slow down, Ralph. Please sit down and repeat yourself, but in English."

The mayor sat down, caught his breath, and counted to ten before opening his mouth again. "The president said he's sending two ex-Navy SEALs to help catch Lucky, and I have a few more days to do it, or that's my ass. But I do have good news. He gave me his word that millions will be available to rebuild New York."

"That's great news. New Yorkers will be happy to hear that. I'm concerned about those two agents he's sending in, but at this point, we need all the help we can get. We don't even know if Lucky is still in New York."

Just as the mayor was about to reply, his secretary came in and said he had a call. The mayor gave her the evil eye for barging in like that, but he knew it must have been important.

"I'm sorry to come in like that, but you have to take this call."

"If it's not the president, take a message."

"Mr. Mayor, I have the Arundel Police Department on the line. They're located in Maryland. Lucky has been spotted at a Holiday Inn hotel."

Both the mayor and governor jumped up when they heard Lucky had been spotted.

The mayor took the call after his secretary left and pressed the speaker button. "This is Mayor Ralph Gulliano. It was brought to my attention you have some information on the whereabouts of one of our fugitives."

"Good day, Mr. Mayor. My name is Captain George Sneed from the Arundel County Police Department down in Maryland. We received a call from a young lady who claimed she met the suspect in question at a mall, and that after they had dinner and drinks, they then proceeded to rent a room at the Holiday Inn in Glen Burnie."

"Captain Sneed, have you dispatched any units to the hotel as of yet?" the mayor asked.

"That's a negative. The young lady claimed they were there only for one night and they both left in the morning. However, she did state she left first."

"I will bet my career he's still at the hotel. He used her for her ID in order to book the room. Call the hotel and have them run the girl's name and see if the hotel stay has been extended. If so, dispatch a few units over there and please call right back. This is my cell number, 646-555-1212. I also need you to call the mall and get in touch with security and ask to review their cameras. I'm sending some of my guys down as well."

"I don't think that would be necessary. We can handle the situation."

"Listen, Captain, this is the governor. I'm also on this call. Three minutes ago the president walked out of here, giving us the green light to apprehend this suspect at all costs. Get off your high horse. Call the hotel and mall like we asked, and we will see you soon."

There was about a three-second pause before Captain Sneed responded, "I will call you as soon as I hang up with the hotel."

Annoyed, the mayor ended the call without saying good-bye. "The nerve of him! Lucky would destroy his bullshit police department."

Both the mayor and the governor were making calls on their cell, trying to get a team together to send down to Maryland. Right in the middle of all the drama, the two ex-Navy SEALs the president had sent walked in the room.

As the mayor was about to introduce himself, Captain Sneed called his cell phone.

"Mr. Mayor, according to hotel staff, the room was extended for an extra night. I didn't want to alarm the hotel, but I did make the manager aware of the situation. He said that the suspect is still in his room and had just ordered room service."

"That's great news. Dispatch a few units."

"I already have."

"How many?" the mayor asked.

"I sent one, and I have about another five units that would be there within minutes as well."

"Great. Listen, he's extremely dangerous and smart. He will shoot on sight, so please tell your boys to be careful. I will have agents down there within four hours, but I will call my friends over in Baltimore and ask for their help as well."

"You are going to call the Baltimore Police Department? We don't work with those pigs. They are giving us all a bad name."

"Listen, to even come close to catching Lucky, you are going to need cops who are known for getting dirty. I don't have time to worry about a beef between police departments. Thank you for the call."

After the mayor hung up his cell, he introduced himself to the ex-Navy SEALs. "Hello, fellas. Please tell me your names."

A black, muscular brother, about six-two, head shaved clean, with numerous tattoos around his neck and arms, said, "My name is Marquis Jenkins, sir."

"My name is Angel Mendez, sir," a five-nine Hispanic brother said. His long black hair was in a ponytail, and he also was tattooed.

Usually, the mayor would have been turned off by their looks, but in this particular situation, this was a perfect fit. Even though Captain Tuna and his boys were dirty, clean-cut guys would get killed easily. In order to fight dirt, he had to get dirty.

"Okay, listen, fellas, we have intel that Lucky is in a hotel room down in Maryland. He may be there for only one night. It will take us about four hours to get there."

"Not if we fly. We flew here, and it only took about an hour," Jenkins said.

"Then that settles it. You two fly down to Maryland. My secretary will provide all the information you need. Remember, fellas, shoot to kill on sight."

After the two ex-Navy SEALs left, the mayor looked at the governor and said, "I hope we catch this son of a bitch once and for all."

"I agree. I think we should just let those two SEALs handle it. We don't need to send anyone else. Plus, our department has suffered enough embarrassment. We don't need to add any more. If that police department doesn't want to work with our Baltimore team, then so what?"

"You're right. Besides, we have a funeral to plan for the commissioner."

Chapter Twenty

The Holiday Inn

Lucky decided to walk over to the hotel gym, which was on the same floor as his room. He wanted to make sure he stayed in shape because running from the law was harder than a marathon. When he got there, no one was using the facility, so he felt comfortable working out. He didn't like the big glass windows in the gym, which gave a clear view of the front of the hotel.

After about thirty minutes of lifting, he decided to jump on the treadmill and run a few miles. While running, he noticed a police cruiser pulling up with flashing lights. He quickly jumped off the treadmill, ran toward the corner of the gym, and peeked out one of the big windows. When he saw two police officers jump out with their guns drawn and running toward the entrance of the hotel, he knew they were there for him.

He ran as fast as he could to his room, grabbed one of his guns and money, and headed toward the stairwell. As he was going down the flight of stairs, he heard one of the officers running up the stairs. He assumed the other cop jumped in the elevator.

Lucky stopped, dropped to one knee, and pointed his gun. Once the officer made that turn toward him, he was going to shoot him. Lucky figured the way those cops had the guns drawn, they were coming to kill him. The officer didn't have any idea what was waiting for him at his next turn.

Once Lucky saw the officer make that turn, he let off two rounds from his 9 mm at the officer's chest. The impact of both shots knocked the officer backward, slamming his body against the wall and dropping him down a flight of steps. As soon as he hit the floor, Lucky was right on top of him. He took his gun, extra ammo, and his radio. Right before he left, he kneeled down to the young officer and whispered in his ear, "I knew you were wearing a vest." Then he got up and continued running down the stairs.

There was a lot of commotion in the lobby, especially after everyone had seen the two officers running in with their guns drawn. Also, the sound of gunfire had the entire hotel concerned. Once everyone saw Lucky busting out the stairwell with a gun in his hand, they started running and screaming for their lives, while ducking at the same time.

Lucky ran out the front door and noticed a guest pulling up. He ran up to the driver's side and opened the door. He pointed the gun at his head and yelled at him, "Get the fuck out or lose your life!" As the nervous driver was exiting his car, Lucky shot out the tires of the police cruiser.

Once the guests at the hotel heard more gunfire, a mini stampede broke out.

As the other police officer was able to make his way through the crowd and reach the front door, he saw Lucky jump into a blue Nissan Maxima. He yelled out, "Freeze!"

But Lucky was already peeling off, so the officer began firing his weapon, and within seconds, Lucky was out of his sight.

The officer called the dispatcher. "Officer down, officer down! I need a bus. This is Officer Lenny Wilson. Suspect has fled the scene in what looked like a dark blue four-door sedan. He disabled my unit by shooting out the tires. I discharged my weapon four times at the suspect, but I missed the target. He made a right out of the hotel. He may be heading toward 895 North."

"This is dispatcher twenty-one. I have already dispatched a bus and alerted all units. We are also contacting the transit department. Are you injured?"

"No, but I believe my partner is. I heard two shots inside the hotel, and my partner is not picking up his radio."

"Please, stand by as help is on the way."

Lucky was listening to the whole conversation. He did make a right, but made the first U-turn available, and pulled into the first shopping center to his right. He parked behind Pizza Hut and jumped out of the blue Nissan.

As soon as he parked, he ran across the parking lot and saw a man in his early twenties about to exit his white 325i BMW. Lucky approached the young driver right before he was about to exit the car and pistol-whipped him before he even knew what happened. He was passed out cold in the backseat of his car.

Lucky got in the driver's seat and peeled off from the parking lot. He made a right, then continued driving on Ritchie Highway. He was listening to the police radio and heard that the cops were still looking for him in a dark blue Nissan. He figured he had at least thirty minutes before they found the Nissan.

Lucky also heard two ex-Navy SEALs were arriving by jet. That was surprising, but he knew it only meant that not only was the federal government involved, but now the president had officially joined the hunt. That made him nervous because soon the CIA would come in the picture. "Damn! Now the alphabet boys are really after me," he whispered under his breath, referring to all the government agencies known only by initials, like the ATF, DEA, FBI, CIA, and even the IRS. Once you were wanted by those agencies, the chances of not getting caught were zero to none.

Lucky knew he couldn't drive all night with a white dude passed out in the backseat. He began making turns at different streets, not knowing where to go. He knew he had to get rid of the car, so he was just waiting to pass the next big shopping center. That way, he'd at least have a little bit of time to steal the car he wanted without the owner in it.

While on Crain Highway he pulled up to a big enough shopping center. He thought it was the perfect spot to find a car. He drove to the farthest part of the lot and parked the BMW. He walked around and noticed there were no security guards present and no outside cameras in sight. Lucky was amazed at how easy it was going to be to steal a car in the plaza. Wanting to play it safe, he walked around just to make sure.

Once he stole his next car, he didn't want any additional attention. He just wanted to be able to jump on I-95 and head back up to New York. He walked over to the Sunoco gas station, and right before he entered, someone approached him.

"What's going on? I got some good green."

Lucky paused, looked at the young kid, and smiled. "What's good, li'l man? Are you sure you got some fire?"

"All you have to do is follow me back to my apartment. I got vicks for thirty-five, halfs for seventy, and onions for one-forty."

"I'm not driving. I live right across the street," Lucky said, pointing at the complex across Crain Highway.

"You live in Village Square? That's what's up. I just came from there. One of my regular customers lives there. I could drive you to your car. Then you could just follow me. I'm like five minutes from here. I live in Hidden Wood apartments."

"My wife has the car. How about I give you an extra fifty dollars if you take me and then bring me back?"

The young hustler looked at Lucky up and down and quickly became suspicious. "How about I just bring it back once you show me where you live? What you need?"

"Listen, I know you don't know me and shit. I don't know you, either. I just need a favor, that's all. I will snatch an ounce off you, plus give you fifty dollars for your trouble. I just want to get high. Your call. I'm trying to be your new number one customer in Village Square."

Lucky said all the right things the young hustler wanted to hear. Buying an ounce plus fifty was easy money.

"A'ight, I don't usually do shit like this, but I'm going to look out for you. C'mon, my car is parked by the pump."

Lucky caught the break he was looking for. He could hide out at the young hustler's crib for a day or two. He just had to play it smooth. When they got in the car, Lucky didn't waste time in sparking a conversation.

"What's your name, young homie?"

"Haze. Everybody calls me Haze. What about you?"

"Donald. Everybody calls me Don. Haze, let me ask you this. What the fuck is a vick? You said you had vicks for sale?"

"A quarter is seven grams. Michael Vick's jersey is number seven. In Maryland, we call a quarter a vick. Where are you from? You sound like you from Up Top."

"Yeah, I'm from New York."

"What part?"

"I'm from the Bronx. You been up there before?"

"I go up to New York all the time. That's where my connect lives. We almost here. I live in these apartments right here."

Lucky had a decision to make when he got upstairs to Haze's apartment—kill him or make him part of his team. He didn't have a lot of options, or too many friends. Once he smoked a few blunts with Haze, then he would make the call. If Haze was a real cat and about his business, then Lucky might have to take a risk on him. In reality, he didn't have any other options.

When they got in the apartment, Haze asked him, "You fuck with Henny?"

"Yeah, I drink, but let's roll up and get high first."

An hour later, they both were leaning back on the sofa, high as a kite, watching the movie *Heat*. In that one hour, Lucky had enough information on Haze to take the risk. He knew li'l man wasn't scared of the police or to bust his gun. Lucky was about to commit suicide with the next move he was about to pull, but he had to take his chance. The kid earned the opportunity by his whole swagger, but if li'l homie didn't agree to roll with the plan, he was going to put a bullet through his head.

"Listen, Haze, turn the movie off and put it on the news for a second."

"News?" Haze laughed. "I don't watch those gay-ass shows."

"I want to show you something. You want to know who I really am, put it on the news."

Haze's facial expression changed. He knew it had to be serious. He turned the movie off and switched it to cable. He pressed GUIDE and surfed the local news channel. While searching, he asked, "What's on the news?"

"I want you to know who I am."

"Now you making me think I made the wrong decision by bringing you to my crib," a serious-faced Haze said.

"Maybe, but if you built like I think you are, everything will be okay."

After locating the news channel and watching it for less than a minute, Haze realized he'd just smoked with the most wanted man in New York, maybe in America. They were reporting the shooting that took place at the Holiday Inn.

As soon as Lucky noticed Haze finally knew his identity, he pulled out his gun and cocked it back. "Now you have a decision to make, Haze. I don't want to kill you. If I did, I would have done it when we first came in."

"So what the fuck you want?"

"I need a little help, like a place to stay for a day or two. You look like a down nigga, so you let me know. Are we good? Can I trust you?"

"Hell yeah, we are good. You like a fucking legend. Everybody is looking for you, and you here in my crib getting high with me. Whatever you need from me, you got."

"I'm going to put my gun away. Are you sure you straight?" Lucky asked.

"I will be, once you put that bullshit-nine millimeter away." Haze laughed.

Lucky lowered his gun and began laughing with Haze, but still was trying to read him. He knew he'd picked the right person.

"What you know about guns, li'l man?"

"I'm not on your level yet, sniping muthafuckas, but I got guns."

"I didn't kill the commissioner. I was set up."

"Word? What about that girl they said you killed right in front of the police station? Did you really kill your female protégé like they say you did? That was an ill move, better than the commissioner hit."

"Well, I did kill that girl, but she wasn't who they thought she was. They were looking for Diamond, who's my real protégé. I needed to clear her name. I made up the story of her turning herself in. Then I shot her right in front of the police station."

"You see, I knew it. You are ill. Yo, I want to roll with you," an overeager Haze said.

"Slow down, Haze. This is not a video game, fam. This is real shit. I got federal agents hunting for me. If they catch me, they are going to kill me. You feel me?"

"I feel you, but do you feel me? I'm a ride-till-I-die muthafucka. This is what I do all day, every day. I smoke weed, make money, and I keep my guns clean."

Now Lucky was beginning to become a bit nervous. He was starting to sound like DMX in that movie *Belly*, when he played an out-of-control thug with an ego bigger than life. He almost second-guessed his decision to pick Haze. He thought he was acting immature, or maybe he was just happy to be around a real criminal. It was time to start testing the little dude.

"Have you ever shot anyone with one of your clean guns?" Lucky asked sarcastically.

"I haven't shot or killed anyone. I been to the range a few times, and I know I could shoot."

"Haze, I'm talking about real cowboy shit. Real blood and dead bodies. Are you up for the task?"

"I'm up for it. This is what I been waiting for my whole life. I'm a thug, yo, you hear me? I'm not like these other cats. I got like six thousand in the closet and another five at my mom's crib. In total, I got four guns, big joints, too. I don't have any kids or a wifey. I have shit to lose."

"I can't front. I'm a little impressed. I busted a lot of hustlers, and most of them fronted like they had money. When we raided their house, we would find like fifteen hundred dollars. Right now, I just need to call my man in New York. He's our contact and our only hope of sneaking into New York safely."

"Are we going to New York?" Haze asked, wide-eyed.

"Slow down with the whole *we* thing. I still haven't decided if you rolling. All I said was I was impressed," Lucky said, messing with him.

"C'mon," Haze pleaded, "you know you need the help."

"Let me just call my man. We'll talk after this phone call."

Lucky reached for his black bag and got the cell phone Sergio gave him and called him.

After a few rings, Sergio picked up. "Lucky, is that you?"

"Yeah. What's up?"

"Where in the fuck are you? There were reports they had you blocked in a hotel and that you shot a cop. Luck must love your black ass."

"It was Diamond, that fuckin' bitch. She was the one who snitched us out."

"Diamond, nah. Are you sure? Not her. I can't believe it."

"When I got down to the house in Glen Burnie, it was empty. She never went to Maryland. The bitch took the money and ran, and put the boys on me. I guess she figured out I was never coming back."

"I guess she figured one hundred thousand was enough to start a new life."

"I don't know about a new life, but it sure cost her her life."

"Where are you? Are you safe?" Sergio asked.

"Yeah, I should be good for a day or two. I'm coming up there, though."

"Up here? Are you crazy, Lucky? Turn the news on. The fuckin' president was up here and made a statement about capturing you. Stay as far away as you possibly can. New York is too hot."

"I don't give a fuck. I still have unfinished business. I'm not running for life. I need you to get in contact with Pee-Wee's brother—his name is Blood—and get me his number. Did you find a way to get my money?"

"I'm working on it."

"A'ight, call me back with Blood's number."

"Lucky, I have followed your orders for years. All I'm asking is this once you consider my advice. Don't come up to New York right now. Lay low and chill."

"Just get me the number and call me back. This is not the time to stick your chest out. It's my life, and I'm making the call. I'm not scared of dying. I'll be waiting on your call."

"Okay."

Lucky hung up the phone. He was upset, which clogged up his thought process. It was hard for him to admit it, but he had to agree with Sergio. He couldn't go back up to New York right away. That was when Haze's apartment came in the picture. Haze could make all the moves for him while he stayed inside and out of sight. He was just nervous that Haze might run his mouth, not to the police, but to his friends.

Lucky walked back toward Haze.

"Okay, look, Haze, I'm going to give you a shot and see how you roll. I need to stay here for like three days. I'd rather stay in a hotel, but I just had to shoot my way out of one. When I go up to New York and everything goes right, I will give you twenty-five thousand dollars."

"Twenty-five thousand? Shit! For that kind of bread, you could sleep in my bed."

They both laughed and shook hands. Haze, eager to prove he was a real thug, would have done it for free, just for the rush of it.

As they rolled up a few more blunts, Lucky began filling him in on his current plan. He didn't waste time on the past because he didn't think it needed addressing.

"Look, li'l homie, from this point on, what we talk about stays between us. If you leak this information, I will kill you, and I'm not even joking. I used to run a storage company, and we stored large quantities of drugs and monies for the mob and kingpins. About eighty percent of the drugs that came up to New York was stored in my storage facility. Then, like many drug corporations, there is always a snitch within the team. The bad part about the snitch is, it was my girlfriend. We got raided, they killed two of my guys, and I escaped. The storage was burned to the ground. I need to get back in the storage because I have an underground stash room with a couple million. I'm going back up to New York to retrieve my money and get some payback on this bitch for snitching. Everything sounds easy, but there will be bloodshed."

"Sounds like a plan. I'm down. And don't worry, yo. I won't run my mouth. I barely hang with niggas. All I do is get money and fuck bitches."

"That's another thing. You can't have company over while I'm here. We can't take chances."

"But I have customers who come to this apartment," Haze quickly shot back.

"Well, when your customers come, I will go into your room while you handle your sale. I don't care about that. I'm talking about having anybody over. That includes bitches."

"That's cool. As long as I can serve and make my money, then I don't have no problem with that."

They continued to smoke and talk. Lucky, at that point, was leaning back and enjoying his high. His mind drifted off, and he started thinking about Diamond. He was puzzled by her betrayal. In his mind, she crossed the line of death. He had to kill her, but he was going to ask her why first. He needed to know why.

Lucky knew she didn't act alone and that maybe there was another man in the picture. He had his suspicions, but he was going to have to wait till he got back up to New York.

He also started thinking about his baby mother, Tasha, and daughter, Tamika. He wanted to call them, but if he did, they would try to persuade him to return to Atlanta. Hearing their voices wouldn't help the situation. Tasha would just have to understand that when he got back to Atlanta. He couldn't give up just yet.

Haze tapped Lucky on his shoulder, interrupting his thoughts.

"Hey, I have a customer who's about to come in here in like two minutes."

"Get that money, li'l homie," Lucky said as he walked toward Haze's bedroom.

While Haze was handling his business, Lucky lay on the bed and started thinking about his daughter again. He couldn't wait to get back to her. He had already lost a lot of years and wasn't about to add to the count. He wanted to settle down and become a father, something his mother could be proud of. He knew he'd been living a life his mother would have never approved of, and imagined her to be flipping in her grave.

Lucky had gotten away from his original home upbringing. After joining Captain Tuna's team, he really turned for the worse, losing all his morals. He'd joined the force to change the stereotype that black people from the hood had about becoming a cop. He wanted to prove that you could come from the hood and be a great officer, not a sellout, like everyone thought.

Lucky was getting tired, and as soon as he closed his eyes, he fell asleep.

Chapter Twenty-one

America's Most Wanted

The mayor was upset when he heard that Lucky had escaped and shot a police officer in the process. He'd warned the police department down in Arundel County that Lucky was considered armed and dangerous and would shoot first. He couldn't believe Captain Sneed didn't take him seriously. One of his deputies almost died for his foolish mistake. He got on the phone, called up his new help, and asked for an update.

"Jenkins, are you guys in Maryland yet? What the hell is going on?" a furious mayor asked.

"Mister Mayor, we're at the scene Lucky escaped from. We found the car he hijacked less than a mile away, in a shopping plaza, abandoned. I'm sure he stole another car. They are reviewing security cameras as we speak. Once we find the car he jumped in, we will hunt him down. I will keep you posted."

"Hurry up and find this cocksucker," the mayor said as he hung up.

The mayor didn't need the extra publicity because, in reality, the whole world was laughing at him. He couldn't catch one individual who tore his city apart and killed his commissioner live on TV.

Not more than five minutes after the mayor hung up the phone, the governor called, asking for an update as well. Lucky had escaped so many traps, they were starting to feel like they were wasting their time chasing him.

Aside from all the drama, today was the funeral of one of the mayor's best friends, Commissioner Fratt. With all the recent events taking place, it was going to be hard for the mayor and the rest of New York to feel any sorrow or pain for the commissioner.

***

As thousands of police officers marched alongside the white stretch Cadillac hearse, the streets weren't crowded. Many New Yorkers were still rebuilding their homes and businesses. They could care less about the corrupt commissioner, who might have been responsible for the worst riot in New York history.

The funeral was one of the quickest and quietest funerals ever for a city official. His wife and kids were stunned that not many of his close friends attended the funeral. Many felt embarrassed to show their support, another indication that they believed he was indeed dirty. The mayor didn't even stay till the end. The city had bigger issues calling for his attention.

The mayor headed back to his office to meet up with his spokesperson, Richard. He needed to get a few updates, and he still had to deal with the whole Captain Tuna and Speedy situation. They were still sitting in lockup at the Booking, in private cells. For their protection, it was best to keep them in Booking rather than transfer them to Rikers Island. The protective custody unit at Rikers had one of the highest murder rates of all the prisons in the United States. They didn't want to take a chance at both Tuna and Speedy getting murdered.

After the mayor arrived back at his office, he told his spokesperson, "Okay, Richard, lay it on me. What have you been hearing down in Maryland?"

"Well, let's first talk about the budget situation. We need to get in contact with the president or someone in FEMA. We're running out of money, and we still haven't received one dollar from those millions they promised."

"How much have we spent so far?" The mayor didn't really want to know the answer.

"In less than forty-eight hours, we have spent a little over ten million dollars, and we still haven't helped the small businesses and the residential community. At this rate, we'll be broke in thirty days. Experts are predicting it will take at least a year to fully recover from the riot, but if we run out of money, it could take three to five years."

"I will make the call. What else?"

"Well, we have to address the whole Tuna and Speedy situation real soon. I heard Internal Affairs is working on both of them. I received confirmation that Internal Affairs feels like Speedy will run his mouth and cooperate. We have to monitor that situation and make sure Speedy remembers which side he's on. At this point, we don't need any more leaks.

"I spoke to the DA. They're willing to give Tuna and Speedy plea deals for the Coleman case. Instead of murder, they will be charged with manslaughter. I don't know how we could get them out of this mess. They're both looking at a minimum of ten years."

"Ten years, Richard? We can't do better than that?"

"Not with the kind of heat and pressure New York is under. We're under a microscope. If they receive a slap on the wrist, it will slow up the healing process in the city. I'm sorry to say, but we're going to have to use those two as examples. And we can't wait until we capture Lucky, either. We need to get them in court as soon as possible."

The mayor sat there in silence because he knew what Richard was trying to imply. He basically was asking him to turn his back on the situation and let the system take its course. That was a hard pill to swallow because he believed in the code of blue, death before betrayal.

The mayor knew he would receive harsh criticism from the police department and the union, but he had to go with his gut feeling, which was following Richard's plan for the moment and seeing where it led. If he had to make a last-minute decision, he would, but at the moment, he was going with the flow.

"Fuck it, Richard! Advise the DA we will accept any deal on the table for the Coleman case. I'll head down and speak to Tuna and Speedy myself."

"I don't think that would be a wise decision, Mr. Mayor. I will have their lawyers break the news down. If they don't cooperate, we pull the plug on their funds and completely abandon them."

"Great idea! Have their lawyers tell them. Also, did anybody find that girl? What's her name again?"

"Who? Diamond?"

"We need to find this girl. She's the final piece in capturing Lucky. Once we put her face and her real identity in the news, he will be rushing back to New York, and we will be waiting," the mayor said with conviction.

"I like that plan. We need to find her quickly. With regards to Lucky, the parking lot cameras captured him jumping in a white BMW after knocking out the driver. They were unable to get the license plate number, but they're running a check on all BMWs in Glen Burnie. A white BMW was spotted in another plaza a few miles down. When officers arrived on the scene, the white car was gone. Right now, they have no leads. I hope those two SEALs the president provided come through in the clutch because right now we need a game-changing play," Richard said.

"We don't have any leads on Lucky. That's not good. He could be on his way to Mexico, for all we know."

Before Richard could answer, the mayor's secretary barged in the office and informed him that there were two men in suits outside his office. The mayor, along with Richard, headed out of the office to see which agency was now snooping in their business.

"Good day, Mr. Mayor. My name is Special Agent Scott Meyer, and this is my partner, Special Agent Marie Summit. We are with the Central Intelligence Agency."

"The CIA!" the mayor said aloud. "First the FBI, now the CIA. Who's next? NASA?"

"We apologize for the inconvenience, but how long did you think we were going to mind our business? When a commissioner gets assassinated live on TV, it becomes our problem."

"The president didn't mention anything about the CIA getting involved."

"The president? You think we're governed by the president? When Commissioner Fratt got assassinated, you invited every terrorist to an open party. We're the nation's first line of defense. We put our country first and the agency behind self. We are here to resolve and stabilize the situation," Agent Meyer said.

"You guys are going to help capture Lucky as well?" The mayor sounded desperate.

"Can we please continue this conversation in your office? And your answer is no. We are here to really find out who killed the commissioner."

"But Lucky killed him," the mayor snapped.

"Based on our intelligence, he's not a suspect."

The room quickly got quiet because, up to that point, Lucky was the prime suspect. When Agent Meyer said Lucky was not a suspect, it made the mayor and his spokesman nervous.

"What are you trying to imply? That his assassination was an inside hit for hire? But who else would dare to pull off such a hit?"

Agent Summit stepped in front of her partner. "That's a question we would love to ask you, sir."

"Excuse me. You better watch your mouth, young lady," an angry mayor said.

Agent Summit reached for her briefcase and pulled out a folder. The mayor took one of those long swallows because he didn't know if the folder she was holding was sent by Lucky. When Lucky had sent those folders out exposing all the corruption, the mayor's name never popped up. He was worried that now his luck had also run out and that he would now be exposed.

Agent Summit threw the folder on his desk. "Then please explain why you made two payments of one hundred thousand dollars from your private offshore account. The first payment was made a day before the assassination, and the second one right after."

The mayor looked through the papers in silence.

Richard was shocked to hear about the new allegations against his boss. "Boss, is this true? You were involved in the assassination?" Up until then, there had been no secrets between them.

The mayor didn't answer his good friend of over twenty-five years. He just kept looking through the folder, which not only contained his bank statements, but also phone records between him and the hired helped, one of the mob's best hit men.

Richard didn't allow the mayor to continue ignoring him. He slapped the folder out of his hands. "You are going to answer me right now! Answer me, goddamn it! Is it true? Is it true?"

The mayor, too embarrassed to admit he was the one who actually ordered the hit on the commissioner, kept his silence.

Agent Meyer decided to help ease the pressure off the mayor. "Listen, Ralph, only the CIA is aware of your involvement. We're willing to keep our mouth shut and roll with you on the whole Lucky conspiracy."

The mayor quickly snapped out of his daze. "How?"

"Oh, now you want to speak? You're not even going to answer my question, boss? You are going to answer me. Did you have the commissioner assassinated?"

The mayor finally looked up at his old friend. "Yes, I was the mastermind behind it."

"Are you fuckin' serious? I have kept my mouth shut on a lot of things, but you are alone on this one. You're not bringing me down on this one," Richard said as he was walking toward the door.

"Not so fast, Richard. We know you were not involved in the assassination, but you were involved in many other illegal activities. You can't leave. You are now involved in this situation, too," Agent Meyer said.

"What do you mean, I can't leave?"

"The CIA will not sit back and allow you to jeopardize this investigation. You already know too much. Please close the door and come back in. Don't make this hard on yourself or your family."

Richard was obviously shaken by the harsh words coming out of the agent's mouth. He closed the door and walked back over toward his boss like a little bitch with his tail tucked.

"Listen, Mr. Mayor, the CIA has handled all the major conspiracy and terrorist threats against the United States of America for over fifty years. There have been thousands of threats that never went public. They were kept under the radar for a reason. This current situation fits the under-the-radar file. We can't afford another major corruption case. If this information hits the press, we will have another riot, and this time many more will die."

"Sounds good to me. What do we have to do?"

"Not so fast, Mr. Mayor. You're not getting away so easy. There will be harsh penalties handed down to you, which will include your resignation."

"My what? That's unacceptable," the mayor quickly responded.

"Unfortunately, you don't have options. You are a disgrace to the United States government and its history. Please, don't think our services are to help you. We're here to keep the good faith of this country. The plan is to frame Lucky. In order for that to happen, you have to capture him. We need you to capture him as quick as possible, before he starts revealing evidence about the truth. Tomorrow morning I will have a team of analysts back here reviewing all your files on Lucky, his ex-partners, Commissioner Fratt, and the Coleman shooting. I expect your full cooperation in this entire investigation."

"So you expect me to just hand over information that will crucify all of us in court?" the mayor shot back.

"Again, our investigation will be silent. We just want to make sure we destroy all evidence. That way it doesn't resurface years later. We're protecting our end. We don't want our involvement to be known. Trust me, your resignation won't be a surprise to the city. Most of the people are calling for it, anyway. Just consider this an early retirement. But if you decide not to cooperate, then you will have to answer to your involvement in the assassination and possibly face life in prison. Your choice. I will give you sixty seconds to decide."

"I don't need any time, if you guarantee no jail time or public humiliation. Richard and I will fully cooperate," the mayor said. "So, Agent Meyer, what's the plan? What kind of support are we going to receive in framing Lucky?"

"Let's get one thing clear. We're not here to play your little cop-and-robber games. We are not capturing Lucky. Our job is to help frame the son of a bitch. We will provide national attention. We will feature him on *America's Most Wanted* tonight. That way we'll receive the audience we need. Lucky can't keep running around in other states so freely and not be recognized. Once you guys capture him, we will then start releasing different bogus footage of him at the crime scene. In order for it to work, we need him in custody first. Here is my business card. I will see you soon."

"Wait. What about me?" the mayor asked.

"If I was you, I would start rehearsing my resignation," Agent Meyer shot back as he walked out of the office.

"Excuse me, if I may. Elections are about eleven months away. Right now, this city is not ready to lose its mayor. I know some are calling for his resignation, but it will cause more damage than good. At least the mayor could finish his term. Can we work something out where he would just make it public that he won't run for a second term?" Richard begged for his boss's job, even after his betrayal.

"I will bring this information to my superiors. As long as you guys fully cooperate, I don't see why they won't agree," Agent Meyer said.

As soon as the agents left the room, and the mayor and Richard were finally alone, Richard didn't waste any time letting his boss know how he felt. "I'm extremely disappointed. How can you kill one of your best friends? You know what? Don't even answer that question. I have a lot of work to do before Agent Meyer gets upset. I will see you in the morning."

"Listen, Richard, I'm sorry I didn't tell you, but I had to do it. The commissioner fucked up by not taking care of Lucky right after the Coleman shooting. If he'd done his job, Lucky would have never shown up in court, and we wouldn't be in this situation we're in now."

"Fuck you! Agent Meyer was right. You are a disgrace to the U.S. government," Richard said as he left the office, slamming the door behind him.

After Richard left, Ralph Gulliano just sat there in complete silence, his whole life flashing right in front of him. He thought about his wife and kids and felt ashamed. He wasn't only raised better, but he took an oath to protect and serve. He was no different than any other common criminal. In fact, he was below a criminal. More like a scumbag, a worthless piece of shit. He was basically the top dog, so that made him a kingpin, but with legal and political powers.

Ralph kept picking up the phone and hanging up. He was scared to call his wife. He didn't even know how to begin. He couldn't just call her and say, "Hey, I killed Commissioner Fratt and I have to resign, but the good part is I don't have to go to jail." His wife wouldn't even know how to handle such a confession.

As the mayor sat in his office, trying to figure out a way to call his wife, the governor made his way in the office. The mayor was thrown off by his visit. He thought the governor knew about the CIA leaving his office.

"News travels fast, I see," the mayor said.

"What news?"

"So you don't know?"

"Do I know what?" the governor asked with a confused look.

That was when it hit the mayor. He realized that the governor's main connections were with the federal government, and he might not be aware about the CIA's involvement. He kept his mouth shut about the assassination, but he had to tell him something because now he was curious.

"Right before you left, Richard and I were talking about my future, and I decided not to run for reelection. I think the city needs a fresh start."

"I don't know. The way you handled the riot and restored order, you may get reelected. You're a hero. Don't let those small accusations scare you. Just take your time and think about it. Anyway, I'm here to see if you have any new leads on our prey."

"No new leads, but I do have great news. John Walsh from *America's Most Wanted* is doing a whole show on Lucky tonight."

"That's great news. I don't know why we waited to get on the show. We need all the national attention we can get. We need to make it a two-million-dollar reward."

"A two-million-dollar reward would make anyone talk." The mayor flashed his trademark smile. "But where are we going to get the money from?"

"I have connections. Plus, after the *America's Most Wanted* feature, it will be a lot easier to come up with the money."

They continued talking for the next forty-five minutes, forty of which were spent on Lucky. They both had not slept in days. Chasing Lucky had drained them and destroyed their personal lives.

***

Lucky was back in Haze's room, doing push-ups and sit-ups, working out in complete darkness. He was revisiting some of the old training he used to do right after his mother had died. He knew, once he stepped back in New York, he would face the fight of his life.

As Lucky sat there motionless, concentrating, Haze came in and interrupted his training. "Lucky, hurry up! You have to see this! You are on TV again!"

Lucky at first was upset but then understood why Haze had interrupted him. He ran into the living room, turned the volume up on the TV, and couldn't believe his eyes and ears. He was actually on *America's Most Wanted.*

> *"Good evening, America. My name is John Walsh. For years I have captured criminals, but tonight it will be a different show. Tonight, America, we need your help in capturing an ex-police officer from New York. His name is Donald Gibson, but he is known as Lucky. This ex-police officer is wanted for numerous crimes, which include murder and drug trafficking. He's also believed to be the main suspect in Commissioner Brandon Fratt's assassination. He's considered armed and dangerous, so if you have any information on the whereabouts of this fugitive, please contact 1-800-OUTLAWS.*
>
> *"Lucky was last seen in Glen Burnie, Maryland, where he was almost captured, but he shot a police officer and escaped. Based on information from our sources, he's believed to still be in Maryland, but he could be anywhere. If you have any information that could lead to his arrest, call the hotline. There's a two-million-dollar reward."*

Haze jumped up and turned the TV off. "Yo, he said two million dollars. Fuck *America's Most Wanted!* Don't worry. I'm not a snitch. There's no need to watch this show. You just let me know when we're making our next move."

"You a real muthafucka, Haze. They don't build criminals like you. Today, snitching is like a new style."

"Ha! Ha! You are right. But that's why I barely have friends. I can't trust these cats out here today. Muthafuckas are cruddy out here."

"*Cruddy?*" Lucky asked, confused.

"That's some B-more shit. It means a foul, grimy-ass nigga. I grew up in Baltimore, over east. Let me tell you. Baltimore got some cruddy-ass dudes, especially in Park Heights and Cherry Hill."

"Ha! *Cruddy.* I never heard of that saying before. I heard of Cherry Hill before, though. I pulled over some Baltimore cats years ago. They were looking for Washington Heights but were lost in Spanish Harlem. They had like sixty thousand cash and three guns on them. We took everything, put them back on the highway, and sent them back down here."

"Y'all kept the dough and gats?"

"Hell yeah, we did. That was an easy come-up. That's how we carry it. I guess we were cruddy cops, you could say."

"Damn! I should have became a cop. I didn't know you could get paid like that."

Haze sparked another blunt, but Lucky passed on it. He wanted to stay focused, and the weed was only going to make him tired. All he wanted was to return to the room and continue working out.

"If you're not smoking anymore, then I'm not smoking. We have to stay focused. I feel you."

Again, Lucky was impressed with his dedication. He was a bit concerned that Haze might later change his mind and go after that two-million-dollar reward. He believed the young soldier was true to his word, but couldn't trust him 100 percent.

At the time, Lucky wasn't too concerned. He had major issues to worry about. Like, why Sergio still hadn't called him back. His phone was turned off, and all calls were going straight to voice mail. The frustration was building inside of Lucky, and it was making him second-guess himself about Sergio as well. Plus, he didn't like something Sergio had said to him in their last phone conversion earlier in the day. All he needed was Blood's phone number. He needed to get in contact with Blood as soon as possible. That way he'd know when he'd be heading up to New York. He felt safe in Haze's apartment, but he was eager to get back up there and find Diamond and his money.

Lucky wasn't about to let *America's Most Wanted* stop his flow. He needed another plan, one that would get him up to New York safely. He was going to give Sergio till the morning to call him back before acting on his own. With Captain Tuna and Speedy still in jail, Lucky knew the mayor was receiving federal help in capturing him, especially after the president's visit. That was the reason why he was waiting on Blood's number. He needed soldiers who were ready to kill. He knew Blood wouldn't turn him down and would do anything to avenge his brother's death. It was a fight he couldn't do all alone. He needed a team, but not just any regular squad. He wanted certified players with experience to play along with him.

That was when he thought about his best friend, Divine, the one person he could count on for anything. Their friendship was solid as a rock and went back to their high school days. They'd actually played football together and graduated in the same class. After high school, Lucky stayed home, while Divine went away to school in Philly. He lasted only a year in school before he was back on the block, hustling. Divine was the one who'd convinced Lucky to invest in the storage facility.

Lucky dropped a few more tears for his comrade and best friend. There was nothing like losing a loved one, but when they got killed in front of you, that memory would haunt you forever. Then he continued to work out, hoping it would help him stop thinking about his homie.

Chapter Twenty-two

Going Back to New York

Around two in the morning, Lucky's phone started ringing. Sergio had finally called him back.

"Damn, Sergio! I been trying to fuckin' call you all day. What's up with you?"

"I'm sorry. My girlfriend, she's crazy. She turned my cell phone off. She didn't want anyone to interrupt us."

"I'm over here hiding from the federal government, and you up there playing little sex games with your girl? I just ask for one little favor, just one. I need Blood's number, that's all."

"I have the number for—"

Lucky interrupted him. "Just give me the fuckin' number, Sergio."

After Lucky wrote the number down, he ended the call without notifying Sergio, making it known he was disappointed in him. Lucky dialed Blood's number, and it rang for about six times before he picked up.

"Who the fuck is this?" a grouchy, intoxicated Blood asked because it was so late.

"It's me."

Blood jumped off the couch. He knew who it was. He grabbed another phone off the coffee table and walked to his kitchen. "I'm going to call you right back," he said before ending the call. He called Lucky back from a prepaid cell phone.

Lucky picked up on the first ring.

"Hey, no need to say names. I know who this is. I've been waiting on your call. These rats burned and killed my brother and Divine. What's up? Where you at? They got the heat on you hard for killing the commissioner."

"I know. I'm still out of town, in Maryland. I need to get up there. For the record, I didn't shoot the commish. They're trying to pin that on me."

"Whatever you need, talk to me. You need help getting to me? I have a minivan with a secret compartment large enough to fit you in. You will get into New York safely. Just give me till about noon. Give me the address."

"Bet. It sounds good. I need about ten thousand when you come down."

"No problem. I will holla. One."

Lucky turned toward Haze, who was anxiously waiting for the plan. "We're leaving noon tomorrow," he said.

Haze started clapping his hands in excitement. It was the moment he'd been waiting for. "I'm going to start packing."

Lucky sat down and leaned his head back. He felt bad for Haze. The reason why he asked Blood for ten thousand was to leave it with Haze. Lucky couldn't risk that boy's life. He didn't care if Haze was ready to ride or die for him. He just couldn't risk it, especially if he didn't have to. Once he got in contact with Blood, Haze's services were no longer needed. Lucky decided not to inform Haze about the new decision. He didn't want him to get upset that he wasn't going and get any funny ideas about collecting the $2 million.

As Haze packed, Lucky jumped in the shower. He decided to wash up and kill time. In the shower, all he thought about was Diamond. He was devastated and embarrassed by her lack of judgment. Lucky felt like he did what any other real man would have done. He set her free to live her life because his was already occupied. He didn't want to continue holding her back.

As the warm water was hitting his head, his emotions were getting the better of him. He let the water continue to bounce off his head. He leaned against the wall, finally realizing Diamond was officially out of his life. After his shower, he went straight to bed and called it a night.

As Lucky slept, the mayor received a call from Jenkins, who was still down in Maryland.

"Good evening, sir, I have new intel, and I couldn't wait until the morning to call you."

"This better be good."

"Remember the suspect who died at the hospital? The one you guys mistakenly identified as Lucky?"

"I remember. His name was Dwayne Mooks. What's your point? I'm about to hang up if you called me to talk about a dead suspect."

"Bear with me, sir. Dwayne Mooks is better known as Pee-Wee. He has a brother named Daquan Mooks, nickname Blood. These brothers as a team were vicious, and their rap sheet is unbelievable. We're on our way back to New York. We believe Lucky will get in contact with him. Blood always worked together with his brother. If Lucky knew Pee-Wee, I'm sure he knew Blood. We are going to stake out several of his hangouts and see what we come up with."

"That's great news. Keep me updated, and let me know if you need additional help once you arrive in New York." The mayor hung up the phone in excitement.

Things were going to get real interesting in the next few days in New York. Lucky and both ex-Navy SEALs were heading to the same location. It was going to be another shoot-out similar to the night the storage facility was raided. New York was not in a position to handle another gun battle. Most of the city's cops were out in the streets, working with the community, building the city together as one.

By the time the sun started rising, Lucky was already on the floor, doing his exercise. After three hundred and fifty push-ups and two hundred sit-ups, he jumped back in the shower. When he came out, he saw Haze doing push-ups in the living room.

Lucky laughed to himself because little man was a rider for real. "I see you bustin' those push-ups out," he yelled.

Haze jumped up. "Shit! I'm trying to be like you. I just did eighty."

"Ha! Eighty? That ain't shit."

"How many you did?"

"A quick three-fifty. I usually do five hundred, but I'm a li'l out of shape."

"Three-fifty, for real? Damn! I need to get my weight up. We still have time before the ride gets here. I'm going to try to do at least two hundred."

Lucky just laughed as he walked away and went back in the room to take a quick nap. As he lay on the bed, he started thinking about Tasha. He knew she must be a nervous wreck. He had to call her. He already knew what she was going to say. Plus, he'd always feared Tamika would snatch the phone from her mother and ask him to come home. He just hoped one day they would understand and forgive him. He missed them so much. He couldn't wait to reunite with them. He made a promise to his little girl and wasn't about to let her down like he did in the past.

A few hours later, Lucky's phone started ringing.

"Yo."

"Hey, it's me. According to the GPS, we should be there in, like, ten minutes, my nigga."

"A'ight bet, I'm ready."

Lucky jumped up and threw his shirt on. Then he grabbed his gun and bag. When he got out to the living room, Haze was waiting by the door.

"I heard the phone ring. What's up? When we are leaving?"

"Listen, Haze, sit down. We need to talk."

"Aw shit! That's what my father used to say to me all the time when he was about to break some bad news."

"It's not bad news. It's just some shit you don't want to hear. Listen, I can't bring you with me to New York. This is a suicide mission, li'l homie. This is a real war, a war that's beyond guns and money. I'm always going to keep it real. The chances of you coming back alive are slim to none."

"C'mon. What the fuck are you talking about? I know the risk."

"You are not listening. You are not going."

"I thought you said it wasn't bad news, 'cause right now I'm feeling like shit. You fucked my wet dream up."

"When my boy Blood gets here in a few minutes, he's going to come in with a bag filled with money, ten thousand to be exact. That's all for you, li'l homie."

"Get the fuck out of here! For real?"

"I told you I appreciate all you have done for me, and I'm going to need you to keep your mouth shut after I leave."

"You still questioning my heart. You never trusted anyone in your life? I'm not a snitch."

"I have in the past, but not lately. Money makes humans act like scavengers."

Right after Lucky finished speaking, his cell phone started ringing, and someone was knocking at the door. He walked toward the door, looked through the peephole, and saw Blood in a medical uniform. He opened the door and let him in.

"Blood, what the fuck you doing in a medical uniform? You are a funny muthafucka. I'm sure glad to see you, bro," Lucky said as he hugged him.

"I'm glad to see you, too. You ready? Let's hit the road. We'll talk on the road."

"Oh, I'm ready. Did you bring the money?"

"It's in the black bag." Blood handed him the bag.

Lucky passed the bag right over to Haze and told him, "I'm a man of my word. I'm going to miss you, li'l homie. I haven't met good youngblood in a long time. Stay focused and invest this money in something positive. Open up a store or something. I need one last favor. Call this number from a pay phone and let her know I'm okay and that I will be home soon."

"You got it." Haze walked up to him and hugged him. "Thanks for the life lessons. I paid attention to everything you said to me. I'm going to miss you, and, remember, you're always welcome back. Please, tell the mayor to kiss my ass right before you kill him."

"I got you. I will make sure I tell him to kiss your ass. Hey, you never know, I might be calling you to come up to New York."

"I'll be waiting."

Lucky grabbed his bag and went out the door with Blood. He was bugging when he read the sign on Blood's van—MEDICAL TRANSPORTATION SERVICES.

Blood turned to Lucky. "Who in the fuck was that, Lucky?" he asked.

"A street hustler I bumped into. I offered him money if I could stay at his house."

"Doesn't he know you have a two-million-dollar reward on your head? You took a big risk in trusting him."

"I didn't have any other choice. I took a chance on him, I know, but I had to. Little man is legit. I really do want to bring him with me."

"Then bring him. It's not like there isn't any room."

"Nah, it's better this way."

"Okay, here's the deal. You can ride in the backseat. My windows are tinted enough, so they won't see you."

"What you mean? That's it? I was just on *America's Most Wanted*, and you just want me to ride in the backseat because you have dark tints? I don't think so, bro."

"Ha! Nah, this minivan is equipped with two large refrigerators. I transport body parts, mainly hearts and kidneys. The larger fridge in the back is the secret compartment. You will be able to jump in there if we get pulled over. Once we get close to the George Washington Bridge, you'll have to get in until we get to Harlem."

"Sounds a lot better now. C'mon, let's roll out of here."

As Blood was driving up I-95 North, Lucky felt like shit. He didn't come clean about leaving Pee-wee alone and bailing out on him. Lucky knew he couldn't come clean, because he needed Blood's help more than anything at the moment. Why ruin it by coming clean? Maybe one day he would tell Blood the truth, but not in this lifetime.

Lucky decided to ask Blood about the body-part gig, to get his mind off things. "So, what's good with this body-part shit? How you into this business? You caught me off guard with this genius move. I never heard of anything as slick as this."

"I got this idea from this bitch I used to fuck with in Atlanta. She told me her father ran his own business for twenty-five years. He actually helped me get all my licenses and permits. This is the slickest shit ever, Lucky. I even get special treatment if I get pulled over by police. They usually let me go. You can't hold up a heart or a lung from surgery when there are people dying."

"Ha! Damn, Blood! This here is a gold mine."

"Who are you telling? This minivan could hold up to twenty bricks of cocaine and about ten pounds of weed. I'm about to get about three more of these bad boys and just take over I-95. If you want in, let me know. I got you."

"Oh, I want in, but first I need to get back in the storage facility. I still have a lot of money in the stash room that's fireproof. I know my money is safe."

"Just let me know the plan. I'm down, just as long as we kill a few cops in the process. I'm not worried about money. I got plenty of it."

"It's not about just killing cops," Lucky quickly said, to get the idea out of his head.

"Maybe it's not, but I'm killing cops."

"I have a bigger plan. We're going after the big boy. The mayor."

"You want to kill the mayor? Damn, Lucky! I know I said let's go hard, but killing the mayor is extra hard. Didn't you already kill the commissioner?"

"I keep telling people I didn't pull the trigger. I didn't kill that pig. I wish I did. But don't forget, Blood, the mayor is the one responsible for your brother's death. We just can't let him get away with it. Trust me, I will work on a plan once we get back to New York. First, I have to find that bitch Diamond. She's the one who dropped dime on us."

"Diamond? She was your bottom bitch. What happened? You see, that's why you can't bring bitches into the game. They get all emotional and personal."

"You don't have to tell me. I'm living proof that theory is true."

As they drove up in the middle of the afternoon, Lucky let his mind wander. In the back of his head, he knew it was going to be hard to kill the mayor. The whole ride up to New York, he kept trying to replay the morning Commissioner Fratt was assassinated. He couldn't understand why his memory was blurry. It was killing him not knowing what happened that morning. He was upset at himself for being weak and losing the battle with addiction.

If he hadn't snorted all that cocaine, he wouldn't have been in this cloud of darkness. He knew in his heart that he didn't pull the trigger. He wasn't equipped with the right type of weapon. In fact, Lucky thought maybe the mayor was the mastermind behind the hit. He didn't have proof, but he could try to make him confess, which would be almost impossible.

The long, quiet drive was making Lucky doze off.

About three hours later, Blood tapped him on his leg. "Wake up, son. I need you to get in the fridge. We coming up on the George Washington Bridge. And, don't worry. You'll be able to breathe in there."

"A'ight, but head to the Bronx first. I want to visit Sergio real quick. I need to ask him a few questions."

"A'ight. I'll jump on the Cross Bronx Expressway. Once we clear, I'll let you know. Don't close the fridge door all the way unless I ask you to."

Lucky went in the fridge and couldn't believe how easily he was able to fit in there. He was only in there for like twenty minutes before Blood called him out the box.

As they headed toward Sergio's house, Blood asked, "How come we need to visit Sergio?"

"Something he said over the phone just stuck in the back of my head, and I need to clarify it."

Blood quickly picked up on Lucky's vibe. "Oh, so this won't be a friendly visit. Damn! Is everybody snitching now? That's the new hustle, I see."

"I don't know if he's snitching, but my hand will be on my gun when I go in his apartment."

As they got near Sergio's building, Lucky asked him to park up the block and watch the building for a few. As they sat there, two suits came out of the building.

"You see that shit, Lucky? They look like homicide."

"Nah, they're either the feds or the CIA. Those are thousand-dollar suits they're wearing."

"You think they just came from out of your boy's crib?" Blood asked.

"I don't know, but we about to find out. Let's wait a minute or two before we go upstairs."

They sat there and only waited about thirty seconds. Lucky was eager to find out what was going on. They slowly crossed the street, and when they reached the building, they ran upstairs to Sergio's door and rang his bell.

Sergio looked through the peephole and saw it was Lucky. He wondered if Lucky had seen the agents leave his building. He couldn't see Blood, who was leaning against the wall, out of sight, waiting for the door to unlock.

Sergio was hesitant to open the door, but Lucky's knocks kept getting louder. When he finally unlocked the door, both Lucky and Blood forced their way in.

Lucky jumped on top of him and put his gun right in his mouth. "Explain why the feds just left your apartment, muthafucka."

Sergio couldn't speak, because the barrel was down his throat. He was choking, and spit was coming out his mouth. When Lucky removed the gun from his throat, Sergio began to cry, saying, "Please, let me explain. I will never snitch. That wasn't the feds. It was the CIA. They approached me. You have to believe me, man. Please don't kill me."

As soon as Lucky heard the *CIA*, he picked up Sergio and threw him on the sofa.

"Let me shoot this piece of shit, Lucky!" Blood yelled as he cocked back his gun. "He's already crying like a bitch. Let me shoot him."

"Chill. Not yet, Blood," Lucky said, pushing him away. "Let him talk first. Maybe, just maybe, he can save his own life. So, Sergio, please tell us what they wanted."

Sergio looked around his living room before answering. He was looking around for some type of weapon, and trying to think of a way to escape. After not seeing anything, he realized his only chance of staying alive was to tell Lucky the truth.

"They came in here looking for you. I don't know how they knew, I swear to God, and I didn't tell anyone. Those muthafuckas just showed up at my door. They're blaming you for the assassination. They kept mentioning some conspiracy theory shit. I don't know. They just want my help."

Lucky backhanded him across his mouth and grabbed him by his hair with his right hand. He pulled his head back, placed his gun on his lips, and looked in his eyes. "Stop bullshittin'! What kind of help?"

"They want me to call them next time I hear from you. They offered me five hundred thousand dollars to testify that you were the shooter. They want me to frame you for the assassination." Sergio wiped the blood that was dripping from his mouth.

"It doesn't make sense. I know the CIA has ways of locating individuals, but how in the fuck did they track you down? is the question. Something is missing. Your story sounds funny."

"That's because he's lying," Blood yelled. "Slap that bitch-ass nigga again, or let me do it."

Lucky, still holding Sergio by his hair, pushed the barrel in his mouth. "Listen carefully to the next question. Your answer will determine your fate. When we were on the phone, you mentioned the one hundred thousand I gave Diamond. No one knew how much money I gave her, except Diamond and Divine. Divine is dead, so how in the fuck you know about the money?"

Sergio once again attempted to lie. "I remember one time you said—"

Lucky moved the gun around in his mouth. "C'mon now, Sergio, you know better than that. I never reveal info about my plans. How did you know? This will be my last time asking. I'm not playing," Lucky said as he placed his index finger on the trigger.

"Okay, okay. Diamond never left New York. She didn't want to live in Maryland. She knew you were never coming back. She was devastated. I let her stay here a few days before she went back home. She never told me where home was, but that's how I know about the money. I'm sorry I never told you."

Lucky let Sergio go, took a few steps back, and just stared at him. He wanted to empty his whole clip in his face, but he needed more answers because now it was getting deep. Those missing pieces were coming to life. He paced Sergio's living room back and forth, thinking about the bomb Sergio had just dropped. It really left him at a loss for words, but it gave him a lot to think about.

"Last time I was here, you left to visit a female friend. Were you talking about Diamond?"

"Hell fuckin' no. I would never touch Diamond. She slept right on the couch. She didn't have anywhere else to go, and she didn't want to stay in a hotel with all that money. After she left, I never heard from her again, I swear," Sergio said, pleading for his life. "Please, believe me."

"I'm still not convinced. If she was here, you must have known about her dropping a dime on me. You didn't stop her. Oh, now I fucking get it. She either called the cops from here or your cell phone. That's why the fuckin' CIA was here, right? They traced the call."

Lucky grabbed Sergio by his hair again and threw him back on the floor. "Blood, go in his bedroom and grab a few pillows. This bitch is dead."

"No, wait. C'mon, Lucky, you were like a father to me. I looked up to you."

"I'm glad you understand why I have to kill you. You violated the code. I also looked at you as my son. I'm going to punish you like our ancestors punished their kids when they betrayed the family. Capital punishment."

Lucky used Sergio's belt to tie his hands behind his back and turned the volume on the radio up high. Blood came back with three pillows. Lucky placed one over each of Sergio's kneecaps and told Blood to hold one over his face.

Sergio began screaming, hoping one of his neighbors would hear him and call 9-1-1. "Help, please help!" he screamed.

"Shut the fuck up, bitch! Apply more pressure, Blood! Keep him quiet!" Lucky said as he pointed his gun at Sergio's knees and shot both of them.

The pillows actually worked, muffling the sound of the gunshots. Plus, with hip-hop blasting through the speakers, Sergio's neighbors were unaware that he was getting tortured to death.

As he lay there screaming, losing consciousness, and damn near bleeding to death, Lucky decided to give him one last chance to come clean.

"Blood, move the pillow away from his face," Lucky said as he leaned over. He pointed his bloody gun at Sergio and said, "This is your last chance to save your own ass. Where did Diamond go? And is the CIA on their way to meet her?"

Sergio was coughing blood, trying to catch his breath. "All I know, she said she was going back home, and that was it. The CIA didn't ask about her. They asked about your daughter."

Lucky quickly got worried, because the CIA knew how to find their prey. "Everyone is looking for my daughter," he said, trying to play it off. He didn't want to show Sergio he was concerned. "Is there anything else you want to add? Because, right now, I'm thinking you don't care about your life too much. You're not giving me anything to work with." He'd just about had it with Sergio.

"I guess I'm not such a good criminal, after all. Maybe I needed better training. You never—"

Lucky grabbed the pillow from Blood, put it over his face, and shot him twice. He wasn't about to allow Sergio to disrespect him. He was the one who'd crossed the line.

Sergio did mess Lucky's head up with the new twist. Now his family wasn't safe down in Atlanta. Sergio could have told them they were down there.

Lucky was mad that he'd killed him before asking him. He got caught in the moment and acted off his reflex. With a gun in his hand and his mind set on using it, the power of holding the weapon manipulated his thought process and made him pull the trigger. Caught in the moment, he forgot all about using patience in his approach. He had wanted to kill Sergio within the first ten seconds of entering the apartment and was surprised he'd waited as long as he did. At least he had confirmation that Diamond indeed was the one who leaked the info and called the cops.

Lucky made a living out of reading people's eyes, and he honestly couldn't tell if Sergio was lying. But he sounded believable. The only way to be sure was to find Diamond and get her to explain herself. He still didn't know where she was located. She could either be back home, like Sergio stated, or she was under protective custody. One way or the other, he was going to find her.

But now he had a new concern. His family down in Atlanta might be in danger. He was going to have to call Tasha himself. He couldn't send anyone else. He needed to speak to her directly and explain the situation. The call was not going to be an easy one. Tasha could very well tell him to fuck off, or she could ride, like he was hoping.

Lucky was glad he was back in New York, where he had connections. Down in Maryland, he was a sitting duck in unfamiliar territory.

After Lucky and Blood wiped down whatever furniture they might have touched, they left Sergio's apartment. Blood wanted to know where Lucky wanted to go next.

Lucky said, "I need a hotel room to lay low for a few days."

"A hotel room, never. You could stay with me, Lucky."

"Nah. I already lost two good friends because of my past. I don't want to have to lose you, too. A hotel room is all I need."

"A'ight, but around here all we have is fuck motels. I know you don't want to stay in one of those nasty places. I can't allow that."

"Ha! I feel you. I can't stay in New Jersey. I'm not trying to cross any tolls."

"Look, I got this bad bitch that's out of town, in Atlanta, for a few weeks, handling business. I got the keys to the apartment, which is my personal stash house. You could stay there if you want. No one knows about the place."

"Where she live?"

"She's right in Harlem, right off Riverside Drive, on 168th Street. It's a three-bedroom condo. You'll have it all by yourself. Plus, it has its own security camera system. I know you love the sound of that."

"For real, or are you bullshitting me?"

"For real, fam. This is where I keep my money and most of my product. I have to keep an eye on things. I paid like twenty thousand for the alarm, and I have a few computers as well. You'll have all the technology you need to keep you busy while we find this bitch. Are we still going after the mayor or what?"

"Hell yeah, we are. The apartment sounds perfect."

Lucky thought the apartment idea was great. He would get a chance to hide and relax a bit until he came up with his next plan. He was glad to hear about the security setup.

Blood drove him straight to the apartment, and they went in unseen. Blood showed him how to work the security system, and he showed Lucky where he kept his guns, which included two AK-47s, at least twelve different handguns, and what looked like a few pipe bombs.

"Are those bombs, Blood?"

"Listen, after my brother was murdered, I was going to run up in city hall and blow a few muthafuckas up. My peoples talked me out of it, so now I'm looking for one of these Hala muthafuckas."

"I don't understand, Blood. Why are you looking for an Arab?"

"So I can sell this shit to him. I don't need them anymore. They might strap them on themselves and run up in city hall."

Lucky couldn't stop laughing. "You are one crazy cat."

"Shit! Them Halas kill themselves all the time. I'm sure if I offered them six figures, they will do it. I'm dead serious, too."

"Like I said, you are loony, but those bombs could come in handy."

"I'm ready when you ready. They're not getting away with killing my brother. I have to bounce and take care of business. Don't worry. No one should show up here, so if anybody rings the bell, you know what to do."

"Oh, trust me, I will be up and ready. I won't get caught with my dick in the dirt." Lucky grabbed his private parts.

"Here, take this phone. My number is the only one saved on it. Call this number if you need anything. I'll come back later and bring you food. You'll be good here. I love you, and I'm glad you called."

"Don't worry about bringing food. I'll handle it. Just give me a few days. Then come through. Be careful out there. Remember, we have all kind of alphabet boys after us."

"I feel you. I'm not trying to get caught with my dick in the dirt, either. I'll just call you."

After Blood left, Lucky sat on the plush leather sofa and watched the fifty-inch plasma. He was trying to get his mind off all the drama that took place no more than thirty minutes ago. He wanted to catch up on some of the current news about him. In Maryland, the news channels spoke about him briefly and did bullshit stories on him. In New York it was a different story. Lucky was on TV more than the O.J. trial.

When he turned the TV on, he just caught the end of Destine Diaz's report about the latest on the Coleman trial, and about Captain Tuna and Speedy still being in Central Booking for their own protection, instead of being transferred to Rikers Island. Lucky laughed when he heard about his former partners still in the lockup and with no bail. He knew support for them was no longer existent. He only wished they were a lot easier to reach. Being locked in protective custody was their life support. Once they came out, they were as good as dead. It didn't matter if they were home or up north, serving a bid.

As Lucky finished watching the news, he got ready to jump in the shower. Before turning the TV off, he said to himself, "I need to set up an exclusive with Destine Diaz."

Lucky knew that would be impossible. The only way that could happen was if he kidnapped her and forced her to interview him. He doubted she would accept his invitation without warning the cops, or at least he wasn't going to take that chance. He figured the interview would allow him to give his side of the story, and so the public might take it a bit easier on his character. He wasn't going to try to fool the public and lie. He was going to admit his guilt. He just wanted to make sure he cleared his name on certain charges, since the media and government made him look like a monster. For Lucky, it was very important to him the way he was remembered. He just wanted to remind all New Yorkers and Americans that corruption still existed and was acceptable across corporate America.

Chapter Twenty-three

117th Street and Seventh Avenue

After a forty-five-minute shower, all Lucky could think about was Sergio's last words. The CIA was now looking for his daughter. But he also couldn't stop thinking about Diamond. He believed she was still in New York and was plotting with Sergio to get his money. They both were money-hungry snakes.

He had two plans. One was to set up an interview with Destine Diaz; the other was to locate Diamond. If she was hiding in her hometown, Little Rock, Arkansas, it was going to be a challenge. If she was still in New York, then it was going to be easy to capture her.

Lucky didn't waste time in working on his blueprints. He logged on the Internet and into his private e-mail account. He needed to get in contact with a few of his old connects. He sent an e-mail to his Department of Motor Vehicle's connect, Asia, with Diamond's real name, Tracey Sanders, and her hometown. Asia, reliable as a bulletproof vest, would get back to Lucky within twenty-four hours. Asia didn't know Lucky's true identity. They'd met on a Web site called MyPlace.com. Asia ran her own private investigation business. Lucky conducted all his business through her Web site and communicated only via e-mail. After he sent her the e-mail, he logged off the Internet, turned the computer off, and unplugged it. He was covering his tracks, just in case the CIA or the feds were spying on Asia's company.

Lucky was paranoid. He plugged the computer back in and waited as it booted up. As he waited, he turned his attention back to the TV when he heard the Colemans were having another press conference. He jumped off his seat, got closer, and turned the volume up.

***

Laura was at the front stage like the strong black woman she was.

"Good evening. We decided to call this press conference because we wanted to update and address certain issues concerning our situation. I remember last time I held a press conference at my front door, we were shut down. The TVs went blank. Just in case that happens this time around, you could log on to our Web site, Perrycoleman. org. We are streaming live, and you will be able to see the entire press conference.

"Okay, let's get back to the serious matter at hand.

"I know New Yorkers have suffered enough, and right now, most are only concerned with the recovery process after the riots. I just want to bring closure and also begin my own personal healing and rebuilding process.

"I have met with the district attorney, and they have confirmed that both police officers who are in lockup have agreed on a plea deal. Each officer will face manslaughter one charges and will be sentenced to nine years to life. I couldn't believe the district attorney offered this deal without our approval. I would have loved to see the charges remain at murder one and they each get twenty-five to life for killing my son. We are bitter, but the district attorney has also made us aware of the numerous charges still pending against the dirty cops. They are still facing life in prison, which I hope they get. I'm just happy to hear that the trial is over, and they will at least serve nine years and spend the rest of their lives on parole.

"We, as a family, just want to turn the page on this book. I want to thank New York for all their support during these hard times. The city already has contacted our lawyers about a settlement before the civil trial begins. I want to go public and say, I promise to donate twenty percent of our settlement to the city. We want to help rebuild this great city.

"I also want to send a personal message to Donald 'Lucky' Gibson. Thank you. Thank you for coming forward and telling the truth. Thank you for the help. And I know in my heart you are not behind the assassination. Lucky, if you are listening, thank you. When the smoke

clears, everyone will see that because of your bravery, we have won the battle with corruption. You sacrificed your own life to save others and rebuild the truth. I understand you were not a saint and you have done your share of dirt, but I just want to let you know that in our household you are considered a hero, a misunderstood one, but a hero. Thank you."

As soon as Mrs. Coleman finished speaking, her husband grabbed her by her hand, and they both walked in their house. In their minds, they were hoping it would be the last time they had to face the media.

Lucky was touched by her words and admired Mrs. Coleman's courage. "This old lady has balls," he said to himself. He was happy to hear that a settlement was already in the works. He knew the city was going to have to break the bank to satisfy the Colemans.

He was shocked to hear about the plea deal. He thought the nine years to life sentence was another sign that Tuna and Speedy were on their own. The city had stopped supporting them.

Lucky walked back over to the computer and logged back into his e-mail account. He sent another e-mail. He wanted more info on the mayor's whole operation. He wanted to know exactly which agencies were involved and how many special agents were in the streets, looking for him.

He needed to tap into the mayor's personal files and e-mail accounts. There was only one hacker capable of pulling off such a task. His name was Cyber Chris. He specialized in hacking into top-secret government files. Lucky had saved his ass thousands of times in the past. Because of Lucky's old ways, instead of arresting Cyber, he put him on his payroll.

Lucky sent him an e-mail with the information he needed and a thirty-thousand-dollar promise of pay. Lucky's credit was good, so Cyber wouldn't hesitate to accept the job. Lucky again logged out, shut down the computer, and unplugged it.

It was going on eight o'clock, and Lucky was hungry. He found a Domino's coupon and called to place an order for delivery. After eating a large pie and drinking almost a two-liter soda, he became sleepy and went straight to bed. He figured that eating that kind of meal would enable him to sleep through the night and first part of the morning. Once he got up the next day, he would log on and see if he received any replies from his two contacts.

Around midnight, the phone Blood left Lucky started ringing. It rang about six times before it finally woke Lucky out of his sleep.

"Hello," a hoarse Lucky said.

"Wake up. It's Blood. We have a problem."

"What's wrong?" Lucky asked as he jumped off the bed and started getting dressed.

"I think the feds are onto us. My boys said they're watching two of my spots."

"What? Are you sure they not those suits from Sergio's apartment?"

"The CIA? I don't think so. Plus, from what we know, they in regular clothes. One van is parked on 147th Street and a Crown Vic on 117th Street. There's only a driver in the van, but in the Crown Vic, there are two pigs sitting inside. We are making our move and taking all three of them out. You are safe in the apartment, so just stay there. I will call you when it's done."

"Let me ask you this. Have you noticed this kind of heat before?"

"No. Why?" a curious Blood asked.

"Then that means they know I'm in New York and that we are together. Anyone else in the crew know about you driving down to Maryland to pick me up?"

"I see where you heading. Only two people knew, and I trust them with my life. In fact, I trust them more than I trust you, real talk."

"I feel you, but I'm just saying, look at all the facts. Now that I'm back in town, the feds are watching you. Sergio didn't know I was on my way back up to New York. Maybe they know who your brother was." Lucky tried to throw off Blood and defuse what could've turned into an argument.

"Maybe, but the block is hot. After I handle these pigs, I'm going to lay low for a few days myself. I'm going to see my white bitch in Long Island."

After Lucky got off the phone with Blood, he couldn't sleep. He was half dressed, and his heart was still beating at a fast pace. He was ready for war, but if Blood told him he was safe and not needed, he was going to keep his black ass in that apartment.

Lucky still couldn't calm down. He wanted to drive to 117th Street and jump out with two guns in his hands. A nervous wreck, he was ready to set it off.

He was in the same state of mind he was in when he was a dirty cop. He didn't care about anyone, and less about his own life. His daughter didn't even come to mind. He was too selfish. Once he set his mind on a target, it was like going undercover. He blocked out the real world. The fantasy life became a reality role.

Lucky was feeling indestructible, but a little overwhelmed. With all the alphabet boys on his ass, his chances of surviving were slim. He couldn't keep killing everybody and surviving at the end like Rambo. His luck would run out one day. He knew his fate. The problem was, he didn't care. He knew that if he stayed and continued the war, he was left with two options, dying or going to jail for life. And jail wasn't an option for him. In other words, he was ready to die.

He took his clothes off and just lay on the bed. He was trying to calm down and go back to sleep, but he couldn't. He figured he'd start working on how to set up the interview with Destine. Getting her number and address was going to be easy. How to approach her was going to be the hard part. He didn't know if he should show up at her job or at her home.

While Lucky thought about his next move, Blood was right on his FBI theory. Ex-Navy SEALs Marquis Jenkins and Angel Mendez were both parked across the street from one of Blood's operations on 117th Street and Seventh Avenue. They hadn't seen Blood or Lucky, but they felt like they were getting close.

"Marquis, you should call the mayor and give him an update."

"Chill, Angel. We don't have to call him every minute of the day. We are here under direct orders from the president. Fuck the mayor! Besides, I don't think he likes the fact we are on the case."

"I still think we should call him. He's still the mayor."

"Let's just wait until we have more proof. Right now we don't have shit, so why call?"

"Cool. Let's check in with Lee and see if anything changed on 147th Street."

"Lee, come in," Marquis radioed in.

"Everything is still quiet," Lee radioed back.

Marquis looked at his partner, and they both were on the same page. They knew something was off.

"Hey, when have you ever heard of these two streets being quiet? Maybe 117th Street, but not 147th Street. They must be on to us and shut shit down," Marquis said.

"Or maybe it's a setup," Angel added in a nervous tone.

"Setup? These muthafuckas don't have the balls to pull hits on cops. I worked in D.C. all my life, and for years it was known as the murder capital state. D.C. is no bigger than twenty miles. I survived the streets of Southeast. I know real killers. These fools are not killers."

"*Papi*, this is not D.C. I grew up in these streets. In New York they will smoke cops faster than crack. Either call for backup, or let's get the fuck out of here. Radio Lee and tell him to bounce as well," Angel said.

Marquis was a bit too cocky and ignored his partner's concerns. Being an ex-Navy SEAL and protecting the president, fear was never an issue for him. As they sat there, a car was coming down the street with the lights off. Marquis picked up on it quick and tapped his partner.

"Angel, it's time. Get ready. A car is creeping with their lights off. Unlock and crack your door. We may have to jump out that way," Marquis said as he cocked back his gun.

"About time we see some action. My Puerto Rican ass was getting tired. I'm up and ready," Angel said as he also cocked back his gun.

The car crept up and stopped right next to their car. The only reason Marquis didn't open fire was because he noticed the car was a Crown Victoria just like theirs, which was usually a cop car.

Good thing they didn't open fire. It was two narcotics detectives making their rounds. They rolled their window down, and Marquis did the same.

"To what do we owe the pleasure of having you guys snooping around in our turf? I'm Marquis, and this is my partner, Mendez. And you guys are?"

"I'm Detective Johnson, and that's my partner, Detective Simmons. We from the Thirty-third. This is our turf. You need permission to snoop in our block."

"We are working on a special assignment under direct orders from the mayor and president. Please continue driving down before you blow our cover," Marquis shot back.

"Oh, so you think the mayor has ranks out in these streets? I'm going to need some identification, since you are a smart-ass," Detective Johnson said as he stepped out of his car, his badge hanging down from his neck.

"All of this is not necessary. Fuck with us, and you will be on desk duty for the rest of your career!" Marquis said.

When Detective Johnson got out of the car to check for their identification, Marquis attempted to exit his car as well, but Johnson closed his door with his left hand, leaned over, whipped out his gun with his right, and emptied his clip inside of the car. Johnson didn't have time to look and see if they were wearing a vest, so he just aimed straight for their faces, shooting Marquis at least seven times, and hitting Angel at least four times.

Angel was able to let off a shot, but he ended up shooting his partner in the side of his stomach.

They were ambushed, caught off guard by Blood's crew posing as undercover cops. The trap worked, and they used the same tactic on Special Agent Lee Chang.

Blood's crew just finished pulling off three more hits, two of whom worked directly under the president. The city didn't need more bad attention, especially the killing of more police officers. It was going to be a rude awakening for most in the morning.

Lucky was anxious in the apartment, not knowing what was going down. He knew Blood was a killing machine. He didn't care who or where he was dedicated to thuggin'.

It was going on six in the morning, and Lucky was working on about three hours of sleep. The first thing he did was turn on the TV and watch the news. As he sat there, his worst nightmare came true as the news anchor reported.

"Again, three federal agents were killed in Harlem. We will be right back with more details."

Lucky was frozen still. He just sat there motionless and didn't blink. He was hoping what he just heard was still a bad nightmare. He was so tired, he thought maybe he was hallucinating. He started pinching himself. He didn't move from the sofa and waited for the news to come back on.

Lucky already knew Blood was responsible for the killings and was more concerned with the identity of the federal agents. He wanted to know their names and their ranks. When the news came back on, he finally moved his body, sitting up and listening.

"We are back. I'm John Silverman. Three federal agents were gunned down in Harlem. We have Destine Diaz with the latest. Destine."

"Thank you, John, and yes, you are correct. Today, around three in the morning, three federal agents were killed in Harlem. Two were killed on 117th Street and one on 147th Street in Harlem. The information we are receiving is very conflicting. According to the police spokesperson, it seemed like an ambush, but one witness told a different story.

"We have a witness who claims she saw the shooting out her window and that the shooter had a police badge around his neck. The police department has rejected those accusations, claiming that many professional killers are now posing as police officers. That matter is still under investigation.

"So far the identity of only one of the agents has been revealed. He is Special Agent Lee Chang. He was killed on 147th Street, shot three times in the face at point-blank range. The other agents, who are being labeled John Doe number one and number two, were also shot multiple times in the face. Again, the police department isn't saying much, except they still have no suspects, and they are not ruling out Lucky's involvement in the shooting.

"A source has stated that the agents were following leads on capturing Lucky. We will release more information as we receive it. The police are also asking anyone with information to please come forward. They are not letting us get close to the shooting scene here on 117th Street, but I will say this: There are a lot of suits down here. I'm assuming these two officers were of high rank or well loved. This is Destine Diaz reporting live from Harlem, Channel Five News."

Lucky didn't know how to feel. He was a little shocked to hear Blood had pulled off such a brazen move. The attack was too early, but you couldn't stop a man from getting his revenge. Blood's mind was made up, and no one could change it. The loss of his brother took him over the edge. He was ready to join him in the grave, but not without taking a few cops with him.

Lucky did love the slick move he pulled off, posing as police officers. He was sure the public was going to feel like the corruption in New York City would never end. With the past accusations against the city, many New Yorkers wouldn't be shocked to learn that cops were behind the killings.

Lucky didn't like that Destine mentioned his name in a negative way. He wasn't surprised, but he was bothered. Destine's tone and body language gave the impression that he was indeed involved in the shooting.

Lucky's cell phone started ringing. He knew it was Blood.

"You are one crazy muthafucka," he said. "You must have a death wish," Lucky said.

"I told you, once those pigs killed my brother and burned him, they created a monster. Anyway, I'm going away for a bit. Keep this cell with you, and I will keep in contact. But I will be off the phones for a while. The combination to the safe is 012449. That's my mother's date of birth. I have over two hundred thousand in there. You already know where all the guns are located. You do what you have to do. I will catch up with you later."

"Hold on, Blood. You sound like you're never coming back. What about your turf and transporting business?"

"Hey, I might not come back at all. I already shut down three locations. The heat is coming, so I'm out before I get burned. I'm not caring about any businesses right now, you feel me? If I was you, I wouldn't leave that apartment. You are safe as long as you don't show your face. Don't worry about my girl showing up. I will call her and make sure she stays in Atlanta a few more weeks."

"You take care and stay alive. They will hunt you down till they find you, and they will shoot to kill. Two of those agents were high-ranked. For now, I'm staying in here until I'm ready to go find Diamond, and then I'm bouncing back with baby moms. Take care, fam. You are the realest nigga I have ever known. Be easy." Lucky hung up the phone.

Lucky was still distressed. The whole situation was moving too fast for him. He still didn't know if Blood's move helped or hurt him. It was in his favor that Blood's crew posed as police officers. Though Lucky didn't like the rampage Blood was currently on, it was going to help his case. Once the FBI figured out Blood's motives and involvement, some of the heat would shift his way. Then maybe, just maybe, Lucky could clear his name. A lot of the accusations were not warranted. And though he wasn't expecting to be pardoned for his ways, he wasn't trying to be remembered as an animal.

Lucky went into the back room and cracked the safe open. Blood wasn't lying. The safe was filled with money. After counting it, he was shocked that it came to two hundred thousand and ten dollars. Lucky felt like he was back on top of the world. He had access to money, guns, and a computer. "I'm back, baby," he said to himself.

Lucky logged on the Internet to check his e-mails to see if his connects replied. Both Asia and Cyber Chris had replied. He opened Asia's e-mail first. She had great information, giving Lucky a current address for Diamond's mother, and another address for one of Diamond's sisters. He knew he could count on Asia.

Then he opened Cyber's e-mail. He promised to start working on it ASAP and to e-mail information before the day was up.

Lucky was happy that the momentum was finally starting to swing back his way. Down and out since the night the storage got raided, he had forgot the feeling of living on top. Once he opened the safe, that feeling came right back. When a man had complete power, such as money, guns, and balls the size of King Kong, the feeling was indescribable. The sky was the limit.

But Lucky was celebrating a little too early. He thought he had all he wanted, but in fact, he needed an extra body, someone who could move around town for him. With Blood out in Long Island, he had no one else he could trust. He called up his little man from Maryland.

"Who is this?" Haze asked.

"What's good, little man?"

"Is this who I think it is?" Haze asked, a smile on his face.

"Yeah, it's me. Come to find out, I still need you up here with me. Do you still want to roll?"

"Hell yeah. I still have most of the money you left me. I will just bring it with me."

"Aw, man, that money is yours to keep. I don't want it back."

"No problem. I just need an address, and I'm on my way."

"Once you are in New York, just call this number, and I will have an address for you."

"You want me to come to Harlem?"

"Yeah, once you in Harlem, call me."

"Bet. I know how to get to 145th Street and Lenox Avenue."

"Perfect. Just call me."

After Lucky hung up the phone with Haze, he immediately started working on the plan. He wanted to drive to Arkansas himself, but he couldn't risk it. He was going to send Haze first and have him check both addresses. If he spotted Diamond, then he would head out there. He had a few pictures of Diamond in his e-mail and was going to print them and have them ready for Haze.

He started plotting his kidnap move. He had Destine's home address, so he was going to start off by staking out her house. He kept the TV on channel five, to keep up with any new updates.

The mayor was at the crime scene on 117th Street, walking around, shaking his head back and forth. He was speechless. Good thing he had Richard with him to serve as his mouthpiece and handle the press, since he was running out of excuses.

What the mayor was really scared of was a phone call from the president, who had two ex-Navy SEALs killed, and he didn't have any answers or suspects. As Richard was gathering all the information, the mayor got on the phone, called his secretary, and asked to get in touch with the Secretary of Defense, Hilda Canton.

When the mayor got off the phone with his secretary, Richard was approaching. "What's the latest?" the mayor asked. "And please tell me Lucky was behind this."

"Well, Lucky's name, so far, has not come up. All the details are still sketchy, but according to a few witnesses, the shooter had a police badge around his neck. We doubt they were real police officers. So far, no leads."

"I can't believe we don't have any leads. Three federal agents are dead and we have no suspects, not even one clue? We are doomed. The press is going to have a field day with this bullshit."

"I will go handle the press. You, in the meantime, have other issues. Don't turn around, but the governor is heading this way, and boy, he doesn't look happy."

"God must hate me. He really does." The mayor waited to hear the governor's voice before he turned around.

"Ralph! Ralph, what in the hell happened here?"

"I'm still trying to figure it out myself," the mayor replied.

"Did you approve this operation?" he asked angrily.

"Listen, the president gave the two ex-Navy SEALs the green light to find Lucky. They didn't need my permission. They called me and said they were going to watch Pee-Wee's brother's several locations, and I said no problem, as long as they keep me updated."

"Who is Pee-Wee again?"

"The burn victim we pulled from the storage, the one we all thought was Lucky. He has a brother named Blood. They were the worst brother tandem the city ever had to deal with. They figured Blood and Lucky might be working together. Maybe they were right, or their cover was blown."

"Three more dead agents, and two of them were ex-Navy SEALs. Next thing you know, they're going to ask me to step down as governor. What are our options?"

"I don't fuckin' know, but we don't have many. The press, the city are going to demand answers as to why we can't get over the hump and end the killing spree going against police officers and FBI agents."

"We need to come up with a quick solution. You don't have any other ideas, anything?"

"I do have one," the mayor said in a low tone, knowing the governor wouldn't approve. "Hear me out first. Maybe we need to release Captain Tuna and Speedy back out in the streets."

"What was that?" The governor got closer to the mayor and whispered in his ear, "Did you just say release Tuna and Speedy? That's the dumbest idea! Are you serious?"

The mayor took about three steps back. "Think about it. Lucky will come out the hole he's crawled into. It will basically be bait. We will just post bail for them and have them sit at home under house arrest."

"Then what?"

"We'll just watch Tuna and Speedy, and Lucky will show up. That's a guarantee."

The governor started walking in circles, holding his chin, thinking about the new proposal the mayor just threw at him. At first it sounded dumb, but the whole bait theory made sense. He walked back to the mayor.

"Okay, I'm going to agree with you on this one, but expect the city and the media to come down on you for the decision. They're going to eat you alive, and you won't be able to hide behind Richard for too long. You're going to have to face the press one day."

"I'm aware of the backlash, but once we finally capture Lucky, they will back off a bit," the mayor said in a confident tone.

They continued their conversation for a few more minutes before the governor left.

The mayor waited for Richard. Then they left together. On the way back to the office, he said to Richard, "We are going to authorize bail for both Tuna and Speedy, and get them back out in the streets. Lucky will show his face once he sees his two enemies released. He's not going to sit around while Tuna and Speedy are walking the streets of New York. Lucky wants them dead. We will need twenty-four-hour surveillance for both of them. Lucky will attack, and when he does, we'll be waiting."

"I like the idea, but are you ready to explain it to the city? The people are not going to take it lightly."

"It can't be any worse than the way they've been treating me these past few months. I don't have anything to lose. I have to resign on the last day of my term. What other choice do I really have but to put the pedal to the metal? If we capture Lucky, then the CIA will handle the rest. If this plan goes accordingly, the CIA will be able to help clear our image by exposing Lucky as a liar, whose plan was to set up the government." The mayor turned on the radio, a clear indication he didn't want to speak about it anymore.

Chapter Twenty-four

The Mayor's Last Desperate Move

The mayor needed the support of the governor in order for him to make calls and get the ball rolling. After a few phone calls, he set up a special arraignment the following morning. The judge was going to set bail at a million dollars apiece, and they both would be monitored by ankle bracelets and curfews upon their release.

After they arrived back at the mayor's office, Richard decided to leave. He couldn't take it anymore. He knew his boss was making a mistake by releasing Tuna and Speedy. The plan sounded good, but it was too risky.

Richard couldn't believe, with all the alleged corruption, that any government official would still do favors for the mayor. He was already bothered by the fact that he was kept in the dark about the assassination plot. He knew the mayor couldn't be trusted and would do whatever to clear his name. Richard knew it was time for him to look out for himself for once. He couldn't wait for the bomb to drop, because when the smoke cleared, the mayor would blame everything on him.

He decided to get in contact with Destine Diaz and start working on a plan of attack to clear his name. He pulled out his BlackBerry, found her number, and called her.

"This is Destine."

"Hello, Destine. This is Richard Claiborne."

Destine sat up in her chair and kicked everyone out of her office. She'd been waiting on his call for about four years now. "Surprise, surprise! I thought you didn't know my number, mister spokesperson," she said in a flirtatious voice.

"I didn't call to chitchat or catch up on things. Do you want the story of your life?"

"What do you have for me? You know I'm ready. You wouldn't call me if you thought I couldn't handle it," a cocky Destine shot back.

"I can't speak over the phone. We need to meet this evening, and not in public."

"Can you come by my place? I have a condo on Twenty-second Street and Park Avenue. Can you stop by around nine, or is that too late?"

"That's perfect. I will call you when I'm outside, and please, no cameras or tape recorders."

"I promise," Destine said before she hung up the phone.

Destine couldn't believe the phone call she'd just received. Richard, always known as the mayor's pet, and a loyal one, too, was not known for sharing information. Destine knew the information had to be top secret. She couldn't wait till that night. She was upset she didn't say seven instead of nine. Destine didn't trust anyone in her office, or the entire building, for that matter, so she decided to keep the conversation with Richard to herself. She knew the media was a cutthroat business where you had to keep your story to yourself until you confirmed the facts and you had your name stamped on it, or the next reporter would steal your story.

Destine went about her day as usual and tried her best to ignore the clock.

Richard, on the other hand, was racing against time. He knew he had to relocate once he sat down with Destine and revealed the truth, but he was having second thoughts about it as well. He kept thinking about his family. It wasn't fair for them to move last minute and change their identities, and he wasn't sure they would understand.

Richard was upset that the mayor kept him in the dark about Commissioner Fratt, but somehow he felt like he was committing a sin. On the other hand, if he didn't relocate and change his name, he would risk his freedom. Richard Claiborne wasn't built for the penitentiary and wasn't about to go to jail for the mayor. He was concerned his wife wouldn't bite on relocating. He was going to have to make a decision. But if he had to leave on his own, he would, since jail time wasn't an option. If he cooperated, he would be in the same position, anyway. His former boss would have him killed if he found out he was the one who leaked the information, and his family would have to go under protective custody. He just hoped his wife would roll with the plan.

As the day unfolded, it was getting worse for the mayor. While in his office, he received a call from Hilda Canton.

"Hello. It's Hilda. We are extremely disappointed on the current events. The president is overseas and will return shortly. He wanted me to express his frustration. It will be in your best interest to resolve this manhunt and gain control of your city before the president returns," she said.

"With all due respect, the president said he was leaving me the best two ex-Navy SEALs available, and they both were murdered with ease. Hopefully, he will understand what kind of monster we are dealing with. This character has already proved to be one of the most dangerous wanted men we have sought after. I need more help. Two SEALs won't get the job done. People are starting to call him the American bin Laden."

"Well, we'll just have to wait and see about that, but the question you should be asking yourself is, can you afford the wait?" Hilda hung up.

The mayor looked at the phone and didn't know how to take the threat. He didn't know if she meant they were going to fire or kill him. At that point, he didn't give a fuck. They had to get in line if they wanted to kill him. The mayor's only concern was capturing Lucky, and releasing Captain Tuna and Speedy was his last hurrah. If it backfired, he was going to kill himself, anyway. He wasn't about to face the embarrassment of corruption and possibly spending life in jail. If he killed himself, it would be easier for his family to move forward and mourn.

The mayor went home to spend time with his loved ones. He knew in the morning, after Tuna and Speedy were released on bail, he was going to face a media riot. He wanted to be well rested and maybe spend his last night at home with his wife and three daughters.

***

The governor didn't get a chance to go home and spend time with his wife and kids. He was too worried for the mayor. He knew his career was over. He wanted to save it before it was too late. Even though he agreed with the plan, he wanted to keep his involvement to a minimum. That way, if everything blew up in the mayor's face, it wouldn't affect him, but if it worked out, then, of course, he'd jump on the bandwagon and take credit for his involvement.

It was going to be a long night in New York City. Once word got out about the release of Captain Tuna and Speedy the next morning, the city would turn chaotic, especially after the Laura Coleman press conference where she made it clear on live TV about their plea deal and additional charges. The city was also right in the middle of negotiations with the Colemans on a lump sum settlement for the wrongful death of their son. How did you explain that the cops who pleaded guilty to manslaughter and were due in court for sentencing in four weeks were released on bail while fighting other corruption charges? It would actually set back the relationship between the city and its people, and erode the trust that was slowly building.

Lucky was glad to see Haze when he finally arrived after they went back and forth on the phone. Haze had been lost and couldn't understand the directions Lucky was giving him. After he arrived, Lucky showed him the apartment and wasted no time in getting ready to execute his next move.

"Listen, Haze, I don't have too much time to explain everything, but right now we need to go watch this apartment in downtown Manhattan."

"So let's go."

"You don't care who it is?"

"Nope. You called, and I came."

"That's gangsta. I could respect that. I'm thinking about kidnapping this reporter. I need her to record my side of the story."

"I understand. If you approached her straight up, she might call the boys on you. I'm with you."

"Exactly. So we are leaving in a few minutes." Lucky went in the room to freshen up and change his clothes.

It was going on nine o'clock. Destine was sitting on her sofa, sipping on Moscato, staring at her cell phone, waiting on Richard's call. Five minutes later, her phone started ringing.

"Hello," she answered in a sweet, low tone.

"It's me, Richard. I'm on the corner."

"My building number is seven hundred. I left your name with the doorman. Just show your ID, and he will give you access to the elevator. I'm on the last floor."

Right after Richard entered the building, Lucky, parked across the street, turned to Haze. "And the plot thickens," he said, rubbing both his hands together.

"Who is that, Lucky? He looks like a fed boy."

"That right there is the mayor's right-hand man, Richard Claiborne. There's no way he's hitting that, so I'm assuming he's there to drop a bomb. I guess he and the mayor are having a falling-out. This is perfect. I think we are going to have to switch our kidnapped target. I'm more interested in speaking to Richard than the reporter. This is why I love stakeouts. Listen and learn, li'l homie. Watch your enemies first before attacking them, and you will find better and easier strategies to eliminate them."

"Oh, I'm listening and learning. I still can't believe you're a cop. You like a hustler's mentor or some shit," Haze said in amazement.

"You like or watch sports?"

"Just football. I'm a die-hard Baltimore Raven fan."

"Perfect. I'm a Giant fan, but I'm a sports fan, period. You learn a lot from studying games and your opponents. I only study weaknesses, though, because that's how you beat the game, li'l homie. Offense is always good, but defense should always take precedence over everything. You feel me?"

"Got it."

Meanwhile Richard was upstairs spilling his guts. But before they began to speak, Destine had to be clear on his reasoning.

"So, tell me again," she said. "Why are you here? Are you pulling a trick on me?"

"No. I'm here because I could barely live with myself. I have protected this man for years, and I can no longer do it. I will not lie anymore."

"Okay, so what do you have for me that's so important? When you say 'this man,' are you talking about the mayor?" Destine thought that maybe Richard was just a bit crazy, and that she'd made a mistake inviting him to her apartment.

"Yes, this crazy man has arranged a secret hearing to set bail and release those bastards back into the streets."

"Are you referring to who I think you are? Are they letting those two dirty cops out on bail? Why? For what? Did you guys see the Colemans' press conference where she clearly stated they pleaded to manslaughter? You are going to release these two animals after all the mess they've caused?"

"Let me finish, Ms. Diaz. Why do you think I'm here? I don't agree with the decision. It was the mayor's idea, and the governor gave it the green light. They are hoping, by releasing Tuna and Speedy, they can make one last run at Lucky. I think the idea is dumb, especially after those three federal agents were killed."

"Are you serious? You mean both the governor and mayor are working together on this? I will be there tomorrow morning as they exit the courthouse. Secret, my ass. I'm glad you came forward. So, did Lucky really kill those three agents?"

"We don't know where he is. After he shot that officer in VA, we have had no contact. We don't know if he's still in Virginia or if he went to the fuckin' North Pole."

"What about those two agents killed on 117th Street?"

"Those two agents were assigned by the president himself. They were both ex-Navy SEAL, ex-secret agent, or some mess like that. Anyway, they were supposed to be the best. They were in the streets no more than a week, and they both were killed."

"Is the federal government helping on the situation? I saw Lucky was featured on *America's Most Wanted*. I know that must help."

"Both the FBI and the CIA are involved. There are all kinds of conspiracies going around."

"What kind of conspiracies? Are you referring to the assassination?"

"I won't get into details, but let's just say, Lucky wasn't the shooter."

"Are you serious? If he didn't kill the commissioner, then who did?"

"We're still trying to figure it out. The CIA knows who the shooter is, but they are not telling. We are clueless. I'm just trying to jump ship before it capsizes," Richard lied to her. He didn't want to say the mayor was responsible.

"And how deep is your neck tied up in this mess?"

"I made his dirty work look clean. I overlooked and turned my face on many occasions. I could have blown the whistle a long time ago, but when you know the information I know and how corrupt this city really is, you keep your mouth shut. I've seen informants disappear in thin air."

"So why are you speaking now?"

"Because the empire is crumbling and I'm going to disappear. I'm not going to stick around."

"What part of our conversation is off the record?"

"Well, I want you to show up at the arraignment tomorrow, but about the assassination, please keep that off the record. Well, at least give me about three to five days to clear all my accounts and move my family. After that, I don't care what you say, but please don't quote me."

"I will respect your wishes, and may God bless you. Would you like a glass of wine?"

"Oh, no, thank you. I have to leave now. You be careful who you share this information with. It could cost you your life. Good night." Richard got up and let himself out.

Destine walked toward the door, shut it, and looked through the peephole, hoping Richard wouldn't come back and say he was playing. After a few seconds, she realized it was all true. She sat back on her sofa and poured another glass of wine. Her hand was shaking as she took a small sip of her Moscato. For the first time in her professional career, she had doubts and was scared. She had always wanted her shot, and this story could be it, but it came with a risk.

Then it finally hit her that Richard was leaving town because maybe the mayor was involved in the assassination.

As Destine sat there contemplating her next life-changing decision, Lucky was tailgating Richard.

Lucky turned to Haze. "At the next light, just pull up on the driver side. I'm going to try to jump in his car. Once I make my move, I want you to drive in front of him and block his path. Once I have control, just follow me. I'm not going to kill him unless he decides not to talk. He just left a reporter's house. I'm sure he was up there cooperating. Hopefully, he's still in a talkative mood. Okay, Haze, just roll up slow like an ordinary driver. I'll handle the rest."

As Haze pulled up next to Richard's black S600, Lucky quickly jumped out and stuck his gun through his half-open window.

"Turn the fuckin' car off and unlock the doors."

As soon as Richard noticed it was Lucky, he did as he said. He knew he was dealing with a killer and wasn't going to take any chances.

"Okay, I know who you are," Richard said as he turned his car off and unlocked the doors. "Please don't kill me. What do you want from me?"

As Lucky opened the door, he said, "Jump over to the passenger seat before I shoot your white ass."

Terrified, Richard jumped over.

Lucky jumped in and drove off while pointing his gun at Richard. Normally, he would knock out his victim, but Richard was no threat, so he gave him a break. He pulled over at the next available parking spot and then turned to him. "Okay, so why were you at that reporter's house?" he asked him as he pointed his gun at his face.

"Okay, wait. Don't shoot. I don't have any problems with answering all of your questions. You could actually just put the gun away. I want to help."

Lucky lowered his gun to make Richard feel more comfortable. "What was the meeting about?"

"Your ex-partners are getting out on bail, and the government is paying the bill."

"What? Are you fuckin' serious?"

"Yes, I am. The mayor is hoping this is their last shot at capturing you. He's pushing for one final plan. They want to charge you for the hit on the commish."

"But I didn't kill the commissioner. All I did was expose the truth."

"I'm about to tell you something that is top secret. Not even the feds are aware. I know you didn't kill the commissioner. It was Ralph. The mayor pulled off the hit. The CIA stopped by the office. They were the ones who figured out he was behind the hit. The CIA has agreed to help frame you, but the mayor has to do what no one has been able to do. Capture you."

"So the mayor hired the hit man, the CIA has proof, but somehow they still want to frame me?"

"That's correct. I'm done. I'm on my way home to pack, and I'm leaving town. If you have any more questions, now is the time."

"What is Destine going to do?"

"She'll be at the secret arraignment tomorrow morning with cameras. I want everyone to see how corrupt they are. Your best move is to disappear just like me."

"Who snitched on me? Who told ya about the storage facility?"

"I don't remember the girl's name."

"Where is she? Is she in protective custody?"

"No, she disappeared as well. Since she called the hotline, we haven't heard from her at all."

Lucky raised his gun and pointed it at Richard's face, erasing the confident swag he had three seconds ago.

"Listen to me carefully. Please don't make me shoot you. Where is she?"

"I swear to God, we don't know where she is," a frightened Richard quickly shot back.

Lucky had believed him the first time he said it, but he just wanted to make sure. He lowered his gun, and right before opening the door, he said, "If you tell anybody about this meeting, I will find and kill you."

"Don't worry, Lucky. I will be on the run myself. Thank you for sparing my life."

Lucky jumped out of the car and got back in the car with Haze, and they headed back uptown. Lucky decided to drive by the storage facility first. He wanted to see what kind of security was around. He needed to get his money out of there quickly, before a construction worker found it.

When they arrived there, he was surprised to see only one police cruiser on the block. Other than that, the property was burned to the ground, and was unprotected as well. That was all he needed to see. He decided to go in.

"Park right over there, Haze. Tonight is a perfect opportunity for me to go in. All you have to do is call me if you see the police cruiser move."

"A'ight, I got you."

Lucky got out of the car down the block and entered his storage facility through the back. The place still smelled like fire, and there was a lot of burned-up wood and trash all over the place. As he walked around, he thought about that fatal morning when he lost two friends. With every step he took, he was replaying the night. He could actually see Divine and Pee-Wee both holding guns, ready to die for him. It was a terrible feeling.

He finally reached his stash box. When he went to punch in the combination next to the door handle, he noticed it was already open. He quickly swung open the door and noticed the box was empty. All the money, drugs, and guns were gone.

Lucky stepped back and rubbed his head. "What the fuck! Where is my shit?" he asked himself, dumbfounded.

He snapped out of it and ran out of there like it was a setup. He jumped back in the car, and they drove off.

"My money, everything is missing, Haze. I don't know what the fuck is going on."

"What you mean, gone?"

"It's all gone, empty. Good thing Blood left me that money and guns behind. If not, we would have been fucked."

"Now what?"

"We are going back to the apartment while I try to figure out who stole my shit."

When they arrived back at the apartment, Lucky was mad as hell about his money. Different suspects ran across his mind. He logged on to the Net and checked his e-mail to see if Cyber Chris had found any information besides what Richard had already told him. When he logged on, he was happy to see that Cyber had finally sent him an e-mail, but he was disappointed after he read it. Cyber told him he was unable to break into the mayor's computer system, but he was able to get two very important addresses.

Since Cyber Chris didn't come through like he was supposed to, he didn't charge Lucky anything, not even for the little information he provided. But Lucky was still satisfied.

"Haze?"

"What's good, boss?"

"You don't need to call me that, Haze. I think I'm going to hold off on searching for Diamond out of town. I have a funny feeling she's still in New York and might've been behind my money vanishing. I can't think of no one else who could have done it. She's the last one alive who knows about the money, unless Sergio opened his big mouth to the CIA and they got me."

"How you know this bitch is involved?"

"Please, watch your mouth. I want her dead, but you don't have the right to disrespect her. We clear?"

"My bad, boss. It won't happen again," Haze said, confused.

"Anyway, we are talking about a couple million dollars. That kind of money doesn't get stolen quietly. We just have to sit back and wait. Tomorrow morning will be a big day for us. Once the news camera catches these dirty cops leaving the courthouse, all hell will break loose. We'll just keep a low profile tonight and wait until the morning news."

Lucky was feeling like Blood, ready to explode and start killing everyone. He was really puzzled about who robbed him. He could only pray for their families, because they were all dead.

As he sat on the sofa, watching a movie, Haze came over and said, "Lucky, I need to talk to you, and I need your big brother advice."

"What's good, li'l homie? Talk to me."

"Back home, I been fuckin' with this chick for like six months. Right before I came up here, she told me she was knocked up. She's, like, three months now."

"Congratulations!"

"You see, that's the issue. I'm not ready to be a father. She's talking about not having an abortion. I'm not in love with this chick. We just been kicking it for, like, six months. I know I fucked up by not using a condom. Shit! After a few months, I knew the pussy was mine, so I was just going raw. The pussy is good as shit, too."

"Ha! Ha! I feel you. Good pussy will make a man act unmoral. What kind of advice you want from me? If she's having it, then you going to have to step up and play the father role. You feel me?"

"We're not on the same page. I'm not ready to be a father, and she's not ready to be a mother. If she doesn't have the abortion, I'm going have to do the unthinkable." Haze grabbed the handle of the .38 on his hip.

"Slow the fuck down, Haze! You can't kill a pregnant woman. I understand you frustrated, but you have to find another solution."

"I need someone to talk her into an abortion."

"You sure the baby is yours?"

"I'm positive. I got shorty strung the fuck out. She's at my apartment right now, watching over my cousin. I left him there so he could serve my regulars. She's there to make sure my cousin don't fuck up and turn my place into a shit hole. She's a down-ass bitch, but we not ready to bring new life into this world."

"After this last job, with the kind of money I'm going to give you, you shouldn't have to sell drugs anymore. You could still be hustling, but running your own legit business. You could open a barbershop."

"I don't even know how to cut hair."

"You don't have to know. You could just run it and hire muthafuckas who know how to cut. Maybe open a clothing store. My point is simple. Having a baby will change your life, so you need to start making some life-changing decisions."

"But that's what I keep trying to tell her and you. I don't want to change my life. I'm up here with you, and you're the most wanted criminal in all of the United States. I'm here by choice. You didn't force me. If I had intentions of changing, I wouldn't be up here with you, ready to die."

"You're right, and I could respect that, but it's a little too late. The girl is pregnant. You can't kill her and the baby because you not ready to settle down. A man faces his responsibilities, not run from them. Trust me, I made the same mistake once with my daughter, and I wish I could take that decision back."

"What decision?" Haze asked.

"When my li'l girl was born, I didn't change. I was in the prime of my dirty career. I was making too much money and was snorting coke like a vacuum. Baby mama didn't take too lightly, and she bounced on me. For years, I blamed them and never once realized that it was me who pushed them away. For my ignorance, I lost time that I can't make up. You might be in the same situation."

"Trust me, I'm not. That bitch is dead if she doesn't get an abortion. I hear what you saying, but I thought you would be more on my side. If you ask me to kill someone, I wouldn't ask why. I will just do it. I don't understand why you can't side with me on this one."

"You asked for my advice, li'l homie. I don't just say what people want to hear. I say what's on my mind. Killing her would make things worse, especially if you get caught. You rather spend the rest of your life being in jail than being a father? That's crazy."

"It sounds crazy, but if you were in my shoes and at my age, you would be thinking the same. This bitch is trying to trap me, and I can't let her. I'm going in the room. I need to lay down and think about this shit here."

"A'ight, li'l homie, you will make the right decision," Lucky said to boost his spirits. "You will see."

Haze went in the room and closed the door behind him. He dropped backward on the bed, then stared at the ceiling, pondering his next move. He knew Lucky made sense, but he just didn't want to accept the reality.

Haze's childhood wasn't the greatest. He knew his parents weren't ready for him and his sister. Their upbringing was rough and came with a great deal of embarrassment. He remembered a lot of hungry nights, and kids at school making fun of their clothes and hairstyles.

Haze, at an early age, had to learn how to defend himself on his own. His father never spent time with him, and by the time he was seven, his father already had disappeared. Three years later his mother died of AIDS.

From then on, Haze bounced around from family house to shelter until he was about sixteen years old. That's when he went to Job Corps, where he acquired survival tactics and the tools to be successful. Haze utilized the job program as a benefit to find shelter and gain an education.

After a year and a half, Haze returned to Glen Burnie, Maryland. He'd made a weed connect while in Job Corps, and when he went back, he called him up and from that day on never looked in the rearview mirror.

Haze lost contact with his sister about four years ago. He tried hard to locate her but was unsuccessful.

As Haze lay on that bed and dwelled on the past, thinking about his sister made him emotional. Those feelings led him to see Lucky's point. It was not worth killing his baby mama and risk going to jail for life.

Haze walked back out to the living room, where Lucky was still watching TV. "You are right, Lucky," he said. "It's time I become a man and handle my responsibilities. When I get back home, the change is coming with me. Thanks for making me realize the reality of my actions. It's not like if I own my business and pay taxes, I'm a square. I don't have to be a thug to gain respect."

"I'm glad you came to your senses. If I didn't believe in you, I wouldn't have given you real advice."

"That's why I approached you, because you will keep it real. I'm going back to the room to get some sleep."

"A'ight. I'm going to stay up for a bit. I'll see you in the morning."

As Lucky lay across the sofa, channel surfing, he couldn't stop thinking about who stole his money. He went through his list of suspects. Diamond couldn't pull off the job alone, even though she was a great student. Lucky knew, somehow, there was a twist or a surprise. He just couldn't figure what it was. In his mind, the only person who could have helped her was Sergio.

Lucky sat up and thought to himself, *Damn! We didn't even check Sergio's apartment.* He jumped up and was about to get dressed. Then he paused. *I'm bugging. With that kind of money and product, it would have been visible.*

He sat back down on the sofa, but his mind kept playing tricks on him. He was breathing hard, and his heart was pounding out of his shirt. He went to the kitchen and poured himself a glass of cold water. After drinking the water, he leaned his head against the kitchen cabinet and let his mind work.

Next on his list was the CIA. They were capable of pulling off the job. But, to Lucky, it seemed too easy to pick them. He couldn't put it past them, since they were known for their dirty tactics as well. Lucky knew there was a third suspect involved, but he just couldn't figure out who. And it was killing him inside, since no one else knew about the money.

Lucky started banging his head against the cabinet.

Haze came out of the room and walked toward him. "Are you all right, Lucky? Why are you banging your head against the cabinet?"

"I'm good. I'm just trying to figure out who the fuck stole my money."

"I thought you said it was either Diamond or the CIA."

"I know, but there's a third person missing, and I can't figure out who it is."

"No disrespect, but what about Blood? He look grimy. Did he know about the money?"

"I can't lie. I thought about it, but I just can't see it. He would have called the cops on me. I don't see it. You feel me?"

"I feel you. So are you good? I'm going back to bed."

"I'm good. Good night, li'l homie." Lucky walked in the bedroom as well to get some rest.

It was going on three in the morning, and Lucky couldn't fall asleep. For some strange reason, he decided to call Tasha.

It would be the first time he'd be calling her since leaving Atlanta. He was scared to make the phone call, but he knew he had to make it.

He dialed her number. Her phone rang six times, and then it went to voice mail. He hung up and dialed the number again.

"Hello."

"Baby, it's me," Lucky said.

Tasha said, "Hold on." She got up because Tamika was in the bed with her. She walked over to the kitchen area. "Lucky, what the fuck? You finally decided to call? What the hell have you started? Did you kill the commissioner?"

"No, baby."

"I thought you were going to New York. Why the fuck were you in Maryland? You were looking for that other bitch? You fuckin' another bitch and I'm down here waiting on you. Fuck you, Lucky! You're not going to change."

"Please, baby, let me talk for a second. I did not kill the commish. The mayor did. I was down in Maryland, following some leads. Somebody stole my money. I'm almost done. I'll be down there soon. Give me a few more days. How is Tamika?"

"Don't switch up the conversation. Why can't you leave right now? They had you on *America's Most Wanted*."

"C'mon, how's Tamika?"

"She can't stop talking about you. Every day she asks me if you call and when you coming home."

"Damn! That's why I didn't want to call. Anyway, you make sure you tell her that her daddy loves the shit out of her and that I'm sorry I made the wrong decision in the past."

"You could tell her when you get here. I don't understand why you can't just walk away, but I understand my man. So, hurry the fuck up and stay alive. We miss you, Donald."

"I miss you guys more. Love you. Good night. I'm going to bed. I will call you."

"Good night. *Mwa!*"

Chapter Twenty-five

Bail Is Set

As the sun came up, Lucky was already on the floor, doing push-ups, and getting ready for the day. First thing he did after his workout was turn on the TV. It was going on six-thirty in the morning. When he went to knock on the guest room door, Haze came out sweaty. He was also in there working out. Lucky loved the kid's dedication.

"I thought I was going have to come in there and wake you up."

"Not me. I'm learning from the best. It's only right I follow your routine to the T."

They both went to the living room to watch TV. They weren't going to move until they saw Destine Diaz with cameras on those pigs' faces when they left the courthouse.

The mayor was at home having a nervous breakdown. He started having second thoughts about his decision to set Tuna and Speedy free. After spending the night at home with his family, he realized how much he didn't want to end up in jail. His wife wouldn't be able to handle the pressure of holding the family down on her own.

The mayor didn't mind losing his job. His loss of freedom was his biggest concern. The CIA knew he was responsible for pulling off one of the most brazen attacks against the city of New York. He had everything to lose and was backed against the wall. That was the reason why he'd decided to take yet another risk and release both Tuna and Speedy. The mayor was basically showing his selfishness. He was concerned only about his freedom and safety. If the plan was effective, he would at least guarantee his get-out-of-jail card.

He didn't care about the safety of either Tuna or Speedy. He knew their lives were in danger. At least in jail, while under protective custody, Lucky wouldn't be able to touch them, but in the street was a different story. Lucky had already proved to be a determined hunter, and unstoppable, too.

The mayor was almost certain Lucky would go after Tuna and Speedy. Before he left his house and headed to his office, his wife gave him a kiss and hug, something she hadn't done in a long time. It felt awkward, like his wife knew today would make or break their family and future.

As he walked toward his car, again he started second-guessing himself, but it was too late. All the chips were already in place. The hearing was set for seven in the morning, right before the morning court rush. The mayor wasn't going to be present. He went into his office. He was going to let Richard be his eyes and ears, and face the press afterward.

The governor, who'd also had a long night, joined the mayor at his office.

"I couldn't sleep. How about you, Ralph?" the governor asked.

"I haven't slept, either. We can't pull the plug now. I just hope this last attempt doesn't backfire on us," the mayor said in a low, sleepy voice.

"What about the media? Are they still in the dark?"

"So far they are. I haven't heard from Richard. That usually means the media still don't know. It won't take them long, though."

"I just don't want the media present at the hearing or near the courthouse," the governor shot back.

"Don't worry. We should be fine."

They continued their short talk as they killed time. It was going on seven in the morning, and they both were on the sofa, watching the morning news.

The mayor was a bit worried that he hadn't heard from Richard. He tried calling his cell phone, but it went straight to voice mail. The mayor couldn't remember the last time Richard's phone went straight to voice mail.

Around seven-fifteen in the morning, right after the weather report, anchorman John Silverman came on.

"Good morning, New York. In a few minutes, we will be coming live from the front steps of the supreme court down in Manhattan. Destine Diaz will report live on a breaking story that will sure shock all New Yorkers. Please stay tuned."

Both the mayor and governor looked at each other. They picked up their cell phones and started making calls.

The mayor called Richard numerous times but got no answer, so he called his secretary. She also hadn't heard from Richard. The mayor was beginning to sweat.

He turned toward the governor to see if he was able to reach out to any of his people. "I wasn't able to reach Richard. Have you heard from the DA or anybody else?" the mayor asked.

"No, I haven't. This is not good. How in the hell did the media find out about this so quick? We have a leak in our team. We need to head down to the courts right now. Once New Yorkers see these two police officers walking out the courtroom, their lives might be in jeopardy."

"Well, let's see what the report is about first," the mayor said, trying to bring calm to the situation.

"C'mon, Ralph, we both know what the report is about. Why would they be at the court steps?" The governor was furious.

The mayor didn't reply, because he was right. They both sat back down and waited like the other millions of viewers.

Speculation was rife around the local coffee shops and breakfast locations. Everyone thought they'd finally caught Lucky, who had turned into public enemy number one. After the assassination and the riots, the love for Lucky had vanished, and the people had actually started blaming him for everything. However, the catch-22 was that those two rogue cops roaming the streets, free on bail, proved Lucky's point—New York was a corrupt city.

The Colemans, along with Kim, were watching the news as well. They were also crossing their fingers, hoping they didn't catch Lucky. As they sat in suspense, so did Lucky and Haze.

Right before Lucky was about to get up for a glass of juice, the news came back on. He jumped back on the couch and turned the volume up.

"Welcome back. I'm John Silverman. Before the break, I reported we have an exclusive report with reporter Destine Diaz, who's down at city hall."

"Thank you, John. I'm here on the steps of the Supreme Court of the State of New York, where we expect to see Captain William 'Tuna' Youngstown and Detective Jeffrey 'Speedy' Winston, labeled the worst rogue cops in NYPD history. They have already pleaded guilty to manslaughter charges in the Perry Coleman case and have numerous charges pending, including murder, drug trafficking, money laundering, and all sorts of other corruption charges. They were sitting in jail with no bail, but somehow this morning, about five minutes ago, they were in a secret arraignment approved by the mayor himself, and they both received bail, which was paid within seconds after the ruling.

"We will try to interview these officers as they exit the courthouse. After what the city has gone through, I'm not sure New Yorkers will be able to handle yet another government scandal. Releasing these two officers will cause an ugly stir.

"I think the officers are walking out right now. Let's see if we can get any answers."

Destine walked up the steps with her camera crew to get a closer look at Tuna and Speedy. When Tuna walked out of the courthouse, another man threw a jacket around his head and rushed him down the steps.

"Detective Jeffrey Winston, can you please answer a few questions?"

Speedy actually stopped when Destine called his name. "Please, call me Speedy," he said in a stressful voice.

"Okay, Speedy, what happened in there? How did you guys manage to get bail, and who paid for it?"

"I don't know what happened. I was told by the correction officer last night that I had court today. I didn't know, and I didn't pay the bail."

"Then who paid the bail, Speedy?"

Speedy looked straight into the camera and slowly said, *"Taxpayers. Who else do you think paid the bail?"* He pushed the camera aside and walked away, ignoring Destine's calls.

"Well, there you have it, New York. These cops were set on bail with your tax dollars, according to Detective Jeffrey 'Speedy' Winston, one of the prime suspects in one of the worst corruption trials in New York history.

"Again, the two police officers, who were labeled rogue cops and were sitting in jail with no bail, were just released on bail. I'm referring to Captain Tuna and Detective Speedy. We will have more on this story as it develops. This is Destine Diaz, reporting live from city hall. Back to you, John."

Everybody who just heard the report went ballistic, many feeling double-crossed by the city once again, especially right after the riots. It was another setback.

The Colemans were beyond shocked. Laura herself stayed frozen. It took her husband almost a minute to get her to snap out of it.

"What the hell just took place, honey? Did I just see Tuna and Speedy walk out of the courthouse?"

"Those crooked bastards!" Perry Sr. said. "How can they give them bail and then try to have a secret arraignment? I'm glad the reporter was there and recorded them leaving out the hearin'."

"Once we get our money, I want to move as far away from New York as we can."

"What about Perry's body?"

"We'll have Perry's body transferred to whatever city we move to. I'm tired. I don't have the energy to fight anymore. Let them roam free in the street. I hope Lucky kills both of them."

"Laura, how can you say that?"

"All I wanted was for these officers to pay for what they done. Now they get a chance to sit at home while they go through another trial. Oh Lord, I'm sorry. Please pardon my behavior. I'm tired of playing Mrs. Good Lady, Jesus. How much longer does this nightmare last? I just want to move away, honey." Laura threw her body on the sofa in surrender.

***

Meanwhile, the mayor and governor were both throwing tantrums. They couldn't believe they'd really allowed Tuna and Speedy to walk out the front door.

"Where the fuck is Richard? How could they walk right out the front doors? Richard would never allow that to happen."

"Well, that didn't go well, did it? Not a good start for the final hurrah. Where is Richard? You think maybe he's the one who blew the whistle?"

"Who? Richard? I don't think he would cross me like that. We've been friends for over twenty years."

"Well, I'm sorry to be the one to break the bad news to you, but I think your boy gave us up. He's the only one who's unaccounted for at this moment. Did you guys have any type of confrontation?"

"Well, sort of, but it was nothing. Maybe you're right about him blowing the whistle, but until I speak to him, I'll hold my judgment."

"Fair enough, but you need to get in contact with him soon."

Lucky and Haze were watching TV with smiles on their faces.

"You see, Haze, all you have to do is sit back and watch everything unfold. It's like playing chess by yourself. You feel me? These idiots are making it easier for me. I'm going to hunt down Tuna and Speedy and kill them both."

"Ha! Ha! Let's do it. Are we also going after Diamond?"

"I'm more concerned about killing my ex-partners. Right now, I don't give a fuck about my money or Diamond. Tuna and Speedy, those are the only two names I want to hear around this muthafucka. Wait, did I just say I don't care about Diamond? I must be high."

"I was going to say something, boss, but—"

"My bad. While we hunting down these two cocksuckas, I'm going to have my peoples hunt down Diamond. I have a connect over in Motor Vehicle."

Lucky stood up, logged in the computer, and sent another e-mail to Asia, asking her to do a national search on Diamond's real name. He wanted her to check hotel reservations, flights, car rentals, real estate, rental properties, and bank accounts, if possible. Asia was good at what she did and had connects that could perform the kind of search Lucky was requesting.

As he was typing, Haze walked over and read the e-mail. "Is this bitch that good?"

"Who? Asia? She's the best. She would slap the shit out of Waldo and tell him to step his game up. That's how good she is. Once we know what city she's at, we will make our move. If she did take the money, she'll make a mistake. That's too much money for a female not to get tempted to spend in a wild shopping spree."

"You're right about that. She will go shopping. But what you mean, 'if she did take the money'?"

"Well, remember I told you right before we killed Sergio, we seen two suits walking out the building? Sergio confirmed they were CIA agents. Who knows what he told them. If he mentioned the money, then I know they went and retrieved it."

"That make sense. So who took your money? The CIA or Diamond?"

"That's the million-dollar question. If the CIA took the money, they would have brought it to my attention already. They would have used it as leverage. I didn't see any notes lying around. Maybe they'll use the media and send a message. If Diamond took the money, then her name will pop up somewhere."

"If you had to bet, who would you pick?"

"Diamond. Her and Sergio had this mapped out for a long time. I feel worse than I did before. She betrayed me. Once I catch this girl, hell will seem like paradise after I'm done with her ass. I'm going to torture her for like two days."

"Two days? Damn! I feel sorry for her already. Well, I'm about to roll up and get my mind right while you wait for Asia to get back at you." Haze got up and went back in the guest room to handle his business.

Lucky sat there in front of the computer and was browsing the Internet while he waited on Asia's reply. It was still early in the day, and he figured Asia should respond any minute now.

The TV caught his attention when the news showed clips of different political figures displaying their disappointment in the latest collapse within the government. It was obvious to the naked eye that Captain Tuna and Detective Speedy should have never had their bail status changed.

Every time Lucky thought about it, he laughed to himself. "The mayor has finally fucked his own self in the ass." All he could hope for was that the city would start to reconsider its quick judgment on him. He could never be considered a hero, but he was damn near close to one. He did what many wouldn't have done. He risked his life to tell the truth, not once, twice, or three times, but a bunch of times.

As Lucky was about to start making something to eat, he noticed he had a new e-mail. It was from Asia. She told him that Diamond was given a speeding ticket in Little Rock two days ago. That was perfect news. He didn't need to send Haze out there first. He could go and find her himself.

He called Haze back in the living room.

"What's going on, boss?"

"I told you about calling me that. Anyway, Asia just replied to my e-mail and said Diamond was given a speeding ticket near her hometown in Arkansas."

"So, when are we leaving? Tonight?"

"Nah. At least we know where she's at. I don't have to send you out there first. As bad as I want to find Diamond, my ex-partners are first on the list. I might not get another shot at them. They're both facing hard time."

As Lucky went over the new plan with Haze, the mayor was in his office, preparing to face the media and give a statement. He still hadn't seen or heard from Richard, whom he could always rely on to face the media and take the bullets he dodged.

The mayor knew something was off, because he even called Richard's home number and there was no answer. Maybe Lucky got to him and killed his whole family. Worried, he called his secretary and told her to send a police car to Richard's home.

The mayor would have never thought his good friend was actually the rat, as the governor pointed out. As he continued to sweat, trying to prepare the statement of his life for the press, his secretary called his phone. The CIA was back at the office and wanted to see him. He almost caught a heart attack. He fixed his tie and opened the door.

Agent Scott Meyer and Agent Marie Summit stormed in and slammed the door behind them.

"Don't walk in my office in that manner. What's the problem? I thought Richard gave you guys all the files you needed."

"Well, that's why we are here. You are not keeping your end of the bargain. We don't have all the files. We haven't heard from Richard. Where is he?" Agent Meyer asked.

"If you find him, let him know I'm looking for him as well."

"Are you saying he's AWOL, Mr. Mayor?" Agent Meyer asked.

"Correct."

"That's not good. What's this new mess about releasing those two dirty cops? You're making it harder for us to clear your name out this mess."

"Well, that's basically my last attempt at capturing Lucky. You guys want me to capture him, so that's what I'm doing. All we have to do is watch Captain Tuna's and Detective Speedy's homes, and Lucky will appear. He will make an attempt at killing both of them, and we'll be waiting."

"I will admit, I like your plan. The clock is ticking. You have about seventy-two hours before our offer expires. We also have new intel that may help your investigation. We tracked down who really called in the storage tip. It wasn't his female protégée. One of Lucky's students set everything up to steal the money he had stashed in the storage. His name is Sergio.

"Sergio had his girlfriend call and pose as Diamond. Of course, he was hoping nothing would be traced back to him. He just wasn't as smart as he thought he was. He should have never used his cell phone."

"That's great news. You mean to tell me a former student is willing to help us?"

"*Was.*"

"What you mean, was?" the mayor asked, looking at both Meyer and Summit.

"We went back to his apartment, and we found him dead. He was tortured pretty bad. We're assuming Lucky saw us when we stopped by the first time."

"There goes the great news. What the fuck happened? Why you guys didn't protect him? How can ya leave him there? He was a prime witness. We could have protected him."

"Sergio told us Lucky went to his apartment after the storage shooting and then headed down to Maryland to look for his protégée, but she's actually back home in Little Rock, Arkansas. Her real name is Tracey Sanders or Stevens. He wasn't sure. Lucky believes she's the one who leaked the information. He wants revenge. Sergio also said that Lucky's ex-girlfriend and daughter are now living in Atlanta. Lucky is not back in town just for revenge. He has a couple million dollars stashed in the storage facility."

"Well then, his money burned with everything else," the mayor said.

"Not exactly, sir. According to Sergio, Lucky had a fireproof room. We went back to search for this secret room. We found it, but it was empty. No money or drugs."

"Damn! He already got his money?"

"We don't think so. We're following other leads, but Sergio was after his money, as was Diamond. Maybe she went back, who knows."

"That's great to know. I could use that as bait. I can't believe he moved his family so quick. I really hope you are right about him not having his money, because he if does, he's long gone."

"Sergio also said that the day the commissioner was assassinated, he found Lucky passed out on his roof. He said Lucky had snorted so much cocaine, he passed out naked with his rifle by his hand and doesn't remember what happened that morning. It should be easy for us to pin everything on him."

The mayor's eyes opened up like a little kid's on Christmas morning. "That's fuckin' perfect. If he was found like you said, then it should be easy."

"Not so fast," Agent Summit said, finally breaking her silence. "You have to catch Lucky first, which obviously for you is hard to do."

The mayor looked at Agent Summit up and down. "When you see men conversing, please play your role and be quiet." He then turned back toward Agent Meyer. "I feel confident we will catch Lucky within forty-eight hours. I will call you if otherwise. Now, please, let me show you to the door. I have a press conference in a few minutes."

As both agents were walking out of his office, the mayor checked with his secretary to see if the police had arrived at Richard's home.

"Nothing yet, sir," she answered.

The mayor walked back in his office and started adding the finishing touches to his prepared remarks for his press conference.

Meanwhile, the news stations were already reporting that the press conference was taking place.

The mayor wasn't focused at all, with all the new info he had, and couldn't wait to start making moves. He could get the FBI to locate Lucky's family in Atlanta, while he followed up with his female protégée, who was still unaccounted for. Now they had her real name and the city where she was from. That should be an easy find.

There were all kinds of news reporters outside of city hall. New Yorkers were concerned with the new direction because, so far, it was still looking like the old corrupt one. The people were again demanding more assurance. The mayor's word wasn't good anymore. They didn't understand why those police officers had been released.

The mayor had about another thirty minutes before walking out to the podium. All of New York was once again glued to their TVs, radios, and logged on the Internet.

The Colemans were watching, and so were Lucky and Haze.

Lucky just wanted to hear what blame would be thrown his way.

Chapter Twenty-six

The Mayor's Press Conference

The mayor was going to update the city on recent developing stories. Richard wasn't around, but he'd sure picked up a few tricks watching Richard handle the press. He was going to use the press conference as his last plea to win the city back. As the time got closer to face the press, the mayor began to sweat heavily once again. He looked like he had run on the treadmill for ten miles with a three-piece suit on. What also made him nervous was the fact that the governor wasn't present. He was hoping they didn't kill him.

The mayor walked toward the podium, praying and asking God to forgive him. As he got closer to the microphone, he kept looking around, trying to locate any snipers. Before he even opened his mouth, spectators were already yelling obscene language at him. Those yelling obscenities were removed by the NYPD, according to their no tolerance code, and there were extra police present to prevent any outburst.

"Good afternoon. I want to thank everyone who waited so patiently. I'm here today to speak on certain matters that are slowing down our process in growing as a community. Especially after the riots, we need to put our differences to the side and stick together. It's easy to point fingers, but harder to stand up and make a change. I'm not here to place blame on anyone. However, I do take responsibility for everything. All the conspiracy theories of corruption happened under my watch. I accept the criticism. I watch the news and read the paper. I hear the harsh comments thrown my way. All I can say is that every day I gave it my all. I spent hours on top of hours serving this great city. I missed so many family functions because I'm in the streets, shoulder-to-shoulder with the people running the city. That being said, ladies and gentlemen, let's get down to business.

"I first want to give the final update on the Perry Coleman case. I know recent events have the minds of many wondering. The officers involved, Captain Tuna and Detective Speedy, have pleaded guilty to manslaughter charges and their guilty plea has not been revoked. I believe in six weeks they are getting sentenced for that case. They are each getting nine years to life. As we know, their civil case was already settled.

"The Coleman case was a tragedy and a wake-up call for all. Because of the outcome of the case, the NYPD has implemented new training for the cadets. These training classes will teach our officers how to use multiple tactics of restraining a suspect without the use of their handguns. I'm deeply sorry for the shooting. We lost a good man and great father. Perry Coleman, may God bless your soul and the souls of your loved ones. From the city of New York and the entire police department, we apologize."

The mayor paused and sipped on a glass of water. He kept looking around, trying to find the shooter. He knew for sure that in only a matter of seconds he would hear the sound of a gunshot that would put him out of his misery.

The opening part of the mayor's statement caught everyone off guard, and now they were listening with open ears. Even Laura Coleman, who was at home watching, thought it was a nice gesture. He was fooling everyone, and it was working.

"I will also update everyone about those famous envelopes that shocked us all. We have information that leads us to believe Lucky was responsible for mailing out these envelopes. His plans were to expose the government for corruption. I just want to give everyone an update on those accusations. In the case against Rell Davis, I'm glad to announce this matter has been settled as well. We cleaned his criminal record, including previous charges that were not relevant to his last case. He will get a chance to start a new life. Also, Captain Tuna, Detective Speedy, and Detective Lucky are now facing double murder charges for the death of Rodger and Connie Newton. Each count of murder carries a twenty-five to life maximum sentence. It seems like in Rell's case, the city failed to live up to its constitutional standards, and for that, I also apologize. I will say that his settlement was one of the highest we ever paid, right behind what we gave the Coleman family. They will get a chance to move forward and start the healing in peace.

"The next envelope involved the case of Juan 'Pito' Medina. I'm not going to get into too many details on his situation because of an ongoing appeal. We are still fighting his situation. This is a dangerous man who, we believe, belongs behind bars for life. I want the city to please not place this man on the same pedestal as Rell Davis. We understand there were some questionable tactics performed in his arrest, but we are talking about a drug kingpin. He was still running his operation while incarcerated. Even behind bars, he's still responsible for most of the cocaine moving in and out of Washington Heights and all the gang-related murders. If we let Pito walk out of jail, the drug and murder rate will increase dramatically. This man is a monster.

"The envelope involving the Wiggins family is also still under investigation. The Wiggins are not participating in the investigation. They have chosen to remain silent. It's hard for me to give any update, or confirm the raid that killed one and left another paralyzed actually took place. Without their cooperation and no evidence, I can't update this case. I will say we are still investigating the matter at full force.

"There were also allegations of corruption against the late Commissioner Brandon Fratt. The commissioner was prepared to resign and fight for his freedom through our judicial system. The assassination prevented that from happening, and we were all left puzzled. He's not alive to defend himself. We are still conducting our investigation on the allegations against him. But, at the moment, that's all we are doing, just gathering information. We will make public what we can. I'm not giving him any special treatment. If he was corrupt, then he will be exposed.

"I also want to address the allegation against the cardinal Joseph King III. This case is a personal one, because as we all know this man married my wife and me. He baptized my kids. He ate dinner at my house many times. We have taken vacations together. I have let my own kids stay over at his house. However, I do want to address the critics. It is absurd to imagine that I knew of his secret life, if the allegations are true. In no way would I support child pornography.

"The cardinal's trial is set to start within a few months. I haven't spoken to the man since the charges went public. If there are videos of him with underage boys, I don't need to hear his side. There is no explanation for such devilish acts. It upsets me when I hear comments about how I'm good friends with the cardinal. I'm here today to say, that's not the case. I will not interfere with the case, nor will I provide any type of support. We are not friends.

"Let's talk about a more serious issue. We're currently still in search of Donald Gibson, better known as Lucky. This man is wanted and is considered armed and dangerous. Please don't help hide this criminal. Call us today if you know his whereabouts. His name has been cleared from the Coleman case, but he's still a suspect in about ten other murders. He's the prime suspect in the assassination of the commissioner. Right now, our main concern is capturing Lucky. Lucky, if you are listening, I have a few messages for you. We have your money you left behind at the storage facility, and we are also in Atlanta, looking for some of your old friends."

The mayor paused and took another sip of water. He looked around again but felt more confident that he wasn't about to get shot. He knew if Lucky was watching, he was shitting in his pants when he heard him mention Atlanta.

"I felt it was important for me to come out today to personally speak on incidents that shook up our great city. I wanted to assure everyone that we will not stand for it anymore. We will change and turn this horrific page and begin our new chapter. Especially after the riots, we need to rebuild our bond, our confidence among each other. We can only do it if we stick together and work as a team.

"I know there have been whispers about me as well. I read the papers and listen to the radio shows. The comments hurt, and they hurt my family as well. My kids get taunted every day in school. My wife, the other night at Bible study, had to answer questions about my character. Please, leave my family alone. Call me all the names you want, but attacking my family is out of line. I can't let these distractions get in my way of running this city.

"Yes, I'm hurt, but I can't show my emotions. I can't stand up here, start to cry, and beg for your forgiveness. I'm not a quitter, and I'm here to fight till the end. I won't be forced to resign on false allegations. Once we capture Lucky, the truth will come out and put a lot of these accusations in perspective. But, again, I take full responsibility.

"I will now do something mayors usually don't do. I will open up the floor to a few questions. If I feel like the question doesn't need an answer, then I will say, 'Next question,' and we will move on. The longer you guys respect the rules, the longer I'll stand here. You guys start to ask anything out of context, I will walk away."

All the reporters present were shocked that the mayor opened up the floor for questioning. They were all looking around at each other. It took about ten seconds for the first question to come out.

"Mr. Mayor, Chris Whitley from the *City Paper*. Can you explain how Tuna and Speedy received a new bail hearing? Can you please elaborate on it?"

"I hear the outcries about police officers receiving special treatment, but that's not the case. These officers have dedicated their entire lives to protecting civilians. They risk their lives every day they put on those uniforms. A lot of these allegations will get cleared once we capture Lucky and prove he masterminded this whole corruption theory."

"So are you saying Lucky is really behind all the corruption? That he is the one responsible for setting up our government?"

"Exactly. But I will hold my judgment until we capture Lucky. I don't want to make any overstatements. We feel highly confident things will turn for the better once we truly have him in custody."

"Mr. Mayor, I'm Susan Murray with Channel Seven News. Do you have leads on Lucky? So far he's been able to elude the police in every attempt and more officers are losing their lives, including federal agents."

"I'm aware of the losses this city has suffered, and my prayers are with the families. We are not in business to lose police officers or FBI agents. That's unacceptable. With regards to the prime suspect, well, let's just say Lucky has been real lucky. We have reasons to believe his run will come to an end very soon. We are working around the clock to bring him to justice, and we will this time around."

"Mr. Mayor, what do you say to those who consider Lucky a hero?" another reporter asked.

"I don't consider him a hero, do you?" the mayor asked the young reporter.

The reporter didn't reply to the question. He just looked at the mayor with a blank expression.

The mayor bailed him out by not waiting on his answer. "Listen, I'm not going to stand here and say that I haven't heard the word *hero* thrown around. I refuse to accept that. This man has admitted to abusing his authority and disgracing his badge. He's a cocaine addict, has committed murder, sold and stole guns, distributed drugs, and the list continues. I know, in my book, no one with that kind of résumé is considered a hero. Next question," an annoyed mayor said.

"Are you considering resigning in the midst of all the corruption allegations?"

"No. Didn't you hear the press conference? I made that clear. C'mon, guys, any real questions?"

"Are you running again when your term expires?" the same reporter asked.

"I haven't made that decision. Look, if the city feels like they want a new face to sail the ship, I would understand. I'm not a quitter. I'm not resigning. But I understand if the city needs a new voice. I'm just trying to make sure I clean up the mess made under my watch."

"Mr. Mayor, what last message of hope do you have for the people who are at home watching?"

"Please be patient, please have faith, and we will all turn the corner in triumph. Thank you for coming out today, and God bless you," the mayor said as he walked away.

As the mayor left, a few reporters were still asking questions, which went unanswered. The mayor jumped in a waiting black Suburban truck and headed back to his office. While in the car, he called his secretary to find out if she had an update on Richard.

"Sorry. Nothing yet. The police searched his house. No one was home. His neighbors stated they saw them load up the family van like they were going on a vacation."

"Okay, thank you." The mayor hung up the phone.

The mayor finally realized that the governor was correct about Richard. He didn't want to believe it at first, but it was obvious Richard jumped ship on the team. He felt betrayed but understood maybe his good friend was upset about the assassination plot. He just couldn't believe he would go to the media instead of having a conversation with him. Richard was the least of his problems at the moment, so he brushed it to the side. He needed to refocus and pull it together.

He went to visit Captain Tuna and Speedy at their homes to discuss their next move. While on his way to Long Island, he called up the governor.

"Ralph, about time you called. The press conference was excellent. You looked and sounded sincere. I did notice you kept looking around as you spoke. Did you think you were going to get shot?"

"Ha! Of course I did. I was looking around for snipers. I was scared to death standing on that podium. What's the overall feedback? Positive or negative?"

"I would say half and half. I would guarantee you, your press conference helped ease the mind of a lot of voters, especially as you opened up the floor for questions. That took a lot of guts."

"I was just trying to be as authentic as possible. I'm buying us some time to catch this son of a bitch. I'm on my way to Tuna's house first, then Speedy's. They're both under house arrest. As a matter of fact, I'm going to wait until the morning to visit them."

"What's the plan?"

"That's the plan. Making sure they stay home, and we wait for Lucky to make his move."

"That's it?" the governor asked, confused.

"That's it. Lucky will come for them, trust me."

"I hope everything goes that easy. Call me after you visit both of them tomorrow and give me the latest update." The governor ended the call.

***

Lucky was walking back and forth in the living room. He couldn't believe the police knew where Tasha and Tamika were. He thought Sergio must have told them.

"Fuck, Haze! They know where my family is at."

"Oh, that's why the mayor said Atlanta? I guess we also know who took your money."

"I have to call Tasha and tell her to get the fuck out of Atlanta. They will find her quicker than me going down there. These muthafuckas took my money, and now they're going to take my family. I don't think so."

"So let's start taking theirs," Haze said.

"That's a good idea. I know the mayor has a few daughters. Fuck!" Lucky yelled at the top of his lungs. "This changes everything. Oh, they're going to give me my money back. Haze, roll up. I need to get high."

"Now you are talking my language."

The weed would help Lucky relax and think of his next move. He knew the mayor was using Atlanta as bait to get him to make a mistake. Truth be told, if they knew where his family was located, they would have taken Tamika and Tasha already. They'd pulled the same stunt in Cape Cod, and Lucky almost fell for the trap. This time, he was going to call Tasha and tell her to bounce. Last time he'd spoken to her, he told her everything would be okay. He was hoping when he called her, she would listen to him and leave.

Within minutes, Haze was already sparking the blunt. Lucky couldn't wait to take a few pulls. He needed to calm his nerves. He took a long, slow drag, exhaled through his mouth and nose, then inhaled the cloud of smoke.

"Damn, Lucky! You have to show me that trick. That was one hell of a pull."

Lucky laughed and took a few more pulls. He knew he heard the mayor say they had his money. For some strange reason, in the back of his head, he felt like the mayor was bluffing. As he passed the blunt, Haze inquired about their next move.

"So, who are we going after now? Are we killing the cops or kidnapping their families? Or are we heading down to Atlanta to get your family and make sure they are safe?"

"I'm not going down to Atlanta. The drive is crazy. I'm just going to call her. I'm pretty sure she already heard the press conference. I know they don't know where she's at in Atlanta. We renting a villa from one of her friends. Nothing is under her name. In fact, they don't even know her name. They're trying to get me to come out there. They tried that in Cape Cod."

"I remember hearing about the Cape Cod shooting on TV."

"They did the same exact thing. They mentioned they were heading to Cape Cod, and I headed out there because I thought they knew where my daughter was staying. They didn't know shit. They just knew they were in Cape Cod but didn't have an address. I just so happened to bump into them first before they bumped into me. That's when I saw them at the post office and took two of them out in broad daylight."

"You are a crazy muthafucka, Lucky."

"Hey, when you trying to defend your family, you do whatever is necessary. Those pricks were going to kill them just to get back at me."

"Do you want me to call your baby mama like last time, or you are going to handle it?"

"I got it. I just hope this doesn't scare her off and she decides to disappear."

"Why would she disappear?"

"She bounced on me before for not changing my act. I know she'll bounce again. She begged me not to come up to New York. Tasha loves me, but she's the definition of a real independent woman. She doesn't need any nigga to be happy."

"Damn! Sounds like my girl."

"I was really sincere about coming back and beginning a new life with her. I even told my daughter things will be different when I return. I don't want my baby mama to take away my last chance of fixing my family."

"She will wait. She's a rider, right?"

"She is. She knew I had to finish my business here first before moving forward. On our last convo, she told me to hurry up and finish so I could go back home."

After smoking two more blunts, Lucky was still hyped. He loved how the mayor was trying to pin it all on him. He wasn't surprised or upset, but he did think the press conference was a nice touch. The mayor made it seem like, for the city to move forward, Lucky had to be captured or eliminated.

Lucky didn't care and wasn't going to run, either. He wanted to go against his own rules because he couldn't wait anymore. He was done with the fucking patience game.

"Damn, Haze! I want to run up in Tuna's house tonight," Lucky said as he cocked back the 9 mm lying by the computer desk.

"I'm ready. Let's use those fuckin' pipe bombs." Haze let a cloud of smoke out his mouth, trying to do the trick Lucky did.

"Shit! We have to wait for Blood. We need his help. I can't lie. For the first time ever, I can't be patient. I'm going to take Tasha's advice and quickly finish this mess. As bad as I want to kill those muthafuckas, I need to be smart as well. I'm trying to walk away alive after I'm done. I'm not ready for either box."

"Either box?" a confused Haze asked. "Oh, I get it," he quickly said before Lucky could respond. "You mean jail or a coffin. I got you."

"Exactly, li'l homie. I'm not going to either one."

"Shit! Me either," Haze shouted as he pulled out his gun and cocked it back as well.

As they both were playing wild cowboys, they heard the front door unlock. They both ran toward the door, their guns pointed.

As they got closer, to their surprise, it was a sexy brown-skinned babe about five-five, with long, silky black hair down to her big ass. Her beauty and booty threw Haze off. He lowered his gun and mumbled, "Damn!"

Lucky quickly grabbed the unidentified female by the mouth and neck as Haze closed the door. He threw her on the floor and pointed his gun at her. "Listen, we don't want to hurt you, but if you scream, I'm going to shoot you. Are we clear?"

"Yes," the terrified girl replied.

"Is this your apartment?"

"Yes," she mumbled, tears coming down her face.

"We both know Blood. He said we could stay here. He told us you were away handling business. Where were you at again?" Lucky asked her. He remembered Blood said she was in Atlanta. If she lied, he was going to put a bullet right through her head.

"I was in Atlanta. Where is Blood? I need his new number. I been trying to reach him for a few days now." The young lady felt a lot more comfortable when they mentioned her boyfriend's name. "Can I please get off the floor?" she asked.

"Yes, my bad. We had to make sure first." Lucky lowered his gun and helped her up. "What's your name, sweetie?"

"My name is Krystal. And you two? Y'all look like a father-and-son team."

"Oh, you got jokes. Don't make me put my gun back in your mouth. My name is Rick, and that's Chris."

"So who are you guys? The ones who pulled off the storage hit?"

"We don't discuss business." Lucky walked behind Krystal and hit her with the back of his gun, and she passed out from the unexpected blow.

After she dropped to the floor, Haze took a few steps back. He was also taken by surprise. "What the fuck, Lucky! I thought that was Blood's girl."

"Didn't you hear what the fuck she said? Are you paying attention? The bitch just said you guys are the ones from the storage hit. Whose fuckin' storage just got hit?"

Haze was upset at himself for not picking up on that. "My bad. That slipped by me."

"Ever since the bitch walked in, you been mesmerized. Don't think I didn't notice when you lowered your gun earlier. Don't let her beauty trick you, li'l homie. If you ever live by any of the codes, live by that one—always stay focused. Look for something so we can tie this bitch up and wait for her to wake up."

As Haze looked around for rope, Lucky was staring at Krystal. He was wondering why the pretty young lady decided to come back to the apartment. He started checking her for wires to see if she was an informant. He didn't find any wires or weapons. He started to feel bad for knocking such a sexy thing out.

Haze found some rope and two pairs of handcuffs in the closet.

"Damn! Shorty's a freak," Lucky shouted, and they both laughed.

Lucky went to the dining room and grabbed a chair. They both picked up Krystal and sat her up. They handcuffed her hands behind the back of the chair and tied the rest of her body with the rope. As they attempted to stuff a sock in her mouth, she started gaining consciousness.

"Lucky, she's waking up."

"I see," Lucky said as he finally got the sock in. "Welcome back, bitch."

By the time Krystal realized what happened, it was too late. She was already tied up. She knew she shouldn't have tried that joke about the father-and-son team.

As Lucky and Haze were both looking at her like prey, she quickly realized they didn't give a fuck about Blood. Lucky pointed his gun near her eye. The barrel was so close, she could actually see the slug. She began to cry and tried to yell, but the sock was too deep in her mouth.

"Again, I'm going to ask you a few questions. When I remove the sock, all I want to hear is the answer. If you scream or attempt anything, we will kill you. It's your choice—live with a bump on the back of your head, or die. Are we clear?" Lucky said in a slow but deadly tone.

Krystal could feel through his voice that he wasn't joking. She started nodding her head up and down.

"Okay, you asked if we were part of the team that hit the storage. Do you know which storage they hit?" Lucky removed the sock.

"I don't know the name," Krystal said. "But it was in the Bronx. Blood's childhood friend worked there. His name is, well, was Divine. He was killed along with Blood's brother, Pee-wee. I swear, I don't know the name of the place."

Lucky paused. Krystal just fucked his head up by mentioning Divine's name. He couldn't believe Divine was behind it as well, because the night of the shooting, Lucky personally went in the safe room to grab the big guns. He saw all the money there, unless Blood still carried out the plan after the shooting and fire. Divine gave him the code, so he must have gone in and cleaned house.

"That sneaky muthafucka. I see why he's flossing so much money. What else you know?"

"That's pretty much it. I know after his brother and Divine were killed, he carried the plan out with new help. I thought it was you guys who helped him."

"I'm actually the guy they robbed. Where is the rest of my money?"

"I don't know."

"That bitch is lying, boss!" Haze yelled. He thought he'd been standing on the sideline for too long and just wanted to get in on the action.

"I know. I'm going to give her five seconds to rethink her answer." Lucky slowly screwed in the silencer.

"I swear, I don't know about the money. I'm not allowed to ask about his business. I just spend the money he gives me."

"You just spend the money, huh? Let me paint the picture I see. You are his bottom bitch, his main squeeze. He trusts you with his money. I'm sure you know more than what you are telling us. You could help us find the rest of the money. Your five seconds is up."

As soon as Lucky tried to stuff the sock back in her mouth, Krystal said, "Wait. How do I know my safety is guaranteed? You still might kill me."

"Are you willing to risk it and find out if I'm bluffing?"

Krystal thought about her options for a few seconds and quickly started running her mouth to save her ass. "Okay, there's about another eight hundred thousand dollars in the bedroom. It's stuffed in the closet behind a fake wall Blood built. The only way in is to break the wall down."

"You better not be lying, bitch." Lucky turned to Haze. "Go check out the wall in the closet and see if she's telling the truth." He turned back to Krystal. "Okay, there's still a lot of money missing, so where is it?"

"I have at least three hundred thousand that's under the mattress, inside the box spring, but that's about it. Where he stashed the rest of the money, I'm clueless. I know he has other bitches on the side, but I don't know where the rest of the money is."

Lucky believed her and lowered his gun. He put the sock back in her mouth and covered her face with a pillowcase. He went and helped Haze break the wall.

Krystal was telling the truth. There were two duffel bags filled with money and a few pieces of jewelry as well.

"Are we taking the ice as well, Lucky?"

"Hell yeah. We taking everything. You could keep the ice."

"For real. That's what's up."

As Haze was packing away the jewelry, Lucky was ripping up the box spring. Krystal again was telling the truth.

Haze removed the money and packed it with the rest. In total, they now had about 1.1 million dollars, enough money to bounce and start a new life.

"Damn, Lucky! Don't we have enough to—"

"Don't say it. I know what you about to say. Let's stay focused. I know never in your life have you touched so much money before. Don't let it poison your mind. We just need to wait for Blood to call."

"That's what I wanted to ask you. How we going to lure Blood in here?"

"I got it. I will wait until he calls me. Trust me, he will show up."

"What about all this money? We can't leave it here."

"You're right. Take both bags to your car and lock them in the trunk."

"Bet."

"Wait. There's like over a hundred and fifty thousand in the safe. Take that shit, too."

"What about all the guns?" Haze asked.

"Take some of them, but grab all the bullets you can. Once we kill Blood, we'll rent a room till we take care of our business."

"What about Krystal?"

"Collateral damage, li'l homie."

"We killing her?" a shocked Haze asked.

"Don't forget, she knows how you look. She saw your face. Right now, the media is just after me. Let's keep it that way."

"You're right. Fuck it then! The bitch has to die."

As Haze packed up the rest of the money and guns, Lucky walked back over to Krystal and removed the pillowcase.

"Sweetie, you said you didn't get in contact with Blood, right? So far, you been telling the truth, so don't fuck up."

Krystal nodded yes.

"Well, I'm going to have to leave you tied up for a few more hours before I let you go. I'm sorry we had to meet under these circumstances. You seem like a nice lady. You just fell in love with the wrong guy. I'm going to cover your face up again. It's better you don't see what we're doing."

Lucky placed the pillowcase back over her face and waited for Haze to come back. It was going on ten minutes, and Haze hadn't returned from the car. Lucky thought the worst. Maybe Haze jumped in the car and bounced on him.

As Lucky began to get worried, in came Haze through the door.

"It took you long enough."

"I was moving the car. I parked it down the block. Here are the keys." Haze threw the keys to Lucky.

"Good idea. Watch this bitch while I go in the room and call Tasha. I'm going to be a minute. If anybody comes to the door, empty your clip on their ass."

"I got you," Haze replied.

"I'm not playing. I don't care who it is. Start blasting."

Chapter Twenty-seven

Another Harlem Shooting

Lucky went in the room and dialed Tasha's number, and she picked up on the first ring.

"Tasha, it's me."

"I know. Are you ready to come home now?"

"Did you see the mayor's conference?" Lucky asked, ignoring her question.

"You know I did. What you want me to do?"

Lucky paused. The last thing he expected to hear was Tasha was still willing to follow suit. "Well, I first called to make sure you were okay. I know hearing the mayor mention Atlanta had you nervous."

"I knew he was bluffing. They just knew you were down here, but I knew he was bullshitting. No one knows we moved down here except my friend, and she doesn't know who you are."

"That's my baby girl. That's why I love you. Listen, I'm almost done, but every time I turn around, there's something new involved. I should be ready within the next day or so."

"For real. Are you serious?"

"I'm positive, but we can't stay in Atlanta. In fact, I want you to leave today if possible."

"Okay, we could go to either Florida or Arizona. We have relatives in both states."

"Let's go with Arizona. We could keep a lower profile there. I will call you back in a day or so and get the address. Tasha, you have to bounce quickly. The mayor may be bluffing, but I'm not taking any risk."

"Okay, I will. Hold on. Your daughter wants to speak to you."

Lucky's heart paused. He hadn't spoken to Tamika since leaving Atlanta a few days ago.

"Hello, Daddy. You there?"

"Hey, sugar. How are you?" Lucky said, his voice cracking.

"I'm fine. When are you coming home? I miss you."

"I will be home soon, sugar."

"Remember, you promised you would. Mommy has been crying a lot. I know why. She thinks you are not coming back."

"Mommy just likes to worry a lot. Daddy will be home. I can't lose any more time apart from you. You keep your mommy strong till I get there. I love you, and I will see you soon."

"Okay, Daddy, hurry up. I want to go to the mall. I love you. Good night. I'm going to give the phone back to Mommy."

"Hello. Baby, are you still there?" Tasha asked quickly, hoping Lucky didn't hang up the phone.

"I'm here."

"So, you will call me?"

"Yeah, I will hit you. Remember, start packing."

"I got it, baby, whatever you say. I'm sorry I was tripping last time we spoke. I was out of line. I know why you are doing it. I shouldn't add any stress. You need my support. I love you, be safe, and get those muthafuckas, baby."

"Ha! That's the support I want to hear, baby. I gotta go. I will see you soon. Remember what I taught you—stay on point. "

"Always. *Mwa!* Love ya!"

Lucky sat on the edge of the bed and took a few deep breaths. Hearing Tamika's voice took him through a ride of emotions. It was critical now that every step going forward be mistake free. Everything was on the line.

As Lucky got up to walk out the room, his cell phone started ringing. He turned back around. He thought maybe it was Tasha calling back, until he saw the number on the caller ID.

"Yo, who's this?"

"It's Blood. What's good? I'm going to stop by there, lay low for a day or two, then I'm bouncing out of town."

"When are you coming? It's going on eight o'clock."

"I should be over there in, like, thirty minutes."

"See you then." Lucky was relieved. He didn't even have to lure Blood in.

He opened the door and called Haze in.

"What's up, boss? Everything all right with the family?"

"Yeah, they're good. Listen, Blood just called. He said he's like half hour away."

"Damn! We need to get ready, then."

"I know. I need you to load up and wait outside for him."

"Outside in the streets? Are you sure?"

"Yeah, man. I just want you to watch him and make sure he enters the building. I want you to look around and make sure he's alone. Once you see him get in the elevator, hit me on the radio, then run up the stairs. But don't let him see you. Stay low. I'll be waiting for him in the hallway. Once the elevator doors open, the first thing he will see is this big-ass gun. If he makes a move, I'm going to light his ass up."

"Okay, I'm going to get ready. What about the bimbo sitting in the living room?"

"One to the head."

Haze walked out and started loading up the guns and threw on his black hoodie. Before Haze went downstairs, Lucky passed him a two-way radio. That way they could communicate instantly. He went downstairs and waited, like Lucky instructed.

Lucky grabbed the bulletproof vest and the 12-gauge shotgun. He wanted to blow Blood's face away.

As they both waited, Haze hit him up on the radio. "I think I see him. He's getting out a car from almost two blocks down."

"So how you could tell it's him?"

"It's just a feeling. I'm going to get a closer look to see if that's him."

"Be careful."

"Copy." Haze felt this was the perfect moment to prove to Lucky he was a real thug.

Haze was correct. It was Blood getting out of a cab down the street. Blood always played every situation safe, just like Lucky. He knew the cops and feds were looking for him. As Blood got closer to the building, he noticed something, so he stopped.

Haze was behind him, so he also stopped.

Blood noticed Krystal's white BMW parked in front of the building. That caught him off guard, so when he turned around to look at the car again, he noticed Haze behind him, wearing a hoodie. He didn't waste any time, pulling out quicker than Haze and shooting as he ran for cover.

Haze wasn't as quick as Blood, but he was also able to pull out. Haze let off a few shots, too, and then ran for cover. Haze leaned against a parked car. That was when he realized he was shot twice, in the stomach and right shoulder. There was blood pouring everywhere. From the look of things, Haze could easily bleed to death. Haze was still letting off rounds, though. He figured, if he kept shooting, Blood would never know he was hurt.

Haze was so busy running for cover and attending to his own wounds, he failed to see that Blood was hit as well, on the upper thigh. The shot wasn't life-threatening, but it was enough to keep a good distance between the both of them. Blood slowly was creeping closer to Haze and letting off more shots than him.

Haze felt overmatched and decided to preserve his bullets. He was praying for Lucky to come down and save him. He wasn't ready to go yet. He thought about his pregnant girlfriend and unborn child. Now it was looking like a big mistake coming up to New York to help Lucky.

All that gangster tough talk was no longer in his vocabulary. He finally realized he wasn't built for this part of the game. He realized what every other wannabe killer realized—bullets did hurt, and burned like hell.

As Haze sat behind a parked car, bullets were still flying past his ears, the shots getting closer and closer.

When Blood paused to reload his .40 Glock, Lucky sneaked up behind him and blew a hole in the back of his head. His body slammed against the concrete, and brain fragments splattered everywhere. A close-range shotgun blast would disfigure any body parts. Lucky didn't even get a chance to ask Blood why or where the rest of the money was. He just knew his li'l homie was in trouble and he had to help him.

Lucky ran over to aid Haze, but it was too late. Blood had shot him two more times. One shot caught him in the back of the head and came out his left eye. Lucky almost fainted when he saw Haze's lifeless body lying in between two parked cars. When he heard sirens in the background, he ran down the block and spotted Haze's car. He jumped in and sped off.

Lucky had tears coming down his face as he was driving, not knowing where to go. He knew he endangered Haze's life by inviting him to help him out. He just didn't think anything would happen to the young buck. All Haze wanted to do was prove himself to Lucky. That was a hard burden to carry.

As he was driving around Harlem, he decided to head over to the Bronx. With Haze and Blood gone, Lucky was back to square one, no help on his side.

Lucky was driving around, trying to find a place to lay his head for a day or two. After driving for about a good forty-five minutes, he decided to drive to the Capri. The Capri was listed as a hotel but was basically a fuck station. They were one of the only hotels/motels with a bar inside with hookers waiting to provide all kind of freaky shit. You needed an ID to rent a room, but Lucky also knew that the owner was a low-down, dirty hustler. He figured he would just approach the bullet-proof window and slip them five hundred dollars.

When he arrived at the hotel, he was a bit hesitant. He didn't want to risk his face being exposed. He pulled up to the parking lot, where the hotel's front desk manager was having a smoke.

Lucky approached him. "Hey, do you work here? Because I have a question."

"I'm the manager on duty. How can I help you, my friend?"

"Listen, I want to rent a room for the night, but I don't have any ID on me."

"I'm sorry, I can't help you, and we need ID, just in case something happens in the room."

"Here is five hundred dollars. All I need is room keys. I'm not interested in tearing up the hotel room. I just need some sleep."

"Are you joking, sir?"

"I'm not joking. Take the money. Go inside and bring me out a set of keys."

"Okay, give me, like, five minutes."

Lucky was glad to hear the manager was willing to accept the five hundred, which was more than his weekly paycheck. As Lucky waited, two sexy females dressed like strippers were leaving the hotel, mad as hell. Lucky quickly stopped them and asked what was wrong.

Only one of the girls stopped. The other jumped in the waiting cab.

"This nasty old man upstairs was supposed to pay us to have sex with him, but once we get to his room, the old bastard said he only had enough to pay for one girl. We left five seconds after he said that dumb shit."

"Damn! That's fucked up. Don't leave just yet. I'm checking in myself."

"Are you alone?" she asked as she got closer and placed her hand on his dick.

"Yeah, I'm alone. I'm just waiting for a new set of keys."

"You *are* checking in alone. Do you need some company, daddy?" the girl said, hoping Lucky had enough money to keep her pretty ass in his room. "What's your name, daddy?" She let go of his balls and wrapped her hand around his dick.

"My name is Larry. I would love some company. How much is it going to cost me?"

"Well, my name is Princess. I will give you a special price. If you just want head, it will be one hundred dollars, but if you want to fuck and do it all, and I mean whatever you want, daddy, it will run two hundred."

"That's it. Two hundred? You better tell your friend to go ahead and leave, because you are staying with me for the night, Princess."

"I sure will, daddy."

As the girl went to tell her friend that she could leave, the manager came out with his set of keys. The girl returned and asked if her friend could join them in the room.

Within seconds, Lucky had a change of heart. "You know what, baby girl? I'm sorry to have wasted your time. Here's a hundred dollars for your trouble. I changed my mind. I need to spend this night alone."

"Damn, daddy, you are a big balla. Niggas don't give bitches a C-note for no reason. Let me come upstairs and make you feel happy. My girl and I will suck the head off your dick."

"Sounds lovely, but after the night I had, the last thing on my mind is pussy. I could go home for that. I just want to spend the night alone. I'm good, baby. You have yourself a good night," Lucky said as he went in the hotel.

Princess felt hurt by Lucky's rejection. She stood there for a second after he went in the hotel, hoping he would come out and say he was just joking. That never happened. She jumped in the cab and went about her business.

Lucky sat on the old chair in the room and finally had a moment to mourn Haze's death. It brought more tears to his eyes. He really broke down when he remembered he had an unborn child. He felt like it was his fault, even though the young buck had his mind made up, ready to die, and no one could change his mind. Lucky knew the risk, but it was still a shocker. Haze had so much to look forward to.

Lucky felt like his luck was running out. Everyone around him either died or betrayed him. It only meant his fate was looming and getting close. He was just hoping that it had a happy ending.

He'd accomplished what he wanted, which was to kill Blood. He was upset that he didn't get a chance to get some info out of him first. That police in him always thought about an interrogation first. A tied-up Blood with guns in his face would have talked. Lucky had witnessed the hardest thugs snitch for nothing and would have loved the chance to speak to him under duress.

Lucky was down on himself, but he wasn't going to lose sleep over it. He did feel bad for shooting Krystal, but it had to be done. He didn't have second thoughts when he shot her. That was who he was and would always be, a natural at it. It didn't matter what he did, he always wanted to be the best. So, once he crossed the line and started killing, his feelings went numb.

Lucky knew in his heart he could change and start a new life. He was just hoping it wasn't too late. He had that one relapse episode at Sergio's house, but ever since that night he hadn't had any cocaine calls. He knew he had his addiction under control. Well, at least, he felt like he did. As long as his life was drama free about his past, he would be okay.

He wiped his tears and realized he had to come up with new strategies. He'd just lost two individuals who were going to help him take down Captain Tuna, Speedy, and the mayor. Leaving town was starting to make more sense to Lucky. If he quit, he would walk away with over a million dollars, 1.3 to be exact, enough to give it a big consideration.

By killing Blood, he eliminated any chance of finding the rest of the money. He was puzzled and helpless. He couldn't pull the job off alone. He had to pick one target out of Tuna, Speedy, and the mayor. It was really between Tuna and the mayor. Lucky hated both of them with a passion.

He decided to take out Tuna. He could live with Speedy and the mayor staying alive. Hopefully, they each would serve long prison terms, but Tuna, he wanted him dead.

He jumped in the bed and turned on the TV to get his mind off his li'l homie. The news was already reporting the shooting that took place that left three dead, including a female who was killed execution-style. Lucky was surprised his name wasn't mentioned as a lead suspect. He figured his name would pop up after they checked the apartment for fingerprints. "I should have burned that building down," he said to himself.

He turned the TV off and just lay there. He put his hand in his pants and began rubbing his balls. He smacked himself over the head for turning down Princess and her friend.

He ended up dozing off. He needed the rest. Tomorrow was going to be judgment day. The day it came to an end.

The mayor was tossing and turning when his phone started ringing around midnight. "Hello."

"I'm sorry to bother you, sir. My name is Anita Flowers, police spokesperson. We can't get hold of Richard Claiborne. We have a problem, sir."

"What's going on?" the mayor said as he got up and off the bed.

"There's been another big shoot out in Harlem today. We have fatalities."

"Please, don't tell me there were police officers."

"No, sir, they were civilians, two males and a female. The female was found tied up with a single gunshot wound to the head."

"Oh my God! We have any leads?"

"The identities of the two males have been confirmed. One of them is Daquan 'Blood' Mooks. He was a person of interest in the shooting that left three agents dead."

"I'm aware of the first victim. He was second on the most wanted list, behind Lucky. What about the other suspect?"

"According to the ID we found in his wallet, he's from Glen Burnie, Maryland. His name is Dante Jones. He has a felony conviction on his record, two years in jail for drug charges. He'd been on parole ever since. We still don't have a connection as to why he's up here. However, after running fingerprint checks in the apartment where the female was found, we have confirmed Lucky was in the apartment. In fact, his fingerprints were all over the dead female."

"We are positive those were Lucky's prints?" a skeptical mayor asked.

"Yes, we are," a confident Anita answered.

"That explains why the other victim from Maryland was up here. He must have helped Lucky come back to New York."

"Do you want me to follow up with Richard? Who do I contact if I can't reach Richard again?"

"No, I'm afraid Richard is on leave for a few months, until further notice. Please call me and keep me up to date. I have to call the governor and then face the media."

"Is there anything you need from me?"

"How good are you with handling the media?"

"With all due respect, Mr. Mayor, I'm the one who's been thrown on the front line to speak to the media on behalf of the department. It's no secret these past few months have been historically challenging."

"Ms. Flowers, if you could step in and take the lead on the investigation, it would be greatly appreciated. You will get complete clearance. Are you up for it?"

"Yes, I am, sir. Thank you."

"I can't offer you Richard's job, because my term is currently in jeopardy. But I will make sure you receive nothing but the highest recommendations, and secure you a slot with the next mayor as their spokesperson."

"Again, thank you, sir. I will give you a call as soon as I receive any updates."

The mayor felt confident Anita would be able to handle the situation. Even though he had been half awake and couldn't sleep, he really wished he hadn't picked up the call. Last thing he wanted to hear was that there were more dead bodies. He wanted to jump back in bed and act like the call never happened.

Chapter Twenty-eight

Tuna, the Last Catch

Around seven in the morning, Lucky finally woke up. For a second he was hoping when he opened his eyes, he was back with Tasha and Tamika. After snapping out of his fantasy dream, he jumped out of bed and turned on the TV. While he waited for the news to come on, all he was concerned with was taking care of Tuna. After he was done with Tuna, he would go down to Arkansas and handle Diamond.

It was time to start putting together the plan to catch Tuna slipping. He was an easy target, so Lucky knew exactly where to find him. As Lucky was going over the details, the TV caught his attention when Destine Diaz's live report came on. He stopped what he was doing and sat back up on the edge of the bed.

"Hello, New York. I'm back with more news and dead bodies in Harlem. Well, first I want to let everyone know about the dead body in the Bronx. This body may be connected to Lucky. According to police officers at the scene, they found Sergio Martinez tortured to death. According to the police, fingerprints taken from the scene match Lucky's.

"Then, in Harlem this morning, three more bodies popped up. We have two male suspects found shot to death outside in the streets. There was also a female found tied up and killed execution-style with a single shot to the back of the head. This shooting happened right in the middle of the upscale Riverside neighborhood of Harlem.

"The two dead males have been confirmed as Dante 'Haze' Jones from Glen Burnie, Maryland, and Daquan 'Blood' Mooks from Harlem. Details about Dante's identity are still sketchy, but investigators believe he's

connected with Lucky. After Lucky's shooting at the Holiday Inn, he disappeared in the Glen Burnie area. The police are trying to determine if Dante was the one who assisted Lucky while he was down in Maryland. One of our sources has confirmed that the Arundel County Police Department in Maryland is working with the NYPD in conducting a proper background check on the suspect.

"Now, here is where it gets interesting. The other suspect, Daquan Mooks, is the other half of the deadly Mooks brothers, known for pulling off memorable crimes. These brothers have terrorized the Harlem community for years, killing people for money and sometimes fun. They were charged but never convicted of many crimes, including a diamond heist, armored truck jobs, and suspected involvement in Lucky's underground operation as the cleanup team. Everyone always wondered why they were roaming the streets as free men.

"Daquan's brother, Dwayne, was burned alive in that shooting in the storage facility owned and operated by Lucky. Daquan 'Blood' Mooks was on New York's most wanted list. He was a suspect in the shooting that left three agents dead the other day in Harlem. Investigators are trying to figure out what took place. If both Dante and Daquan were working with Lucky, how come they are dead and he's not? Did Lucky pull the trigger on his own team, or did someone else come to kill them and Lucky got away? Police believe the mysterious girl found shot in the head may be Lucky's girl. They say his fingerprints are all over her body. It looks like detectives will have their hands full.

"I've lost count of the amount of murders since Perry's trial began, but there's been nonstop warfare, which looks like it won't end until all parties kill each other. This is Destine Diaz, from Channel Five."

Lucky sat there with a smirk on his face because they'd found Sergio's corpse, but something didn't make sense. He and Blood had wiped everything down at Sergio's apartment. If the police found prints, then the CIA must have made that happen, to make the public aware that he was responsible for all the killings.

Lucky needed to make his move. Checkout was in a few hours, and he needed a new car. Haze's car was too hot to drive. He ran outside and cleaned everything out of the car.

On his way back to the room, he noticed a cab dropping off a couple. He walked up to the driver's side. "Hey, I need a ride to 125th Street and Lexington Avenue."

"Twenty-five," the African cabdriver said.

"I just have to check out. Give me five minutes, and I will give you forty dollars."

"Thank you. I wait here. Hurry please. Thank you."

The mayor was down the street from Tuna's house. Tuna was waiting outside and got in the car when it pulled up.

"What the fuck took so long to get me out?" Tuna said before he sat down.

"Things have changed a bit, especially after the commissioner was killed."

"That's bullshit! But fuck it. Anyway, what's up? I know there's only one reason why you muthafuckas bailed me out. You need help with Lucky."

"You right. We need your help. He's kicking our asses bad," the mayor said.

"Well, we'll see, because I have a perfect plan to get him out of hiding."

That wasn't what the mayor wanted to hear. "Listen, I just need you to lay low for at least three days. You have to stay away from the public's eye."

"I can't stay here for three days straight."

"Okay, well, maybe two days, but I need you out of the spotlight. We don't have the power like we used to. The federal government is about to take over the whole police department's daily operations. We need to catch Lucky and return things back to normal."

"What about my situation? We already are going to do heavy time for shooting that black boy," Tuna said.

"If we capture Lucky, the CIA is going to help us flip everything back on him. Most of those charges will be dropped."

"What about the Perry case?" Tuna asked with a look of desperation. "I can't get a lower sentence?"

"There's nothing we could do about the Perry Coleman case. I'm sorry."

"So I'm just supposed to accept a nine-to-life bid. That's nine years, Mr. Mayor."

They continued to talk for about fifteen minutes. The mayor could only hope that Tuna followed his instruction to lay low.

After the mayor left, Tuna said to himself, "Shit! Stay here for three days straight? Never." He pulled out his cell phone and called up The Candy Shop. He told Dimples to have a girl at his spot on 102nd Street in about three hours.

Tuna wasn't about to stay confined in his own home. He broke off his ankle bracelet, kissed his wife, and left. He worked for the commissioner, not the mayor. He knew he was going back to jail, so he was going out with a bang.

Meanwhile, the mayor was driving with a smile on his face. All he needed was for Tuna to stay put in the house. The mayor was on his way to Speedy's house. He knew Speedy wouldn't mind staying home.

When the mayor arrived, Speedy invited him in. The mayor told him his plans about capturing Lucky.

"No disrespect, I'm not interested in doing nothing else but spending time with my family until I go back to prison."

"You can't turn your back on us now," the mayor said in a low, disappointed tone.

"There is no *us*. I finally figured it all out. These last few days of confinement have cleared my head."

"Well, it's your decision, but if we capture Lucky, a lot of those charges will get dropped, and you would be able to spend more time with your family."

"I don't care about the charges we have pending. I'm more interested in the one I pleaded guilty to. I already made thousand of mistakes. I don't need to add any more. My time is valuable, and I need to spend it with family, not chasing a rat. I'm done."

The mayor realized Speedy was sincere about his commitment to staying home until his next court date. That was all he wanted, but he had to make it at least seem like he was disappointed in his actions.

"Okay, I see I wasted my time coming out here. I could have just called you. Remember who made it possible for you to come out and spend this precious time with your family. You dwell on that. You know how to contact us," the mayor said as he walked toward the front door.

Speedy didn't respond to the mayor's last comment. He didn't even make eye contact with him. Speedy knew the mayor was right, which made him question his decision. Speedy was raised in a household filled with cops. In fact, both his parents were detectives. One thing he'd learned from birth was the code of honor among the blue. He had to make a decision. He didn't know if he should stay home with his family or join his work family, which was all he had known for the last fifteen years.

The mayor called the governor to give an update.

"I just finished visiting both Tuna and Speedy," he said. "And the plan is in motion. They're both going to be in their house for at least the next forty-eight hours. We need to set up surveillance teams on both locations ASAP."

"I'm on it. What kind of manpower we need?"

"Well, judging from our luck, we need as much as we can get at both locations. But make sure they are our veteran team. Lucky will spot them from a mile away if they're not careful. We can't fuck this one up," the mayor said. "This is our last chance."

"Understood. I will start making calls as soon as we get off the phone. Are you on your way back to the city?"

"Yes, I'm on the Long Island Expressway right now. Call me, once the team is set up. We need to post up within hours, if possible."

"Got it," the governor said.

Chapter Twenty-nine

The Final Stakeout

It was going on four o'clock in the afternoon, and the surveillance team was intact. A team of twelve staked out Tuna's house because they felt confident Lucky would attack there first, while a team of four staked out Speedy's.

The mayor checked in with his surveillance team. He radioed his lead agent, Captain Mark Schuler, who was watching Tuna's house.

"Captain, come in. What's the latest?"

"It looks like he's not home, sir. We been here for almost two hours, and so far there are still no signs of Tuna."

"Damn! I don't know why he couldn't just follow simple directions. What about Speedy? What's the update?"

"Speedy's car is parked in the driveway. His wife and kids are running all over the house, but still no visual on him, either. He was last seen about forty-five minutes ago. We believe he's actually sleeping, sir."

"What about their ankle bracelets?" the mayor asked.

"They are indicating that they are both home. That's why we are confused. We are certain Tuna isn't home. We been outside his house, and there is still no sign of him."

"They must know how to tamper with the devices. Okay, Captain, please have your eyes open for Lucky. He doesn't know they're not home. Remember, he's a former detective. He will do what any other cop would do—stake the place out first. Hit me as soon as you have visual contact. Remember, shoot first as soon as you have contact."

"Affirmative."

The mayor was disappointed to hear Tuna wasn't home and that Speedy wasn't willing to cooperate, especially after speaking to both of them earlier in the day. It was delaying his plan to capture Lucky.

The mayor was becoming nervous again. He was starting to feel like it was his last day on earth. He was glad he'd spent a great night at home with his family. He didn't jump the gun and call the governor, figuring the best plan at the moment was to be patient and wait for Lucky to show.

Captain Schuler radioed in. "Sir, come in."

"Tell me some good news, Captain."

"Speedy is on the move, sir."

"Stay on him and keep me updated turn by turn."

Five minutes later, Captain Schuler reported, "It looks like he's heading toward the Triboro Bridge."

"He's coming to Harlem, maybe to meet up with Tuna. I know they had a secret spot somewhere in Spanish Harlem. I don't know the address. Stay on him, Captain, and please don't get made. Speedy was part of an elite team of officers as well. They were the best in their field."

"We understand, sir."

Captain Tuna pulled up to his old hangout spot on 102nd Street and Lexington Avenue and saw a yellow cab sitting in front. He rolled up next to it, his gun on his lap. He saw a female in the cab. That was when it hit him. She was one of the girls from the escort service, the Candy Shop.

He lowered his window. "Candy Shop!" he hollered.

"Yes, my name is Mindy. Are you the sexy Tuna guy all the girls talk about? You late, pretty boy."

"Listen, let yourself in the building. Let me park, and I will be right back."

As Mindy paid the cab and got out, Tuna drove around the block a few times to make sure no one was following him. He knew Lucky knew about the apartment, so he wanted to be extra careful.

After about ten minutes, Tuna finally made it in the building. "I'm sorry, baby. Parking is hard to find around here."

"I was starting to wonder if maybe I scared you off."

"I wouldn't leave something as pretty as you stranded. I haven't been in this apartment in a few days. I'm hoping everything is still intact."

"As long as you have the money, baby, I don't care where we fuck." Mindy grabbed Tuna's dick.

As Mindy and Tuna walked up the steps, Speedy was pulling up on the old hangout spot. He knew Tuna had to be up there. His plan was to see what Tuna's intentions were. If he felt like Tuna was going to turn into a rat, he was going to kill him, then kill himself. But if Tuna was okay with him falling back on this last push for Lucky, then he would just walk away and go home.

Speedy was tired of all the bullshit. He wanted to find a quick resolution. He parked and started walking toward the building. He looked down the street and waved at the surveillance car that was following him.

"Sir, come in."

"Yes, Captain. Where did he stop?" the mayor asked.

"He just entered a building on 102nd Street and Lexington Avenue."

"Okay, I'm dispatching additional help. Stay put and out of sight until more help arrives."

"He already made us. Right before he entered the building, he waved at us."

"Well, still stay put and out of sight," an angry mayor said. "Didn't I warn you to be careful? Never mind. Don't do anything until help arrives."

"Affirmative."

As Tuna tried to open the front door, Mindy couldn't wait until they entered the apartment. She started kissing him all over him. She wanted to fuck him in the hallway.

"Calm down, baby girl. Let me open the door first."

As Tuna swung open the front door, Lucky was standing there waiting, pointing the same 12-gauge he used to blow Blood's head off.

"What the fuck!" were the last words Tuna said as he looked right into Lucky's eye.

Lucky shot him in the chest and watched his body slam against the hallway wall. Mindy began screaming and ran downstairs as fast as she could.

Speedy grabbed her right before she ran out the front door and covered her mouth.

"Sshhh! Calm down! Please, calm down. I'm a police officer. I heard the shot. What's going on? Who's up there? What happened?" Speedy removed his hand from her mouth.

Mindy yelled hysterically, "He shot him! He shot him!"

"Who did?"

"A black guy shot him as soon as he opened the door. Tuna is dead. A black guy shot him."

Speedy released the girl and raced up the flight of steps in time to see Lucky standing over a barely breathing Tuna.

Lucky placed the barrel in Tuna's mouth. "You racist muthafucka! I told you I would kill you." He pulled the trigger and watched part of his face smear all over the wall. As Lucky was about to shoot him again, he was met with about four shots from Speedy's 9 mm.

Lucky ducked while letting off two shotgun blasts and dropping the gun on the floor. As he ran in the apartment for cover, he pulled out two 9 mms of his own and let off about another twelve shots toward the front door, keeping Speedy at bay.

As Speedy and Lucky were facing off on the third floor, Captain Shuler was on the radio, calling the mayor.

"Shots fired, sir! Shots fired!" the captain yelled.

"Secure the perimeter. Help is minutes away."

The mayor quickly called the governor and told him, "We got him!"

"Where?"

"He's in Spanish Harlem, 102nd Street and Lexington Avenue. He's trapped inside, we believe, with Tuna and Speedy. They are currently in a shoot-out as we speak."

"We'll dispatch the entire department to 102nd Street. He can't get away this time."

"I'm a step ahead of you," the mayor said. "I already made the call. I'm also on my way there."

"I'm on my way as well."

About twenty minutes later, the mayor had the entire block shut down. He had about a hundred police officers and about thirty SWAT members posted all in front of the building. And news reporters were all over the scene, which was being broadcast live. The potential shooting and hostage situation involving Tuna, Speedy, and Lucky caught the attention of the city, which, once again, was glued to the TV, and watching in anticipation.

The negotiating team at hand attempted to communicate through a bullhorn. They were only going to give them another five minutes before entering and shooting everyone.

As the countdown was nearing its end, the mayor was getting anxious. He was hoping it didn't lead to them having to rush in. He was afraid of what the death toll might be. Lucky could be waiting inside, plucking them off one by one.

With one minute left, an officer yelled, "I see someone coming out!"

Everyone got in their firing positions, and snipers were locked and ready. No one knew what to expect, and out came a suspect dressed in all black, wearing a black mask and waving two guns.

As soon as the mayor saw he was armed, he yelled, "Fire!" and ran for cover.

The gun party began. Snipers hit him first, and then a few officers also discharged their weapons. The suspect's body dropped like rain while shots were still being fired. They rushed toward the suspect and quickly became confused. The handguns were taped around his hands. They removed the mask and noticed it was Detective Speedy.

Lucky had duct-taped his mouth and hands, pushed him out the door, and had run for his escape. And since no one could hear Speedy beg for his life, he was murdered. Once again Lucky embarrassed the police department nationally.

Before the cops had arrived, Speedy ran out of bullets in his standoff with Lucky. Once he noticed he was out of ammo, he gave up, tired of fighting and playing the villain role. If he had had an extra bullet, he would have shot himself.

The second Lucky got ahold of him, he heard the sirens outside. That was the only thing that stopped him from killing Speedy's snake ass. He handcuffed Speedy to the stair rail in the hallway while he ran toward the nearest window.

Lucky couldn't believe the amount of cops outside. With that monkey wrench thrown in his plans, he needed to think fast. He looked over at Speedy and decided to use him to buy him time to escape through the roof.

Right after Lucky pushed Speedy to his death, he turned to run toward the roof, but he noticed a door that led to the back. He decided to skip the roof idea because, knowing the mayor, snipers would be on the roof. He had a better chance of escaping by staying low and out of sight. He didn't have time to map out the area. He was going to have to improvise as he went.

It turned out it was a good decision. The back door led to a small, junky backyard with a bunch of broken refrigerators and air conditioners. Lucky made his way through it. He even had to avoid a few cat-sized rats in the process. He jumped the fence and entered the back of another building and came out on 103rd Street. When he got outside, there were still cops flying past him on their way to 102nd Street. No one noticed him as he calmly walked down the street, his backpack filled with over a million dollars.

Meanwhile, police officers swamped the building, desperately searching for Lucky. Instead, they found the dead body of Captain Tuna, his face on the wall.

When the mayor heard about Tuna's death, he dropped to one knee. It was a wrap. Everything he hoped for went down the drain. A few officers helped the mayor back on his feet. They didn't know what happened.

The mayor refused medical attention, and his staff led him back to his awaiting truck. While the mayor sat there and tried to gain his composure, the lead agent in charge reported back to him.

"Sir, we have searched the entire building, and there are no signs of another suspect."

"Listen, Detective Speedy didn't tie those guns to his hands himself. I want your team to search the building again. Are we clear? As a matter of fact, search every fuckin' building in Spanish Harlem."

"Clear, sir."

The mayor sat there in disbelief. "How can this son of a bitch keep getting lucky?" he said to himself. He just couldn't understand how every plan they came up with backfired on them. This was going to cost him his career and was his first-class ticket to prison. As he thought about his demise, he noticed the governor flying toward him.

The governor got in the truck and didn't even close the door before he started moving his mouth. "What in the hell happened here, Ralph? I'm hearing both Speedy and Tuna are dead, and Lucky is nowhere to be found. Please tell me those reports are not accurate."

"I wish I could."

"You wish you could. That's all you can say? I risked my neck helping you in this final fantasy of yours. We broke a lot of rules to get them out of jail. We promised the public that these police officers would be under our watch at their own homes. Explain how in the world they were both found dead on 102nd Street."

"I don't know, and I don't give a fuck. I already killed myself by blowing this last opportunity. Lucky will now disappear. He has gotten his revenge and killed all his ex-partners. He won't stick around. I'm fucked."

"We both are," the governor said.

"Look around. I'm the one that fucked up. What am I going to say to the city now? Once this nonsense hits the news, I'm dead. Not more than twenty-four hours after those three dead bodies in Harlem, we have two more cops. That's a total of five dead cops, three of them feds. All the murders are connected to Lucky. Everything happened within a week. One fuckin' week!"

"I'm going to make some phone calls and start kissing ass now. I'll see you in the morning. Don't be hard on yourself. You always had the city's best interest. Once your laundry hits the media, it's hard to move forward without scrutiny." The governor hugged his political friend.

"Thanks. I'll be okay. I just know I hear the fat lady loud and clear. Don't forget to stop by in the morning. I'm going to stick around for the media and give them my last report. I'm sure I'll be asked to resign."

The governor left with a clear understanding that it was every man for himself. He started making his calls to clear his name and slam the mayor under the bus. Plus, he didn't like his attitude and sensed he was quitting. Quitters usually started snitching.

As the mayor watched him walk away, he quickly called up Anita Flowers.

"Hello."

"Mrs. Flowers, it's the mayor."

"I know, sir. Please call me Anita."

"I need you on 102nd Street and Lexington Avenue."

"I'm on 108th Street and Lexington Avenue. Once I saw it on the news, I got dressed and jumped in a cab. I should be there in five minutes. Have you made a statement?"

"No, that's why I'm calling, Anita."

"Okay, sir, just send a police captain out to the media. Have him tell them a statement from the mayor is coming within minutes. I'll be there to handle it."

"Sounds great. Please hurry," he said as he hung up. It was a blessing to have Anita's help. He didn't have the right energy to face the media. His behavior would have been out of line.

Within minutes, Anita arrived and was quickly updated on the situation. Without hesitation, she turned around and walked straight to the podium.

As Anita played her role, the mayor disappeared, jumping in his ride and heading down to his office. He needed peace and quiet, and that was usually the only place where he could find it. Both his personal and business phones were ringing, but he ignored them as he sat there in complete silence.

Chapter Thirty

Little Rock, Arkansas

Lucky was sitting at a Popeyes on 125th Street and Park Avenue. It was going on six o'clock, and he didn't have time to waste. He calmly bit into his chicken. While he ate his food, his brain was racing with different emotions.

The first thing on the list was a car. It was too risky to pull off a carjacking. He had to steal one quietly. By the time the owners realized their car was stolen, he should be halfway to Arkansas, a sixteen- to eighteen-hour drive.

After he finished his food, he jumped in a cab, headed toward the Bronx, to the Yankee Stadium area, figuring that would be a great area to take a car. On his way there, he saw a used car lot and asked the cabdriver to stop.

"Let me out right here."

"Are you sure?" the cabdriver asked.

"I'm positive. Here, keep the change," Lucky said as he handed him a twenty.

Lucky jumped out of the cab and ran across the street. When he walked toward one of the cars for sale, a Hispanic male came out of the little trailer they called an office.

"What's up, *papi?* What kind of car you looking for? My name is Pedro. I'm your man."

Lucky was relieved Pedro knew English. He threw on his acting suit and came up with a story. "Look, Pedro, I'm not going to lie. I have a family issue I need to attend to down in Virginia. I need a car."

"Well, you came to the right place."

"Pedro, here is the deal. I only have cash, no ID. I just need a car for a few days."

"Well, hello, Mr. Cash. How about I let you rent a car and you leave a deposit? Which car you want?"

"I'm looking at that black Explorer with the light tints."

"For how many days you need the truck, Mr. Cash?"

"I need the truck for a week. Just let me know how much it's going to cost to rent it and the deposit."

"I want a thousand to rent for a week and another five thousand for deposit, *papi*. You bring truck back in same condition, I give money back. Any damages, I will keep money. We got a deal?" Pedro extended his hand.

"We got a deal. I'm going to give you ten thousand dollars. When I bring the truck back, just give me back five thousand dollars. You are doing me a big-time favor."

The transaction was a win-win situation for both of them. Pedro bought the truck at an auction for only thirty-eight hundred dollars, so he had nothing to lose if Lucky didn't bring it back. He was going to make a profit, regardless. Lucky leaving ten thousand dollars in total made the deal even sweeter.

For Lucky, he bought himself a ride with no paperwork, and it only cost him ten thousand.

Lucky waited as Pedro changed the oil and fixed up some minor issues, like the brake light and car radio. The Explorer truck was a 2006 model, so Lucky felt comfortable it would be able to handle the long trip.

"Hey, Pedro, let me sit in one of these cars to count the money."

"Go in my office. It's going to take me another fifteen minutes to finish up."

That was exactly what Lucky wanted to hear. Pedro fell in his trap.

Lucky didn't need to count his money, since most of it was already in ten-thousand-dollar bundles. He wanted to get in his office and look around to see if he could find Pedro's personal information.

As soon as Lucky went in the trailer, he found bank statements right on the small desk. He grabbed one of the statements, memorized the address, and placed it back on the desk. He came out of the trailer just as Pedro finished working on the car.

"Just in time, Mr. Cash. The car is ready, and it has a full tank of gas as well."

"Great. Hey, listen. Just so that we understand each other, this meeting never took place. We never met."

"No worries, *papi*. I don't know you."

"Just to make sure, let me make a call." Lucky pulled out his cell phone and acted as if he dialed a legit number. "Hey, it's me," he said. "Listen, if anything happens to me, and I don't come back, pay a visit to Pedro Soto, nineteen-forty-two Sedgwick Avenue, apartment four-b." Lucky then hung up.

"How did you get my address? You were in my office, snooping around?"

"Listen, I'm leaving you with ten thousand dollars. I just want to make sure, when I leave the lot, you don't report the car stolen."

Pedro didn't like it but understood. "Hey, *papi*, I'm a man about my word. No worries. Have a safe trip, and I will see you in a week."

Lucky pulled out of the parking lot, jumped on the George Washington Bridge, and headed toward Little Rock. As he drove, he thought about what he would do to Diamond once he found her. He knew she didn't steal the money, but she was still responsible for calling the cops on him.

In reality, the only thing Diamond did wrong was not go down to Maryland. She decided to go back home and reunite with her family. She wasn't about to be stuck in Maryland all by herself. She knew Lucky was never coming back. She felt she was grown and strong enough to face her family again.

Unfortunately for Diamond, Lucky blamed her for everything. He was going to torture her to death, worse than Sergio. That was how much hate he had for Diamond.

As he drove, he would tighten his grip on the steering wheel. It was beyond frustration. It really hurt him, because he fell in love with her and never would have thought she would drop dime on him. All he kept thinking was, Why couldn't she just leave and go back home? Why would she call the cops on him and cause all the additional headaches?

The mayor was back at his office, still in a daze. His secretary kept screening his calls and taking messages. She even stopped going in the office, because he kept yelling at her every time she went in.

After the governor never got any of his messages returned, he decided to show up at his office. As soon as he turned the knob, he heard a single shot come from inside the mayor's office. The governor ran in to find the mayor's head lying on his desk. He had killed himself with a single shot to his temple with a .38 special. The governor instructed the secretary to call 9-1-1. He checked for a pulse. "C'mon, Ralph," he said, "you have a family. You can't check out like this."

The governor stood back and let the medical staff do their job. He was staring at Ralph, as his own life flashed in front of him. He was hoping he didn't have to commit suicide. It was sad and a low point in the governor's career, but if he played his cards right, he could come out on top. He was going to use the mayor's suicide to his advantage and play the blame game.

Reporter Destine Diaz had reported that she had learned from a reliable source that the mayor was the one who had the commissioner assassinated. Her accusations raised some eyebrows and got her suspended from her job. She was only reporting what Richard Claiborne made her aware of. Destine didn't have any evidence to back up her story. Her only hope was if they captured Richard. Then he would come clean. But, knowing the CIA, she thought they would probably kill him to keep his mouth shut forever.

Thirteen hours into his trip, Lucky decided to pull over and catch about an hour of sleep. He had driven through the night, stopping only for gas and snacks, and was tired. His eyes were starting to hurt, and he couldn't keep them open.

With so much on his mind, Lucky couldn't rest. After about thirty minutes of tossing back and forth in the driver's seat, he'd had enough. He went in the bathroom, washed his face, and got himself a large coffee and two five-hour energies. Within minutes, around ten in the morning, he was back on the highway, with another five to six hours to go.

***

Back in New York, all the morning stations and national media outlets were reporting the mayor's suicide and his alleged involvement in the commissioner's assassination. Some media outlets mentioned that the CIA was involved to some degree, but no one could verify it.

Then, there was Lucky's mysterious disappearance. It still baffled the public that he wasn't captured. That was why he was labeled the American bin Laden. New Yorkers, at the end of the day, loved Lucky. They just didn't like the amount of dead bodies they claimed he was responsible for, especially that female found tied up and shot.

That raised the question of him being set up. Maybe the police department wanted payback because he exposed their dirty deeds.

Lucky was the number one enemy among the boys in blue. From the moment he'd testified, every police officer in the world had hated him. You didn't cross the line. That was worse than working with Internal Affairs.

New Yorkers understood how much he was hated. They were assuming he was framed. The public just wanted to hear from Lucky himself to make an independent judgment.

Back at the Colemans', a bit of a celebration was taking place. Laura Coleman had had her wish granted. She wanted all the officers charged with her son's murder dead and didn't feel one ounce of sympathy for them or their families, because the same courtesy wasn't extended to her.

Before Lucky came forward, it was believed that her son indeed had a gun on him when he was killed. They began calling her son a criminal, saying he was armed and dangerous. Laura knew better and pleaded with the public to hold back judgment on her son's character. She knew he was innocent and didn't shoot at the officers, as alleged.

If it wasn't for Lucky, the truth would have never been revealed. Laura questioned her faith throughout the ordeal, but she still prayed every night before going to bed. That same ole prayer she recited had a new name added, which she always thanked as well. *Lucky*.

Not everybody was ready to label Lucky a misunderstood hero. The governor was still on the hunt and made it part of his business to continue tracking down Lucky. His department reached out to the CIA, and after numerous attempts, he was able to track down Agent Scott Meyer.

"Hello, this is the governor. Are you still on the line, Agent Meyer?"

"Yes, sir. How can I help you? How did you find me?"

"C'mon, just because the FBI and CIA personally don't like each other doesn't mean we don't have friends in each other's departments."

"True. So how can I help you?"

"I understand you visited the mayor on a few occasions. I want to know the business behind those meetings."

"I can't disclose that information. That was between the mayor and us."

"Well, how about I release your name and your pretty little partner's name to the media?"

"Okay, listen, let's meet in about an hour. I will give you what I have. I think we know where Lucky is heading to."

"Now, that sounds a lot better. I will be waiting on your call."

The governor was excited that he was going to receive exclusive information about Lucky's whereabouts. Catching Lucky would help him in his bid to run for the presidency down the road. He couldn't wait until the meeting with Agent Meyer.

The past few weeks had been the most challenging of the governor's career. The only good out of it was, all parties involved in the corruption plot were now dead. It would be easy to start all over. Besides, his name never came up. For the time being, until the new acting mayor was appointed, Governor Andrew Silver was taking over all responsibilities.

After all the alleged corrupt officials were dead, there was a collective sigh of relief all around the streets. The healing process was going to take time. Many were not fully recovered from the riots yet, but at least the worst rogue cops in the NYPD's history were now gone.

By the time the six o'clock news came on, the tone of the broadcast had changed. Only ten minutes of their sixty-minute segment was spent on the mayor and the dead officers. The media was trying to help New Yorkers forget about the drama.

It was going on seven in the evening, and Lucky was staying at a crappy motel off Willow Mills Highway in Little Rock, five minutes away from the address Asia gave him. He was unaware of what was going on back in New York, and he didn't care. All he was concerned with was taking out Diamond and getting back to his family.

Lucky got dressed and packed up like he was gone for the night, even though the room was paid up for three more days. Though he was just going to do a routine stakeout first, he knew there was a possibility he might not return to the room.

Diamond's family lived in a house on S. Chester Street and Wright. He drove over there and parked down the street. He noticed a white two-door Mercedes with temporary tags. He knew that was Diamond's car. The one she used to always talk about when they were together.

Lucky was out there for at least three hours before he saw any movement. Someone turned on the light on the front porch. He sat up. He saw someone come out of the house, but by the time he tried to get a closer look, they had already jumped in the white Benz.

He started following the car. In his mind, it could only be Diamond. He followed the car for about ten minutes and ended up in a quiet, fancier neighborhood. When the white Benz parked, Lucky parked as well and kept watching. The driver jumped out, and it was Diamond.

Lucky paused. He had to catch his breath, and himself. He wanted to jump on her right in the parking lot. He decided he would wait and see which building she walked into, and after that, watch which lights she turned on. Once he saw which apartment she was staying in, he would make his move and ambush her ass.

It was going on two in the morning, and everything was going according to plan. He knew which apartment she lived in, and he waited until the lights went off. Lucky finally decided to make his move, slowly walking in the apartment building and up the stairs to the second floor.

As Lucky attempted to unlock the door, out of nowhere, it swung open. It was Diamond standing by the front door.

"About time you fuckin' found me," she said. "What? You didn't think I knew you were following me? Don't forget, you taught me all the tricks. Come here, baby," Diamond said, not knowing Lucky was actually there to kill her. Once she saw Lucky standing there, it meant the world to her. She thought he was there to reclaim her as his woman.

Lucky slapped her so hard, he lifted her body off the floor, and she landed flat on her back.

She grabbed her face. "What the fuck was that for? You can't be mad that I didn't go to Maryland."

"Oh, you think I'm just mad about that? Is there something else you want to tell me?" Lucky went to slap her again.

"Wait, baby. Just wait. What are you talking about?"

"I'm talking about the fuckin' cops raiding my storage facility. You didn't have anything to do with that?" he said as he cocked back his gun.

"I swear to fuckin' God I didn't. So, now you are going to shoot me, Lucky? What the fuck!"

Lucky tried to read her and felt like she was telling the truth. That was puzzling. He'd believed in his heart Diamond was the one who snitched.

"Listen, Lucky, when I left that night for Maryland, I actually went to Sergio's apartment. I didn't want to go to Maryland and be alone. Fuck that! I decided to come back home. I felt I was strong enough to face my demons. That's all I did. Why would I call the cops on the love of my life?"

"Maybe you were mad because I sent you down there without me. I don't fuckin' know. All I know is, my spot got raided, and all signs point to you. You better come up with a better story than that, bitch."

"Bitch? How dare you call me that! Now you are disrespecting me, Lucky?"

"So I'm supposed to believe you stayed at Sergio's apartment a few days and nothing happened?"

"Whatever. You don't fuckin' believe me, let's call Sergio."

"We don't have to. I already confronted Sergio about that."

"Well then, you know I'm telling the truth. Why you all in my face like that, Lucky? Like I'm a fuckin' mark. That's how you treating me."

"If you was a mark, you would have been dead already, but we can't call him, anyway."

"You killed him? Why? Sergio didn't do anything. I was at his apartment for a few days, and that man never attempted anything. He had too much respect for you. Oh Lawd, you killed Sergio. He was like a son to you."

"Why everybody keeps fuckin' saying that? He wasn't my son. When I went to visit him, the CIA was leaving his apartment. I'm assuming they traced the call and that's how they found him. The call was made from Sergio's phone, so if you didn't, then who? According to my sources, it was a female who made the call."

"I don't know. I didn't. That's all that should count. I seen this look before. It's the same look before you pull off a job. You're making me nervous."

"You should be, because I didn't drive all the way down here for hugs and kisses. I want the truth. You should be a real woman and own up to it."

"Nigga, please. I'm a woman. A real one who will never double-cross her man. If the call came from Sergio's phone, then maybe he had his girl call."

"That's a possibility, but all signs still point toward you," Lucky said as he picked her up from the floor. "Sit over there on the sofa. We're going to get to the bottom of this."

"C'mon, baby, why would I call the cops on you? It doesn't make sense. You saved my life, Lucky. I owe you more than my life. Yes, I was mad that you left me, but that doesn't mean I want you in jail for life. I have to respect the fact that you wanted to get your family back. I know your daughter means everything to you. I can't come between that. Fuck your baby

mama! But I knew that's what you wanted. It didn't matter
how many nights I woke up with a soaked pillow, crying my
eyes out. I think about you every day, Lucky. I thought you
changed your mind and came back for me. I guess I was
wrong."

"Whatever. If you love me like you say you do, then you
would have followed the plan and went down to Maryland.
Why come back here to your hometown?"

"Because this is all I know."

"What? Being abused is all you know? When you left, you
were a little girl. Now you are a grown woman. You had the
opportunity to start a fresh life somewhere else. Why come
here, where it all went wrong?"

"I know, but I didn't want a fresh start. What part of *you
were my all* don't you understand? Remember, you left me
and lied to me. You weren't going to meet me in Maryland.
Let's be honest with each other."

"You didn't know that. I'm not going to lie. I didn't have
intentions of coming back at first. When you left that day,
well, when I thought you left, I was down. I couldn't stop
thinking about you. I was going to wait a few months before I
popped up. I love you too much to abandon you."

Lucky pulled out some handcuffs and cuffed her to one of
her kitchen chairs. He moved her to a corner far away from
any objects she might use as a weapon. After he secured
her, he sat across from her and stared at her. He was really
stuck on killing her. He didn't know what to do. She sounded
believable, but he'd already reached the point of no return. If
he let her walk away, he would second-guess himself for life.

It didn't help Diamond's situation that she was most likely
there when Sergio made the call. An angry black woman's
revenge was the number one fear among black men. They
would do the unthinkable.

Diamond sat there quietly. She couldn't believe Lucky just
popped up out of nowhere. She never thought he would find
her here. As bad as she talked about her family, it was the last
place she thought he would check. She didn't like how Lucky
was looking at her. She knew she was in trouble.

"So, are you just going to stare at me?" she said to break the ice.

"I'm just thinking. That's all."

"About what?" She licked her lips. "How much you miss me?"

"Please, girl, that sweet talk is not going to help you today. I'm trying to decide if you should live or die."

Diamond exhaled and looked at Lucky. "You have to believe me. I didn't call the cops, and I didn't know Sergio called the cops. Baby, you have to believe me."

Lucky didn't reply. He continued sitting there in silence.

Originally, he wanted to torture her so bad, her mother wouldn't have been able to identify her. He had about a hundred different ways to make her suffer and die slowly. He thought about locking her in a room with two hungry and mad-as-shit pit bulls while she was handcuffed.

Then he started thinking about how much he loved her. All recent memories with Diamond were good ones. Truth be told, he wasn't going back for Tasha. It had always been about Tamika. If he could swap baby mamas, he would. He was disappointed that she didn't go to Maryland and at least try. He'd spent money on the house and given her a hundred thousand.

Lucky had to take a deep breath. He was starting to get upset. He caught himself before he started getting mad.

"C'mon, Lucky, say something, my love. Why are you doing this? For real, why?"

"It's the trust issue, Dee. You sound believable, but I don't feel right. It's a hole in the story, and I can't pinpoint it. I'm just waiting to see it if comes to me."

"C'mon, let me go, Lucky. You know in your heart I didn't do nothing."

"I wouldn't go that far. The whole Sergio situation is throwing me off."

"I'm telling you, baby. Nothing happened between Sergio and I. The only thing he did was encourage me to go back home."

"Encourage you? What you mean?" Lucky said as he sat up.

"Calm down, honey. I told him about our situation, and he agreed it was a little fucked up, and that I should do what's best for me. You had too much heat on you," Diamond said, feeling a bit more comfortable. She saw it in his eyes. He wasn't going to kill her. He was just trying to scare her, and it was working.

"So, it was Sergio's idea for you to come back home?"

"No, but something like that."

Lucky stood up, cocked back his 9 mm, pointed it at Diamond, and aimed for her head.

Diamond still wasn't alarmed about it. There was no way he was serious.

"It's about trust. I always want to feel like I could trust you." Lucky blew her a kiss. Then he shot her twice, knocking her backward.

She ended up in a sitting position with her legs up, blood leaking from the two holes in her head, and her eyes open.

Lucky kneeled down and closed them for her. He kissed his index and middle finger and touched her forehead. "I will always love you, baby."

He got up and quickly ran the hell up out of there. He couldn't believe he'd just pulled the trigger. He felt like he was left with no options. Diamond was cuffed, but his hands were tied behind him as well. If he let her live, then he wouldn't get an opportunity to make a clean move forward. She would always be in the middle. He needed her out of the picture. He did think about letting her slide, but when she said Sergio encouraged her to move back home, the trust issue came to mind again. He just could not risk her living and knowing his past, if he was going to move forward. She could still be an informant.

Lucky's decision to go back to Tasha and his daughter was Diamond's death certificate. She didn't move down to Maryland as planned and stayed a few days at Sergio the snitch's house. She just couldn't be trusted, so she had to die.

He jumped in the black Explorer and found his way back to the highway. He was moving fast because he felt like maybe a neighbor or two could have been looking out the window when he peeled off. If the police showed up, he would be long gone.

As he was driving, tears were coming down his face. He didn't want to kill Diamond, but it was what it was. He'd created her, so he felt like he could destroy her. Once he reunited with his family, he would get a fresh start, and Diamond, along with his ex-partners, would all become a distant memory. To start his new life, all he would need was plastic surgery to change his look.

He reached for his phone and started calling Tasha. Speaking to her would make him forget about Diamond.

She picked up on the second ring. "Hello. Please tell me you are on your way," Tasha said in excitement.

"I'm on my way. I should be there in another six to seven hours."

"Please don't bullshit me. I don't have time for any new games, Lucky."

"Why would I play like that? It's all over. I will be there. Please, tell my li'l princess the king will be there soon."

"I sure will. But what about the queen? I don't get any special shout-outs? I've been waiting for this moment for a very long time."

"I have something special planned for the two of us. Don't worry, sweetheart. Now you have me until I grow old. I will never leave your side again."

"I love you, Lucky. Drive safely. Oh, I almost forgot to tell you. The mayor committed suicide."

"Get the fuck out of here! He did? That's great news. Ha! So he pulled the trigger on himself. What a coward! Thanks for the news. You just made my ride a better one. I will see you in a few."

Lucky hung up the phone, happy to hear the mayor was dead. That meant everyone involved in the corruption allegations was gone. It worked out perfect, almost like he drew it out. He'd never expected to kill Diamond, but casualties were a part of the game. It got to the point where he was starting to believe his luck was running out. Now, after a few close calls with death, he still didn't know how he was able to escape all the drama unhurt.

As he drove, he tried to stay awake by counting how many blue cars he passed. Lucky couldn't get Diamond or Haze out of his mind, the only two individuals who he wished didn't get caught in the cross fire. He felt bad for Diamond only because he truly loved her. He just couldn't accept that there was a possibility that she'd indeed snitched.

On the other hand, he really felt fucked up about Haze. Even though Haze picked his own destiny, Lucky still felt awful. Haze had made up his mind, but Lucky didn't step up and make him change it, like he did when Haze was talking about killing his baby mama. Crossed by his associates in the past, Lucky had a feeling Haze would have been by far the most loyal. It was too bad he was gone, leaving another single black mother to raise his family.

Once Lucky was back with Tasha, he planned to hit up Asia and find out Haze's real name and address. He would send like a hundred thousand dollars. It wouldn't bring Haze back, but it would help his family get through the hard times.

Chapter Thirty-one

Finally Reunited with Tamika

It was going on noon, and Lucky was about five minutes away from hugging his wifey and daughter. It was a long time coming for that moment. He'd had many sweaty nights when he felt like that day would never arrive. He called Tasha.

"Where are you, Lucky?"

"Damn! A simple hello would have been better."

"Whatever. I've been waiting on you all this time. Where are you, honey? Stop playing. I've been a nervous wreck since you called and said you hours away from us."

"I'm at the gas station."

"What the fuck for, Lucky?"

"Calm down. The gas tank is on empty. I wanted to put some gas in it. I'm not parking the truck with no gas, just in case I have to make a run for it."

"Okay, but hurry up. We'll be waiting outside for you. Tamika has been up since, like, five this morning, waiting for you. I don't know who's more excited between the both of us."

"No one is more excited than I am. I'm in a black Ford Explorer. I should be pulling up soon. Don't wait outside. It will bring attention."

"Why not?" a curious Tasha asked.

"Baby, don't wait outside. We don't need the extra attention."

"Okay, I will just look out the window, then," she said, disappointed.

"Did you cook?"

"You know I did. I made one of your favorites, but hurry up and get your butt over here before I throw it in the garbage."

"Yeah, right. Here I come."

Lucky hung up the phone, smiling ear to ear, but still looking over his shoulder. He couldn't forget the *America's Most Wanted* piece they did on him. He had to be cautious. Two million dollars would give an old dude 20/20 vision.

After filling up the tank, which cost almost seventy dollars, he jumped in and headed to his family. As he pulled into the gated community, he parked his truck and jumped out. He got out and could see both Tasha and Tamika waving from the window like he was the first human contact they had seen in years. That made him smile and wave back.

After Lucky went to the back to retrieve his bag, he started walking toward the front door. He looked back up at the window to see Tamika blowing him kisses. Lucky so happened to look up toward the roof and noticed what looked like a marksman. Before he could even react, two loud shots erupted in that quiet community.

Bang! Bang!

Lucky dropped to the ground after getting shot twice in the head.

Both Tasha and Tamika began yelling and crying. At first they felt like they were daydreaming. When Tasha realized it wasn't a bad dream, that Lucky was actually shot, she asked her mom to hold Tamika and she flew down the steps. When she made it to her man, he was dead. There was blood everywhere.

Tasha started yelling, hoping someone would call 9-1-1. "No! Oh my God! Please don't do this to us. Oh God! Please help! Someone help!" She looked up at the window and could see and hear Tamika still screaming for her father.

Tasha grabbed Lucky around his neck and lifted his head up. She wanted to make sure he was dead and there was nothing for him to say. While doing that, she noticed the bag he was carrying. She grabbed it and put it behind her back. She knew it was stuffed with money, because that was one of the main reasons he went back to New York.

Within a few minutes, there were police officers everywhere. Tasha started looking around, and when she saw what looked like FBI agents on the scene, she put one and one together and knew the feds must have assassinated him. She ran upstairs, grabbed a few things, and told her mother and Tamika they were leaving.

"Mom, wait a second! What happened to my father? Is he dead?" a hysterical Tamika asked.

"Now is not the time to talk about it."

"But, Mom, that's Daddy. They shot him in front of us. Who would want to kill my father? I want to see him. Please, take me downstairs. I want to see him. Please, Mother, please," Tamika begged.

"Listen, Tamika, your father was a wanted man. He did some bad things that we can't discuss right now. I'm sorry I never told you the truth about him."

"So he wasn't a cop?" she asked and started wiping her tears.

"No, that part is true. He just wasn't a good one. We will talk later. I promise I will sit you down and explain everything. Right now is not the time. We need to disappear before they come after us."

"But why? I don't understand."

"Girl, just bring your ass and stop asking so many fuckin' questions." Tasha had to pause. She had never lost her cool and cursed at Tamika. "Listen, I'm sorry for cursing. Your father sacrificed his life in order for no one to know our true identities. He arrested powerful, bad people who usually go after the family of the arresting cops. Your daddy never told anyone about us. Now they have found him. I'm sure they want to look for us. No more questions. I'm sorry you just witnessed the murder of your father, but we have to go."

"Okay, Mommy." Tamika ran back toward the window. Her father's lifeless body was still lying on the ground. She blew her daddy a kiss. "Thank you for giving up you life for me. I love you. God will protect you."

Tasha, her mother, and Tamika disappeared through the back entrance of the three-story building. Tasha didn't pack any clothes. She just grabbed her money and the money she snatched from Lucky. She always parked her car out of sight just in case she had to make a quick getaway.

Tasha thought she was getting away, not realizing the feds had been watching her for two days now. As she was driving out of the gated community, one of the SWAT members radioed in to find out if they should stop them.

"Sir, come in. This is Captain Ortiz."

"Yes, Captain," Governor Andrew Silver said.

"The target's girlfriend is trying to make a getaway."

"Pull her over and hit me on the radio."

"Affirmative."

The governor, along with the CIA, was able to track down Lucky's family. When the CIA had visited Sergio before Lucky killed him, Sergio told them the number Lucky gave him when he asked him to call Tasha. The CIA was able to trace the cell, and that was how they found Tasha. When Lucky called her and told her he would be on his way, they were waiting for him as well.

The governor gave one order—kill him on sight. They weren't going to give him another opportunity to escape.

"Sir, come in."

"Yes, Captain Ortiz," the governor shot back.

"We have detained the target's family."

"Okay, Captain, put the radio near the girlfriend's ear."

"They can hear you, sir."

"Good. I'm going to make this short. A lot of people have died and suffered because of Lucky and his ex-partners. We are not going to hold anything against you. We're sorry you had to witness what you saw. Enjoy your fresh start. Captain Ortiz, let them go." The governor turned off his radio.

Even though the governor hated Lucky, he wasn't a monster. He wasn't about to ruin their lives. Since Lucky's ex-partners' families were left alone, he decided to give Tasha the same courtesy.

Tasha was scared to death and didn't know what to expect. When she heard they could leave, she put the car in drive and peeled off. She didn't even look through the rearview mirror. She jumped on the highway and headed to Florida.

The governor was at the crime scene, staring at Lucky. He couldn't understand why that pig was so hard to find. In a way, he was glad he'd exposed corruption in the city.

The governor headed to the airport, on his way back to New York, where he would be labeled a hero. The news traveled fast, and all the news stations were reporting the death of Lucky. It was big news. A lot celebrated, some cried, but a breath of fresh air was felt throughout the gritty streets of New York.

Destine Diaz was sitting on her sofa, sipping coffee. The longer she stayed out of work, the more depressed she became. TV was her life, and she didn't have a backup plan. It was going on six o'clock in the evening when her doorman buzzed her from downstairs.

Destine was short. "Yes, Fred?"

"I'm sorry to bother you, but you have a package."

"A package this late? From whom?"

"It just says, 'To Destine Diaz from Donald Gibson.'"

Destine spat the coffee out of her mouth. "What name did you just say?"

"Donald Gibson," the doorman repeated.

"Please, bring it up. I'll be by the elevator."

When the elevator doors opened, Destine was waiting in anticipation. She was so excited, she'd walked out in her T-shirt and panties.

Fred was taken aback. "This package must be pretty important," he said, looking at her up and down.

When Destine realized what the hell she'd just done, she snatched the package and ran back in the condo. Right before she closed the door, she yelled to Fred, "I'm sure this package will get me my job back!"

Destine went in her living room and leaned against the door. She couldn't believe she'd just walked out in her underwear. Her face was red with embarrassment. Good thing Fred was in his sixties and a gentleman.

She ripped open the package and found a DVD disc and a note inside. The note read:

Destine
It's me, Lucky. The DVD, it's an interview I recorded.
I wanted you to interview me, but with all the drama
going on, it was impossible. On this disc, you have my

confession, and you have my life. I just want to ask for one favor. Don't play this until after I'm killed. I might be dead by the time you get this DVD, anyway, so it wouldn't even matter. I just want New York to hear my side of the story.

Lucky

A tear came down Destine's eye. She could only imagine what was on the DVD. She felt honored that Lucky chose her and had faith in her abilities.

She popped in the DVD. Once she confirmed it was Lucky, she stopped it and called her boss. She didn't even get a chance to see the whole story. When she told him she had Lucky's video confession, he offered her job back with a few extra perks. Destine accepted his offer over the phone and headed down to the station, where they were going to broadcast live at eight instead of ten o'clock.

The news station was already promoting the breaking news. Once New Yorkers heard they had a video of Lucky confessing to his wrongdoings, it caught everyone's attention. No one had ever heard his side of the story, except maybe those present at the Coleman trial. Plus, so much had happened since the trial. Everyone was eager to hear his side.

When Destine arrived at the station, it was going on seven-thirty. She quickly gave the DVD to her production team while makeup was being applied. The news of her firing was made public, so New Yorkers would be shocked to see her back in front of the camera.

Destine didn't lose a beat. She was prepared like the veteran she was. As eight o'clock rolled around, she was back in the limelight.

"Good evening, New York. Thank you for tuning in at this special time for this exclusive interview we have with Donald 'Lucky' Gibson. Today, around six this evening, I received a package, a DVD, from Lucky with a note that read, 'I know I'm going to get killed. Please make sure you play this DVD.'

"Ladies and gentlemen, here we go. If you have young children, please use your own discretion, but I wouldn't let my children watch this clip."

"Hello, everyone, if you are watching this video, then you all are aware that I'm dead. I recorded this because I wanted an opportunity to say my side. I know these past few weeks have been a nightmare for all of us. Throughout these allegations, I have been silent. The time has come for me to clear my name in some of these allegations made against me. I know nothing I say will change the past. Heck, it won't even bring me back to life. I just want to get the opportunity to rest in peace, so I'm cleansing my soul.

"I first want to touch a li'l bit about myself and why I became a police officer. I was raised by a single mother. I never once met my father. My mother did an excellent job in raising me. I was able to stay out of trouble, though I had no father figure in my life. I had an opportunity to become either a baseball or football player. I rejected all kinds of scholarships to play for national schools. I wanted to stay close to home and be with my mother.

"I was raised with great morals and respect, so I just thought it was the right thing to do and join the police academy. I always wondered why there weren't any black cops in my neighborhood, so I wanted to make a difference and show the rest of my community that it was okay to become a cop. After my mother was killed by a drunk driver, it changed my life for the worse. My morals died with my mother. I still followed my dreams of becoming an officer to keep my mother happy, but the passion was not there.

"After joining the force, the first few years, everything went as expected. I was getting promoted left and right for my outstanding achievements. I did everything by the book. I was the perfect cop, and everyone in my neighborhood loved me. Once I became a detective and I joined the elite unit called Operation Clean House,

everything went wrong. The unit was run by Captain Tuna, and then it was Detective Loose Cannon, Speedy, and Tango. Tuna was the captain, but the real brain behind it all was Commissioner Fratt. At first I dealt with the pressure of being the only black man in the unit. As time went on, I just adapted, and the dirty tactics became second nature. I honestly thought, in order to close some of these cases, we had to play criminals. We put away some very dangerous men. I can't lie. I saw how easy we were getting away with the illegal shit we were doing. I got greedy and started committing crimes on my own. I was making a lot of money. That's how I opened up the storage facility in the Bronx along with my dead associates Divine, Pee-Wee, and Blood. We were a deadly force in the streets.

"I'm not proud of what I'm revealing here today. I just want to get the truth out. After one of my partners in the unit, Tango, was set up and killed in one of our undercover missions, I became suspicious. I thought Tango's murder was in-house. I bugged my own team. I knew we were a dirty unit, but I knew it went deeper than just the commissioner. That's when I found out the damn mayor was the king of the mud. I became my own internal affair team, keeping all evidence instead of destroying it. I was going to put all the files together and submit them to the federal government and the media.

"After putting together my plan to come forward and confess, I suffered a setback. My ex-partners decided to kill an innocent black man just because he blew our high. We were on the job, snorting cocaine and hanging out at a strip club. Well, once I heard the murder charges were about to get dropped against my ex-partners, I stepped forward and decided to testify.

"Once I took that stand, my life became a nightmare. I was the number one target. First, my ex-partners tried to kill me in broad daylight in Central Park. They thought I was meeting with the Colemans and I sent a look-alike, a stunt double, you can say. They killed him on sight.

"Then they hired a crew of contract bounty hunters out of Florida. They kill their targets. There were, like, four of them. They were good, but not that good. However, they figured out I had a female companion with me, which is true. Once she became a target, I came up with the story of a young girl turning herself in. Now, I'm going to admit I made a crucial decision that I had to live with. I shot and killed an innocent woman. I did it because I wanted to save the identity of my female protégée, who I was in love with.

"After she disappeared as planned, that's when the folders were coming to light. Everything was going well until they found where my baby mother and daughter lived in Cape Cod. They were seconds away from kidnapping my baby mother. I interfered, and I killed both of them. I know for a fact one of them was a fed. The federal government was now helping my dirty ex-partners and doing it at all costs.

"I gathered up my family, and we all left Cape Cod. I took them somewhere safe. After I returned back to New York, I went to my storage unit, and that's when we had the face-off with police. Snipers killed my friend Divine, while the police burned up my other friend, Pee-Wee. I was able to escape, and I stayed over a friend's house to lay low.

"I passed out on the roof, high off cocaine 'cause I relapsed, and then the king of all corruption, the commissioner, gets assassinated. Then, minutes later, they are blaming me for it. I run down to Maryland, where I was trapped in a hotel. I shot the police officer only because I knew he had on a vest, nothing personal. If you are watching, I'm sorry. I knew what I was doing. Again, I'm sorry for the bruise.

"After that, I make it back up to New York. I wanted to clear my name and prove I didn't kill the commissioner.

In the process, about another ten dead bodies popped up, including the murder of Captain Tuna and Detective Speedy. Another thing, I'm not responsible for the death of those three federal agents in Harlem. Also, if you find Richard Claiborne, the mayor's assistant, you will find out who truly killed the commissioner. I will give you a clue—he runs the city. Once I took care of my ex-partners, the plan was to reunite with my family.

"Before I left, I decided to record this video. If I know the federal government like I do, they are going to kill me. I caused too much embarrassment.

"I want to take this time to thank the people first. I want to apologize to New York. I did the city dirty. I want to apologize to the Colemans. That's one strong family. I'm sorry I couldn't stop them before they killed your son. I'm sorry.

"Now it's time to talk to one special lady out there who I love, my daughter. I'm sorry, baby girl. I'm so sorry."

The tears were flowing once Lucky mentioned his daughter.

"I know I made a promise to my daughter, and if you're hearing this recording, I didn't make it back alive. I'm sorry. You are the last person in the world I wanted to let down. I'm sorry. Please forgive me. Please understand I did it all because of you. I know you are hearing all the news channels talking about your father, and it has you confused. Trust what your mother tells you. She knows the truth. I didn't abandon you, baby. For your safety, your mother moved you away. I was just too stupid to see it back then. I'm going to ask you for one favor, baby girl. Please take good care of your mother. I know she's watching as well.

"What up, baby? You are a great mother. I really wanted to start over and do this family thing with you. I'm sorry. I let cocaine ruin my life and cause pain in yours. *I can't believe I let you slip through my fingers. Take care of my daughter, and make sure she grows up to be a woman like you. I have to go now. I love you guys.*"

He broke down again and could barely speak as he added:

"*This is Donald Gibson, better known as, well, I guess not anymore. I guess I wasn't so lucky, after all. Good night and God bless ya.*